GAME TIME

"Look," Phil Elliott said to Dickie Blades as pro football's hottest prospect pressed the elevator button, "if I write that you offered me cocaine, I'll get published and make five thousand. Hell, I could probably renegotiate my fee up to ten-K if you had a nude white woman in your apartment."

Blades broke into uncontrollable laughter. He fell against the side of the elevator and tears ran down his cheeks. Phil Elliott had to smile.

The elevator doors slid open.

Standing just inside the penthouse, her arms wide open, her long hair flowing over her shoulders and full breasts, was the best-looking blonde Phil Elliott had ever seen.

She was stark naked.

NORTH DALLAS AFTER 40

The game is the same—but they play it even harder . . .

"YOU'LL LOVE THIS BLACK-AND-BLUE SEQUEL THAT CONTINUES THE MAYHEM, THE RAUNCHINESS, THE EXPOSÉS OF PRO FOOTBALL."

—*The Short Pump Express*

"GENT WRITES WITH GREAT INSIGHT on the ugly corporate character of football and dark human nature."

—*United Press International*

NORTH DALLAS
After 40

Peter Gent

A SIGNET BOOK

SIGNET
Published by the Penguin Group
Penguin Books USA Inc., 375 Hudson Street, New York,
New York 10014, U.S.A.
Penguin Books Ltd, 27 Wrights Lane, London W8 5TZ, England
Penguin Books Australia Ltd, Ringwood, Victoria, Australia
Penguin Books Canada Ltd, 2801 John Street, Markham, Ontario,
Canada L3R 1B4
Penguin Books (N.Z.) Ltd, 182–190 Wairau Road, Auckland 10, New Zealand

Penguin Books Ltd, Registered Offices:
Harmondsworth, Middlesex, England

Published by Signet, an imprint of New American Library, a division of
Penguin Books USA Inc. This is an authorized reprint of a hardcover edition
published by Villard Books, a division of Random House, Inc.

First Signet Printing, December, 1990
10 9 8 7 6 5 4 3 2 1

 REGISTERED TRADEMARK—MARCA REGISTRADA

Printed in the United States of America

This book is dedicated to my son Carter Davis Gent in memory of his grandfather Charles E. Gent, Sr. (1906–1988), and my friend and teammate Bill Mayhak (1942–1988)

In walking, just walk, in sitting, just sit.
Above all don't wobble.

Yun-men

Elliott—*Now*

Phil Elliott was excited and tense as he stepped around the corner and down into Charlotte Caulder's den.

Bob Beaudreau was sitting on the couch, alone. He was dressed neatly in a light blue suit and a wide red-and-blue-striped tie. He watched calmly as Elliott entered the room.

"I thought I heard somebody," he said, crossing his legs. Large dark stains covered his trousers. "She's in the bedroom." He pointed down the hall, then used his finger to scratch his cheek. "With the nigger."

Lying on the low coffee table in front of the couch was Beaudreau's fat blue-steel .357 magnum. He had placed it on a magazine to keep it from scratching the tabletop.

Elliott continued down the hall to the bedroom.

Charlotte Caulder and David Clarke were just shredded pieces of flesh, brown and white. Lumps of nothing. The bullets had knocked away great hunks of meat and bone.

Charlotte had died quickly. The first bullet struck below her eye and tore off the side of her head. The second slug ripped open her breast.

David had bled to death through the awful holes torn by three hollow-point slugs.

Charlotte suddenly reached out to Elliott and tried to sit up, blood pouring from her wounds.

Soaked in his own sweat, Phil Elliott woke from one nightmare into another. He felt the familiar discomfort of

the hard metal bunk, the cold of concrete and steel suck
at him from the blackness.

Jail, again. Jail, still.

The plastic bunk pad turned his skin clammy inside the
white coveralls. His bare feet were cold, dry, and cracked.

The line between waking and sleeping was no longer
clear. Only the pain was constant: arthritis, old injuries,
scar tissue, useless muscle and joints. Awake or asleep,
there was no refuge from the agony of emptiness. Jail,
the horror of captivity, life in a cage. The Experience as
absence. The absence of Experience. Nothing to *fear*.
Nothing to fear.

The terror of awakening slowly pushed the dreadful
nightmare aside. Elliott began to gag. He sat up, leaned
over the open commode next to his bunk, and tried to
vomit, but nothing came. His ravaged nervous system hit
full general alarm: the fight-or-flight syndrome gone berserk. Fight whom? Fly where? Nothing helped. Everything hurt.

It was not yet dawn but the naked bulb in the adjoining tank reflected pale green off the wall of Phil Elliott's
jail cell.

It was just another day.

Phil Elliott hurt worse than any morning in recent
memory, but his subjective senses of pain and memory
had been challenged many times before. It did occur to
him to wonder how many more times he'd be up to the
challenge.

Elliott's sense of time told him it was 3:00 A.M. A
glance at his luminous watch would remove all doubt, but
in jail, with great effort, a man could cloak himself in
Time for short but pleasant moments. It was important to
learn to *feel* time, since one's sense of place was in
constant danger. So Phil Elliott sat in the darkness, alert
for clues. Then, closing his eyes, he returned to his head.

He conjured up Charlotte Caulder. Quickly. This time
unblemished and beautiful, full of life, walking alongside
him on her ranch east of Dallas.

"You ought to write a book about all this," she had
told him long ago, lacing her fingers in his. "Tell people
what really goes on in professional football."

"No one would believe it." He laughed. "Worse, no one would buy it."

"You write it"—she grabbed his hand in both of hers and drew it to her breast—"and I promise you people will buy it."

"You gonna loan them the money?" Elliott mocked. "I'd rather it was a profit deal."

"It will be." She turned his hand loose and danced away, her yellow dress swirling. "Grant Grinnell, a very dear friend, just happens to be the best literary agent in New York. If he likes your book, it'll sell millions of copies. You'll be famous."

"Or infamous." Phillip Elliott grinned. "The book has to be written first. I don't know if I can do that."

"Sure, you can," she argued. "Write the same way you tell me those stories. Phillip, please promise me you'll write the book. Please. Please."

"Okay."

"Okay what?" Wisps of fog snaked around her legs and coiled up her body.

"I promise I'll write the book."

"I can't wait to read it." Charlotte's face was wreathed in mist and she just seemed to fade, to move away into the fog. Suddenly, he was alone in the whiteness. Then violent back pain jerked him back to the dark cell.

Phil Elliott glanced at his watch. It *was* 3:00 A.M. He was doing his time accurately.

He was sad, lonesome for his dream of a living Charlotte Caulder. He worked hard to conjure his dream of her alive, vital, happy, real. The nightmare of violence and death came uninvited and often. Bob Beaudreau grinning malevolently, Charlotte and David twisted and forever frozen in postures of death.

It would be four more hours before enough light would reach Elliott's cell to allow reading or writing. Until then, he did his morning ritual: thinking, stretching long-damaged muscles and joints, walking, remembering, sitting, trying to forget. Forget the bad and the good, forget the past and the future, forget the outside. There was only here; the rest did not exist. The walls had only one side, there was no other side to the fence, and to think about grass, however green, was madness.

There was only here and now.

There was only jail.
And time.

"Elliott!" the turnkey yelled through the slot in the heavy door. "You got a visitor."

It was 9:00 A.M. and John Wilson, dressed nattily in suit and tie, smiled nervously at Phil Elliott, shuffling clumsily into the Attorney's Room, just off the jail kitchen.

"I love what you do for those white coveralls and county-issue bath thongs." Wilson looked him over, stopping his gaze at the bare, red, chapped feet, uncomfortably wedged into the purposely small rubber sandals. "As always, your socks match your gloves."

"Oppression only sharpens my sense of fashion." Elliott slumped down into the steel chair and stared at the peeling green paint on the wall. The clatter of pots and pans mixed with the chatter of Spanish as the trustees worked on lunch next door in the galley.

"You didn't get the writ," Elliott said, finally.

"I can't find the judge I want," John Wilson explained.

"William O. Douglas died." Elliott frowned, keeping his eyes on the puke-green wall. He tried to slide his chair closer to the table but it was bolted to the concrete floor. The futile effort depressed him, a bad sign. It should have made him mad.

"So." Elliott finally looked at his friend. "Why are you here?"

"A social call from an ex-teammate to cheer you up." John Wilson smiled with relief and picked up his heavy briefcase, dropping it on the gray metal table with a bang. The table did not move. It was also bolted to the floor.

"I would prefer a successful professional call from my attorney." Elliott looked from Wilson's broad face to the briefcase and back. "I hope you are a better attorney than you were a safety."

"Whaddaya mean?" Wilson protested. "I was a great safety. B.A. just went with them young high-dollar kids."

"Well, you don't have to worry about the high dollar here," Elliott said.

"Don't worry, Phillip, I'll have you out of here by tomorrow at the latest. The judge is one small tactic in a much larger game plan."

"I hate it when you use football terms," Elliott complained.

"Scott sent you a drawing." Wilson changed to Elliott's favorite subject: his ten-year-old son. "I've got it right here." The football player-turned-lawyer began unstrapping the overfilled leather case.

"How *is* Scott? Have you been taking good care of my boy?" Elliott's face brightened and a sense of purpose entered his voice and posture.

"You bet." Wilson smiled. "He loves the ranch and all the animals. He misses you and his dog but he seems to understand all this court and jail mumbo jumbo."

"I wish I did."

"That makes two of us."

"Does he ever ask about his mother?"

"Not yet, but if he does, I'll call Courtnay's lawyer, the honorable Mr. Stein, and see if she is available to talk to him over the phone." Wilson narrowed his eyes. "I heard she was back in the house in Austin."

"That makes sense." Elliott nodded, his eyes dropped back to the floor. "She always pictured herself at the center of things. It never mattered what things, as long as she was the center of them."

"Well, she is running with the talent scouts now," Wilson said, "and you are paying for it. The Bar Association ought to vote her a Natural Resource. I will never handle another divorce and custody fight again. I can't deal with people who think divorce is a solution to their problems. Goddamn, it is just another problem that you have to pay in advance for."

"Why are you complaining?" Elliott asked. "There are damn near a million lawyers out there looking for work . . . making work, if they can't find it. They've got the franchise rights on misery and there just ain't anything much more miserably vengeful than a woman when she wants to be. The woman's movement didn't change that. Courtnay is my problem and Scott's mother and always will be. We're stuck with her no matter what some idiot judge says or lawyer promises. The boy's life has been ruined by his mother and me. I'm paying you *not* to make it any worse."

"Does this mean you got a plan other than fighting her?" Wilson was suddenly interested. "If you got another way out of this mess, I would certainly like to hear it."

"Being mean and vengeful don't make her or her lawyer smart or right," Elliott pointed out. "It may make David Stein rich and it seems to be emotionally rewarding to Courtnay in the short run." Elliott rubbed his eyes. "But in a fight, short-term tactics must not be mistaken for long-term goals. B.A. taught me that. I didn't want this fight but I am in it. All I know to do now is fight and keep fighting."

"Until then?" Wilson had an anxious look on his face. "When does this insanity end?"

"What don't kill, fattens." Elliott smirked. "B.A. also said adversity makes us stronger."

"*Adversity*," Wilson moaned, "not *insanity*."

"What do you think Courtnay wants out of this divorce?"

"Everything," Wilson paused, "but you."

"Precisely." Elliott nodded. "This is not a divorce, it's a ritual killing and she won't be satisfied until I am dead or an acceptable equivalent of dead."

"So what do you want to do?" Wilson pulled a pen and yellow pad from the briefcase. He would not write anything down. If he did he would just misplace it.

"Let Courtnay and David Stein win anything except Scott and the things that belong to him."

"Okay. That's easy. They been constantly kicking the shit out of you anyway and she does not seem to want the boy with her in Austin." John Wilson smiled. "What about the resort property and house in Purgatory?"

"That belongs to Scott." Elliott was firm. "They can never have that. It's all he'll have left by the time this war is over."

"I do have some good news." Wilson put down his pad and pencil. "Decker McShane over at the *Southwest View* is considering filing an *amicus curiae* brief in your behalf. I'm trying to convince him that every time Courtnay files a *subpoena duces tecum* against you it makes this case relevant to the protections promised in the First Amendment." Wilson held up his big scarred hands. "Decker is concerned about the larger ramifications of domestic law on a free press."

"What is larger than being in jail?" Elliott was skeptical of Decker McShane's motives. "Everytime you guys use them Latin words, I lose more of my rights and money."

Wilson reached into his case and withdrew three pill vials. "I'll have you out of here no later than tomorrow." He showed the bottles to Elliott. "The Doc filled your prescriptions. I'll give them to the turnkey. And I brought your TENS unit. The turnkey said Jo Bob would have to approve before you could wear it."

"My neck and back are killing me. I need that unit." Elliott scowled and sat back down on the immovable metal chair. "Is the ball club's big reunion on again this year?"

"Haven't you been reading the sports pages?"

"No. I've been sleeping on them."

"Yep, it's on. We all go back and check waistlines, hairlines, the current wives' looks. Then try and guess everybody's wallet size." Wilson paused thoughtfully. "You know B.A. is coming back this year?"

Elliott was without interest. "I'll go back and scratch the date on my cell wall."

Wilson was slightly put off by Elliott's disinterest but he quickly recovered. "Well, there are certain possibilities to be researched here, Phil. The Hunters sold the club to the Denham-Laughlin Group. Conrad's dead and Emmett's fortune is rapidly on the decline. They kept Clinton Foote on to run the franchise and brought Danny Raines back from Denver to coach. And B.A.'s seeking a second term as governor."

"That's a fine summation," Elliott said. "So?"

"So I've been working on a couple ideas. One of which is you are going to this year's team reunion and write some stories."

"Who's going to make me?"

"Me. It'll get you out of here."

"Be my guest," Elliott smiled slowly.

"I thought as much."

Elliott pushed to his feet. His whole body felt leaden. "Kiss Scott for me and tell him I love him."

"You bet." Wilson frowned and closed his briefcase. "It sure is strange," he said thoughtfully. "Who would have thought I'd be a lawyer, Tony Douglas would be a game warden, Alan Claridge a congressman, Seth Maxwell a number-one-rated television star, Jo Bob Williams the Purgatory County Sheriff, O. W. Meadows his deputy and B.A. getting ready to run for a second time as governor?"

"Who would have thought I would be in jail?" Elliott asked.

Wilson squinted at him. "You want a list?"

Raul

"So what they got you in here for, Raul?"

Elliott had asked the question daily of his cellmate. He'd been asking it for one whole week now, ever since they'd arrived simultaneously at the Tri-County Jail and been tossed together in the same cage.

Every day Elliott got the exact same response from the big dark man in the white coveralls. And that response was: *nothing*.

All he knew about Raul was that he'd been living in Los Cruces City, having become an American citizen, and after four years as a Marine, had the not particularly brilliant idea of sneaking back into Mexico so he could bring his wife and children to live with him in the land of the free and clear. It turned out that his wife was now living with another man. She didn't really want to leave her happy home for Los Cruces City. So Raul headed back north by himself, trusting in Jesus and his certainty that his American papers and discharge orders were on record somewhere. Between there and jail, Elliott wasn't getting a whole hell of a lot of info.

"Come on, what did you do besides cross the border?"

"My lawyer told me to say nothing."

"He meant to the law," Elliott pressed. "What are you charged with?"

"My lawyer did not say, but . . ." The big knuckled hand pulled at his face; the high cheekbones stuck out even more. "He said not to worry about it and to have a nice weekend."

"It's Wednesday, Raul. You've had a nice *long* weekend."

But that was all Raul was going to say. Raul wasn't interested in talking. He was interested in figuring out what had happened and why he was in jail.

Raul had fallen behind the main group after spraining his ankle just before they crossed the Rio Grande. Raul had paid the six hundred dollars to join the others the coyote was guiding across the border into Texas. An eighteen-wheel trailer truck was waiting at a rendezvous just below the Purgatory Plateau. The illegals would be loaded inside and hauled east to San Antonio. Raul would then make his own way west to Los Cruces City.

There were twenty-five others in the group, including an old man, three women, and a nine-year-old girl from El Salvador plus two young men, Emeliano Rivera and his cousin Cruz who had come all the way from Costa Rica. The rest were Mexicans: five women, three children under ten, plus ten men ranging in age from seventeen to fifty.

All were pursuing the same hope of work and a share of the wealth in the United States, except Raul who just wanted to document his U.S. citizenship and bring his family out of Mexico.

The first night he talked with Emeliano and his cousin Cruz from Costa Rica. They claimed to know people in San Antonio and Purgatory, Americans who had business interests in Costa Rica and who had employed Emeliano and his cousin back home.

"They told us to come to Texas and they would have work for us." Emeliano did not say what kind of work. Raul was too polite to ask.

The next day, Raul's ankle slowed him more and he found himself in the company of the small band of Salvadorans. They were silent and scared, running a thousand miles from the death squads that roamed their country. Their hopes, grown in desperate terror, were great; their chances were slim.

Finally, as his ankle worsened, stumbling through the rugged brasada country below the Plateau, Raul fell behind even the old people.

The coyote came back to him and frowned.

"I will try to wait for you at the truck." He was a

decent man and didn't want to abandon anyone in the harsh brushland. "I have never lost a customer yet, friend, and I am not going to have your ghost disturbing my sleep." The coyote pointed out the distant mountain peak. "That is Sierra Maga. Keep walking toward it until you come to a dirt road. Turn east on the dirt road and we will be waiting in a truck two miles up in a big grove of trees. If we have gone, *don't* leave the road. This country will kill you. If it doesn't, the Border Patrol will eventually find you and, who knows, maybe they'll check out your story in Los Cruces City and all your problems will be solved."

Raul nodded and sat to rest his aching leg. The coyote led off and soon he and his ragged band were out of sight. Raul pulled off his old Marine fatigue jacket and dug through the pockets for his small Spanish-language Bible.

The next morning at daybreak, Raul found the truck, out of gas, deathly silent in the high desert stillness.

He was yanking at the trailer door latches when Purgatory County Sheriff Jo Bob Williams stepped around the front of the tractor and leveled his pistol.

"Habla inglesa, motherfucker?" Jo Bob waved the pistol at Raul.

"Yes sir!" Raul's hands shot up in the air and he stammered, "I am American. I fought in Grenada." He pointed at his fatigue jacket. "Marine Corps. I am from Los Cruces City. I got people there."

"Then what in the goddamn hell are you doin' here?" Jo Bob Williams kept the big pistol pointed right in Raul's face.

Raul kept silent. One of several things he had learned in the Corps was when to keep his mouth shut.

"You know anything about this fuckin' truck?" Sheriff Jo Bob Williams was a terrifying sight: a six-foot seven-inch 270-pound gringo with a gun and a badge, the stuff of Mexican nightmares. *"Comprende,* motherfucker?"

Raul shook his head.

"Well, back your ass up, Pancho, and we'll both find out what's in here." Jo Bob Williams kept his eyes on Raul as he unlatched and pulled open the doors of the truck. The smell that rolled out and over them caused Jo

Bob to gag and Raul to vomit up what little he had in his stomach.

"Jesus fucking Christ!" Jo Bob Williams looked at the bloated, contorted bodies of the men, women, and children and then looked back to Raul. "Well, Pancho, I'm taking you to jail until I decide what to do." The giant sheriff glanced back at the frightful cargo.

"Motherfucker!" was all he said.

That had been a week ago. The same day Sheriff Jo Bob Williams delivered Raul to the new Tri-County Jail, Jo Bob's old teammate Phillip Elliott turned himself in to begin serving his contempt sentence.

Elliott had refused to take the oath before taking the stand. "If what I've heard today is the truth, as each witness against me has *sworn an oath* that it is, then I choose to be called contemptuous, rather than be called a *liar.*"

Raul liked Elliott and they got on well but he never told the Anglo what had happened or how he came to be in jail. The sheriff had promised to check out his story with the law in Los Cruces City. Meanwhile, his court-appointed attorney listened without interest to Raul's story that he had just wandered off the interstate while hitchhiking from El Paso and warned Raul to keep his mouth shut and hope somebody in the Los Cruces City Courthouse remembered him.

Raul watched Elliott sitting in the tank marking time, thinking his head would burst with what he was keeping secret. But Elliott had told him that he knew the sheriff from the past and that was enough connection with the law to keep Raul fearful of confidence.

Maybe tomorrow, Raul thought as the lights-out signal told them to return to their cells. *If tomorrow came.*

It was just past midnight when Deputy Sheriff O. W. Meadows pulled into the lot behind the Tri-County Jail.

Using his key, O.W. let himself in through the outside door to the kitchen. He walked directly to the cells.

The turnkey was off duty and sleeping in the small office in the front of the building. He would not make his rounds until 2:00 A.M.

O.W. pulled the levers opening the tank door and cell number three.

He walked swiftly and silently across the tank floor and was into Raul's cell before the big Hispanic was awake.

When Raul opened his eyes, he was looking down the barrel of O.W. Meadows's big revolver.

"One squeak outta you, Cisco," O.W. hissed, "and you die trying to break jail."

Raul nodded. His eyes wide, fully awake, and terrified, he grabbed his Bible and shuffled barefoot out of the jail ahead of the deputy, who quietly locked up everything behind him.

In cell number three, Phil Elliott was having another nightmare about the murder of Charlotte Caulder. Three hours later, he would wake up soaked in a cold sweat.

"Okay, Cisco, strip!"

Raul was standing in the glare of the deputy's car headlights. The voice came from somewhere behind the glare.

They had driven up the river several miles before the deputy made him get out and walk in front of the car. Raul walked barefoot on the sharp limestone rocks for another mile before the deputy stopped. The prisoner's feet were cut and bleeding.

Raul knew the deputy was going to kill him. He frantically searched for escape.

"I must lay down my Bible."

"Go ahead." O.W. laughed. "But don't lose it, you'll be needin' it."

Raul placed his Bible on the thick club-sized piece of driftwood he had spotted as he stood in front of the car. Then, he began to pull off the jail coveralls.

The deputy came around in front of the car. He was a giant man and cast a monstrous shadow. In one hand, he carried a heavy nine-cell flashlight, in the other the big revolver.

"So, Cisco." O.W.'s voice was friendly, yet did not hide the menace in the words. "You crossed the border with that bunch of wets that died in the back of that truck Sheriff Williams found you snooping around."

"No, sir. I am a U.S. citizen. I was in the Marines." Raul was stark naked.

"Don't fuck with me, boy. Anybody can get themselves a Marine tattoo." O.W. swung the flashlight.

Stars exploded in Raul's head as the flashlight struck just above his left ear. He staggered but kept his feet. He could feel the blood running warm into his ear, down his neck and across his chest. The second blow caught him full across the forehead.

Raul went down on his back.

"Now, one more time, greaseball." O.W. growled. "Tell me what you saw."

"I tell you, sir, the truth. I saw nothing." Raul pushed himself to his feet.

"Fuck, Cisco, I ain't got all night." The deputy raked the hammer back on the pistol and placed the barrel right between Raul's eyes. The barrel felt ice cold.

"Please, if I am to die," Raul begged, "may I be holding my Bible?"

"Sure, Cisco," the deputy said. "I ain't a fella who wants to piss off God. But you ain't got a lotta time to pray."

Raul stumbled forward slightly, as he bent down. The calculated movement, though it looked as if he was barely conscious, had placed his body between the deputy and the large stick of driftwood where he had laid his Bible.

Once he gripped the piece of wood, Raul turned and swung so fast that the deputy didn't get an arm up to protect himself. The blow caught O. W. Meadows on the temple and he was out cold on his feet.

Raul swung again, hitting the deputy at the base of the skull, and he crumpled like a sack of ashes.

Grabbing his Bible and nothing else, Raul ran for his life off into the darkness of the river bottoms.

The Limo

In the morning when Elliott came out of his cell, Raul was gone.

They probably had him on *the circuit* from one county jail to the next, a different jail every couple of days, Elliott thought. If anyone was looking for him, with a writ or a real lawyer, they would have hell finding him.

The number of people *lost* in the Texas jails any one day boggled Phil Elliott's mind.

Elliott worked through his morning routine of dry heaves, panic, agonizing physical and mental pain, walking, stretching, thinking and forgetting.

It went slow.

He missed Raul.

Lying on his aching back, Elliott waited stubbornly for lunch to see what would happen.

He heard the turnkey at the door, but his sense of time told him it was too early for lunch. The noise of the heavy door opening did not turn him. A new prisoner most likely and Elliott was in no mood to swap stares for space and power right now. He stayed on his back and stared up at the green concrete ceiling.

The face that loomed over Elliott and blocked his view could not have been more surprising had it been old Jesus Christ himself.

"Well, hidy Phil." Seth Maxwell chuckled and charmed, his face upside down in Elliott's vision. "Nice place you got here."

"Can't beat the rates," Elliott said, refusing to move.

"You got a summer place like this?" Maxwell just kept grinning.

"I got my people looking." Elliott tried to act unsurprised, as if Maxwell was expected, possibly even late. "Your people might want to meet with my people. We could do a time-share. You do my time and I will do yours."

"Naw, I think not." Maxwell reached out his hand and Elliott grabbed it. "Let's have lunch instead." He pulled Elliott to his feet.

The tank door was still open. The turnkey stood aside as, to Elliott's amazement, Seth Maxwell led him out of jail.

Outside, John Wilson was waiting and walked them all to the back of Maxwell's gray stretch Lincoln limousine. Phil Elliott did not speak again until they were in the vehicle and moving away.

Far away.

"How long have you been in there?" Maxwell asked, as the car hummed along.

"About a week, this time."

"How long is this going to keep on, John?" Maxwell turned to the safety-turned-lawyer.

"In perpetuity, throughout the universe, by any and all means to be yet devised," Wilson replied.

"Let us just say a long time," Elliott said.

"You got any strategy besides sitting in jail for long periods of time?" Maxwell asked Elliott.

"We are working on a change of venue," Elliott said. "John is meeting with Spielberg's people, trying to get the whole case moved to Andromeda. He is going to argue temporary sanity."

"You ain't got much of a witness in Elliott here," Maxwell said. "Do you, John?"

Wilson watched Elliott puff on his cigarette and hunker forward in the seat like it was a jail bunk and not the backseat of an $80,000 limousine. "Uh uh," he told the ex-quarterback.

"So, what do I owe for the bust-out?" Elliott finally asked.

"I guess you heard." Maxwell seemed to ignore the

question. "Governor B. A. Quinlan is going to be in Dallas and take part in the reunion celebration on the twentieth anniversary of our first championship team."

"My invitation must have gotten lost in the mail." Elliott's jaws caved in as he smoked. He looked thin and haggard, with scared eyes.

"You are on the B List with the recalcitrant niggers," Maxwell said.

"There are worse places to be," Elliott replied. "Like the A List."

"B.A. is going to announce for a second term as governor," Maxwell continued. "It only seems proper, since I turned it down."

"I wish you had taken it," Elliott said. "You could commute my sentence."

"Only God Himself can commute your sentence."

"And God is going around thinking he is B.A.," Elliott added.

"That pretty much sums up your prospects," Maxwell replied. "So you better do what we tell you."

"It's what you *don't* tell me that I worry about, Seth."

"The smart money is backing B.A. for president in '96, as long as he runs as a Republican."

"Who is the smart money?"

"Laughlin, Denham, me," Maxwell explained.

"What about Emmett Hunter?"

"He's *no* money," Maxwell said. "Conrad did not sell the football team because he wanted to do it. Ten-dollar-a-barrel oil and Japanese microchips killed the old man. Emmett's been running on empty for a year. He filed for Chapter Eleven reorganization and Joanne divorced him about the same time Courtnay was dragging your ass through court."

"The deal I cut with Decker is for you to go to the reunion and do an article for *Southwest View*," Wilson explained. "Go see some of the old guys and find out where their lives have taken them."

"Especially my old coach?" Elliott asked. "An article on a great coach turned governor?"

"See!" Wilson said. "It's not all that hard to figure out what people want, when you really put your mind to it."

"Why should I put my mind to it?"

"Because, you need the money. Do you really want

out of jail or not?" The raw-boned lawyer sighed. "Grant
Grinnell, your literary agent, is having one hell of a time
negotiating any contracts for a jailbird. You ain't a goddamn Russian dissident and the prisons are full of serious
criminals who can write better than you . . . for nothing.
Zip. No cash. Nothing. *Nada. Habla inglesa,* you asshole?"

"I'll do it."

"Fine. You see, Seth? He is as easy to deal with as he
always was, just older." Wilson took no joy in his statement. "Also, your ex-wife called and said we are late
with the alimony and child support."

"Child support?" Maxwell interrupted. "I thought *you*
had custody of the boy?"

"I do. I pay her support to leave us alone. Sometimes
she does and sometimes she don't," Elliott explained. "It
is all hormones and lunar phases."

"That is why we call them cunts." Maxwell did not
conceal his gleeful dislike of women. "I don't hate them
as a group, Phil. I hate each one individually. 'More
bitter than death is woman!' " Maxwell loved quoting the
Bible.

"So," Wilson spoke directly to Elliott, "you will use
your writing talent and type yourself to safety. Agreed?"

"They'll crucify me," Elliott complained.

"They already crucified you," Wilson pointed out. "But,
these bastards are scared of you. Laughlin and Denham
especially."

"They ain't afraid to throw me in jail," Elliott said.

"Let us worry about that," Wilson said.

"That is big of you, but I'll do my own worrying, just
like Seth does his own stunts on television."

"I don't do my own stunts."

"Believe me, Phil," Wilson said. "Some of these people are afraid of what you might say. They don't think
they can do enough to you to keep you from writing the
truth."

"Oh! That is great!" Elliott interrupted. "It is hurting
them more than it is hurting me."

"Maybe they think you *really know* something."

"I don't."

"Well, for Christ's sake," Wilson said, "don't tell *them*
that. The article you wrote on Bobby Laughlin cost him
his chance to be chancellor of the university."

"I didn't intend for that to happen," Elliott protested. "Who knew he was *really* with the CIA?"

"God, Phillip! How in hell do you get on *everybody's* wrong side?" Maxwell was amazed.

"I didn't have you to send me on routes through life's little minefields, Seth."

Maxwell suddenly ducked his eyes. "I been busy making myself a media star of incredible proportions. I am apolitical, myself."

"You are amoral," Elliott disagreed. "That qualifies you for politics in Texas."

"Just like Congressman Alan Claridge," Wilson pointed out.

"You two are certainly the social analysts." Maxwell looked suspiciously from Wilson to Elliott. "How did I end up mixed up with you two?"

"That is the question they will eventually ask you, Seth," Elliott said. "When did you mix with them and why? What did you think and about who?"

"Well," Maxwell sighed, "I didn't get here by being stupid. And to quote from one of your better-known works . . ." He changed to his deep broadcaster's voice. "Life is hand-to-hand duck hunting. I won't go down."

Elliott closed his eyes and listened. Charlotte Caulder appeared and he smiled at the visage. Maxwell mistook the smile.

"Hah, you got it," Maxwell continued. *"Down?"* He turned to Wilson. "Duck feathers, do *you* get it? *Down?* I won't go *down?"*

"Pretty funny." Elliott kept his eyes closed, gazing at the delicate face of his Ghost Lover, unchanged after all the years, all the miles. It all seemed like yesterday. Elliott just slipped quietly into sleep and his breathing fell into an even cadence.

Seth Maxwell watched Elliott sleep. Wilson reached over and took the cigarette from Elliott's hand.

"He starts smoking every time the judge throws him in jail," Wilson explained.

"Damn, John, what turned him so old?" Maxwell stared at the lines in Elliott's face, the gray in his stringy hair. "He looks terrible."

"He didn't stop taking beatings because he left football," Wilson said. "His writing got him pounded a lot.

Christ! So did his talking. You ever see him on a talk
show?"

Maxwell nodded.

"The first time in front of this judge, Elliott tells him
that he has a First Amendment duty . . ." Wilson shook
his head. *"He called it a duty* . . . to point out an asshole
when he saw one."

"And he saw one, right there in court?"

"In black robes, sitting on the bench."

"He is crazy," Maxwell said.

"Sometimes. But who can say anymore?" Wilson said,
"Being his lawyer has been an experience. I was a happy,
relatively well-to-do man when I began representing Phil
Elliott. I have never seen the world the same again."

"I wouldn't walk in his shoes," Maxwell said.

"Neither would he if he could figure out how to get
'em off. So you be certain you want to get involved
before you do much more," Wilson warned. "Phil Elliott
is the Tar Baby."

"The football stuck to him like he was the Tar Baby,"
Maxwell said. "He could catch a goddamn ball in a race
riot. But God . . ." He paused and shook his head. "I
never expected him to look so old."

"Give him a couple days and he'll be an anarchist's wet
dream. He is all beat up, but he is as pissed off as ever."

"I liked his books." Maxwell stretched. "It was a real
tragedy what happened to Charlotte Caulder. She was
good for him."

"It's sad. Beaudreau never did one day in jail. He had
David Stein defend him." Wilson watched Elliott sleep.
"Now, Stein is attorney for Elliott's ex-wife. When Phil
made the connection, paranoia set in. Beaudreau's kept a
low profile, but lately he's been raising money for B.A.'s
reelection campaign."

"No shit?"

Wilson nodded. "Elliott does jail time for contempt,
and that goddamn Beaudreau walks on a double murder
charge because he can pay a million-dollar legal fee."

"She was a good gal." Time had changed Maxwell. He
hadn't been very enthusiastic about Charlotte while she
was alive. But, as Elliott had said in his first book:
Things don't change, people do, and dead people do all
sorts of crazy shit.

*   *   *

After Phil Elliott buried Charlotte Caulder, he returned north and spent a year watching Lake Michigan change color and temperament.

The second year, Louie Nance got back from wherever it was he disappeared for a year or two at a time. Louie and Phil Elliott went to high school together. Then Louie had spent six months in the Central Highlands in Nam with five other Americans and a tribe of Montagnards. They had an artillery unit on a mountaintop. Under fire every day, they were completely overrun by the Vietcong three times in six months.

"I just hid under the dead guys and hoped daylight came before the Cong found me."

Elliott loved it when Louie moved into the log cabin with him, and not just because he did all the cooking and light housekeeping. Elliott began to write the book on professional football he had promised Charlotte Caulder he would write.

Famous American Ducks was the title, because Charlotte loved ducks and he had to start somewhere. The book was about professional football and what was happening in American sports. It took him a year to write the novel and mail it off to the literary agent that Charlotte had known in New York.

In June the phone rang.

"Phillip Elliott? One moment for Mr. Grinnell."

"Mr. Elliott, this is Grant Grinnell. I would very much like to handle *Famous American Ducks*. If you don't object, I would like to suggest a few changes in the manuscript and, after you do the rewrites, we will go right into the market."

Elliott liked Grant Grinnell. His manner was attentive, respectful, and most of all without pretense. Grant Grinnell was *really* on the other end of the phone line, a presence that was necessary to Elliott, who had experienced so much that was transitory.

Grinnell returned the manuscript with his editor's marks and marginal notations. Elliott went right back to the typewriter and rewrote *Famous American Ducks* in five weeks and mailed it back to New York City.

Two weeks later the phone rang again.

The next day, Phillip Elliott flew to New York and met

Grant Grinnell in the bar of the Sheraton Russell Hotel. A little over six feet tall, Grinnell looked like he sounded over the phone. He was thin with a smallish head, overflowing with gray curly hair. His style was gleefully conspiratorial and, as he talked, he kept his left hand in front of his mouth, covering his thin lips, while his fingers stroked his long nose.

"First," Grinnell began, "the rewrites were fine and it looks like the deal is going to be better than I expected. You are a good novelist."

"I'm not sure how it happened."

"It just happens." Grant Grinnell nodded sympathetically. "You just write, there are no real rules for novels." He chuckled. "There's a strain of insanity that runs through the book like a river. Any special reason why you chose ducks?"

"Rabbits were already taken," Elliott said, wondering if Grinnell thought he was crazy. *He* decided he was crazy, for writing a book that would give the authorities all the proof they needed to catch him. He decided he would blame the craziness on living with Louie.

"You had better get ready to deal with success," Grinnell advised. "I believe the industry has already decided *Famous American Ducks* is going to be a blockbuster. The sports magazines have been calling my office all week. The hardcover advertising budget and the first printing alone will push your book to the major best-seller lists around the country."

"Well, success makes me anxious," Elliott said. "It's a kind of *too-much-too-soon* syndrome."

"You don't enjoy success?" Grinnell asked.

"It's not that," Elliott explained. "I just know how fast things change and if I get *too much too soon,* I am always afraid that someone will come and take it all away that much faster. Big success breeds gigantic failure. If you get too big a pile of money, somebody notices and starts planning how to take it away. It's called paranoia, I guess."

Phillip Elliott knew he had a lot to learn about being a famous writer, just like he did when he became a famous football player. It was interesting, in retrospect, that he made almost all of the same mistakes.

He made the right decisions for the wrong reasons, and

the wrong decisions for the right reasons, and, as always, had to live with the consequences.

"This deal just fell into place. The timing in the market is incredible." Grant Grinnell reached into his inside coat pocket and pulled out a letter-sized piece of paper. "I am getting calls from the movie people and I got a sixty-forty split on paperback rights. The hardcover and paperback people will want you to tour the country and promote this book for twelve to fourteen weeks. Can you handle that?"

"Sure. No problem."

Right.

In the first twelve weeks of the fourteen-week tour, Phillip Elliott traveled the United States promoting *Famous American Ducks* and never missed an appearance. He worked five days a week, starting at 6:00 A.M. on the local morning television show. He did eight interviews a day, often ending after midnight. He was the hottest author on the publisher's fall list and was on a first-name basis with everybody from the sales director to the president. He was planning a trip to the chairman's house in Barbados when the tour suddenly ended just before Christmas.

Elliott was on his second pass through Dallas when they canceled the remainder of the promotional tour. The publisher found him at the Stoneleigh Hotel registered as O.M.R. Kyam from Odessa. The previous night he had passed out on a live television show in Ft. Worth. That had followed The Great L.A. Coliseum Bust, which made the front page of the Los Angeles and New York papers and had convinced the publisher to pull Elliott off the road.

The fracas in Los Angeles sold five thousand hardcover books in one day but it made responsible people nervous. It also cost Elliott a free trip to Barbados.

Later, in New York, rested and filled with Valium, Elliott dropped by the Grant Grinnell Agency.

"Too much, too soon, Phillip?" Grinnell asked.

"Naw." Elliott shook his head. "Too little, too late. If I had thought earlier to rent those ambulances, I could have toured for three more months."

"The publisher is refusing to pay for those ambulances," Grinnell explained. "And, they will not pick up any of the legal expenses involved in your skirmish at the L.A. Coliseum."

"I'm not surprised. I told you things change fast." Elliott stood and shook hands with his agent. "I am outta here."

"When can I expect another book?" Grinnell stopped him at the door.

"It will be five years before I am healthy enough to do this again, Grant." Elliott was out of the office and the door closed slowly behind him.

That night, after work, while walking down Madison Avenue, Grant Grinnell was run down by a New York City Police cruiser driven by a thirty-year veteran sergeant with fifteen martinis under His belt. Grant Grinnell suffered a broken leg and was cited for reckless walking.

Things change. Fast.

The rain pounding on the gray limo woke Phillip Elliott. The last thing he saw in his dream was the ever-unchanged face of Charlotte Caulder.

Help me Phillip. Please.

They were heading east on the Ranch Road, toward the town of Purgatory away from the new Tri-County Jail Building. The live oaks glistened a wet green, the Spanish oaks spotting the rugged landscape with lumps of bright red. The car tires hissed on the wet pavement. The tail end of Hurricane Horace had stalled right over them.

John Wilson was talking on the car phone while Seth Maxwell watched the small television built into the walnut bar console. The peculiar hieroglyphics of the stock market crawled across the bottom of the screen.

The market was back over twenty-six hundred with no sign of stopping, nor any reason for climbing. It was all a giant crap shoot.

Elliott was fairly positive that New York was financing the end of the world.

He closed his eyes again, the humming of the tires and the steady beat of the rain pushed him back toward the unconscious.

"That is the *only* reason you wrote about *ducks?*" Courtnay Howard's face loomed out of the dark. It was the second time they met.

"Yep," Elliott nodded, some sixth sense urging him to back away. "George Orwell had a lock on *pigs*." She seemed so friendly, so generous, so harmless. He had forgotten the first time they'd met, but she hadn't. Courtnay was a stalker.

"There *must* be more to it." Courtnay Howard's blue eyes searched his face. She moved forward, as he backed away step for step. It appeared as if they were almost dancing.

"Well, it's a *roman à clef*," Elliott said, "and I had to disguise my characters to avoid lawsuits. I'm just practicing my interview." He looked nervously for an escape route, but the professor's house was small and clumps of people, talking and drinking, blocked the doorways. It was a reception for Phillip Elliott, famous author. He had just finished speaking to an English class at Texas Christian University. He never did understand what Courtnay Howard was doing there. It was only much later that she reminded him they had met several years before in Dallas at Harvey Belding's house. Elliott had stopped by after practice to score some dope. She was at Harvey's with Felice McShane who was, at the time, putting together one of her women's coalitions.

Just networking on Harvey's waterbed.

Years ago.

"So." Courtnay pressed Phil relentlessly, finally cornering him by the stairs. "It is all a posture. You're faking."

"I wouldn't exactly say faking," Elliott stammered. "It just seems important to make the choice of ducks appear as a calculated, literary, metaphorical choice, rather than a late-night, lunatic decision."

"You are lying." Courtnay refused to look at life's nuances.

"No." Elliott was firm. "Explaining the writing of a novel is very similar to the only survivor of a five-car crash telling what happened and claiming he did it on purpose."

"You just want to be certain you have all your ducks in a row," she said, smirking.

"Exactly." Elliott nodded. "You see how easy it is?"

"It doesn't sound easy." Courtnay was suddenly understanding, without aggression. "You look awful."

"I'm just tired." Elliott relaxed, dropping his guard.
He would never get it back up.

Courtnay Howard was small-boned, weighing somewhere near one hundred pounds. Her dishwater-blond
hair hung in ringlets over her bony shoulders. The small
sharp bones made her face interesting. When she smiled,
the six-thousand-dollar investment in the Highland Park
orthodontist seemed worth every cent, except to her father. Daddy was doing two to ten at Huntsville for the
string of holdups he had to pull to pay for the braces. As
soon as he had pulled off enough robberies to pay in full,
his wife turned him in to the law, crying to the sheriff
that "that lazy bum Mac Howard spent every dime on
women and whiskey."

Phil Ellioas not one to hold Courtnay's parents
against her, particularly since she told him they'd been
wealthy cattle ranchers who died in a plane crash. At
least she mentioned them, which is more than she did for
her husband and two little girls in El Paso. Courtnay just
walked out on them and never mentioned them again but
once: the first few weeks after she had met David Stein
in Dallas. Drunk on Bollinger and herself, Courtnay laid
out this hypothetical situation concerning her "friend in
El Paso with two kids and a worthless husband."

Stein saw through her immediately and, within an hour,
he had the husband's name (Tom Reece) and the daughters (Billy Jean, age four, and Billy Jane, age six), plus
their home address and phone number and his Social
Security number. David Stein also had her ass in a sling
and he knew how to keep it there.

Hell, Stein turned her loose on Elliott. Phil was convinced he deserved this special favor she showed him.
This whore-goddess fantasy was a reward for a job well
done.

He had paid his dues. Now he was reaping the benefits
of a decent, honest life of hard work. It would be years
before he learned that he had merely upped the ante.

God does not pay rewards.

Allah doesn't play the lottery.

There is no jackpot for living a good life. There is just
a good life.

But all that was far from Phil Elliott's mind that night in the home of the TCU English professor.

"I haven't read your book," she said, "but I've heard lots about it. My sister read it. She said you are a pessimist." Her eyes seemed to bore into him, then she giggled nervously. "I'll take care of you and look after you. Duckie."

They both laughed and quacked.

It seemed like a good idea, at the time. It *was* a good idea . . . *at the time*.

"You look so . . . so . . ." She searched for a word. "So . . . so sad." She licked her full red lips and smiled. "You should have some *fun*." She glanced over at David Stein.

"What a wonderful idea." Phil laughed.

"Lucky you, for finding me." Courtnay Howard smiled. "Lucky you."

"Lucky me," David Stein would later whisper to himself. "Lucky me."

"I figured a guy who wrote about ducks would be a queer." She looked Elliott over.

"Well, the book is not exactly about ducks . . ."

"Yes, it is!" she snapped. "My sister told me. She read it."

"I *wrote* it."

"So? You could have forgot." She was definitely good-looking and interesting, but at times, Courtnay Howard seemed like a nice room with no furniture.

"Look!" Courtnay pointed toward the front door. A short, pudgy, red-haired man was leading a tall black-headed woman inside. "Those are the *Southwest View* people, Decker and Felice McShane. They have just been hired by D-L Communications to run the new magazine. They brought David Stein and the *normal* people with them."

Phil knew Decker McShane when he was the pro football beat reporter for D-L Communications' first magazine, *Southwest Sports*. The name David Stein seemed familiar but Phil had met so many people lately. He didn't try very hard to remember where he had heard the name. Years later, he was astounded that he ever could have forgotten David Stein, Bob Beaudreau's defense attorney.

"They have normal people?" Elliott mocked. "I should have known better than to come, everybody seems so . . . ah . . . normal."

"God! Even your jokes are depressing." Courtnay kept her quick little blue eyes on the gathering at the door. She was quickly calculating their social worth and entertainment value.

"Oh! Here they come." She turned to face Elliott. Something inside made her feel good. "Give me a big kiss, sweetie." She was on her tiptoes reaching for him.

Elliott picked her up and pressed his mouth to hers, feeling the soft breath on his face. Her eyes were wide and blue when he turned her loose.

"Courtnay! How is my favorite girl?" David Stein walked up, leading a tall willowy brunette. Decker McShane and wife Felice trailed further behind, greeting people, smiling, hugging, shaking hands.

Stein was medium height, dark and stocky, wearing white slacks, sandals, and a red, yellow, and blue orchid-print shirt, open to the navel. He was heavy in chest hair and gold chains. Chiffon Sheffield was thin and into modeling and her freshman year at TCU.

"David!" Courtnay leaned toward him to kiss his cheek. "This is Phil Elliott."

The two men shook hands, while Chiffon shifted nervously from foot to foot.

"Meet my friend, Chiffon Sheffield." David introduced the girl.

"I know you," Chiffon spoke to Elliott. "You played football with Seth Maxwell. I did a tire commercial with Seth last year."

"That must have been wonderful for you, Chiffon," Courtnay's voice sliced her up, "but this is Phillip Elliott, the famous writer."

"I never heard of him," Chiffon apparently contradicted herself.

"Fame is fleeting." Elliott shrugged.

"But you are ridiculous, Chiffon." Courtnay wouldn't let up.

"Girls, let's not squabble." Stein seemed used to the tension and was adept at defusing Courtnay. "I liked your book." He turned to Elliott, smiled and winked.

"Thanks. I hope you buy copies for all your friends."

"So?" Stein was digging in the front pocket of his pants and pulled out a five-gram vial of cocaine. "Does anyone want a blast?"

Both women nuzzled into the heaps of white powder he portioned out, sniffed and snorted, rubbed their noses and smiled with glassy eyes, then sniffed and snorted some more.

"You got another book in the works?" Stein asked, while the women snuffled like they had head colds.

"Yes. I do," Elliott lied. It was his standard reply. He didn't have another book anywhere and had no concept of *the works*.

"He's in the middle of a promotional tour, David." Courtnay took over, her eyes still watering. "He is doing very well. I am going to help him."

"Well. How lucky for you." Chiffon giggled. It was unclear who she thought was lucky.

"Great!" Stein poked some cocaine in his own nose. "That is great!" Elliott thought he meant the cocaine. "Where next?" Courtnay's lawyer grinned wetly.

"You could try your ear," Elliott replied, "but I don't think that will get you very high."

"No!" Stein laughed and coughed again. "No! I meant where do you go next?"

"New York."

"Fly up with us," Stein suggested. "We're meeting with some of the president's people at the Waldorf, trying to keep the DEA out of the mind control business."

"Who is we?" Elliott asked.

"Me, Decker McShane and his wife, Felice." Stein was standing next to Courtnay rubbing one hand across her back. "Felice has political ambitions. She's great at networking."

"No better place to start than the Waldorf," Elliott replied.

"Well, the president is considering massive legislation concerning drugs." Stein's hand never slowed on Courtnay's back. "The social implications of a drug war are awesome: state of mind and body have relationships to basic freedoms. You understood physical and mental oppression as a pro football player; legal chattel, you were chained by law. In fact, rumor has it that B. A. Quinlan's retiring to politics. He's thinking of running for governor."

"So?" Elliott was irritated by Stein. "I played for the asshole, I wouldn't vote for him."

"Well, we have influence in the White House." Stein began to stroke Courtnay's shoulder. "And you ought to consider your own position should Quinlan be elected governor of Texas."

"My position won't change," Elliott said. "And Texas will probably survive. B. A. Quinlan will be a stroll in the park." Phil paused, "Central Park at four A.M."

"You can joke, if you like." Stein was unshaken. "But this system of politics and laws is the best in the world. It works and we want some input. The individual right to choose state of mind will be the political and legal issue of the next twenty years."

"It all seems pretty hopeless to me," Elliott said. "I just came from Michigan, the birthplace of Real Republicans. All I hope is that this book tour has just driven me crazy and not illegal."

"You will find out soon enough," Stein replied.

The lawyer was right. He knew what was coming for Elliott.

"Phil! Wake up, Phil!"

Elliott jerked awake, frightened he was in jail. He looked around wildly. He was still in the back of the Lincoln with John Wilson and Seth Maxwell.

"What happened?"

"You just fell asleep," Wilson said. "I can't give you a complete update, but most of the bad things you think happened . . . happened."

"Phil Elliott," Maxwell sighed, his eyes still on the television. "The man they love to hate."

"Christ! I was dreaming about Courtnay and David Stein." Elliott was thirsty, but instead he dug for a cigarette. "I was at the party in Fort Worth where I met them all . . . Decker and Felice McShane." He struck a match and dragged deeply on the Marlboro. It burned his dry throat. "Damn! I must have been really crazy."

"You were." Maxwell handed him a glass of scotch he had just poured himself. Elliott sipped at it.

"And now I'm depressed."

"Well, if you're looking for *sympathy,*" Maxwell took

back the drink. "It's listed in the dictionary between *shit* and *syphilis*."

"The judge just released Delma from Huntsville." Wilson recradled the phone. "I just finished talking to him. He's out just for the reunion."

"It'll be good to see him," Elliott said.

"You two have a lot in common." Maxwell sipped his scotch.

"How long am I out for?" Elliott finally asked the obvious question.

"Until after the reunion, plus you have some grace time to deliver the story," Wilson explained. "Then, all you have to do is reach some agreement with Denham, Laughlin, and your ex-wife on that piece of land. Otherwise, the judge'll put you in jail until you do."

"I'll never sign off."

Elliott looked out the car window. The high desert land was bladed and scoured into white rectangles. A custom-designed sign read:

ANOTHER DENHAM-LAUGHLIN LAND AND CATTLE COMPANY DEVELOPMENT

Maxwell studied the caliche roads that bordered the development. "I wonder where he's getting the water for his latest Yankee ghetto."

"Laughlin builds for people who drink blood," Elliott said.

Wilson explained. "He's pushing through a municipal utility district while the state legislature meets in a special session to sell all the banks to Wall Street. With a MUD, Laughlin can control it all—the whole Purgatory Plateau. The river, the land, the aquifer, the power plants . . . and the politicians'll give him the power to tax anybody who lives out here."

"He sure is in a good location." Maxwell glanced from Elliott to Wilson. "El Paso, San Antonio and Austin all racing this way with their dicks in their hands."

"And you weep for the Virgin Land?"

"Only because I don't own any," Maxwell said.

"Listen, Phil," Wilson said, "don't go nuts on me, but

Laughlin and Denham will be at the reunion, along with
Bob Beaudreau. It's all just politics."

"Laughlin and Denham control the vote south from
San Antonio to the border," Maxwell said.

"Of what country?" Elliott asked.

"Well," Maxwell paused. "They control the penguin
vote, which can't be good for you, after pissing off all the
ducks the way you have." Maxwell laughed. "So how did
you do in the property settlement?" It seemed like a rude
question.

"All right," Elliott said. "I wanted custody of the
boy."

"She wanted custody of the money." Wilson grinned at
Maxwell. "We got the boy and the right to litigate over
the title to a thousand acres and the house on the
Purgatory."

"Smack in the middle of Denham-Laughlin River Ranch
Estates." Elliott smiled.

"You overestimate your nuisance value, Phil," Wilson
pointed out. "It's a four billion-dollar swindle and they're
not going to let you be a pimple on their ass for too
long."

"I'm not selling. This land will be all Scott has left. I
want to catch these bastards with their hands in the till.
Jo Bob can get me the information that I need. I can
prove they're conspiring to defraud the county."

"Well, shit, Phil." Maxwell was angry. "Don't be stupid. You can't fight everybody. And what the hell can Jo
Bob tell you? He's just a good old boy sheriff. These
guys'll just do a bunch of lawyer dance steps on your
head—and if that don't work, they'll just kill you."

"Well, nobody promised we would live forever."

"Don't you want to see fifty?" Maxwell asked.

"I see it on you." Elliott sneered. "It don't look that
hot. I puzzle over what you did and who you did it to,
pal. You don't *really* need to learn what Jo Bob, Wilson
and I are doing. It would really break Jo Bob's heart if
you betrayed him. And immediately after you break Jo
Bob's heart"—Elliott frowned at the ex-quarterback—
"he'll break your spine."

"Phil, how *can* you even suggest that I would betray
my ex-teammates?"

"Because you're here," Elliott said.

"Look," Maxwell said, "everyone else is selling their land and taking their profit. *Now.*"

"How do you know that?"

"Well . . ." Maxwell looked at Wilson. "I heard. I was contacted confidentially."

"Are you workin' for D-L?" Elliott wanted to know. "Did they send you? If they did, tell 'em that Denham and Laughlin sold me that land on the Purgatory and I plan to keep it."

"Hey! I came on my own. Jesus!" Maxwell grimaced. "I'm just giving you good advice. Why would you think I'm on their side?"

"Because you work for Mitch Simmons productions."

"So?"

"So it's a wholly owned subsidiary of the D-L Financial Group."

"You do have access to some info, don't you," Seth noted, almost admiringly.

"Why should I listen to you? Why should I even *talk* to you?" Elliott asked.

"Because I told O.W. to stay out of oil and downtown Houston real estate," Maxwell said. "He was my teammate. Just like you. But he didn't listen. He and his partners were building a thirty-story office building near Pennzoil Plaza, when oil hit ten dollars a barrel. The day they topped off the building, they went into receivership. Not one square foot of office space had been leased. The goddamn building was brand new, empty and closed up tighter than a bull's ass in fly time. His partners were Steve Peterson and Bob Beaudreau. Both offered me fifty G's to get O.W. into the deal. I told him no. He was my teammate. As I get older, that means a *lot* more to me."

The big gray Lincoln topped the ridgeline and dropped down into the Purgatory Valley and the old town of Purgatory. The driver, Joe, steered slowly into the square, as the three friends in the back stared out the mirrored windows.

"It's a nice little town." Elliott lit another cigarette and offered the pack to Maxwell. "I quit smoking," Maxwell said, "as soon as I got out of football."

"Makes sense." Elliott put away the pack.

They passed the courthouse and the small stone Mexican Catholic church. In front of the church, a small group of people waited for the new sanctuary priest from Wisconsin to open the doors and offer aid and refuge from *La Migra.* All of the people waiting were from below the Rio Grande, having followed the windmills and the rumors north. The Purgatory church was part of the national sanctuary movement set up to aid refugees from political violence in Mexico and Central and South America.

In the churchyard, Emeliano and Cruz Rivera watched the big gray car as it made the square and headed up the River Road.

The two Costa Ricans had escaped the trap set for the coyote and had made it to Purgatory and the sanctuary church. The colonel had picked them up as planned, then told them to go to the priest from Wisconsin and make use of the safety extended to refugees. He promised to return later and take them to San Antonio.

"Do you think that is Señor Laughlin?" Cruz asked his cousin as he watched the big car disappear up the valley. They had seen Laughlin's name on billboards everywhere. "Maybe we should go see him and tell him we used to work for his newspaper in San Jose?"

"No," Emeliano said. "First, we get some money and some new clothes, so we look good. Then, we will get a good job from him or the colonel. We will wear suits and go to offices and screw the secretaries. This is America."

Joe Wood followed the river, heading the big car upgrade as the clear cold water washed past.

Two small fault lines intersected about two miles up from the square, and the narrow canyon opened into a wide flat grass-covered valley. Once good cattle country, the Denham-Laughlin Development signs indicated it was soon to become resort country for the rich and foolish.

An increase in the number of people would result in accelerated use and pollution of the ground water—the only year-round supply, because in drought years the surface streams and, occasionally, even the river would dry up. More people meant more fights over the rights to use water, an unpleasant prospect for everyone but law-

yers and real estate developers—specifically Bobby
Laughlin, Ross Denham, and their lawyer, David Stein.

Crossing to the east side of the river, the car tires
hammered over the cattle guard and they drove into
Laughlin's River Ranch Estates. The water frontage land
was in various stages of development. In the flat pasture
where the fault had slipped and the land sank, Purgatory
Dude Ranch was located in a square of new native stone
buildings resembling an eighteenth-century presidio and
mission. A small shopping mall was planned for the site
and a large sign in red and yellow announced projected
completion dates.

"The big swindle started here. They start with land
flips, selling the same piece of property among their
cronies, sometimes three to six times in one day, inflating
the price with each flip." Elliott pointed out the window.
"D-L then used HUD money to buy from themselves
and build. They loan the money from their S-and-L to
new buyers, handled by their development company, who
purchase the land at the artificially created incredible
prices. The beauty is it's all guaranteed by the U.S.
government."

"Well, maybe Claridge can help you stop the MUD
package from passing the legislature," Maxwell suggested.

"He's as honest as they come in politics," Wilson said.

"Which, unfortunately, ain't too goddamn honest,"
Elliott said.

"Well, he *is* the devil we know," Maxwell argued.

"It is *that* attitude that kept Torquemada in office so
long, Seth," Elliott replied.

They approached the low-water bridge where Frio Creek
flowed into the Purgatory River. Over the bridge, they
passed the eighteen-hole golf course and clubhouse, all
built in the river bottom.

"All this has been made safe from flooding by the
Corps of Engineers and the U.S. Geological Survey,"
Elliott announced.

"How did they do that?" Maxwell looked around in
amazement.

"They sent a lot of majors and colonels and government surveyors and simply announced it wouldn't flood
here anymore. Cut right through all that environmental
red tape and reality."

Large cedar and stone veneer houses on two-acre lots shaded by ancient cypress trees, and more recent pecans, lined the river.

"This is prime land, selling by the running foot. The lots run to the middle of the river bed. The people own the bottom while the state retains the rights to the water," Wilson explained. "Because the last three years have been relatively dry, the river is down and the lots seem bigger."

The road cut back east away from the river past the riding stables and the new hangar that marked the private airstrip.

Beyond the airfield, development stopped and the road cut back west through a wide empty pasture of blue stem grass.

"This is where my property starts." Elliott swept his hand from north to south. "See the way it doglegs around the airstrip while the rest cuts off the condominiums and swimming pools from the golf course. It also fucks up access to the Maquiladora section. The big houses on the river have no direct access to the presidio mall, the tennis courts or the clubhouse restaurant. They have to drive south and cross below the square and then come back along that hogback way to the east."

"How did you end up with all this?" Maxwell asked.

"Ross Denham and Bobby Laughlin brought me the deal while Courtnay and I were still married," Elliott explained. "It looked like a no-lose deal. Laughlin loaned me the money at nine percent and if the development went through, I made a tenfold profit in three to five years. They were just using me to borrow HUD money and hold the land for them. Laughlin brought in lots of people that way, lots of players and ex-players, since he bought the club. Tony Douglas is the game warden out here. Laughlin got him the job."

"How come she didn't get the land in the settlement?" Maxwell was confused. "Christ! She got everything else."

"Greed," Wilson interjected. "She had set the divorce up, secretly over several months, moving all the assets she could lay her hands on; three hundred thousand dollars in CDs and one hundred thousand in gold coins and silver bars, plus the titles to the cars and trucks, bankbooks, all the publishing and film contracts. She turned everything over to her lawyer, David Stein."

"Who, coincidentally, was also Denham and Laughlin's lawyer," Elliott said. "He gets around."

Elliott dragged on his cigarette. He had heard the story so many times, he no longer knew or cared if it was true.

"She grabbed everything but the kid." Wilson continued. "She ran with Stein to Bexar County, filing for divorce from San Antonio. She demanded everything including the Purgatory house and the thousand acres."

"Why didn't she get it?" Maxwell asked.

"Because they had been living in Purgatory County for almost a year." Wilson explained. "The Bexar judge threw the case out and told them to refile in Purgatory. That gave us enough time to protect the boy's interest in the house and land."

"Where is this house?"

"Just up ahead on the south side of Sierra Maga," Wilson replied.

Phil looked ahead at the looming shadow of the magic mountain and the entrance to the long driveway leading to his house. At one time it had seemed so safe, so perfect, so permanent.

"It *is* pretty country, Phil." Maxwell finally spoke. "But it ain't worth dying for."

"Maybe *they'll* die first."

"This guy is always an optimist," Wilson said.

They drove on through the Purgatory toward San Antonio. Phil Elliott slept again, dreaming of an unchanged Charlotte Caulder and of a world that was younger, filled with people who were happier.

Seth Maxwell would fly back to Los Angeles and John Wilson would go on to Austin and the court of appeals.

Phillip Elliott would sleep the night in his San Antonio apartment above the Riverwalk. When he awoke he would feel better but not really know why.

The reunion was two weeks away.

It might as well be a lifetime.

For someone, it would be.

"So, what do I do, Grant?" Phil Elliott was calling the Grant Grinnell Agency from his San Antonio apartment, five floors above the coin shop at the Riverwalk.

"Do you think there's a book in this reunion?" Grinnell's voice was deliberate, thoughtful. He was one of the few people left in whom Elliott placed any confidence.

"*Book*"—Elliott paused for effect—"has come to have a different meaning for me lately."

"We're going to need a new language for you," Grinnell said, chuckling. "Let me call Patrick Greene over at Venture Books. He's stuck with us through everything since the L.A. Coliseum bust. I assume you're broke."

"My liquidity problems rival Latin America's," Elliott said. "I still owe Patrick the Comanche book. What do you think he'll say?"

"I'll see if we can't do a two-book deal. It'll take me a week or two, and Patrick is off in Paris until Monday," Grinnell said. "Will you be able to work for *Southwest View*?"

Southwest View magazine was owned by D-L Media, a wholly owned D-L Financial Group corporation. D-L Media owned magazines and newspapers in Texas, Mexico, Panama, and Costa Rica.

When sex and drugs brought down the ministry of Oxnard Assembly of God Cable Network, D-L Media bought the studios, satellite, and took a short-term lease on the Oxnard offices, planning to move it all to the Purgatory.

Phil thought back over those long, incredible training camps spent at the Oxnard Assembly of God College.

"I get a certain pleasure out of tormenting Decker McShane," Elliott finally spoke. "It's possible to turn that into a working relationship. It's a D-L Media magazine. God only knows what I could learn by accident. I just have to be careful I don't get up to take a fall."

"Well, give it a try. Be careful and I'll get back to you as soon as I can."

The phone rang as soon as Elliott replaced the receiver. He let it ring, weighing the chances of good news versus bad, finally picking it up on the sixth ring.

"Sorry to interrupt, buddy." Decker McShane's voice boomed into Elliott's ear. McShane, the editor of *Southwest View* magazine, was lately considered a possible candidate to become president of D-L Media.

"You *are* sorry, Decker." Eliiott leaned back in his chair and lit a cigarette.

Decker's magazine was a result of the urbanization of the Southwest, the business invasion from the north, the biannual money lobby buy-off of the Texas legislature, the daily robbing of the poor, the halt, the blind, and the middle class. It was all dutifully reported in *Southwest View* magazine. But it was news as entertainment, reflecting the sardonic unreality of the Sun-Belt suicidal Yuppies. Phenomenal advertising revenues had led Decker McShane to the editorial position that all is going to be fine, if we just pull together in designer clothes, Rolex watches, and Gucci shoes. Even the total collapse of the Texas economy hadn't affected Decker. He fired the few good journalists he did have, busted the union, cut out the employee benefits, and gave himself a raise.

After all, Decker reasoned, *can a world be evil that makes me rich?*

So Decker McShane was running *Southwest View* from a big hand-carved desk he found in Jalapa, behind a big hand-carved door he found in Cuernavaca, inside a hand-carved stone building he had shipped piece by piece from Guadalajara along with the Indian stonemasons to reassemble it.

"I want you to hang your reunion story on Delma Huddle's cocaine trial, conviction and sentence." Decker McShane looked out his window at the ever-growing Austin skyline, then shifted the phone to his left hand and wiped the sweat from his right. Talking to Elliott always made him nervous.

"No, thanks." Phil Elliott looked out his window at the San Antonio River and imagined Decker squirming nervously up in Austin, the walls of his office covered with journalism awards. "The legal system makes me nervous, all that justice being parceled out in the courthouse bathrooms, the halls filled with lawyers, judges, and cops, while all the good guys sit around in handcuffs."

"Come on, Phil, a little digging around might get you a decent scoop."

"Bullshit, you're believing your own memos. You're the only news magazine that's worse than television news. You wouldn't publish a good story if you had one," Phil said.

"You need to get back into print on something besides the police blotter."

"Look, I just got out of jail. I'm not anxious to go poking around."

"I know. I helped get you out and Wilson promised you'd do a story on the reunion. I just think Delma's situation offers a lot of range."

"I thought you were interested in B.A. announcing for a second term as governor."

"We're putting someone else on that. B.A. won't talk to you."

"What about Mack Haline, Joe Parten, and Jimmy 'The Bug' Hart?" Elliott asked. "We were together on the first championship team and all three died in the last two years from Lou Gehrig's disease. That's a goddamn pandemic."

"Naw." Decker sighed. "That's no more interesting than Alan Claridge's problem. It'll be old news by the time we're on the stands"

"What about Claridge?"

"AIDS." McShane was matter-of-fact. "Announced it yesterday from the hospital."

"Oh, my God."

"Certainly fucks up his political career." McShane chuckled. "They won't want him kissing no babies. Ross Denham doesn't feel we should cover this kind of stuff."

"You agreed?" Elliott asked. "You got balls the size of mustard seeds."

"So? I guess we're in agreement?" McShane was unaffected. "Delma it is. I might be able to squeeze a thousand plus expenses out of the budget. Would you do it for a thousand?"

Decker McShane knew Phil Elliott needed money. Without considering his immense legal fees, and other divorce-related costs plus his ongoing debts back in Purgatory, Elliott's San Antonio landlord was demanding his last three months' apartment rent in a last gouge before going condo. Elliott loved living on the Riverwalk, near the new high-rise hotels, the trendy restaurants and bars with crowds of strangers wandering from the Alamo to LaVillita. It was a place to lose himself, to forget his pressing problems and to dream of a different world.

"Phil, my man, it's time to use your gridiron experience as commando training for pursuit of the American Dream," Decker insisted. "You had better start working again before there ain't enough of you left to squeegee off the wall."

Elliott looked at a copy of *Southwest View* on his coffee table. The cover was a four-color of a chicken-fried steak, smothered in $500,000 worth of diamonds, emeralds, and rubies with a twenty-cent dollop of cream gravy on top. "The Search for the Best Texas Chicken Fry" was reversed out in red. It was an annual affair.

"I got your latest issue here." Elliott picked it up and thumbed the pages, stopping at a full-page ad promoting "The Maquiladora Program and You," sponsored by the U.S. Commerce Department. The subhead read: "Meet a Mexican businessman face to face." The ad argued the pros of a free trade zone on the border and the cost benefits to employers who exported American jobs to Mexico.

He continued through the magazine, glancing at the slick colorful ads for the Texas-American Dream, all still available, according to the copy, although it cost a fortune.

"It looks good, Decker," Elliott continued. "Not *real*, but good."

"Well? What about the story?" Decker McShane's voice brought Elliott back to the purpose of the call. "Use Delma's story as a hook."

"Why a drug abuse story? Why not focus on Seth Maxwell? An ex-All-pro quarterback becomes successful television star and after twenty-five years of misery our hero finds the rainbow's end."

"Too upbeat," Decker replied. "People want to read about how bad you famous jocks are at real life. It makes them feel good about themselves. Christ! That's why your first book did so well."

"That is a wonderful view of the human nature of the reading public."

"It works for me," Decker insisted. "They want to read about successful people whose lives have gone to shit. A man eventually has to do something real, Phil."

"Is that it, Decker?" Elliott gritted his teeth. "I have to create something for you to prove I am sane, even if what I produce is insane?"

"By whose standards?" Decker shot back. "I am offering you a job that pays one thousand dollars plus ex-

penses, that's more than I pay anybody to exercise their
demented eccentricity toward authority."

"I don't want the job," Elliott answered, "but I'll take
the two thousand dollars."

"The price is *one* thousand. Oh, all right. All right,"
Decker said. "Fifteen hundred and expenses. Only a guy
like you can do justice to this story."

"Fifteen hundred dollars for a guy *like* me?" Elliott
replied. "For *me,* the price is two grand plus expenses.
You'll get two stories for the price of one—what I write
and the story of what happens to me for writing it."

July—*Then:* The Rookie

The 707 nosed down through the smog. The pilot was on approach to LAX in Los Angeles and Phillip Elliott sat in the very last seat in the tourist section of the jet. When the stewardess commented on his choice of seat, the Dallas rookie smiled.

"I never heard of one of these babies *backing* into a mountain," Elliott said.

That had been upon boarding in Chicago. Phillip Elliott, Michigan State University, was flying to Los Angeles to attend the Dallas Football Club Training Camp. Elliott was one of one hundred rookies that Dallas was bringing to camp in California. A combination football/basketball scholarship had financed Elliott's college education. Both head coaches had pressured him for four years to quit the other sport, but neither offered a full scholarship, so Elliott concentrated on sports as a means to an end: his education in communication arts. He never achieved greatness in football or basketball.

"You got to concentrate on one sport in the Big Ten to achieve greatness," both coaches told him, again and again. But neither offered to pick up the tab in full, so Elliott concentrated on one thing: getting his degree. Which he did with honors.

Phil Elliott had been drafted ninth in the National Basketball Association and offered a contract of $8,500 a year, if he made the squad.

Dallas drafted him eighteenth and made him an offer of $500 to sign and $11,000 if he made the team as a wide receiver. When he said he wanted to think about it, Clinton Foote upped the offer $500. When Elliott told the NBA team he wanted to think about their offer, they hung up on him. Clinton Foote signed Phillip Elliott to an NFL Standard Player's Contract in East Lansing, Michigan. "You know," Elliott said to Foote, after the contract was signed in triplicate, "you really fooled me into signing with Dallas."

"How's that?" Clinton Foote was folding up his copies of the contract. "The NBA make you a better offer?"

"No." Elliott shook his head and smiled. "All the time I been talking to you and negotiating to sign, it wasn't until you set out that contract today that I realized Dallas was not in the new league."

Clinton furrowed his brow in confusion.

"I . . ." Elliott paused, embarrassed. "I figured I could make it in an expansion league."

"We all make right decisions for the wrong reasons, Phil. Welcome to the club."

It was the truest thing Clinton Foote ever told Phillip Elliott and he remembered it for years.

During the flight, Elliott reread the glossy four-color brochure the football club sent to all prospects. The booklet described the glamorous life that awaited the successful professional football player in Dallas and America. There were photos of current players and their families, and profiles of the few star players that populated the current Dallas roster.

One of those young stars was the up and coming All-American quarterback Seth Maxwell, who had been on the Dallas team ever since breaking all the NCAA passing records and going first in the draft several years earlier.

The booklet explained everything a hopeful rookie needed to know about professional football, Dallas, and America. It even explained why Dallas held its training camp in California: a combination of weather elements and the advantage of the extreme isolation offered by the newly built Oxnard Assembly of God College.

The one issue the booklet skirted, and the main reason why eighty free agents plus twenty draft choices and all the returning veterans were about to experience a training camp more violent, more physically and mentally

demanding, more exhausting, more terrifying than anything in Dallas's history, was the team's record.

In four seasons, Dallas had won seven, lost forty, and
tied one.

Things were going to change and this was the year it
was going to happen.

And Phillip Elliott was going to be one of the reasons.

The wrong choice for the right reason.

It went so right for so long, Elliott never did notice
when it began to go wrong.

Six feet five inches tall and 215 pounds, Phil Elliott
could run the forty-yard dash in 4.4 and had a vertical
standing jump of forty-four inches.

Now he was following the signs in the airport terminal
to baggage claim.

Phil Elliott only brought one bag; he wasn't confident
of his chances. All he had was one rule: DON'T QUIT. He
would take what they dished out and play the best he
knew how, leaving it all on the field, never easing up,
never cheating himself, or the club. Phil Elliott would
deliver the talents he had contracted for with Clinton
Foote and for the first time in his life *football* became an
end in itself.

They would have to *make* him leave. It was a seductive
release into the joy of a sport. No thinking. No decisions.
No ifs, ands, or buts, just play the best he knew how, the
hardest he could, for the longest they would let him.

As it turned out they let him do it for a long time, a lot
longer than *he* ever thought they would and longer than
they ever thought they would. But there were lots of
reasons. Some of them were even the *right* reasons.

Grabbing his bag, Elliott walked out of the terminal.
He followed the directions on the map that was enclosed
in the form letter to each rookie from owner Conrad
Hunter welcoming him to "the Dallas football family" on
behalf of his brother Emmett, the club president; B. A.
Quinlan, the head coach; Clinton Foote, the general
manager and director of player personnel; and "the rest
of the coaches, staff, and relatives."

The map directed Phil to the far end of the terminal
near the flight insurance counter and as he approached
he could see the others. They were so obviously different
from any other travelers passing through LAX or any

other major airport in the world that twenty years later, given the political climate, they would have set off "profile alarms" administered by every drug, law enforcement, and intelligence agency in the Western world.

As it was then, they looked unusual but were noticed *only* by their own for what they were—a gaggle of Dallas rookies.

There were eight or ten of them in a loose circle with their luggage.

Elliott walked up to a muscular black man on the edge of the crowd and dropped his bag.

"Dallas?" Elliott asked the six-foot man who looked small compared to the others.

"Yeh. Dallas," he said.

Phil Elliott extended his hand. "I guess this is where I belong."

"Don't be too sure." The black man took Elliott's outstretched hand. "I'm Delma Huddle."

"Phil Elliott." Phil knew the name. Delma Huddle was a receiver too, but he had the college credentials to back him up and had been drafted number one, seventeen rounds ahead of Elliott. "How come you're not in Chicago for the All-Star Game?"

"I told them I was injured." Delma Huddle smiled. "I may be from a little nigger school in the South but the worst that can make me is stupid. I ain't crazy. Why should I risk getting hurt just to play in a pickup game with a bunch of jive-ass turkeys that think you can take bein' in the All-Star Game to the bank. I quit playing football for free last December."

"What did they say in Chicago?"

"That I was a lazy, lying jungle bunny, I imagine," Delma replied.

"And?" Elliott was already liking Delma Huddle, although he knew full well the dangers of making friends in the sports business, especially guys who played the same position.

"Sticks and stones." Huddle shrugged. "That's what I tol' 'em. Sticks and fuckin' stones."

"The ball club back you up?"

"B.A. did." Huddle explained. "He's got to win this year or he's gone. He needs what he calls 'impact players.' I like to think of myself as an 'impact player.' "

Delma Huddle was certainly an impact player. He would change the shape of the passing game, and it was Phil Elliott's good fortune to be the other wide receiver when Huddle confused the thinking of every defense that Dallas faced.

As a result, Phil Elliott also became an "impact player." He was in the right place at the right time. It didn't matter *what* the reasons were.

"Well, Delma, who's this here motherfucker?" The guy was six feet seven inches and tipped in at about 265. His head was big and square and covered with curly black hair. The heavy lips smiled, but the eyes didn't. His stare was slightly demented and directed at Elliott.

"This is Phil Elliott," Delma answered.

"Hidy, motherfucker." The big man grabbed Elliott's hand and squeezed. "I'm Jo Bob Williams."

"Jo Bob." Elliott squeezed back. His one strength was his hands and his grip defeated Williams's first attempt at intimidation. There would be many more. It was the nature of the business. "Nice to meet you."

The two men glared at each other and squeezed, until their fingertips went white.

"Hey, O.W." Jo Bob yelled to another man of equal size wearing a soiled Caterpillar hat with the bill bent back. "Get a load of this dipshit."

Jo Bob loosened his grip, Elliott extracted his hand and waved it toward the huge man in the cap.

"Hope you didn't bother to bring a change of clothes," O. W. Meadows said to Elliott. "You don't look like you'll last through the Quinlan Mile."

The Quinlan Mile was run the first day of workouts and was designed by Head Coach B. A. Quinlan to make certain that his players arrived in camp already in physical shape. Backs and ends were expected to finish the mile run in under five minutes, linemen and linebackers had to come in under five and one half. Elliott wasn't worried about running the mile. He had kept himself in shape since basketball season ended. Basketball required incredible physical endurance compared to football, Elliott knew that much. In a regular basketball game, Elliott was likely to run four to five miles, so Phil wasn't worried about the Quinlan Mile. He was right not to worry; he posted a 4.38, the best time in the history of the franchise.

"Hi, Phil." A slender man about six feet two walked up. "John Wilson." He extended his hand and Elliott grasped it.

"Illinois?" Phil asked. "Defensive safety? Picked off two and kept us out of the Rose Bowl?"

John Wilson smiled shyly and nodded. "Say, Delma," Wilson added, "this guy tell you he plays a damn fair game of basketball?"

"I thought you were going on to law school." Elliott turned loose of Wilson's hand. "Academic All-American, weren't you?"

"I'll go in the off-season. If I make the club."

"He'll make it," Delma Huddle observed. "He be one of them 'impact players.' "

"So are those two." Wilson nodded toward Jo Bob and O.W. "Just shows God don't give talent to the gracious."

They had been driving north on the expressway for about an hour. Los Angeles had petered out into sun-burned rolling hills with occasional exit ramps to nowhere.

Wilson was sitting next to Elliott in the blue and white Assembly of God College bus. "Look at that sign. Great, or what?"

A giant green and white sign announced the next exit. There wasn't a tree in sight, just brown hills waiting for a careless cigarette to start the only summer activity in the area:

GRASSFIRES

"El Conejo Boulevard." Elliott read the next sign aloud. "The Rabbit Boulevard?" He translated without confidence.

Wilson nodded. "In twenty years, this will all be part of Los Angeles."

Phil Elliott wasn't sure Wilson knew what he was talk-ing about and it certainly didn't seem important then. "Well, twenty years is a long time."

"Only in the life of a jock, Phil." Wilson stared at the empty brown hills. "Don't you ever forget that. One danger of being a professional athlete is a foreshortened sense of the future."

"I got a real foreshortened sense of the present," El-liott replied.

"Bingo." Wilson turned and pointed a finger right between Phil's eyes.

They rolled through the sunbaked country another twenty minutes before turning off an unmarked exit and turning east on a two-lane road that snaked through the hills past a combination bowling alley, bar, and movie theater.

The bowling alley had open bowling seven nights a week.

"They ain't got enough folks around here for a bowling league," Delma Huddle observed.

The marquee advertised *The Long Ships*.

The theater was open only Friday, Saturday and Sunday nights.

The Long Ships ran all summer long.

Phil Elliott saw the movie five times.

That's how bad training camp was at the Assembly of God College.

Most players ended up with a foreshortened sense of the months of July and August.

The two-lane blacktop led down into a bowl-shaped valley dotted with blue and white metal pole buildings and a three-story stucco dormitory built in a U shape. Beyond the dormitory was the athletic complex, a large blue and white metal building housing the gymnasium and locker rooms with a small football stadium alongside. Farther down in the valley, backing up against the small mountain, the two practice fields and the tracks were set in the basin made by the low hills.

The surrounding country was desolate and in the next valley over the hills, several movie and television production companies did location shooting for westerns, war movies, and films about life on other planets and the moon.

The Dallas football club had certainly found an isolated spot and Phil Elliott had a hard time believing that it would ever look like much more than the far side of the moon, certain desert isles in World War Two, or some lonely stretch of Kansas that might just swallow up Marshal Dillon and most certainly be the end of Chester, with his bad leg and all. He doubted the area's ability to sustain life, much less a major real estate development.

Of course, this was before he'd ever heard of the
Denham-Laughlin Development Company.

The bus dropped them off at the lobby door and headed
right back to LAX for another bunch of rookies due in
from all over the country.

Elliott stood outside in the fading California sun, trying
to imagine the ocean only ten or twenty miles to the
west. All that water and all this dry desert country seemed
so incongruous. It was a feeling that was to become
second nature to Elliott—incongruity.

Everyone had grabbed their keys from the lobby desk
in front of the switchboard and were off in their rooms
unpacking by the time Elliott wandered inside and found
the envelope with his name on it. He tore it open and
dumped the contents on the lobby desk. Inside was his
room key, a mimeographed map of the campus with all
the important facilities labeled, and a photocopied schedule of the activities for the rest of the day. Dinner was
scheduled for 6:00 P.M. in the common dining room, a
square stucco building between the dormitory and the
blue and white gymnasium. The WELCOME MEETING FOR
ALL ROOKIES was scheduled for 7:00 P.M., then FREE TIME
was scheduled from 9:00 to 10:00 P.M.; 10:30 was LIGHTS
OUT.

As he stood in the lobby reading over the day's schedule, Elliott heard the scuffling flop of someone walking
up behind him wearing shower thongs. The shuffling
stopped and Elliott felt the man's presence at his back,
reading the paper over Phil's shoulder.

A long-fingered hand reached over and pointed at
LIGHTS OUT.

"They are really serious about that, kid."

Elliott turned and looked into the familiar and famous
face of Seth Maxwell, the Dallas quarterback.

"They mean that for sure." Maxwell smiled and shuffled off toward the coaches' wing of the dormitory. He
began singing as he turned the corner.

Turn out the lights . . .

Maxwell looked back and grinned at Phil Elliott, then
disappeared down the hall.

It was the beginning of one of the most tumultuous relationships of Phil Elliott's life. He decided he liked Seth Maxwell. It was another right decision made for the wrong reason.

Right and wrong have different values to people with foreshortened senses of time.

Phil checked his room number on the key and started toward the players' wing of the dormitory. The rookies were all assigned to second-floor rooms, the veterans had the first floor. The only veterans currently in camp were the quarterbacks and centers, the rest would begin to trickle in over the next ten days. The final reporting day for veterans was the fifteenth of July. The first ten days of camp was designed to evaluate and eliminate rookies before the veterans arrived. The rookies had to run the Quinlan Mile the next morning. The veterans would all run on the fifteenth. During the intervening ten days, over fifty rookies would disappear from camp. They would be cut, or would quit, or be injured. Often it was unknown what happened to certain rookies, they just vanished; overnight, at midday, between workouts.

Whenever.

Unexplained.

Unquestioned.

Just *gone*.

That would leave fifty rookies in camp when the veterans arrived. That was the mathematics of professional football—simple. But, while discarding fifty players in just ten days, the Dallas club also acquired thirty more rookies who had left other professional camps for various reasons.

Nothing was ever as simple as it seemed.

Phil Elliott climbed the stairs to his second-floor room, carrying his bag down the hall, his eyes cutting from the room number to the number on his key. He passed the open door to the room shared by O. W. Meadows and Jo Bob Williams. Delma Huddle was in his room hooking up his stereo system while John Wilson was across the hall trying to place a call through the switchboard to his fiancée back in Illinois. Wilson smiled and waved as Elliott passed, still checking his key against the numbers on the doors.

The door to his room was open and he could hear someone talking inside.

"I already hate it here and I want to come home."

Phil stepped into the room. A well-muscled wide receiver from North Dakota named Jimmy West was stretched out on one of the two single beds with the phone cradled in his shoulder. With his free hands he was picking at his toenails.

The good news seemed to be that Jimmy West wanted out and he wanted out *now*.

The bad news was, if he stayed, Jimmy West was six feet tall, weighed about 205, and held every receiving record at North Dakota.

It didn't take long to unpack, but by the time he was finished, West was off the phone, wiping tears from his eyes.

"Hi, I'm Phil Elliott."

"Jimmy West," he stuck out the tear-stained hand and they shook. "Welcome to hell in Southern California."

"That bad, huh," Phil tried to casually wipe West's tears from his own hand. It was a peculiar feeling.

"It's goddamn awful." West shook his head, sadly. "This is the middle of goddamn nowhere."

"That's funny," Elliott replied. "I always thought North Dakota was the middle of nowhere."

"It just ain't nothing like that goddamn Clinton Foote promised me it would be," West replied. "He is one lyin' son of a bitch."

"Well, he fooled me," Elliott said. "I thought Dallas was in the other league."

"See what I mean about the lying bastard."

"In all honesty, the misunderstanding was my fault."

"It don't matter whose fault it is now, Elliott. They *own* your ass." West was angry.

"I find a certain comfort in that. I just have to play—everything else is their problem."

"Just my luck," West observed, unhappily, "they give me a looney for a roommate."

"I guess I should take that as a compliment."

"Shit, you might as well. It may be the only one you get."

The dining room was about half full when they arrived and, by the time they had passed through the cafeteria line and found themselves an empty table, another twenty rookies had arrived.

"Look up at the line." Wilson tapped Elliott's shoulder. "The guy with the brown hair and hawk nose, second from the end. That's Tony Laker from West Texas State."

"Another goddamn wide receiver!" Elliott said. "Clinton Foote promised me when I signed that they were only bringing two other wide receivers to rookie camp."

"Clinton meant *white* receivers," Delma said. "Laker's a bitch. He missed most of his senior year with injuries, but his credentials got to rank him right up there with me." Delma Huddle grinned and drank his iced tea.

"Jesus Christ." Elliott looked over at Jimmy West. "When are you gonna quit? I'd feel better if I could schedule that right away before my chances fade completely from my dreams." Elliott glanced back to study Tony Laker at five-ten and 180 pounds. "He looks kind of small."

"Don't you wish, turkey." Delma was cutting his steak.

"The prototype wide receiver in professional football is a guy like Boyd Dowler from Green Bay, or Gary Collins from Cleveland," Elliott said. "Big fast guys who can take a beating."

"Guys like you?" Wilson smirked.

"Maybe so, Elliott," Delma said, "but I'm here to change the game. I tol' you I was an impact player."

Delma Huddle did change the passing game for Dallas, there was no doubt about that, but it took a lot of rule changes before the NFL wide receiver didn't have to be big and fast. Until they ruled out the bump-and-run, clotheslining, blindsiding, headhunting, and the crackback block, NFL wide receivers had to be big enough to give punishment, as well as take it, and fast enough to outrun it when they could. But by the time those changes came, they had little or no effect on Phil Elliott's career, or his health, which by then had become inextricably entwined.

But until then, he gave them all a hell of a run for their money, and when it was over the whys and wherefores mattered not at all. And all that remained were the memories: the men he had played with, the money he left with, and the pain he lived with.

Wrong decisions for the right reasons.
Right decisions for the wrong reasons.
They led inexorably to the same ending.

"Hello, walls, how things go for you today?" Seth Maxwell said as he descended the stairs into the dining room. "Have you missed her, since she up and went away?"

Elliott studied the tall well-built quarterback and wondered how they would get along, if at all. Two big linemen flanked the quarterback; they climbed down to join the other diners. All the rookies were present and only the head table, reserved for management, coaches and staff, was still empty.

"The guy on the left is Bill Schmidt, the starting center," Wilson whispered, as the three vets passed close to their table. "The other guy is Larry Costello. He had to report early 'cause he's forty pounds overweight and B.A. will fine him fifty dollars a pound, from July fifteenth on, for every pound he's over."

"Where do you get your information?" Elliott looked over at the safety from Illinois.

"I plan to be a lawyer someday. Information is my business."

"I could have used you to negotiate my contract," Elliott said.

"I would have gotten you in the right league, that's for sure." Wilson grinned and forked some mashed potatoes into his mouth.

"I want to go home," Jimmy West complained.

"I'll help you pack right after dessert," Elliott volunteered.

"This guy is all heart," Delma Huddle said to John Wilson.

"It comes from playing in the Big Ten. We develop a great sense of social responsibility."

The dining room was filled with the clatter and clang of eating utensils, the ragged hum of conversation interspersed with occasional laughter and nervous chatter, when suddenly Conrad Hunter and B. A. Quinlan appeared side by side at the top of the stairs. The commotion stopped, almost at once. The young rookies, with heads lowered, watched quietly as the owner and the head coach of the Dallas team led the remaining mem-

bers of management and staff present in training camp
down the stairs and to their reserved head tables where
bus boys waited on them and food was served family
style to spare them the time and any possible indignity
involved in passing through the cafeteria line.

Elliott watched the procession with interest. Immediately behind the front rank was Emmett John Hunter,
the team president and owner's younger brother; next to
him was Monsignor Twill, the Hunter family's personal
priest and a religious fixture at training camps and in the
locker room at home and on road games. Following in
the third rank were Jim Johnson, Ray Benroe (the receiver coach), and Buddy Wilks, assistant coaches. Behind them was Eddie Rand, the trainer, and the Dallas
newspaper sportswriter who had just been given the team
beat because his predecessor wrote everything exactly the
way the team told him to and with their recommendation
landed a job with *Sports Illustrated*. The new reporter
was a small, squirrely-looking guy named Seymour
Zolinzowsky; this was his first professional football camp
and the beginning of what he considered the biggest
break in his journalistic career. It never entered Seymour's mind that guys like Seth Maxwell or an anonymous rookie like Phil Elliott could do more to derail his
chances in one day than all the Dallas sports editors
combined.

The last man down the stairs was a beat man for a new
magazine called *Southwest Sports*, financed by D-L Financial, an investment group headed by Ross Denham.
The reporter's name was Decker McShane.

This was just the *first time* Phil Elliott's path would
cross with theirs. It would be the high point of their
relationships.

It was on the eve of Phil Elliott's ascension to the rank
of "impact player" and his star was on the rise.

Phil Elliott chewed what he could of the oversized,
overcooked steak, took a few bites of the instant mashed
potatoes, and scooped up a couple mouthfuls of steam-
table peas, then sat, sipping his glass of iced tea slowly,
while his eyes traveled the room and he tried to take
stock of what he was up against. Eventually, he would
have to confront and deal with every person in this room

who survived. It was an awesome prospect and his first
decision was to take it from one moment to the next, no
long-term planning. Schemes, he decided, should not be
time-framed in increments longer than two to three hours
and personal relationships should be approached with
caution and an infinite capacity for noncommitment.

He felt he was taking the reasonable attitude when his
eyes caught Seth Maxwell's. The two men locked into a
momentary stare, then Maxwell winked, smiled at Elliott
and went back to entertaining the players at his table:
Schmidt, Costello, two backup quarterbacks and a re-
serve center. They were all veterans.

Elliott was still at his table, listening to Jimmy West
plan his early return to North Dakota, when he felt Seth
Maxwell at his side. He looked up at the smiling quarterback and nodded hello.

"You the guy from Michigan State, thought he was
signing up in the other league?" Maxwell rolled a toothpick between his teeth.

"Yeh."

"Well, come on out for a beer and tell me all about
it," Maxwell said.

"I got the Rookie Meeting."

"Fuck the Rookie Meeting, kid. You'll be going drinking with The King."

"I don't drink."

"Never?"

Elliott nodded.

"Well, hell, kid!" Maxwell shook his head. "We gonna
have to fix that. Pronto!"

"Fine, Mr. Maxwell," Elliott replied. "Just not tonight. I already got more than I can handle and I ain't
even had time to suffer jet lag."

"Well, kid," Maxwell sucked at his toothpick. "You go
deal with B.A. and the Hunter family, let Eddie Rand
tell you how to fold your jock and treat your bumps and
bruises, then deal with your jet lag. But real soon, you
and me better go drink together. I'm looking for a receiver who'll drink with me. They traded the last one
who did to Pittsburgh, so I'm lonesome, thirsty, and in a
hurry."

"Why don't you ask Jimmy or Delma here?" Elliott
said. "Or, how about Tony Laker over there? I'd love to

see all three of these guys go to Pittsburgh. Hell, Jimmy wants to go, it's closer to North Dakota."

"You're funny, kid." Maxwell chuckled. "I like you. Stick with me and I'll make you a star."

"I don't suppose you'll commit on *how long* I get to be a star."

"If you were looking for a long career," Maxwell said, turning away with a smile, "you should have stuck with the new league." Seth shuffled away toward the stairs.

"It wasn't for lack of trying on my part," Elliott said to Maxwell's departing back. "This is all one big misunderstanding."

"I don't care about your religious beliefs, kid," Maxwell shot back over his shoulder. "I just want a receiver who'll drink with me."

"I'm quitting first thing in the morning," Jimmy West said.

Returning from dinner, Elliott placed a long-distance call to East Lansing, Michigan.

"Kappa Kappa Gamma." The voice was soft and unfamiliar, a late spring pledge, probably enrolled in summer school because once in the Kappas she drank and screwed her way through April and May instead of going to class. Elliott was hardly one to place blame.

"Jenny Feld, please." Phil lay back on the bed and wondered where West had gone. Home, he hoped.

"May I ask who is calling?"

"You certainly may." Phil switched the phone from his right to his left hand and said no more.

There was a long pause.

"Well?" The girl answering the Kappa's phone was confused.

"I just said you could ask. I didn't say I'd tell." Phil kicked off his low-cut Converse shoes without undoing the laces. They clunked to the floor.

The girl waiting on the other end of the line began breathing heavier. Elliott looked out the window and then into the hall, just in time to see a new rookie arrive, bags in hand. Phil recognized a free-agent running back from Iowa. "Oh good," Phil said quietly. "Someone to keep my crazy roommate company."

"What did you say?" The girl on the Kappa phone was totally without a clue as how to behave.

"I asked *you* if I could speak to Jenny Feld," Elliott said. "So get her to the phone. This is a long-distance call."

"I'm supposed to get the caller's name." The young pledge was whining through her nose.

"She'll know who it is and if you don't hurry I'll be missing an important date."

"Oh, all right." The girl surrendered in dismay. Elliott could hear her calling Jenny's name. There was a short pause and then he could hear the phone changing hands.

"It's some guy who says he's got to hurry . . . something about an important date." Elliott could hear the girl explaining to his fiancée. "He says it's long distance."

"Hello?" Jenny's voice was husky and tentative.

"Hi. I'm running late but I wanted to call . . ."

"Well, damn it!" Jenny's tone turned cold. "I'm dressed and ready to go. This is a fine time to call and say you're going to be late. Where the hell are you?"

"What?" Elliott was puzzled. "I'm in California at training camp. Where the hell did you think I was?"

There was a sudden stillness at the other end of the line. Then:

"Phil! Oh Phil, I've missed you so. How are things in California? Do you like it? I sure miss you!" The questions came machine-gun quick in a staccato, nervous voice. A pitch too high. "How was your flight? Do you miss me? I'm so lonesome."

"It sounds like it. You're not talking, you're raving." Phil paused. "Who did you think this call was from? What do you mean 'dressed and ready to go'?"

"Oh. That." Jenny paused. "I thought it was Gates Ford." Another long pause. "He called. We planned to go to the library and then out to The Gables for a drink. No big deal. He's *your* friend."

"Like you're my fiancée? I love the way you rationalize."

"Oh honey . . ." she crooned into the phone.

Elliott slammed down the receiver.

West looked up momentarily from his packing. Then stopped and sat on the bed.

"Don't let my problems throw off *your* timing."

"I've decided not to leave before the Rookie Meeting."

"And I've decided not to marry the queen of Kappa Kappa Gamma."

Jimmy West left, for the first time, right after the Rookie Meeting. Phil Elliott went ahead and married Jenny Feld. Gates Ford was best man. They were both nuts.

The Rookie Meeting was held in the dormitory lobby and over one hundred folding chairs had been placed in ten rows, facing a blond wood lectern and a large, green two-sided movable chalkboard. The room was almost full by the time Elliott and West arrived. They took two seats in the back row.

Elliott read the daily schedule of daily activities printed neatly on the chalkboard:

Wake-Up . . . 6:00 A.M.
Breakfast . . . 7 to 7:10 A.M.
Taping . . . 7:30 to 8:45 A.M.
Morning Workout (shoulder pads/helmets) . . . 9:00 to 11:00 A.M.
Lunch . . . 12:00 to 1:00 P.M.
Taping . . . 2:00 to 3:45 P.M.
Afternoon Workout (full pads) . . . 4:00 to 5:30 P.M.
Injury Treatment . . . 5:30 to 6:15 P.M.
Dinner . . . 6:30 to 7:00 P.M.
Team Meetings . . . 7:15 to 9:15 P.M.
Injury Treatment and/or Free Time . . . 9:15 to 11:00 P.M.
Lights Out (everybody in their rooms) . . . 11:00 P.M.

"Looks like they got us a full day planned." West nudged Elliott in the ribs. "I hear we get Wednesday nights off after dinner until curfew at eleven."

"Whatta you care?" Elliott replied, his eyes roving the room, checking for familiar faces. "You're outta here after this meeting. I'm going to help you pack."

"Those must be the playbooks." West ignored Elliott's remarks about leaving. "I heard they got the most complicated offense in football here. Look at the size of those notebooks."

Elliott followed West's pointing finger to a long table set up beside the lectern. The table was stacked high with blue loose-leaf folders that were at least four inches thick.

"I hear they got fifteen basic offensive sets and over four hundred different plays," West said.

"Hell, they'll need five or six more years in the league to just run through that playbook once," Elliott replied.

"It gives them a lot of options, makes 'em more dangerous."

"To who? Themselves?" Elliott scoffed. "This don't sound like football, it's nuclear proliferation. We're talking serious overkill here."

It would take Elliott only a short time to change his mind about the Dallas playbook and to understand the basic genius of B. A. Quinlan's multiple-offense football. The system quickly seemed to Elliott like a combination of all the finer aspects of both football and basketball, especially B.A.'s insistence on offensive players understanding how to read defenses. By learning to read defenses, the Dallas offense was soon able to develop the instinctive and intuitive quickness to change pass patterns and blocking assignments after the ball was snapped, catching defenses in blitzes and zones and line stunts, then hitting the weak spots left open. The offense was nearly foolproof. It just took intellect and execution, not the easiest qualities to uncover in ballplayers.

"Men! Men!" Emmett Hunter stood at the lectern and tapped on it with a pencil. "Men! Could I have your attention please?"

The drone of voices quickly ceased and the chairs skidded and squeaked, as the assembled rookies turned their attention to the chubby young man at the front of the room. He was twenty-nine years old and president of a professional football franchise by virtue of the fact his brother was the owner and chairman of the board. Otherwise, Emmett Hunter knew hardly anything at all about football or the business of running a franchise. That was all left in the capable hands of Clinton Foote and B. A. Quinlan.

"Fellas, please." Emmett continued. "For those of you who are from outer space . . ."

"Or North Dakota," Elliott whispered to West.

". . . and don't know who I am, my name is Emmett Hunter and I am the president of this football team. I would like to welcome you all to camp and wish you the best of luck. Your luck has already been running pretty good even to get chosen by Dallas because we are the team of the future . . ."

"I hope he means sometime before my grandchildren are born." Elliott nudged West, who was listening intently. Elliott looked at the square blond face. "I hope this guy ain't romancing you out of quitting."

". . . and you men . . ." Emmett continued his speech, "may well be the future stars of the league. I certainly hope you feel as lucky to be here as we feel to have you with us. So, without further comment, I would like to introduce the man responsible for building this franchise, from the lowliest secretary and clubhouse boy to a star quarterback like Seth Maxwell, and a first-class coaching staff, headed by the most innovative coach in the league, B. A. Quinlan." Emmett started to clap his hands. "With a great deal of pride I introduce to you my friend and older brother, Conrad Hunter. The head of the family."

The rookies quickly took up the applause as Conrad Hunter, dressed out in a Dallas practice sweat suit and brand new sneakers, topped off with a baseball hat emblazoned with a big white capital *D*, strolled up to the lectern. He shook hands and thanked Emmett for the introduction, like they had just met. Then he stepped forward, locked his hands behind his back, and began to roll up and down on his toes as he talked.

"First, let me welcome you all to our little family . . ."

"Only a Catholic"—Elliott nudged West and turned his eyes on Monsignor Twill, standing affably over by the lobby desk next to B.A. and all the assistant coaches—"would welcome one hundred guys into his 'little' family."

"Shut up, will you." West leaned away from Phil. "You're trying to get me in trouble."

"You're *already* in, Jimmy, I'm trying to get you out before you start *believing* all this."

". . . and by the time the rest of the veterans arrive, my own five boys will be here to help out as ball boys, locker room helpers, towel boys . . ."

"And snitches." The voice came from behind Elliott and he turned to see Seth Maxwell slowly walking by, heading for the door. He winked down at Phil. "Don't forget our drink, kid," he whispered. "You'll find you'll need something to kill the pain caused by these meetings. They got drugs for the pain caused by *playing* this game, but only alcohol can keep the worms from breeding in your brain during meetings."

Then he grinned and was gone out the door. Nobody else seemed to have even noticed he had been there.

". . . and I am damn proud to call all my players *family,* and treat them like family. But," he paused and raised one finger ominously, "I expect all my family to behave themselves and follow certain rules, like any good father. You'll find most of these rules written out in the back of the playbook, along with the fine schedule should one be so foolish as to break a rule. Some rules are ironclad and shall never be broken. Those that aren't either listed in the playbook or your contracts will come as directives from either the team office or the league office. I think a word to the wise sufficient and only emphasize the provision against any player involving himself in any kind of illegal gambling or betting, most specifically betting on football games." Conrad Hunter paused and looked around the room. He was still rolling up and down on his toes, his hands clasped behind him. "As I am sure you all know, several quality players were suspended by the commissioner for betting on their teams."

"But," Elliott whispered to West, "it was okay for the owners to do it."

"Will you please shut up," Jimmy West hissed at him. "You want me to get thrown out?"

Elliott grinned and nodded his head. "I think it's the best plan for us all."

West elbowed him hard in the ribs. "Just for that, I'm staying."

Elliott smirked. He knew he was lying.

"Now," Conrad was waving the monsignor to the lectern, "I would like you to hear from a man you will be seeing a lot of around here. A kind and understanding man who will be more than happy to listen to any of your problems in the strictest of confidence, a man whose undergraduate days at Notre Dame instilled in him a love for football that almost rivals his love of God . . ."

"His God is obviously Knute Rockne," Elliott said, dryly, to himself. Phil had played both football and basketball against Notre Dame while at Michigan State.

Games played in South Bend gave Phil a good feel for what being Moorish meant during the Crusades. At the basketball gym, the students came armed with pellet guns; they heated coins with cigarette lighters and threw them at the MSU players during basketball games. It tended to interfere with one's concentration. State didn't start winning basketball games consistently at Notre Dame until the Fighting Irish moved into a large modern basketball facility and the shooting range from the crowd became much more difficult.

". . . so I would like you to meet my dear friend and confessor, Monsignor Twill."

The monsignor seemed to slide up to the front of the room like a high-speed snail, lacking even a hint of the rhythmic movement that indicates human ambulation. He just glided past Conrad as if his long black cassock hid a pair of roller skates.

"Thank you so very much, my dear friend Conrad." The monsignor smiled at Hunter's retreating back and then turned his grin on the assembled rookies. "Bless you, Conrad, and your family, and your extended family that you so generously nourish with your care and concern, especially these boys who are about to embark on a professional football career in Dallas playing for Conrad Hunter and his capable staff. The Hunter family's deep and abiding faith in God and their commitment and dedication to the Dallas franchise make you young men doubly blessed. And, I just want to remind you of the spiritual and social debt you owe to this team for picking you, and to the Hunter family, who work unceasingly for the good of football and America."

Monsignor Twill closed his eyes and his lips moved silently for the better part of a minute, which was a long time to the confused and nervous rookies. Finally, his lips stopped moving, he opened his eyes and made the sign of the cross in the general direction of the assembled players.

Elliott flinched. "I wonder if he's got a pellet gun under that robe?"

"And now, I turn you over to the man who will, more than any of us," Monsignor Twill announced, "mold your lives. He will hone your bodies, minds, and spirits."

Elliott noticed the slight reservation the monsignor left

for himself and unnamed others to also hone and mold his body, mind and spirit.

"He is a man I am certain you will grow to love and respect as much as I do." The monsignor began to clap and back away. "Coach B. A. Quinlan, the coach *Sports Illustrated* has picked as the man to watch." B.A. approached the podium.

"Watch for what?" Elliott continued to needle West, who did his best to ignore him.

Head Coach B. A. Quinlan made his way to the front of the room; the assistant coaches picked up the stacks of playbooks and began passing them out to the rookies.

"Men, these playbooks," B.A. began, "are the property of the Dallas club and anyone who loses his book is subject to a five-hundred dollar fine."

A sigh of surprise rippled through the assembled players.

"Would all the defensive players please raise their hands?" B.A. asked. "We want to make certain the offense and defense books get to the right men."

Ray Benroe, the ends and backs coach, and Hank Henry, the offensive line coach, passed out the offensive playbooks while Jimmy Johnson, the defensive line coach, and Aaron Jones, the defensive backs and linebackers coach, handed out the defensive books. Buddy Wilks, whose coaching position was a subject of speculation for years, stood next to Clinton Foote and picked his nose.

"Men, I know you're tired, so I am not going to take much more of your time." B.A. smiled. "I know you've all had long, tiring trips from all over the country and need your rest. Because tomorrow we are going to start running your butts off and won't stop until you are in the best shape of your lives. Anybody here ain't ready and willing to sacrifice everything to the effort of making this team, *now* is the time to leave."

"He's talking to you," Elliott whispered to Jimmy West.

"Starting at nine A.M. tomorrow, beginning with the mile run, the coaches and I are going to teach you more football technique and theory than you ever thought existed. We are gonna cram your heads with offensive and defensive formations until your eyes bulge out. Then, we're gonna run your legs down to stubs until you know every play in your book." He slammed his hand flat on the thick blue notebook in front of him. "Let me just close with these few words. Professional football offers you young men a great opportunity to test yourself to the limits of your endurance, mentally and physically. You'll learn more about your capabilities as human beings and your potential in the greater society out there on that football field than anywhere else in society. It will be tough, some will find it impossible, but, for those of you who survive, football will teach you the greatest of all lessons, that without pain and sacrifice there can be no success, and the greatest victory of all comes when a man learns he is capable of rising above defeat and over-coming adversity to struggle on to final victory. Because we are all assembled here in pursuit of one goal: *winning*. Winning is the only thing that a professional football team is judged by. Its ability to *win*. Again and again. Our goal, starting tonight, is the league championship, and we must never allow anything or anyone to deter us from our final victory."

B.A. paused and looked around the room.

"Well now, you know it won't be easy and you'll all need help surviving in training camp. That's what the coaches and I are here for, it is one of our most impor-tant jobs." B.A. frowned. "But there are some difficul-ties that are impossible for mortal man to overcome on his own. I know. I have faced them many times and when things have gotten the bleakest, the most desperate, I have always turned to the Bible and the Lord above for his merciful help in facing these tests. He has never let me down and has given me the greatest gift of all: *peace of mind*."

B.A. paused strategically again, his eyes slowly scan-ning the room, as if he could see to the depths of each and every desperate soul there.

"In the back of your playbooks," he began again, "you will find printed the worship schedules of all the churches within a thirty-mile radius, along with departure times from the dormitory. Cars will be furnished each Sunday for those of you who want to go to church. Just sign up on the list next to the lobby desk. Now, go take a few minutes for an ice cream and then get back to your rooms and begin studying your playbooks. Wake-up is at six A.M. tomorrow. Everybody must be at breakfast or expect a fifty-dollar fine. The taping schedule will be

posted and report to the training room at your assigned
time. We will see you on the track tomorrow in just
T-shirts and shorts for the mile run. Good night and good
luck, gentlemen.''

B.A. turned quickly on his heel and, without a glance
either way, he disappeared into the coaches' wing of the
dormitory.

The first night in camp, Phil Elliott slept fitfully. The
other rookies yelled, laughed, howled, and cursed up and
down the second-floor hallway. At exactly 11:00 P.M.,
there was a general scramble and doors began slamming
up and down the corridor. By 11:15 the dormitory was
silent, except for the muffled whimper of Jimmy West
crying himself to sleep, his face buried in his pillow.

Phil had to admit he was lonely and scared, and there
was a tug at his heart to go home, especially since his
phone call to Jenny Feld, the heartbreaker of the Kappa
House. But it would be a cold day in hell before Phil
Elliott cried himself to sleep in a professional football
training camp. Actually, it was a warm night in California
and was only nine days away.

At 11:30, the door swung open and Coach Buddy
Wilks shined his flashlight in Elliott's face and on the
back of Jimmy West's blond head.

"Bed check, kiddies," Wilks said and closed the door.

"Welcome to the big leagues," Elliott said to himself
and rolled over. He fell asleep to the sounds of crying.
He woke just before six to find West gone.

"Oh shit!" Eddie Rand said, when he opened the
door, expecting to wake two men for breakfast. "Did he
slip out after bed check?"

"Yeh, but what are you worried about?" Elliott said.
"He left the bed."

"Whattaya mean? He's gone for *good?*"

"I don't think he's just out breaking curfew." Elliott
swung his feet off the bed.

"Clinton is gonna be pissed." Rand shook his head. "I
just hope he didn't catch a ride."

"Why?"

" 'Cause there ain't no other way out of here and
Clinton will have him back by morning workout," Rand
explained. "It's one advantage to training out here."

Rand turned and ran down the hall, heading for the coaches' wing of the dormitory.

"Jesus Christ!" Phil staggered into the bathroom. "The Yuma Prison theory of training camp location. You gotta love these guys. They're so fucking logical."

Phil ate breakfast with Delma Huddle and a black running back from Tulsa named Thomas Richardson. Elliott told the story of West's disappearance. Huddle said he was going to Hollywood and meet a famous actress on their first off night.

"I been fucking her since I met her raising money for the United Negro College Fund." Huddle laughed his high-pitched giggle. "Her pussy stink, but a pussy is a terrible thing to waste."

Phil laughed and almost choked on his orange juice but Thomas Richardson glared over at Delma.

"Not funny, nigger." Richardson's size and musculature made the remark ominous.

"Thomas." Delma kept smiling and spoke to Elliott. "Thomas is one of them issue-oriented niggers, but he don't mean no harm. But it sure do get in the way of his sense of the more humorous aspects of niggerhood."

"You're all niggers in this business, rookies." Seth Maxwell stood beside their table, looking down through bloodshot eyes. A lighted cigarette dangled from his lips. He turned and walked to the table where Bill Schmidt and Larry Costello (the fat man) had saved him a seat.

All Seth Maxwell had for breakfast was coffee and cigarettes.

At least he won't have a lot of foul-tasting shit to throw up, Phil thought.

What Elliott didn't know was Maxwell had already thrown up the contents of his stomach, which he had filled last night at the bowling alley bar. After curfew. Maxwell sat alone in the bar until 2:00 A.M. drinking alone and looking out the window at the empty desolate valley.

At 1:30 A.M. he watched Jimmy West walking by on the road and drank a silent toast, hoping the poor bastard made good his escape, knowing he wouldn't.

Elliott was scheduled for taping at 7:30 and afterward he pulled on his shorts, shoes, and T-shirt and went

outside to walk in the sun. The Quinlan Mile was scheduled for that morning and he was feeling a little queasy.
Walking sometimes helped Phil to ease his nerves. The
grass on the football field adjacent to the blue and white
Sports Complex Building was wet from the morning dew.
A mist lay close to the ground, hiding the practice fields
and the running track down in the bowl at the end of the
little valley.

Phil felt cold and alone, far from friends and family,
facing an impossible task. He turned and walked back to
the locker room. It was 8:30 A.M. and he was about to
begin a trek to nowhere for no particular reason. He
already understood that, all too well.

He pushed through the locker room door. Halfway
down the aisle toward his locker, Phil Elliott stopped
dead in his tracks. There, sitting by the locker next to
Phil's, dressed in shorts and T-shirt with tears streaming
down his cheeks was Jimmy West.

He looked up at Elliott with a twisted grin and sighed.

"They caught me at the El Conejo exit." West tied his
shoes. "I promised I would try to stay another day.
Clinton said I was letting you other guys down."

"Well, don't do this on my account, you asshole."

"All we got are the physical exams this afternoon."

"I hope you got a fucking heart murmur."

"Me too." West finished tying his shoes and followed
Phil Elliott out to run the Quinlan Mile.

It struck Phil as funny that the physical exams were
scheduled *after* everyone risked a major cardiovascular
collapse trying to run a mile in under five or five and
one-half minutes.

San Antonio—*Now*

Night on the river. From his window, Phil Elliott watched the Fiesta crowds on the Paseo del Rio and listened to the music from the barges carrying the mariachi, country and polka bands. The Evinrude outboard motors thrummed a constant two-cycle accompaniment.

The gray-green river looked dead, barely moving beneath the teeming metal that washed across the bridge and roared down the Commerce Street Canyon. Gleaming machines, polychromatic beasts, lunged, howled, and squawled.

Low rollers.

High riders.

Phil turned indoors to hear the stories coming from the television's fire.

The television news offered a world of structure, but not coherence; the storyteller's indifference did not lessen the horror.

"The trailer truck found by Sheriff Williams of Purgatory had been abandoned in the one hundred-plus temperatures with the human cargo locked in the trailer. Officers of the INS counted the grisly bloated remains of twenty-two illegal aliens, men, women, and children, who had smothered, unable to get the heavy double doors open from the inside." The anchorman smiled and looked into the camera. Sincerely.

"Governor B. A. Quinlan was at the Burn Center in

San Antonio visiting the wounded commandos just back
from the aborted embassy rescue in Costa Rica. We
spoke with him about the illegal alien problem."

B. A. Quinlan grinned out of the television at Elliott,
then reached over and shook a charred hand before he
spoke. "We have begun to take stronger measures and
are in the process of putting a comprehensive border
control program together." Elliott was positive that B.A.
was wearing lipstick. "It will involve combined operations of military and law enforcement. The necessary
legislation is being drafted as I speak. We must secure
our southern borders against drug traffickers and terrorists. We have the plan, men, money, and equipment. . . ."

Elliott turned the sound off and walked away from the TV.

He sat down in front of his typewriter and looked at
the photographs of his son, a child forced to grow up too
quickly, to see and hear too much, and to feel more than
either of them could bear. But he loved the boy and was
loved back, unconditionally, *without reason*. Reason would
never enter into it.

Phil looked at the letters and pictures pasted on the
wall. Crayon and watercolors, a rainbow of love, they
drove the cold from his heart and he turned to the
typewriter.

He paused, glancing once more at the photos on his
desk and the drawings, paintings, and letters on the wall.
Each one was headed *Dear Dad*. Each one was signed
Love Scott.

Elliott began typing:

Dear Scott,
    I'm sorry I can't be with you tonight but I have
been busy the past week and it will take me a few
days to catch up on my work here in San Antonio.
Jaws looks good in his new goldfish bowl. Junior
and Pearl like their new cage and are the happiest
gerbils in the building. Uncle John fed them while I
was away. I will bring them with me when I come
up there to get you next week.
    Well, I've got to go back to work on my book. I
can't wait to see you. I love you and miss you.
    Love and BIG HUGS
                    DAD

Phil removed the letter and typed an envelope, inserted the letter and a five-dollar bill, sealed the envelope and put it on the table by the door.

Returning to the typewriter, Phil glanced outside at the festivities along and on the San Antonio River. From the Commerce Street Bridge, a couple of skinheaded airmen gawked down at the Riverwalk, the trendy cafés and people, the natives and tourists. Both sides of the water were jammed with those in a hot, crowded, intense hurry: to have fun, to experience, to feel, to get rich, to survive.

In 1835 Commerce Street was little more than a rutted dirt trail leading out to the river that was used as horse pasture; *el potrero*.

It was at the bridge during the Battle for Bexar that Colonel Lee Laughlin and his volunteers killed a large number of Mexican soldiers, in a major real estate transaction. With the colonel leading the way Laughlin's Volunteers fought their way down Commerce Street to the Governor's Palace on the Plaza.

The bloody Plaza.

In return for the services of the colonel and his men, the Laughlin family received their first parcel of the land called Texas.

There would be many more claims to come.

There was so much of Texas to be acquired. It got to be a habit with them. Or an addiction.

In 1876, the colonel's consumptive grandson, Clinton Lee Laughlin, was named a captain of the Texas Rangers and set up camp in the old potrero, where he recruited Rangers for a special mission. After two months in San Antonio, Laughlin's Rangers headed out in a heavy spring rain to settle for all time whether the border of Mexico was on the south bank of the Nueces or the Rio Grande and, regardless of the Treaty of Guadalupe Hidalgo, who owned the land between the two rivers.

By 1880 the Laughlin family ended up with another big parcel of Texas.

The Laughlins had definitely developed a taste for the real estate business.

Now, they wanted the one thousand acres in the Purgatory Valley that belonged to Phil Elliott's son Scott and by all the early indications, this one had the makings of another big win for the Laughlins. All that stood between them and the completion of River Ranch Estates was an aging, busted-up ex-football player with a killer ex-wife.

Austin—Now

Courtnay Howard-Elliott woke with a hangover and David Stein in her bed.

The previous evening, after his meeting with Ross Denham and Bobby Laughlin, Stein came by Courtnay's office at D-L Development in Austin. They went to dinner at The Chambers Restaurant, a favorite hangout for lobbyists, legislators, and power brokers. It was only two blocks from the capitol building, making it a convenient place to make deals and hand out bags of money.

David Stein owned The Chambers. He had accepted it as part of his fee for defending the previous proprietor Dickie Lafler against federal charges of smuggling weapons into and cocaine out of Central America.

After dinner at Dickie Lafler's old restaurant, David Stein and Courtnay Howard-Elliott went to the Clear Springs Mall for a wine and cheese party to raise money for Felice McShane's campaign.

Felice was Decker McShane's wife and the Clear Springs Mall was the newest, biggest, totally enclosed, air-conditioned shopping center in Austin. It was financed by D-L Financial and built by Denham-Laughlin Development on the bluff above the Clear Springs, a historic and popular Austin recreation and swimming area where aquifer water bubbled into a natural ten-acre limestone pool at 72 degrees. Year-round.

The mall was built over heavy local opposition. The development succeeded when Felice McShane, then head

of the Capitol Women's Environmental Coalition, re-
versed her position opposing the building and, instead,
promoted the development wholeheartedly as "a way to
provide jobs, convenience, better schools and municipal
services due to the increased tax base created by this
multimillion-dollar project, which I assure you, after careful study of all environmental reports, offers absolutely
no threat to the water quality of the aquifer or Clear
Springs."

After ground was broken, Felice McShane, with husband Decker by her side, resigned from the Coalition
and announced as a candidate for the state senate. She
said she felt she had done all she could for the environment and was anxious to serve a bigger constituency.

The wine and cheese tasting fund-raiser was organized
by D-L Media, the parent company of *Southwest Sports*
and *Southwest View* magazines, and the Southwest Conservative Trust. D-L Financial was the real power behind
both organizations.

"I keep waiting for your ex-husband to show up."
Felice McShane sliced off a cheese wedge and handed it
to Courtnay. "Here, try this. It's fab." Felice scanned the
crowd while Courtnay did as she was told. "I think we've
got a good turnout. Did your boss say whether he was
coming?"

Courtnay shook her head and swallowed. "He didn't
say. This cheese is delicious." She followed Felice
McShane's eyes and together they sized up the turnout.
It was a crowd made up of young upwardly mobile executive types, expensively dressed and desperately greedy;
people who were anxious to trade cash for favors, political deals, or good cocaine. They were all quite handsome
and wore their ambition on the sleeves of their $150
shirts and blouses.

"I figured Phil will show up just to gloat about the
Clear Springs," Felice said. "You remember what an
asshole he was about my decision to support it. God! I'm
glad you divorced that jock prick."

"What about *the* Clear Springs?" Courtnay asked.

" *'Shit runs downhill, Felice,'* " she mimicked. "That's
all he kept saying: *'Shit runs downhill, Felice.'* The dumb
ass never read the environmental report. Typical jock,
thinks he can get his way by bullying people. Well, you

and David sure kicked his ass in court." Felice laughed nervously and gulped her wine.

"What about the Clear Springs?" Courtnay pressed. She didn't care about the Springs per se, she just didn't like the way her ex-husband seemed to be involved in upsetting her friend Felice.

"Some bureaucratic fuck-up. I'll get it straightened out before the election." Felice kept her eyes on the crowd. "It was all politically motivated. They released the new study and took action on the same day I announced for reelection. Hardly a coincidence." Felice turned and looked full face at Courtnay, raising an eyebrow and giving Courtnay *the look:* Them against Us. "You know?"

Courtnay nodded. "I know. But what study? What action?"

Felice turned back to the buffet table and poured two glasses of wine. She handed one to Courtnay.

"Try this. It's a new Texas wine."

Courtnay took the long-stemmed goblet and did as she was told.

"Mmmm." She lowered the glass. "This is good."

"Here's Decker," Felice hissed. "Late as usual."

Decker McShane worked through the crowd toward Courtnay and his wife, smiling, shaking hands, clapping people on the back, as he slowly crossed toward the buffet table.

"Well, honey, it looks like they got out the faithful." Decker leaned over and kissed his wife lightly on the cheek, trying not to damage her makeup. "Hey! Courtnay, you look great! I saw David over by the door. Did you two come together?"

Courtnay nodded and sipped more wine.

"I talked to your ex the other day." Decker poured himself some wine. "He's gonna do some writing for us."

"Maybe he'll pay my back alimony," Courtnay replied.

"I thought he might be here," Decker continued. "He is the kind who likes to say 'I told you so.' "

"About what?" Courtnay asked.

"The Health Department closed the Clear Springs to swimming today," Decker said. "They got some study that says the water is toxic."

*   *   *

Phil Elliott did not show up at Felice's fund-raiser the
night before but that did not keep him from spoiling it
for Courtnay. He had been right about the building of
the Clear Springs Mall and nothing infuriated and depressed her quite as much as Elliott being right.

It was always so much more comfortable for her when
Phil Elliott was shown to be wrong, proven to be wrong,
punished for being wrong; even if she had to lie in court
to get it done.

The judge said he was wrong and put him in jail for it,
several times.

Decker had also spoiled her evening by saying that
Elliott was going to do some writing for *Southwest View*.
That meant that Phil was out of jail again.

"I'll put his ass right back in." Courtnay spoke to her
reflection as she sat at her vanity and studied her face,
looking for signs of age. She had her blue terry cloth
robe wrapped loosely around her, as she planned how to
put on her makeup. What did she want to look like?
Who did she want to be today?

David Stein was still in her bed. He had been no
comfort.

When she told him that the Clear Springs were toxic,
he had replied: "Elliott told Felice that shit ran downhill
and today it hit the fan." Then he laughed.

Sometimes, Courtnay hated David Stein almost as much
as she hated Phil Elliott.

"Goddamn the both of them," Courtnay said to her
reflection. Her mirror image agreed completely and then
reminded her that she had better do something with her
hair.

David Stein was on his back with his hands behind his
head and one of her Virginia Slims hanging from his
mouth when Courtnay walked in from the bathroom and
sat on her bed.

"Phil's out of jail," she said.

"I know."

"Why didn't you tell me?" She turned angry.

"I didn't want to spoil the evening."

"I want him back in jail."

"Not right now," Stein said. "Maybe later and for a lot
longer. Let's just let him go on up to the Dallas team

reunion and write his stories. You'll get most of the money and maybe he'll fuck up real big. You know how he is when he writes."

"No, I don't. I always went shopping."

"He has trouble watching his back." Stein grinned and stubbed out the cigarette. "That was how we nailed him in the divorce. He was so busy writing his Comanche book, we scalped the motherfucker."

"I want . . ."

"What you want isn't important right now," Stein interrupted. "There are bigger strategies than revenge. We do it *my* way. I told you that from the start; *do everything I tell you to do.* It's what I tell all my clients, except I also relieve them of huge amounts of their money at the same time. I haven't charged you a dime. But the other rule is unbreakable. You do everything I tell you to do."

David Stein had built his reputation as a flamboyant trial lawyer with his first million-dollar case, defending Bob Beaudreau for the double murder of Charlotte Caulder and David Clarke.

Charlotte Caulder was a Vietnam War widow who lived on a ranch outside of Lacota in east Texas and David Clarke was her black hired hand.

Bob Beaudreau was second-generation oil money with his own insurance company and had a ranch near Charlotte Caulder's. They had dated a couple of times.

Beaudreau was also a football groupie and friend of Andy Crawford's, one of Phil Elliott's teammates. Elliott knew Beaudreau as a lunatic cokehead and gun nut who always carried a .357 magnum.

Phil Elliott met Charlotte Caulder at a party given by Andy Crawford and Alan Claridge, during Elliott's last season in Dallas.

Phil and Charlotte began dating and the relationship grew serious enough that Elliott planned to move into the ranch house to live with Charlotte.

The day Elliott arrived at Charlotte's ranch with all his belongings, ready to move in, he found Bob Beaudreau and his .357 magnum in the den and Charlotte Caulder and David Clarke shot dead.

David Stein took on Beaudreau's defense and by using the technique of *blaming the victims,* a white woman and a black man alone in a house where the postmurder search turned up quantities of marijuana, Stein got Beaudreau acquitted on a plea of temporary insanity.

Phil Elliott thought they were all permanently insane.

David Stein pushed the soft blue robe off Courtnay's shoulders and it fell to her waist. He ran his hands over her breasts and stomach.

She's starting to lose it, he thought. *The breasts not as firm, the stomach too soft. She'll do until we get this job done.*

"You know he hates you."

"Who could possibly hate me?" Stein grinned. "Everybody loves me. Didn't you read the magazine section of Sunday's paper?"

"Phil hates you."

"Because I beat his brains out in court getting you your divorce?"

"That and the Beaudreau case," Courtnay said. "He was in love with that Caulder woman."

"Really?" Stein was unconcerned. "It never came out in testimony. I established that Beaudreau was in love with her and she was running with the black guy."

"He told me that nobody ever called him to testify," Courtnay said. "And that some Dallas cop named Rindquist told him to get the hell out of Texas before the trial. They had some drug charge on him. It was why he left the football team."

"Well, I'll be darned. I didn't know that," Stein lied. Getting Elliott out of Texas had been an important defense tactic. "I don't think I'll lose too much sleep over it. By the way, I've got some more papers for you to sign. I want to file a few charges against him, just so he'll lose some sleep. They're in my briefcase."

"What kind of charges?"

"Don't you worry your pretty little head about that," Stein smiled.

"You mean my pretty *empty* head, you asshole!" Courtnay stormed back into the dressing room and sat heavily at her vanity, glaring at her unfinished reflection.

"Come on, babe," David Stein called out from the bed. "Chill out. Get yourself looking good and I'll take you shopping. I'll leave my briefcase here and you can sign the affidavits and other stuff later. I'll take the day off and we'll spend ourselves into euphoria."

Courtnay kept staring at herself in the mirror and didn't answer but her skin began to tingle and her nipples turned hard. She loved to shop and her anger quickly began to fade.

"Well?" Stein was standing naked behind her. His face was a perfect oval with a thin long nose, no brow ridges and a high flat forehead from which his dark curly hair had made a premature retreat. His lips were thick and colorless, heavy lines drew down from both sides of his mouth. Crow's-feet spidered out from his large brown eyes and the dark skin of his face reminded Courtnay of a bag that had just unwadded. His small body was covered with dark hair.

"All right," Courtnay said, dropping her gaze to the vanity top, beginning her search for the brushes, pencils, lipsticks, eyelashes, glosses, powders, shadows, colors, and shades she would need.

Courtnay and David Stein had rekindled an old affair when Stein told her that Phil Elliott was not everything she needed in a man or husband. They began meeting in hotel rooms and at his office, primarily as a sexual relationship. Soon postcoital conversation turned to the possibility, then the certainty of Courtnay divorcing Elliott.

They quietly began to transfer and conceal joint assets and lay the groundwork for the quick and final blow.

Courtnay found the conspiratorial theft of wealth and property, plus the desperate eroticism of the illicit sexual relationship and treachery, exciting. The intrigue and deception, the clandestine existence, it all increased her feeling of power and control over Elliott. She found it a profoundly sensual experience. She never felt more alive. The more she beguiled and deluded, the more authentic and self-actualized she felt.

The emotional hallucinations carried her right on through the divorce.

She never noticed that she had completely lost touch with reality.

Reality was now defined in divorce decree and legal opinion. Facts became the currency of settlements and court orders.

David Stein began to lose his energetic charisma for

Courtnay once the divorce was final. Bit by bit she had
seduced him in as many ways as he had her. They had
honed each other to fine edges and, as matched blades,
they cut Phil Elliott to ribbons, while Stein convinced the
court and anyone else who cared that Elliott had done it
to himself.

Elliott and his attorney John Wilson had put up a
terrific fight for the custody of the child. And, when
Stein explained to Courtnay that it was going to cost her
some of her own money to continue the fight, she surrendered the child. He was extra baggage where she was
headed anyway.

The first time Elliott saw David and Courtnay after the
final settlement was when he came by to pick up Scott.
Elliott loaded the boy and all his belongings in the car
and then walked back to the front door of the house
where Stein and Courtnay were standing.

"You may need your client Beaudreau," Elliott said to
Stein.

"Why?" Stein laughed. "You didn't even *know* he was
my client."

"Well, I know now. And you may need him because
you made one big mistake."

"And what was that?" Courtnay smirked.

"You should have killed me," Elliott replied, then
turned and walked toward his car.

"It's never too late to arrange that, asshole," Courtnay
screamed after him.

Elliott got into the car with his son Scott and drove
away.

"Maybe we should have," Courtnay said, as she dug
through her vanity drawer.

"Should've what?" the naked attorney asked. He was
looking at his own body in her mirror. David Stein worked
out every day and was extremely proud of the results.

"Killed the fucker."

"Elliott?" Stein was surprised. "Don't talk crazy. The
poor bastard will *wish* he was dead before I'm through
with him." Stein put on his famous jury face and all the
creases and lines smiled, his eyes danced and charmed.
Whatever *it* was, David Stein hadn't lost one single bit.
He walked back into the bedroom.

"What'll we shop for today?" Courtnay studied her face in the mirror, deciding on the eyes, the angle of the cheekbones, the tones; shadows to cover blemishes, high-lights to bring out other features. Her face was a daily work of art, creating a specific mask. From behind that mask she could perform marvelously. Doing what was needed. Being who was necessary. Playing the role to the hilt.

"David!" Courtnay was dusting powder on her cheek-bones. "Where are we going to shop?"

"Let's go to the capitol," David joked. "Maybe buy us a state senator or two. It's late in the term and they're marking them down."

The Los Angeles Coliseum
—*Then*

Phil Elliott tasted blood and wakened to a shadow
world of strangers and fantastic sights and sounds.
He was being born again with dirt in his mouth and
a roaring in his head, spots of light diffused the blackness, voices spoke strange commands.

"He's okay. He's coming around."

Phil tried to move but nothing worked, he didn't know
if he was standing or sitting. It turned out he was stretched
out flat on his back. His head hurt and his face was
numb. He didn't know where he was, who he was, or
what he was doing. Or, more exactly, what he had *been*
doing, because for the last several minutes he was doing
nothing but lying on the twenty-five yard line of the Los
Angeles Coliseum.

Phillip Elliott had no idea how long he had been there
or how he got there in the first place.

"Can you move your legs?" somebody was asking.

Whose legs?

"Come on, move your legs." The voice came somewhere out of the blackness. "Try!"

The light spots began breaking up the darkness.

Strange faces hovered over him, fading in and out. Life
was blurred, streaked, colors exploded somewhere in his
head, or in the sky.

The roaring grew, then faded. The world went black
again. A ringing started in his ears and he opened his
eyes into a swirling fog. He tried to talk but his tongue
was thick and filled his mouth.

"Can you move your fingers?"

Who were these people? Where the hell was he? What was happening? Who was HE?

He felt hands feeling his neck, prodding and probing, then working their way down his left arm and finally gripping his left hand.

"Come on!" the voice ordered, "grab a hold. Do it. Do it now."

Phil squeezed the hand.

"That's it," the voice continued. "Now, give me the other hand."

Phil tried, but his right hand felt leaden, frozen. Occupied.

"You can let go of the ball, now," the voice commanded. "Come on, turn it loose. Let go. It was a great catch, but they want the ball back now."

Suddenly, his nose and head filled with fumes and fire. Eddie Rand had popped an ammonia ampule under Elliott's nose. Phil jerked his head from side to side to escape the horrible fumes. Rand kept the ammonia under his nostrils and, finally, Phil flailed with his left hand, trying to knock the offensive smells away.

"Is he gonna be okay?" Seth Maxwell stood behind the kneeling Eddie Rand.

Rand nodded. "He just got his bell rung." That was Eddie's standard euphemism for a player hit so hard in the head his brain casing smashed into the inside of his skull, leaving the brain bruised and battered.

It had been the Los Angeles strong safety's forearm, crashing into the back of Elliott's helmet, that had rung Phil's bell.

The safety was pissed off. It had been Elliott's fifth catch, a quick post, Maxwell threw between the linebackers and Phil caught the ball in front of the safetyman. The safety knew he couldn't stop the perfectly executed pass, but he could make this rookie son of a bitch pay an awful price for catching the ball.

And pay Phillip Elliott did. It was the first of many installments.

The Los Angeles secondary was confused and furious. As a unit they had practiced all week to stop the speedburner at split end, Delma Huddle, and this guy

Elliott working at the flankerback had now burned them
for five catches, 123 yards, and two touchdowns.

And worse, after Elliott had hurt them early with his
first three catches and one touchdown, they tried to
change up their pass defense and Huddle had killed them
on two long bombs from Maxwell.

The strong safety blasting his forearm into the back of
Elliott's head was the first good thing that had happened
defensively all night long.

Los Angeles wanted Elliott to stay down. They would
go after Huddle next.

Dallas wanted Elliott back on his feet and in the game.
It was Eddie Rand's job to get it done and Seth Maxwell
stood over him while he worked.

"Anything broken?" Maxwell asked the trainer.

"Nothing important. He's moving his arms and legs
now." Eddie continued to work on Phil. He studied the
pupils of his eyes. "I don't think they got his neck."

"Why is it so dark?" Elliott spoke. His tongue no
longer filled his mouth.

"It's a night game." Eddie Rand held four fingers up
in front of Phil's uncertain eyes. "How many fingers?"

A night game? A night game of what?

Elliott remembered nothing of his life to that moment.
"Who are you."

"I ask the questions, Phil."

That helped. His name was Phil.

"How many fingers?" Eddie shoved them closer, the
fingers blocked out everything else.

Elliott focused and concentrated, knowing he would
learn no more until he counted these fingers that currently made up most of his conscious universe.

"Four."

"Good." Rand moved his index finger from left to
right. "Keep your eyes on my finger."

"What the fuck is going on?" Phil tried to raise his
head. The too-sudden movement made his head ache.
He felt nauseous.

"Look at my finger," Rand commanded and Elliott
obeyed, watching the stubby finger move back and forth.
"Good. Good. Now, let's try to sit up." Eddie cradled
Phil's neck in his hand and pulled.

Phil Elliott was now sitting upright. The football field

stretched out around him in all directions. There were robots moving near him, mechanical men with shiny plastic heads and numbers on their chests and backs.

A man in a black-and-white-striped shirt, white pants and cap, stood nearby with his arms folded. Elliott thought he was God. God's face looked severe. God was deciding whether to let Phil Elliott live or die. And, if it was to be the latter, was he sending him to Heaven or Hell?

"I want Heaven," Elliott yelled at God. "Heaven. Now!"

God looked puzzled then turned and walked away.

"He seems okay." Seth Maxwell was talking to Eddie Rand, who was massaging Phil's neck.

Elliott began to taste more blood in the back of his mouth, dirt ground between his teeth, he spit a red splotch of something onto the grass. He licked his lips and tasted salt; more blood. It was dripping from his face onto the grass.

Eddie Rand reached over and pinched Phil's nose between his thumb and forefinger, then tried to pull it off his face. Pain shot through his cheekbones into his eyes and brain. Rand turned loose of the nose and wiped the bright red stain onto his white pants.

"It ain't broke," the trainer said. "Might have a little cartilage tear. He hit face first."

"Yeh," Maxwell replied.

They talked about Elliott like he wasn't there. And Phil wasn't sure he *was* there; wherever *there* was and whoever *he* was.

"You're doing great, kid," Maxwell said.

Elliott wondered what *that* meant. He was looking past the mechanical men, to where the world ended in darkness. There was something out there in the darkness; he could hear it and feel it. Some giant animal was roaming back and forth, growling and roaring from the blackness.

"Phil, look at me," Eddie Rand ordered. "Phil. What's your name?"

Elliott turned and looked askance at the trainer. "Phil?"

"Yeh. You're Phil," Eddie said.

"Look." Maxwell grew impatient. "Now that you two are through with introductions, get the kid on his feet. I got a football game to win."

A football game.

"Elliott, can you play or not?" Seth Maxwell leaned over and stared into his face.

Phil Elliott.

That's who he was, Phil Elliott, and he was playing in a football game for Dallas against Los Angeles. That was enough to go on. He would figure out the rest as he went along.

"Yeh. I can play."

"Let's get him to his feet, Seth." The trainer grabbed Elliott's left arm.

Seth.

Seth was the guy standing over him in the football uniform. It was football. Those weren't robots wandering around, they were men in football gear. He was Phil Elliott and he knew how to play football and he knew this was a football field. Beyond that, it was all pretty hazy.

"Here, take another whiff of this. Your eyes still look a little glassy." Rand popped another ampule under his nose. It felt like the top of his head was coming off. "Okay, Maxwell. Gimme a hand with him."

Seth Maxwell was the quarterback, Elliott remembered that now and he knew what the quarterback's job was, and he knew he was a flankerback. They pulled him to his feet and the change of perspective triggered even more recall. He knew this field of play. The yard lines and sidelines, the end zones and goal posts, were part of an intuitive geography and life skill.

Instinct told him not to think beyond these boundaries; what lay beyond was an incomprehensible turmoil with which he had neither the time nor presence of mind to deal.

Elliott followed Seth Maxwell back to the Dallas huddle. He had a game to play and he still knew *how* to play it.

Before the night was over, Phil Elliott had three more catches for another touchdown and sixty-five more yards.

Phillip Elliott had become an impact player.

The Middle Linebacker
—*Now*

Newly appointed Game Warden Tony Douglas drove along the Purgatory River in his jeep. The drought had lowered the water level, making the limestone riverbed relatively easy to navigate in the four-wheel vehicle. When he reached the low-water bridge, upriver from the River Ranch Estates development, Douglas stopped the jeep and turned off the engine.

The night was silent except for occasional howls from the coyotes that roamed Governor B. A. Quinlan's Pigskin Ranch on the south fork of the river. Upon Quinlan's retirement as coach of the Dallas football team and subsequent announcement as a candidate for governor, Ross Denham and Bobby Laughlin made him a gift of the five thousand-acre ranch that D-L Financial had repossessed from an unfortunate Houston oil man who had expected West Texas crude to hit a hundred dollars a barrel. He was only off by one zero.

Although B.A. still had a house in Dallas, he quickly changed his legal residence to Purgatory County. It was part of the quid pro quo for the ranch and unlimited financial support for his gubernatorial race. B. A. Quinlan now supported the Denham-Laughlin slate of candidates and issues, which meant he had voted against Jo Bob Williams, his faithful offensive guard, for sheriff.

Jo Bob won anyway, but he never forgot that his old coach had publicly campaigned against him. Nor did he forget that his ex-teammate Tony Douglas sat stoically on the platform behind the governor at an anti-Jo Bob Williams rally.

"Those motherfuckers!" Jo Bob had said to Phil Elliott, who had ridden with him to the rally. "The bastards turned out to be exactly like you described them in *Famous American Ducks*."

"That book was a work of fiction," Elliott replied, making the disclaimer that had become reflexive.

"Fiction this, motherfucker." The sheriff grabbed his genitals.

"Can I assume this is the beginning of a friendship?" Elliott grinned and looked back at the stage. The flags of Texas and the United States hung as backdrops while B. A. Quinlan, ex-coach and current governor, continued to lie and betray one of his most loyal players.

"You know," Jo Bob said, "when B.A. decided to go with the youth movement, he had Buddy Wilks cut me. He didn't have the guts to face me himself."

"What would you have done to him, if he had?"

"Beat the living shit out of the motherfucker."

"So, he may be dishonest," Elliott observed, "but he isn't crazy."

As they moved into middle age and events put them into proximity in Purgatory, Jo Bob Williams and Phil Elliott became friends, while Tony Douglas and B. A. Quinlan moved into the ranks of the enemy.

Things change.

The coyotes started yipping and barking. Tony Douglas would go after them later. They hadn't bothered any of B. A. Quinlan's goats or sheep but three of Mrs. Quinlan's French poodles had disappeared and the governor wanted that stopped.

Douglas hadn't had much extra time to hunt coyotes. Deputy O. W. Meadows had kept him busy working the picketline, prowling the valley and upland looking for wetback signs.

The picketline was Colonel Glanton's plan to secure the border against drug smugglers and terrorists. Glanton was convinced that they were moving across the Rio Grande with the illegal aliens, so his solution was to catch and kill every alien that came through. It was a model program he had developed at Purgatory Military Institute and was certain, after he made it work in Purgatory, he could sell it through the governor on a national scale.

Tony Douglas hadn't seen any signs of wetbacks since they caught that bunch in the trailer truck. A slight fear gnawed at his tiny brain: the big Mexican, Raul, had apparently escaped and Jo Bob had him lodged in jail with that asshole Elliott. If Raul talked, there might be hell to pay with Jo Bob. Colonel Glanton had told them all not to worry and had assigned O.W. to take care of Raul, but Game Warden Tony Douglas would not rest easy until he was sure the guy was dead and gone.

"The big East Coast money people won't invest seriously in plants and industrial capacity until we can assure them that their investments will be safe," Glanton had told his handpicked Picketline Unit. "Northern Mexico is in rebellion. We must be ready to respond to this communist conspiracy at a moment's notice."

The chain of command was simple: Glanton controlled Tony Douglas and Ross Denham controlled Glanton. *Southwest View* magazine had named Denham "the greatest Texan since Sam Houston." He was a man of national prominence and respect who not only controlled Governor Quinlan but had direct access to the Oval Office. It was through Denham's influence that Colonel Glanton had launched his disastrous rescue attempt of hostages held in the American Embassy in Costa Rica. Of course, when the rescue ended so messily—with quite a few deaths and even more questions—Denham disavowed any knowledge, not only of the mission, but of Colonel Glanton. For some reason, probably because he said it so many times and usually on television, people believed him.

Tony Douglas worshiped Ross Denham and wanted to grow up just like him. The ex-football player had no way of knowing that game warden was the highest he would ever get on the totem pole he thought was real life. Football had destroyed what little self-awareness he had ever possessed. Phil Elliott had told him that years ago.

"Ignobility is not a divine attribute, Tony," Elliott had told him on the practice field one day, just after Douglas had clotheslined him during a pass drill and broken his nose. "You might make some money being a cheap shot artist, but you won't get to heaven."

Douglas waited for the receiver to get to his feet and then punched him in the stomach.

"Maybe not, Elliott," the linebacker had said. "But I like the way it feels."

"Blame that on your limited range of feelings and a complete absence of self-awareness," Elliott gasped, before staggering over to the fence to vomit. The front of his white jersey was blood-soaked.

Tony Douglas, the game warden, laughed as he recalled the mess he had made of Phil Elliott. As he sat by the river, he wondered if Elliott was still in jail and whether he might talk O.W. into letting him knock Elliott off the walls for laughs.

The game warden smirked and glanced across the water. This game trail was a popular ford for wetbacks following the windmills north. Tony would sit here and wait a while longer. Later, he might move.

When the moon was high, he would drive up on top of Sierra Maga and park above Elliott's empty house. From there, he could survey the whole valley and would probably catch the Abbott brothers spotlighting axis deer on Bobby Laughlin's exotic game ranch. That was always good for fifty or a hundred dollars from Laughlin and the fun of rousting the cedar choppers.

Tony Douglas was too full of himself to realize the dangers inherent in making trouble with a family of cedar choppers, especially a family like the Abbotts, whose principal weapons in a fight, if not guns, were double-bit axes and chainsaws.

Matthew Abbott, the eldest, had once gotten in a fight in Ingram with another cedar chopper and they *both* used chainsaws. The fight ended with Matthew's opponent lying on the gravel parking lot, screaming and clawing with his left hand, trying to reach his right arm which lay a full ten feet away up under a flatbed truck stacked with cedar logs.

Matthew just tossed his saw in the back of his pickup and drove off, leaving the loser in an ever-widening pool of blood.

Tony Douglas leaned back and gazed into the night sky. The wind picked up slightly and rustled the oak leaves. The constant sound of the moving water entranced him and he slipped out of time.

At first, Tony Douglas thought the sound came from behind him, but the canyon walls can play tricks with noise and it had echoed from across the river.

Probably a deer, he thought.

As the crunch of leaves and twigs grew louder, Douglas realized the sound was coming from across the river, heading for the ford. Instinctively, he unsnapped his holster and reached for the spotlight.

When he heard the slurping and splashing on the far riverbank, as the animal drank, Tony Douglas flicked on his two-hundred-thousand-candlepower light and quickly raked the limestone ledges along the water.

The man was crouched on all fours, drinking from his cupped hands.

He was stark naked. Looking up, directly into the spotlight, the insane shine of his eyes startled Douglas. They were wild animal's eyes. Angry eyes. A wild mane of black hair splayed out from the dark Indian face.

"I better kill this sumbitch quick," Douglas mumbled, half-scared, as he stepped out of the jeep. He kept the light beam on the crouched man and reached for his pistol. The man seemed frozen by the light, his eyes sparkling like a ringtail cat.

Suddenly, to the game warden's right, something moved and he glanced toward the movement. When he looked back, the naked man was gone.

"Shit!" Douglas pulled his flashlight from beneath the seat. "Now I got to hunt him down." He took a closer look to his right where he thought he had seen movement, scanning the beam of the flashlight along the brush. He saw nothing.

Shifting the flashlight to his left hand and holding his cocked revolver in his right, Game Warden Tony Douglas waded across at the ford and began searching the riverbank for the man.

As Douglas worked down the riverbank away from his jeep, Matthew Abbott stepped out from behind the tree. Waiting for a deer to come drink, he had been standing there since before the game warden drove up. Matthew Abbott hated Tony Douglas. The Abbotts had been hunting the Purgatory country for generations and now this snot-nosed new game warden had taken it upon himself to hassle them about where and when and what they could shoot and eat.

Matthew Abbott had figured that one day he might have to kill the new game warden, but he was very hesitant. The game warden and Sheriff Williams had been friends before Williams moved back to take his father's job as the new Purgatory sheriff and Matthew knew if he killed the game warden, Sheriff Jo Bob Williams would come looking for him.

Matthew wasn't afraid of the six-seven, 275-pound lawman (in fact Matthew was six-eight and weighed over three hundred well-muscled pounds), but he knew Sheriff Williams wasn't afraid of him either and it was certain that one or both of them would end up dead.

Matthew Abbott didn't want to die. He was most certainly the meanest man to be found in the breaks of the Purgatory River but that didn't mean he was stupid. He fought only when he had to fight. Because he was poor he had to fight a lot. Fighting Sheriff Jo Bob Williams seemed to be a no-win proposition.

If worse came to worst, Matthew would get one of his brothers to kill the game warden and Sheriff Williams. Matthew had more brothers than he needed.

Across the river, pistol shots echoed out of the darkness.

It was dark on the square in Purgatory. It was 5:00 A.M. and at Doc's Café, the first place to open every morning, began a ritual so precise people set their watches by it.

The routine began when Doc walked through the unlocked door. Then he filled and started the coffee maker, fired up the big stove, made the biscuits and slid the pan in the preheated oven. Then he would go out and sit on the porch, time the biscuits, drink coffee, watch the town wake up and his customers arrive with their stories. The first liar never had a chance.

But this morning the schedule changed and Purgatory never was the same again.

Doc's first match blew out in the draft from an open kitchen window. Doc quickly struck the second, but gas had already filled the oven.

The explosion blew Doc backwards over the salad table and slammed him against the upright freezer.

Waking for the second time that morning, his eyebrows and eyelashes singed off, he struggled over to the stove and turned off the gas. He kicked the oven door closed and left the makings on the batter board. Thus ended a cosmic ritual that stretched back to the first day he took over the café after the war.

Born and raised up north in the breaks of the Purgatory River on the Blaine Ranch, Doc left only once, in 1942, when he hitchhiked into San Antonio and met the Marine recruiter.

Doc didn't get back to Purgatory until 1945. He never left again.

Doc leaned against the stone porch pillars and felt the sweating stones turn his shirt wet. A Blaine Ranch pickup truck rattled in from the north off Comanche Ridge Road, past the military school, onto the square and stopped in front of the café.

L. Ray Prescott, foreman for the Blaine Ranch, closed his bloodshot eyes and leaned forward against the steering wheel, still in last night's blue down jacket, red-and-black-flowered western shirt, blue snakeskin boots, black wide-brimmed hat and starched Levis strung by a leather belt, hand tooled, and fastened with the calf roping buckle that he won at the Negro rodeo in Winnie. L. Ray had respect for black cowboys.

L. Ray had married Ruby Lee Abbott and dropped out of high school. Jo Bob Williams was the best man. "I never went much for reading them books," L. Ray told Doc the day he quit school. "I just like to run my finger in that ol' pussy."

Now, L. Ray lifted his head from the steering wheel, stepped slowly, carefully from the cab and shuffled up onto the porch of the café.

"You look gutshot," Doc told him.

"Been bowling."

"With all those squareheads at the Bowling Club? All night?"

L. Ray nodded. "Beer frames. And whiskey frames, too."

"I'd give up bowling for sex, if I was you," Doc told L. Ray. "You don't have to change shoes so much and the balls ain't near as heavy."

L. Ray staggered into the café, poured himself a cup of

coffee and lit up a cigarette as best he could with his shaking hands.

He was sitting there, reasonably under control, and Doc came back inside to try making biscuits one more time.

They both heard the screech of tires and an engine turn off, but they didn't pay it too much mind. They began to pay closer attention, though, when the two naked women ran in.

"We saw a wild man!" They both spoke at once. "It was horrible! We were sunbathing on Table Rock, the other side of those little falls. He came down that canyon wall like a monkey, then he dug through our bags and searched the car and took our clothes!"

"He didn't look human," one of them said. Her name was Brenda.

"For sure," the other one agreed. She was Mary Ralph.

Doc and L. Ray watched them talk, one tall with thick black hair, tan shoulders and perfect, enormous breasts; the other, less spectacular but pretty, with blue eyes, slender arms and legs and small breasts.

"Could be a wild man," Doc said.

"That's right," L. Ray agreed. "We've had 'em before and we'll have 'em again. No reason not to have one now."

Jo Bob—Now

Jo Bob Williams had been awake an hour when the orange sun finally peeked between the ridge line and the low, gray, cloud-saturated sky. He listened to the quiet of the house. It seemed unnatural. Helene had taken the kids and already left for Dallas. He would meet her up there in time for the reunion.

The reunion. He hadn't seen many of his ex-teammates in nearly fifteen years. Once the team released him, he came straight back to the Purgatory and went to work as a deputy for his father. When his father was killed by the gunrunners in Bahia, Jo Bob was appointed sheriff by Judge Zack Blaine. Jo Bob liked his job. And he liked Judge Blaine, mostly because the old man hated Ross Denham more than anyone in Purgatory County. The hatred burned so brightly because Denham had, more or less, stolen the Purgatory Bank away from the Blaine family when the Texas economy had collapsed. Jo Bob liked anyone who hated Denham or B. A. Quinlan. But he also liked most of his old teammates and he was sorry he had so little time to get back to Dallas and look them up.

When Phil Elliott moved to the Purgatory, Jo Bob had to admit he was glad to see him. They were teammates and shared certain things that just couldn't be explained to outsiders.

He grew to respect and like Elliott even more when his ex-wife took him to war against Bobby Laughlin, David

Stein, and all the D-L Financial henchmen. It took a lot
of guts for Elliott to take the beating they gave him, but
that was one thing every player had respected Elliott for:
his willingness to take a beating, to do his job. Now he
was crippled and broke, but he never stopped trying to
do what he thought was right.

As he awkwardly pulled himself up out of bed by using
the brass bedstead, Jo Bob Williams realized, as he did
every morning, that he too had taken an awful beating,
while keeping crazed defensive linemen from getting to
Seth Maxwell. He had never really healed; instead, like
Phil Elliott he had learned to ignore the pains. That
wasn't always possible but it was the only alternative.

Jo Bob spent many restless, agonizing nights. He was
pushing forty-eight and sleep came hard. His dreams
were few but always of what had been or would soon be
no more.

Youth had flown so fast, he didn't even remember it as
his life. It was like somebody else had been Jo Bob
Williams, the All-Pro guard, and he had always been this
crippled man, old before his time. He hadn't been robbed
of his dreams, he had been sold somebody else's dreams.
Clinton Foote, B. A. Quinlan, and Conrad Hunter had
done the selling, taking his dreams in trade.

He fastened the pearl snaps on his shirt and tucked the
tail into his boot-cut slacks. Pulling on his socks and
boots made his back hurt. He straightened up slowly,
carefully.

"Come on, motherfucker, pull yourself together." The
wooden floor creaked, as the big man walked over to the
closet. "Everybody gets old and sentimental, you *don't*
have to add stupidity," the sheriff scolded himself.

He had dreamed about the old days when he was
young and strong, a force to be reckoned with on a
football field. He saw all their faces and he missed them.
He had loved them, as only men engaged in an intense
struggle for honor and glory could love.

And it had all been a charade.

He learned that the day Buddy Wilks told him to turn
in his playbook.

He wasn't needed.

He wasn't wanted.

Worst of all, he wasn't missed.

But oh, how he had missed football, how he had suffered.

He was a man and he learned to deal with it. But he couldn't control his dreams and those awful yearnings that came with them. He wanted to be young again. He would not be so quick to spend those precious years and those precious friends. Phil Elliott had been a godsend. They talked about those times and the times to come. He used to think Elliott was crazy and now Elliott kept him from thinking *he* was crazy.

The last time Elliott came over to talk, Jo Bob got out his telescope and they searched the sky and the insides of their heads for signs of intelligent life.

They weren't sure they found any in either place. But they did decide that Elliott liked strawberry ice cream better than chocolate or vanilla, that Jo Bob had probably made a big mistake giving O.W. a badge and a gun, that there wasn't a devil—there was just evil, and that they actually loved each other as ex-teammates, friends, and hopeful survivors of the upcoming shit storm.

As he finished dressing that morning, Jo Bob thought about his friendship with Elliott.

But, as he strapped on his pistol, his thoughts wandered to Raul and the mysteries surrounding him. The big Mexican was obviously terrified and now that he had disappeared from jail, Jo Bob *knew* that it wasn't him the prisoner had been frightened of; it was something he knew or had seen.

Jo Bob Williams had a newfound pride in his job as sheriff and he would be damned if a prisoner was going to disappear from his jail. Raul had been under his protection and before this day was out, Sheriff Jo Bob Williams was going to find out what had happened to the man.

He already had a pretty good idea that O. W. Meadows was involved. There were only three keys to the jail: Jo Bob had one, the turnkey had one, and O.W. had the third.

The turnkey had called Jo Bob at 2:00 A.M., when he noticed the prisoner gone during his early morning rounds.

The sheriff had gone there immediately.

Outside the jail, Jo Bob found two sets of prints,

leading from the rear door. One set were boot prints, the
other were bare feet. The boot prints also led into the
jail, starting from the spot where some tire tracks stopped.

Jo Bob recognized O.W.'s radical heel in the boot
prints and the wide track marks made by the radials on
O.W.'s car.

The sheriff said nothing to anybody. He needed time
to think. Finally, late the next day, when he went to get
Elliott out and talk to him, he discovered that John
Wilson already had him out on a writ and they had
driven off in a big gray limousine. The turnkey swore
that Seth Maxwell was with them.

He wished Elliott had stayed around, but figured he
had fled to his San Antonio place or up to Wilson's
Ranch before his ex-wife and her lawyer tried to put him
back in jail.

He would track Elliott down later and discuss the latest
turn of events, but today he was going to nail some things
down on his own.

Assuming O.W. took Raul from the jail, Jo Bob still
had to find out why.

His philosophy was: Never ask a question until you
already know the answer.

O. W. Meadows stood behind his white Chevrolet, parked
at the PMI fenceline. He was a giant man, having put on
sixty pounds of fat since leaving football. The fat hung
from his waist in huge rolls, flowing over his belt, forcing
his holster so low his gun was almost out of reach. He
had to bend to the side to draw it.

A high crowned hat perched on his balding head. His
jowls hung below his jawline and the fat of his neck made
buttoning his shirt impossible.

Fifteen years ago, O.W. and Jo Bob had been teammates in Dallas. The years had not had the same mellow-
ing effect on O.W., particularly since he made no attempt
to reconcile the contradictions of violence in his life, and
a residual rage haunted him.

After hanging out in San Antonio with Andy Crawford
and Dickie Lafler for a year or two, O.W. plunged into
the Houston building market. As O.W.'s first big high-
rise project was going up, the Texas economy was sinking
faster than the *Titanic*. The market was already soft when

O.W. let Steve Peterson and Bob Beaudreau sell him on the idea of building office buildings.

Jo Bob told Phil Elliott that O.W. was going into business.

"Well, you got to hand it to O.W.," Elliott said. "This must be the first known case of a rat swimming *to* a sinking ship."

At the time, Jo Bob didn't know how right Elliott was. The day O.W. topped off his building, the bank foreclosed on him.

Aging had not brought maturity to O.W. as it did to Jo Bob.

While Jo Bob mellowed out and grew to like the slow pace of his hometown, enjoying the rewards of a loving wife and children, O.W. was nose deep in the Houston-Dallas-San Antonio fast lane. And he was sinking deeper. When the bottom fell out of the Texas economy and landed on O.W. (somehow missing Peterson and Beaudreau altogether), Meadows was fourteen million dollars in debt. He had also run several hundred thousand up his nose, which did no good for his already vicious personality.

When O.W. showed up in Purgatory and asked Jo Bob for a job, Sheriff Williams found himself in an untenable position. His brain told him that O.W. neither had the disposition to be a deputy, nor would he be able to live on the meager salary offered. Jo Bob knew that O.W. hadn't made the necessary mental and emotional adjustments required to keep him within psychological parameters incumbent upon a man who enforces the law and carries a gun.

Put simply: O. W. Meadows was crazy as a shithouse rat.

But, O. W. Meadows had been his teammate and there was no way for Jo Bob to discount that relationship.

So O.W. got the deputy's badge, while Jo Bob spared no effort to make his decision work.

But it hadn't.

And, as Jo Bob shut off his truck and stepped out into the sun, he knew he would have one hell of a job making things right again. He knew full well, since O.W. had certainly taken Raul from jail, that things might *never* be right again.

O.W. waddled over to Jo Bob's truck and leaned against the fender. He was breathing heavily from the effort, his lips were stained with tobacco juice and his face distorted by the large wad of Red Man stuffed in his cheek.

Jo Bob studied the boot prints in the loose caliche of the road. They matched the ones outside the jail.

"You going to the reunion?" O.W. asked. He shifted the tobacco and spit. "I can't wait to see Seth and the guys."

"We won't be able to go, O.W., until we find out what happened to that Mexican you let out of jail." Jo Bob lit another cigarette, keeping his eyes on O.W.'s face. There was a lump and a large bruise on the side of his head.

"What are you talking about?" O.W. dropped his eyes, avoiding Jo Bob's gaze. "I didn't . . ."

"Save it," Jo Bob said. He casually rested his hand on the butt of his pistol.

"But . . . I . . ."

"Can it, you back-stabbing motherfucker," Jo Bob ordered. "Now, you are going to tell me what happened to Raul and who told you to do it."

"Fuck you!" O.W. spit at Jo Bob's feet. "I ain't scared of you. The people I work for will squash you like a bug."

"Not before I kick your ass up and down this valley until you tell me what I want to know, you ungrateful tub of shit."

O.W. reached clumsily for his pistol. He hadn't even gotten his fingers around the grip before he was looking down the barrel of Jo Bob's revolver.

"Just unbuckle the belts," Jo Bob said.

O.W.'s eyes narrowed in fury, as he grappled with the gun belt buckle and let the gun, hand-tooled holster and belt fall to the ground.

"Now the other buckle."

"My pants'll fall down," O.W. whined.

"It's called gravity and unless you tell me what I want to know, I am going to give you a crash course in New-ton's theory of falling bodies." Jo Bob waved the gun barrel at the belt buckle. "The operative word here is *crash.*"

O.W.'s pants fell to his ankles. He was wearing boxer shorts with little red hearts on them.

"Those are cute. Pull 'em down." Jo Bob reached into the truck cab and grabbed his lead-weighted nightstick.

"I'll kill you for this, asshole," O.W. grunted, as he bent and pulled his shorts down.

Before O.W. could straighten up, Jo Bob struck him across the shoulder blades with the heavy club. The half-naked fat man fell heavily on his face, raising a thick cloud of caliche dust. Jo Bob relieved him of his expensive nickel-plated nine-millimeter automatic, stuffing the pistol in his belt.

O. W. Meadows lay face-down in the dirt, moaning in agony from the vicious blow across the back.

"You broke my back," he groaned. "Goddamn you. You broke my back."

"What about Raul?" Jo Bob asked, holding up his cigarette and blowing on the end until it glowed red. "Who are you working for?"

"Fuck you, Sheriff." O.W. spit out the words.

Leaning over O.W., Jo Bob ground the lit end of the cigarette into Meadows's huge ass.

O.W. screamed, flopping around in the dust like a fish out of water.

"You got a lot of ass there, O.W., and I got a carton of cigarettes in my truck." Jo Bob relit the cigarette. "You got any answers for me?"

"Jesus Christ!" O.W. howled. "Jo Bob, we were teammates!"

"And you gave somebody else the game plan. You used up our friendship. The game is over. Real life is what we're playing now. Elliott was right about you."

"Elliott! They'll get that cocksucker. He's already dead, he just don't know it yet."

"You want to tell me how you know that?" Jo Bob stuck O.W. in the ass again with the cigarette.

"Stop! Please! Stop!" O.W. shrieked. "I'll tell. I'll tell."

"Where is Raul?"

"He's gone."

"I know that." Jo Bob whacked him across his bare buttocks with the nightstick.

"No! No!" O.W. began to sob in pain. "I mean, he is

really gone. I took him from the jail but he got away
from me up on the river, near the Narrows. Look!"
O.W. pointed to the bruise on his temple. "He hit me in
the head and ran off."

"Now we are getting somewhere," Jo Bob said. "Who
are you working for? It is obviously not me."

"Colonel Glanton told me to get the Mexican."

"Why?"

"I don't know, he didn't tell me," O.W. lied. He
didn't dare tell Jo Bob about the killings of the aliens.

"Why would you take orders from Glanton?"

"I made a mistake."

"You sure did." Jo Bob smacked him across the ass
with the nightstick. "Now, why? What does Glanton
have on you?"

"I worked for him," O.W. cried out. "Several years
back I worked handling cargo on flights carrying machinery and supplies to D-L companies in Panama and
Costa Rica. Glanton flew the planes. He works for Ross
Denham."

"Is it Glanton who told you that Elliott was a dead
man?"

"Oh God, Jo Bob." O.W. started crying. "These people are going to kill me."

"Maybe you better skip the reunion then and start
running," Jo Bob said. "Why did you go to work for
Glanton?"

"Because I was broke and went to Ross Denham for
help. He sent me to Glanton. After I made a few flights,
Glanton suggested I ask you for a job. They had stopped
making the flights and Glanton said if I could land a job
out here, then he and I could stay in touch. Denham and
Laughlin had promised me money for any information I
could get on the Blaine family, especially Judge Zack."

"And you passed the information on to David Stein,"
Jo Bob added.

"Yeah, we would meet in Glanton's quarters here at
PMI." O.W.'s voice had lost its quiver. "Can I get up?"

"Only if you want me to knock you back down."

"You son of a bitch."

"Tell me exactly what Glanton told you about Elliott."

"He didn't say much, except that they had some trap

laid for him in Dallas," O.W. said. "They were going to set him up and use Delma Huddle as bait."

Jo Bob pulled out his handcuffs and shackled O.W.'s hands behind his back.

"Get your ass in the back of the truck," Jo Bob ordered.

"What if somebody sees me?"

"Lay your fat ass down and shut up."

O.W. obeyed and Jo Bob covered him with a tarp.

"Ruby? This is the sheriff." Jo Bob had pulled back on the ranch road and was heading into Purgatory. Ruby Prescott was his radio dispatcher.

"Yeh?" Ruby sounded angry. Her voice crackled out of the receiver.

"Wake up L. Ray and drive him out to PMI by way of River Ranch. The deputy's car is parked there with the keys in it. Have him drive it back to your place and stash it in the barn."

"Jo Bob! Goddammit! This ain't in my job description."

"It is now."

Jo Bob parked his pickup truck in front of Doc's Café, across from the Purgatory Feed Store.

As Jo Bob stepped from the truck, Matthew Abbott, the cedar cutter, walked out of the feed store with a fifty-pound feed sack over each shoulder.

Jo Bob Williams walked softly around Matthew Abbott. He had once watched the big redneck lift the front of a '75 Ford LTD completely off the ground to win a five-dollar bet.

The problem was that the Abbotts were outlaws and the sheriff's job required him to keep an eye on the county's outlaws, so Jo Bob strolled over to the back of Matthew's car just as he was tossing the feed sacks in the trunk.

Matthew was closing the trunk lid when Jo Bob caught sight of a slender bare leg next to the spare tire.

A small girl was curled up around the spare tire. She looked about twelve with pretty dark eyes and hair and wearing only a dirty red dress.

"Whoa there, Matthew," Jo Bob said, catching the lid before it latched and springing it back open. "What we got here?" The pale, dirty girl remained still, curled

around the bald tire. Her frightened eyes moved from
Matthew back to Jo Bob.

"Wife," Matthew said and began to close the lid once
more. Again Jo Bob stopped him. Matthew was getting
angry. Running thick fingers through his dirty black hair,
he gritted his teeth.

"Thought you already had a wife."

"She died." Matthew scratched at his full beard, avoiding direct eye-to-eye contact. He wasn't afraid, but he
wasn't afraid to die either—and there was a correlation.

"How many wives is that, Matthew? Three?"

"Four. Counting her." He pointed into the trunk.

"You go through a lot of wives."

"They wear out just like everything else."

The loose trunk lid bobbed between them as if moved
by the tension between the two big men. The girl lay
motionless on the dusty carpet hugging the treadless tire.

"What's her name?"

"Rae Ann."

"What you got her in the trunk for?" Jo Bob looked
down at the dirty girl.

"Taming her." Matthew looked hard at the sheriff.
"You got a woman, Sheriff, you know better than most
what women are like if you don't tame 'em early. They'll
eat the young."

"Let her ride in front, Matthew, it's too hot in the
trunk." Jo Bob took off his hat and wiped his forehead.
He looked at the sky. Jo Bob wasn't afraid to die either
but today didn't seem the day.

"Sheriff," Matthew said. "I know my rights."

Jo Bob laughed. "That is always the first refuge of the
outlaw. His rights." It was amazing what Matthew thought
his rights were. Jo Bob dropped his gun hand to his side,
watching Matthew's knife hand.

"You really want it to be today, Matthew?"

Matthew let Rae Ann ride in front. She smiled at Jo
Bob when she slipped into the car.

It wasn't yet noon and Jo Bob had already confronted
two men who would kill him the first chance they got.

Jo Bob wrestled O. W. Meadows out of his truck and
walked him around back of Doc's Café, locking him in
the woodshed.

"What's going on, Sheriff?" Doc had been watching out the rear window.

"The deputy is gonna go south to the Estrada place for the winter. I'll deputize L. Ray to take him across the border," Jo Bob explained. "We got niggers in the woodpile."

"Judge Zack's waiting inside," Doc said. "He's talking to two women with a strange story to tell."

"That's all I been listening to all morning. One more can't hurt."

Visions of the Wild Man

Zack Blaine, Sheriff Jo Bob Williams, and Doc Morris sat in the upstairs JP office and listened to Mary Ralph and Brenda, dressed in Doc's flannel shirts, repeat their story.

"Coulda been a crazy wetback," Zack said, lighting a cigarette and leaning back. He still wore his hat. He would not take it off until bedtime.

"Or a hippie or one of the Abbott boys," Jo Bob added. "We get wild man stories from tourists all the time. There's a lot of strange people live up here. You better expect to see things you ain't used to in Austin." Jo Bob *knew* it was Raul but said nothing.

"Well aren't you even gonna go look?" Mary Ralph was angry. "We're not crazy you know. We saw him."

"I don't doubt you girls saw a naked man running the ridges, but so what?" Jo Bob said. "I ain't going kicking around up in that country looking for a naked man. I don't even know if that's indecent exposure. And I don't care." *And,* he paused and thought, *there is a lot of shit up there I don't need to see.* "My advice is stay away from the upland river breaks," he began again. "I'll go up and get your clothes and bags."

The two girls left grumbling.

"I got O.W. locked up in the woodshed," Jo Bob announced. "He's been working for Laughlin and Denham, trying to spy on us. He reports to David Stein."

"So?" Zack rocked back in his chair. "What do you suggest we do?"

"I'm going to have L. Ray take O.W. south to Estrada's," Jo Bob said. "Keep him prisoner. Then I'm going to head to Dallas for the reunion. All the main characters in this drama seem to be headed that way. Since Denham and Laughlin bought the club, they've hired lots of ex-players to work for them in jobs that are extremely vague, if not illegal."

"How is that going to help us here?"

"I'm not sure, but O.W. claims that Glanton has set some sort of trap for Phil Elliott at the reunion," Jo Bob explained. "For some reason they want to put Elliott away for good and they're using the reunion, Delma Huddle, and D-L Media's *Southwest View* magazine. It is the longest unbroken chain of evidence I can find. My hope is that Elliott has been able to dig up some dirt for us in San Antonio and Austin."

"So what if he does?" Zack was irritated.

"Maybe, between the two of us, we can tie together some sort of criminal conspiracy involving the municipal utility district, River Ranch, and Denham and Laughlin. It is pretty obvious that some very heavy money is changing hands but we have to have proof tying D-L Financial into something illegal. Being successful businessmen is not a crime."

"The way they do it must be a crime," Doc said.

"Well, we got to find and prove what kind of a crime it is."

Zack smiled and patted Jo Bob's arm. "I ain't afraid of the son of a bitch. Tell the bastards we'll shoot it out with 'em right in the square."

"I ain't afraid to shoot it out," Doc said. "But we'll be using handguns and they'll have helicopters and rocket launchers."

"Another one of your teammates is having problems," Zack said to Jo Bob. "Tony Douglas' wife called twice this morning and said the new game warden hadn't been home all night. Some teammates you had. Elliott's the only guy who seems worth a shit and you keep putting him in jail."

The Dead Man

Jo Bob Williams drove up the river to Table Rock to retrieve Mary Ralph's and Brenda's clothes, backpacks, and sleeping bags.

The white rock ledges, river bottom in wetter years, were littered with cans and bottles. Tourists drive all the way from San Antonio to float down the Purgatory in rafts, canoes, and inner tubes. During big summer weekends they jam the river with anything that floats, towing ice chests, trailing litter like an invasion fleet.

The river always got a few of the drunk, careless or stupid, especially during the sudden plateau rains and flash floods. This year probably they wouldn't be riding the river, unless the drought broke. There was so little water, the canoes and rafts would be quickly gutted on the rocks. The River Ranch Estates were trying to get a special pumping permit to allow overpumping of the aquifer so the excess water would run into the river, making it more attractive to prospective buyers. River Ranch Estates manager J. C. Bilkeniser had paid to have the clouds seeded by San Antonio Ecological Engineering. He was also negotiating for "an authentic Amerindian rain dance." They needed the water. The attraction of canoeing and rafting the river attracted large numbers of tourists who accounted for the major income percentages of the shops on the square, the canoe livery and raft rentals. Their success, in dollar figures, was in direct proportion to the water in river and creeks. As Jo Bob drove along the riverbank toward the table rock, he knew they would get the water from the aquifer because Governor B. A. Quinlan would make certain whatever D-L Development wanted to make River Ranch Estates attractive, he would use all the power at his disposal to make happen.

Jo Bob listened to the purple-red Dr. Pepper can crunch under the wheels of his squad car.

He found brightly colored items of clothing scattered at Squaw Falls where Squaw Creek joins the river and scanned the cedar breaks for peculiar shapes, forms or movements in the heavy undergrowth. The birds stopped singing, the wind was still. He heard only the rippling of the water, the slow gentle sound of the plateau bleeding to death.

A roadrunner stalked up the riverbank, hunting lizards warming in the sun. The bird moved past Jo Bob as if he didn't exist. The sheriff's mouth was dry, his stomach tightened and he had to make a conscious effort to calm himself and control his breathing. The stillness was suddenly broken, birds began singing and the wind picked up.

He was rolling up Mary Ralph's sleeping bag when he found the blood, a large splotch soaked into the porous limestone. Startled, he looked up, glimpsing the roadrunner disappearing into the cedar break. Upriver he saw another stain on the bone-white limestone, there was another and another up through the rocks, near where the walking bird had just disappeared into the cedar.

It was then he saw the front end of Tony Douglas's jeep, partially hidden by the brush. The jeep was parked on the game trail near the ford. He glanced around and found a large spot of blood where the animal had apparently lain down, like a deer will do when it's gutshot. Further on down upriver was another smaller bloodstain. Whatever it was had lost a lot of blood.

Jo Bob felt his stomach knot as he drew his pistol and followed the blood trail into the underbrush. As he came closer to Tony's jeep, he found a spot where someone had been standing beside a cottonwood tree. Cigarette butts littered the ground at the base of the tree. He picked one up. It was hand rolled.

The Abbott boys hand-roll their cigarettes, Jo Bob

thought, placing the butt in his shirt pocket and continuing up to the abandoned jeep.

Tony Douglas's footprints led toward the ford and disappeared into the water.

The sheriff was about to cross the river when he caught sight of another large bloodstain on the limestone about ten yards further upstream. The animal was lying down more frequently and staying down longer.

Jo Bob was studying the bloodstain when he noticed an opening in the underbrush back away from the water. It looked as if something had crashed and torn its way through the cedars and mesquite trees. He followed the broken trail into a small clearing.

There, curled under a small cedar, was a man's body, covered with blood from head to foot. He was stripped naked.

The skull and facial bones were smashed horribly, beyond recognition. There wasn't another wound on the whole body.

On the right leg, just above the knee, was a large heart-shaped birthmark. It was a mark Jo Bob had seen many times, years ago, in the locker room.

The dead man was Tony Douglas.

The Abbott Boys

Jo Bob drove north of the Twin Peaks following the river, into the breaks of upper Purgatory.

At the mouth of Abbott's Canyon, he turned off the engine. He climbed deftly, weaving his way up the side of the hill to a spot exactly opposite Indian Cave.

He crouched down, studying a dark spot in the limestone shelving of the peak. It was a cave entrance. Moving with a quiet stealth that belied his size and age, he crawled through the four-foot opening and eased through the cave to the iron stakes driven into the side of the sinkhole shaft, leading down toward the lower cavern. He saw the faint light glowing from the big room and could feel the cool wet draft drawing out of the sinkhole; the whispery shuffle of his boots seemed loud as he climbed down the metal rungs of the rock chimney. Reaching the bottom, he switched on his big nine-cell flashlight and swept it around the gallery of bizarre limestone sculpture. Water dripped and seeped, drops plopping and echoing. Stalactites and stalagmites, colored icicles of limestone.

The cavern was carved in monstrous shapes, shadows in the weak yellow light.

He flicked the light off and moved toward the flickering glow down into the bowels of the mountain. The cave was damp and the floor was slippery, the dim light grew out of a small tunnel that led into the Big Room.

Inside were the Abbott boys: Matthew, Little Brother, and Big Brother. They sat around a big copper still. The room was illuminated with several Coleman lanterns. There were bedrolls and piles of clothes. Stacks of five-gallon cans, several crates and boxes filled with tinned food and cartridges. Several rifles lay scattered near the still. Each man had a knife and a pistol in his belt. Hanging in the back of the cavern was a freshly butchered animal. Several double-bit axes and two new chain saws lay near the animal. The carcass was still dripping blood.

"See you boys shot another one of the Governor's axis deer." Sheriff Williams was suddenly standing in the entrance from the outside cavern.

Little Brother jumped to his feet, startled. The other two Abbotts didn't move.

"We heard you comin' down the chimney, Sheriff," Matthew said slowly. "You losing your touch? Can't put the stalk on some drunk old cedar choppers?"

Big Brother laughed.

"Nothing tougher to track than an animal that works at being stupid," Jo Bob said.

He heard a whimper and a shadow moved, chains rattled. Jo Bob turned toward the sound, hand resting on his pistol butt. "Okay you, out where I can see. Move! *Pronto!*" The shadow moved into the light, the tired thin woman had a dog collar padlocked to her neck. A long chain trailed behind.

He turned back to the three men. "Matthew, you can't chain up that woman like that."

"Who says?" Matthew snarled. "I don't and she runs off up to that military school to smoke that marijuana and screw."

"Let them toy soldiers have her," Big Brother said. "They'll never get past that worn spot."

Little Brother laughed.

Matthew glared at them, then leaned over and threw a dry oak stick onto the fire that burned under the still.

"Lady," Jo Bob spoke to the chained woman. "You want me to cut you loose?"

She looked at the sheriff with dull flat eyes and then slid back into the shadows. Her chain rattled as she sat down with her back to the men.

"How do you expect to whip us three?" Big Brother

unraveled his six-foot six-inch frame and picked up a pipe wrench from near the still.

"I ain't thinking whipping," Jo Bob said. "I'm thinking killing. I came about Douglas, Matthew."

"He *needed* killin'." Matthew was chewing a wad of tobacco, loose-jawed, like he was eating mashed potatoes. Matthew never spit. He swallowed.

"That don't mean you can kill him," Jo Bob said.

"I didn't." Matthew rolled his bowling ball head back and looked Jo Bob in the eyes. "Some big goddamn Meskin kilt him. Don't like greasers myself, but any that kill that game warden is all right with me. I watched the whole thing from my deer stand by the Purgatory ford up near the Narrows. That asshole Douglas had the Meskin spotlighted across the river and then lost him. So he grabs his gun and his flashlight and crosses after him. The Meskin didn't have no clothes on." Matthew laughed and tobacco juice ran down his chin. "Anyway, for awhile I hear the two of them crashing around in the brush and then Douglas must've spotted him or something, because bang bang bang, he is blazing away with his hogleg. Then, the next thing I see, the shithead game warden comes running back across the river like his ass is on fire and that goddamn naked Meskin is right behind him swinging a log the size of a fence post. When he hits the bank, Douglas turns and takes another shot. It was the last one he got off. By then the Meskin is on him and hits him smack in the face with that post." Matthew coughed. "Blood flew everywhere. That greaser stood over him and beat his head to pulp, then he stole his clothes. I thought about shooting him but it weren't none of my affair."

"What happened then?"

"I left," Matthew said. "All that racket had scared off any deer that might have been around. When I was driving back here, I found this axis deer dead in the highway. Somebody must've run him down. You know them goddamn *turistas*."

"Where did all this come from?" Jo Bob pointed at the cases of weapons, ammunition, and military supplies stacked along the wall. "You got enough to supply the Eighty-second Airborne."

"We traded for it with one of them toy soldiers up at

the Institute," Little Brother Abbott said. "They got more of this stuff than my hound dog's got ticks."

"What did you trade him?" Jo Bob asked.

"The wife." Matthew grinned. "He gets to use her on weekends. I think he rents her out to some of them other soldier boys. That wasn't part of the deal but I'm a fair man."

Los Angeles—*Then*

Phil Elliott was the last man in the showers. He was letting the hot water pound on the back of his stiff neck. His head ached and he was still tasting and spitting blood.

"Come on, kid." Seth Maxwell stood in the doorway, a towel wrapped around his waist. "It's time we had us that drink."

"I don't feel too good."

"You will after a few drinks," Maxwell said. "There's no curfew back at camp tonight and I got a car." He turned and walked toward the training room, leaving Elliott alone in the steaming showers.

Phil Elliott still wasn't thinking clearly. He remembered only partially the events of his life that led him to this moment. He knew who he was but not very well. There was a lot of detail missing, large parts of his life were just blanked out. His memory was oddly selective. He remembered Maxwell, Huddle, Jimmy West, his roommate, and several other of his new teammates, but he could not recall his parents' names. It seemed as if most of his life had taken place over the past four weeks at the Assembly of God College out near Oxnard.

Elliott turned off the shower and walked toward the training room, grabbing a couple of towels from the stack by the door. He tied one towel around his waist and began drying himself with the other, as he walked slowly toward the brightly lit room furnished with blue rubbing tables, whirlpools, several folding chairs and small stools.

Along one wall ran a Formica countertop covered with tape, gauze, elastic wraps, needles, syringes, pill bottles, a stainless steel medical sterilizer, tape cutters, scissors, splints, plastic pads, and a thick roll of foam rubber.

Eddie Rand was rubbing down Maxwell's arm and Delma Huddle was in the whirlpool when Phil walked into the room. Danny Raines, a second-year running back from Georgia Tech, was sitting on a stool, cutting the tape off his ankles.

"How you feeling?" Eddie continued rubbing Maxwell's shoulder but looked closely at Phil's eyes as he walked past and lay face down on the next rubbing table.

"My head hurts."

"You sick to your stomach?" Eddie asked. "Feeling dizzy?"

"I don't think so. My head hurts too much to tell."

"You got plenty of time to recover," Maxwell said. "B.A. gave us until tomorrow at dinner to report back to camp. You're coming with me, kid. I'm gonna make you a star."

"Where are you taking me?"

"Hollywood. The Polo Lounge." Maxwell smiled. "I got us a bungalow at the Beverly Hills Hotel."

"Goddammit, Maxwell," Eddie Rand complained. "You take it easy. This rookie isn't strong enough to run with you when he's feeling good and he isn't exactly in peak shape. That safety damn near tore his head off."

"Football is a violent game of physical contact played by madmen and misfits," Maxwell recited. "I know this boy is good enough to play the game on the field, now I got to know what he can do *off* it. And there's no better place to put him to the test."

"Jesus Christ." Eddie Rand shook his head. "A bungalow at the Beverly Hills and all night in the Polo Lounge."

Phil Elliott had no idea what they were talking about. He was trying to remember where he was from and how he got all the way out to California to play in a football game with a team from Dallas. He didn't think he had ever been in Dallas. He was right.

Elliott spoke. "I don't want to play polo. I'm scared of horses."

Everybody in the training room laughed.

Danny Raines finished cutting the tape away from his ankles. He turned and looked at Elliott.

"You poor dumb sumbitch." Raines shook his head and left the room.

Twenty years later, Danny would be coaching his own team in the Super Bowl. "Right As Raines," he would be called, and he was right that night at the Coliseum; Phil Elliott was one poor dumb sumbitch. But how was Phil to know? They had given him such a whack on the head, he didn't know whether to shit or go blind. By dinner the next day, he had done both.

"That's some girl." Maxwell said to Elliott. "Joanne Remington. She runs with Mary Jane."

They were standing outside the dressing room in the Coliseum tunnel watching a tall, good-looking brunette talking to a petite blonde who had to qualify as pretty but suffered in comparison. Joanne Remington was the tall brunette and she was waiting for Mary Jane Woodley who was waiting for Seth Maxwell. Phil couldn't take his eyes off of the tall woman.

Poor dumb sumbitch.

"Come on." Maxwell was tugging at Phil's arm. "I want you to meet these two women. They're both first class babes, not your regular road trip dirty legs." He steered his receiver over next to the women.

"Oh Seth!" Mary Jane Woodley, the small blonde, put her arms around the quarterback and hugged him. The top of her head was level with his armpit. "You were wonderful, just wonderful. Wasn't he wonderful, Joanne?" She turned to the tall woman with the waist-length brown hair.

"Yes." Joanne smiled. "Seth was his usual wonderful self." She glanced at Elliott who had not taken his eyes off her. "Who's your slack-jawed friend?"

"This is Phil Elliott." Maxwell patted Elliott's shoulder. "He's only semiconscious but he's great company."

"Oh." Joanne looked Phil over. "You're the guy that got his head knocked off out there. You played very well."

"What does ownership say?" Maxwell asked.

"Conrad loves him and Clinton is taking all the credit for finding him," Mary Jane replied. "Emmett got drunk,

as usual, but I'm sure he'll share his brother's opinion as
soon as he's informed of it." She looked into Phil's face
with a sly smile. "Is it true you thought you were signing
up in the other league?"

"I'm not sure." Phil replied. "Life has gotten sort of
hazy. What league am I in now?"

"The big leagues, kid." Maxwell laughed and winked
at Joanne. She was sizing up Elliott and liked what she
saw.

"I'll tell you what, Phillip," Mary Jane said. "When
the team president sobers up, I'll tell him how good you
are."

"Thanks." Phil smiled at Joanne. "How tall are you?"
He knew immediately it was a stupid question but laid it
off on the head injury.

"Just your size," Joanne replied. "I'll expect you to
call me sometime and return the favor."

"You want me to tell Emmett how good *you* are?"
Phil was trying to be funny.

"No! It would be nice if you found out sometime. Call
me when you get to Dallas. I just moved to Denton.
North Texas State. I'm in the book." Joanne looked past
Elliott to the dressing room door. "Speak of the devil
and out he staggers."

Phil turned to see Emmett Hunter standing unsteadily,
talking to his older brother Conrad.

"Bye, boys. Come on Joanne." Mary Jane brushed
Phil, leaving a lilac scent in the air.

Joanne hesitated, looking at Phil.

"Don't worry," Seth said. "I will look after the kid.
He needs his brain rescrambled tonight and I'm the only
one that can do it."

Mary Jane rose up on her tiptoes and kissed Maxwell
lightly on the lips.

"I'll see you later," she said. "I fly tomorrow. Joanne
goes back to register at North Texas." Mary Jane quickly
led Joanne Remington over to join the group that was
rapidly gathering around the Hunters.

"Come on, let's go," Maxwell said. "The car's supposed to be parked right up by the tunnel gate."

It was a red Ford convertible and Maxwell drove them
quickly to the Beverly Hills Hotel.

"We're supposed to meet Mitch Simmons in the Polo Lounge," Maxwell said, as he turned the car into the hotel driveway. "He got us the bungalow and car. He's a big producer out here."

"It's *pink.*"

"What?"

"The hotel," Elliott said. "It's pink."

"Sure. It's supposed to be. We're talking your basic Hollywood glamour. You'll love it." He pulled the red convertible to a stop beneath the front entrance canopy.

It was a warm summer night, palm trees lined the drive, and the big, pink stucco building was set in a jungle of tropical plants, expensive cars, and well-dressed people. Elliott followed Maxwell into the lobby and past the registration desk around a corner right to the bar.

"Mitch Simmons, please," Maxwell spoke to the maître d'.

"Right this way, sir." The man in the tuxedo led them to a booth in the corner, occupied by a good-looking blonde, a middle-aged guy with a phone to his ear, and an eight-year-old girl who was eating a hot fudge sundae.

The maître d' bowed out. Mitch pointed with the phone at Maxwell and Elliott, indicating they should sit down. He smiled and nodded at Seth.

"Yeh. Sure Murray. Look, we'll talk on Monday." Mitch Simmons nodded, as he spoke into the phone. "I already read the property and I like it but it needs some work." He paused and listened, raising his eyebrows and rolling his eyes at Maxwell. "Okay. Okay. Monday." He cut in. "We'll talk Monday. Call me at the studio." Mitch Simmons laid the phone back down. "Hey, Seth." He stuck out his hand. "Helluva game."

The two men shook hands and then made all the introductions.

The blonde was a twenty-two-year-old actress who was struggling to break into films by sleeping with Mitch Simmons and two other big independent producers. Her name was Stephanie Teague.

The child was Simmons's by his first wife and this was his custody weekend. Her name was Kennedy King Simmons.

Elliott's brain was not so addled that he was foolish

enough to ask how two adults could tag some poor little child with a moniker like Kennedy King Simmons.

"You coming to the softball game tomorrow?" Mitch Simmons asked Maxwell. "We're playing Aaron Spelling's team."

"You a football player too, mister?" the little girl asked Phil. She had fudge all over her fat little cheeks and hands.

"Yep." Phil nodded. "That sure looks like a good sundae."

"You want some?" She held the spoon out to him as melted ice cream ran down her arm and dripped off her elbow onto the table.

Stephanie Teague was sitting next to her and eyed the whole mess rather nervously. Every movement made by the little girl left deposits of ice cream and fudge scattered around the booth. Stephanie had miraculously avoided any hits. Her luck wouldn't hold.

"Kennedy, honey." Simmons spoke baby talk. "Dadda told his baby-waby not to spill any of that."

It was like *asking* her to dump the whole sundae onto her father's girlfriend. She only got Stephanie with about half a spoonful of sundae and made it look almost accidental.

Stephanie jumped up like somebody had shit in her lap.

"Uh. Oh." The little girl said, deliberately, and then frowned. "I am *sor-ry*," she sang, only slightly disguising her glee.

"Goddamn," Stephanie said. "This is my best eggshell dress."

"Don't swear in front of the kid," Mitch admonished. "I *told* you to dress casual."

"I should have worn a wet suit." Stephanie stormed off to the rest room.

"Now, see what you did, Kennedy?" Simmons said to his daughter.

"I am *sor-ry, dad-dy*," she sang, enjoying the turmoil she caused.

"Okay, baby." Simmons turned from his daughter and spoke to Maxwell. "Steph can be a real cunt. I'm losing her after tonight."

Kennedy King Simmons smiled and offered another spoonful of fudge sundae to Phil Elliott.

"Well, Seth," Simmons pitched hard. "It'll be a package deal, television *and* big screen. We've got a couple ideas. One is a dramatic show; a detective series that we'll spin off our successful series *The Texas Ranger.* While you're still playing ball, you'll make a few guest shots as a continuing character on the series."

"What's my character like?" Maxwell was drinking his third scotch. "I don't just want a walk-on. I want my character to have some real input."

Elliott was drinking a beer and nursing his headache, while the eight-year-old ate her second hot fudge sundae.

Stephanie Teague had returned, her eggshell dress repaired, but with a noticeable stain in the front. She purposely sat as far from Kennedy as possible.

"He'll be an important guy, Seth," Simmons said. "Why would I lie?"

"I don't know, Mitch," Seth grinned, "but I'm sure I'll find out eventually."

"The other television deal would be a game show," Mitch Simmons continued his pitch. "*Sports Trivia.* It will be an instant hit, the way the public is going for sports on television."

It seemed like a stupid idea to Phil, who didn't think the public would go for sports in that context.

"Then we'll make independent production deals with the major studios for big-screen movies." Mitch Simmons was fully wound now, believing everything he was saying and convincing Seth Maxwell. "Once the studio people see the big numbers you pull on television, they'll be bidding for you. But, you've got to remember, this is a long-term plan, figuring you'll play another eight or ten years. You really won't be able to do more than the guest-shot stuff until you hang up the old jockstrap."

"What's a jockstrap, daddy?" Kennedy King Simmons looked up from her sundae.

"Eat your sundae, darling."

"What's a jockstrap?" She became insistent.

"It's like a hat, darling." Simmons shushed her and turned to Maxwell.

Phil Elliott looked at the little girl and wondered what

other brilliant bits of misinformation her father had sad-
dled her with already.

It's like a hat.

When, Elliott wondered, would she be disabused of
that notion and under what circumstances. How could
Maxwell believe a guy who lied so openly to his own
child?

"I've got some financial partners out of Texas who
aren't big buddies of the Hunters," Simmons said. "They
want to finance your movie and TV career and they
won't let Conrad Hunter bully them. That way we've got
some leverage against the football club, if they try to stop
any decision you make they don't agree with."

"They don't tell me what to do." Maxwell was ada-
mant. "They never have, they never will. I'm the quarterback of that club and they need me as bad as I need
them."

"Exactly, Seth, that's my point." Simmons pushed.
"When the time comes you want to quit and come out
here full-time, they'll have no financial leverage to stop
you. I've arranged for you to meet my two partners
tonight. They were at the game with me and said they'd
meet us all here."

"Well, Mitch." Maxwell sipped his scotch and carefully
chose his words. "This is a very attractive offer and I'll
want you to put it down on paper for my lawyers to read.
I've already received offers from the network to do cover
commentary and I will have to weigh all the offers when
the time comes. As you know I am already doing a lot of
commercial work and that not only keeps me busy but
also makes me very wealthy."

"I know, I know." Simmons nodded his head grimly.

A tall, slender, red-haired man stepped into the Polo
Lounge and squinted against the dark. Simmons saw him
immediately.

"Ah! There's Jimmy Boxx." Simmons broke into a
relieved smile.

The maître d' led the thin ruddy-faced man over to
their booth and Mitch Simmons quickly made the introductions.

"Where are Laughlin and Denham?" Simmons asked
Boxx as soon as everyone was situated in and around the
booth.

"Right behind me," Boxx replied. "Ross had to make a call back to San Antonio."

Jimmy Boxx was an ex–Los Angeles policeman who, at age twenty-five, had quit the force and joined the movie community as a stunt man. His first affiliation with the movie and television business had been while still an active cop—he had been hired as technical advisor by Mitch Simmons on his short-lived series, *L.A. Cop.* Immediately intoxicated by the glamour and seemingly endless supplies of quick money, Jimmy Boxx quit his job as a policeman and joined the Stuntman's Association. Early on, he got work on a couple of television movies and low-budget films but, except for his relationship with Simmons, he was never able to establish a working relationship with any other producers. As a result, Jimmy began supplementing his income by supplying drugs to the film community through several connections he'd made on the force. These new relationships became quite profitable, both financially *and* as sources of inside information: which stars had drug or alcohol problems, which studios used what methods to deal with those problems, how to supply the drug needs of this high-pressure industry, and who were the contacts throughout the business.

Jimmy Boxx knew the value of information and where to find it, as well as where to sell it. He was currently working as stunt coordinator on *The Texas Ranger,* but he still kept up his other business and subsequent contacts. Jimmy Boxx was well known throughout Hollywood by executives and producers who occupied a peculiar layer of responsibility in film and television. Jimmy Boxx could get certain things done without any interference from local law enforcement agencies.

Jimmy Boxx also did work as a bodyguard for Simmons and any major stars he might have working for him on any particular project.

"Here they are." Jimmy Boxx pointed to the doorway.

Two men stood side by side just inside the Polo Lounge. Ross Denham was five-feet-three and slight of build, wearing a well-tailored three-piece suit and alligator skin cowboy boots. Bobby Laughlin was an overweight six feet two inches and his clothes showed all the unsightly results of bulging flesh and fabric. He looked tattered, although his clothes were new and expensive ready-mades.

His boots were brown snakeskin with white wing tips and his trouser legs were stuffed into the tops of his boots. Both men wore their hair cut in severe flattops.

Walking in lockstep, Denham and Laughlin headed toward Mitch Simmons's booth without waiting for the maître d'.

A brace of Texas moguls, thought Elliott. *I could be hallucinating.* His headache had moved to behind his eyes.

"This has been an evening of severe physical and psychic damage," Elliott announced. "If you'll excuse me, I think I'll go lay down and make room for Mr. Denham and Mr. Laughlin."

"That's fine, Paul," Mitch Simmons said. "You're in bungalow four, just out that side door."

"It's Phil." Elliott stood. "But thanks anyway. Nice meeting you all." Phil nodded to Simmons, Stephanie Teague, and Jimmy Boxx. He noticed a dangerous gleam in Boxx's eyes, a different kind of greed than the type that had been oozing from Mitch Simmons all night.

"It has been very nice meeting you, Miss Kennedy King Simmons." Phil turned to smile at the little girl splotched with ice cream and fudge. "You're very pretty."

The little girl looked up and smiled.

"Will you tell me what a jockstrap is?"

"Not a chance, kid." Elliott turned quickly and was out the side door onto the hotel grounds before Ross Denham and Bobby Laughlin were halfway to the table.

It was a beautiful warm night and the hotel grounds were elegant. The sweet smell of the tropical flowers mingled and floated on the heavy night air as Phil walked along the palm-lined sidewalk to the bungalow.

Once inside the bungalow, Phil Elliott took two of the number three codeine with Empirin compound pills the trainer had given him for his headache, then lay down on the couch and fell asleep almost immediately.

Later on in the night, Phil thought he heard Maxwell and a woman enter the bungalow but he could not claw himself out of the semiconscious fog caused by the drugs and the blow to the back of his head. Phil Elliott had suffered a severe concussion and cervical vertebrae damage. He was never told and the damage would come back to haunt him twenty years later. But that night, by the time he was asleep on the couch, the drugs had masked the pain, and the bleeding of his severely bruised brain casing had finally stopped.

The pain killers wore off about dawn and Elliott woke in severe agony. His headache was worse and now his neck was so stiff he could not rise from the couch. He had fallen asleep in his clothes and quickly dug in his shirt pocket for more codeine pills, popping three into his mouth, chewing them up and swallowing without anything to wash them down.

He was in desperate pain and tried to lay motionless on the green couch with the white print leaves until the pain began to subside. It took about forty-five minutes before Phil could raise his head from the pillow, then it was still an awful process. The room immediately seemed to spin and he quickly but carefully lay his head down again.

"Well, this ain't worth a shit," Phil said. He had enough experience with head injuries in college to recognize the symptoms of concussion but his experience also told him that there was no treatment but rest. A good reputation to avoid in this business was to be known as "injury prone."

He drifted off to sleep again.

"Come on, Phil." Maxwell shook his shoulder gently. "Get up, kid. We got a softball game to see. Celebrities playing jocks. It'll be fun."

"Ah . . ." Phil didn't open his eyes. "Did anybody ever tell that little girl what a jockstrap was?"

"I dunno," Seth replied. "I got drunk pretty early. So me and Stephanie come over here to leg wrestle and rumple the sheets."

Phil opened his eyes. Seth Maxwell stood over him and Stephanie Teague sat in a chair by the door, looking cool and aloof. "Looks like Simmons lost her sooner than he thought."

"The perks of stardom, kid." Maxwell laughed. "Come on, the softball game starts in about fifteen minutes."

"Call room service," Phil said, "and order me a new head and neck."

"Take some more drugs. I can't believe you never even finished your beer last night," Maxwell said.

"I told you, I don't drink."

"You'll learn, sonny." Maxwell grinned. "You'll learn."

"What were those last two guys like?" Elliott asked, as he tried to rise.

"Ross Denham and Bobby Laughlin?" Maxwell replied. "Just about how they looked, only richer. They are into banks, computers and real estate. They drill a few oil wells in south Texas and northern Mexico just to keep up appearances. I think Laughlin owns some businesses in Costa Rica and Nicaragua. Denham's company set up B.A. and Clinton Foote's computer systems. Dallas is the most computerized team in the league."

"Well, they knocked the fucking data outta me last night." Elliott lay back down, aching. "I thought the Hunters didn't get along with these two guys."

"I guess the Hunters don't know it yet," Maxwell said.

"That is the danger of computers—somebody can steal all your software," Elliott said. "They can't get at it if you keep it in your head."

"I don't think *your* head is an especially good place for safekeeping anything." Maxwell laughed. "Besides, I think these guys, especially Laughlin, could be brain suckers."

"Great title for a movie," Stephanie Teague said, in her wonderfully bored voice. "The Revenge of the Texas Brain Suckers."

It would be years before Phil Elliott saw the irony in her statement.

Phil Elliott steered the rented convertible into the dormitory parking lot at the Assembly of God College. Seth Maxwell was asleep and drooling on himself in the seat beside Phil. Elliott's head and neck still hurt, but he was in much better shape to drive than Maxwell, who had gone back to the bungalow after the softball game and finished off Stephanie Teague and a full bottle of scotch.

Phil sat in the lobby, drank Cokes and swallowed codeine and Empirin until he was nauseous as well as suffering from head and neck pain. He found the lobby of the Beverly Hills Hotel a fascinating place and Hollywood life an intriguing enigma. Phil Elliott was seduced by the glamour of the scene just as he had been captivated by the life of an athlete; the intense existence of men who put it all on the line for two or three hours every

Sunday afternoon or Saturday night or whenever a game was being played.

Finally, at a little past four, Maxwell appeared in the lobby without Stephanie.

"She couldn't get out of bed," Maxwell said, as he swayed noticeably. "I rode her hard and put her away wet."

"You have such a way with words." Elliott eased to his feet, his head and neck still sensitive. "How would you describe your own condition?"

"Seriously fucked up," Maxwell said.

Elliott sent for the car and loaded Maxwell into the passenger seat. Driving away, between the palm trees, Phil hoped this would not be the last time he visited the big pink stucco anachronism. He knew he could grow to love this kind of corruption. It was so easy and he felt so deserving.

Maxwell snorted and woke, as the car stopped in the dormitory lot.

"Are we back at camp?" Seth wiped the spittle from his mouth and chin.

"Yep." Phil turned off the ignition. "And with ten minutes to spare."

"I'll see you at dinner, kid. I'm going to my room to puke." Maxwell jerked open the car door and staggered away.

"Later." Elliott took time to put up the convertible top, then pulled the keys and stuck them in the pocket of his Levis.

When Elliott reached his room on the second floor, he saw that Jimmy West had once again emptied his closet and drawers, packed his bag and was gone. Since the first time West had run for it, Clinton Foote had told Elliott that he expected to be notified immediately whenever it looked like West was going to run. Phil picked up the phone and waited for the switchboard to answer.

"Yes? Can I help you?" It was Brenda, the blond girl who usually worked weekdays. Delma Huddle had been slipping off with her on weeknights without anyone in management or affiliated with the college finding out. Yet.

"Yeh. This is Phil Elliott in two sixty-five. Connect me with Clinton Foote's room."

"Sure, Phil. You played a great game last night." She purred. "You and Delma were terrific."

Oh. Great! Phil thought. *I'll bet she thinks of us as a threesome.* He made a mental note to tell Delma that this girl was not the most discreet. Discretion was *quality one* if a black man is going to date a white girl while playing for a Texas football team that is training on an Assembly of God College campus.

"Yeh." Clinton was suddenly on the other end of the line. Phil never heard the phone ring and was certain that the general manager knew everything he had been thinking.

"Ah . . ." Elliott had momentarily forgotten why he called. "Did you? . . . er . . . West is gone again," he suddenly blurted out.

"Goddammit," Clinton shouted. "How long's he been gone?"

"I don't know. I haven't seen him since last night."

"Shit. I'm gonna have to handcuff you to that slippery dumb Swede."

"Norwegian."

"What?"

"He's Norwegian."

"He's a fucking rabbit," Clinton snapped. "Get off the line."

Phil hung up and chuckled at the prospect of Clinton organizing another search for West. It was the fifth time in four weeks Jimmy had run for it. He was a good player and if he would just stick to it, Phil considered him serious competition, especially since Tony Laker tore a hamstring in the first scrimmage and returning veteran flankerback Mac Kine was having contract problems with Clinton. A former All-Pro, not far past his prime, Kine was expected to move right into the starting lineup. But neither he nor Clinton would budge in negotiations and Kine hadn't even come to camp. They were only two thousand dollars apart and Phil figured it only a matter of time before he was battling three men for the flanker's job. One good game would not be enough to hold off a guy like Kine. Phil had seen last year's films of him, all during camp, and he was impressive.

What only B.A. and Clinton knew was that Kine wouldn't be coming at all if he didn't drop his demands.

The computer told them that a man with Kine's statistics was only worth eighteen thousand dollars a year.

B.A. and Clinton never argued with the computer.

Mac Kine had played his last down of football. He just didn't know it yet.

Elliott's phone rang.

It was Decker McShane of *Southwest Sports*. He wanted an interview.

"I don't have time," Elliott told him. "I have to be in the dining hall in five minutes."

"How about after dinner?" Decker McShane asked.

"We got a meeting from seven until nine."

"How about after the meeting?"

"Look," Phil tried to beg off. He didn't like interviews, they could draw the wrong kind of attention. "I'm really tired, couldn't we put this off a few days?"

"Hey, Elliott," McShane's voice turned cold. "I got a job to do and I'm up against a deadline. You ain't my choice but my editor wants you. So he'll get you, with or without your help. It'll be a better story with your help."

What he meant was, without Elliott's cooperation, Decker McShane would make him look like a complete asshole. Phil had learned in college that if they were going to write about you, it was best to control the writer as much as possible. The best way to do that was to have as much input as possible.

"All right." Phil gave in. "I'll meet you in the ice cream parlor at nine-fifteen."

"See you then."

Elliott stared at the phone. He had better start composing the story about himself immediately. By the time he met with Decker McShane, he would have the complete story in his head in order, including amusing anecdotes and a clever finishing paragraph. If McShane was a smart working journalist, all he would have to do was listen to Elliott and record everything he said, the way he said it, then sit down, type it out, and send it in. His editor would love it. Phil Elliott did not hold a bachelor's degree in communication arts for nothing; he had learned by unpleasant experience that sportswriters were not geniuses and few had any serious regard for the business of sports and the business of reporting on the business of sports. Most sportswriters, in Elliott's rookie season, looked

upon the team they covered much as a public relations
writer looked upon a client. Few had played sports beyond
high school, fewer still understood the sports they covered; most had little knowledge of the game and less
respect for the players. They wrote to please readers,
editors, owners, coaches, and, occasionally, a great player;
they did *not* write to increase understanding or to stimu-
late serious thought. And since television had preempted
the job of *actually* reporting the play-by-play of the game,
sports reporters as a species in print media were skating
on thin ice, with a mortal fear of the deep water beneath.

"What's the problem, turkey?" Delma Huddle was
standing in the doorway, studying the frown on Phil's
face. "Your roomie gone AWOL?"

"Yeh," Phil nodded. "But that's not my problem. I've
got to give that guy McShane from *Southwest Sports* an
interview tonight."

"Well, that be the price of fame," Delma said. "He
ain't too bad. Wait'll you talk to that guy Seymour. He's
a real humpback."

"Let's go eat." Elliott was absently rubbing his stiff
neck. "Maybe I'll feel better with something in my
stomach."

"Your head still hurt?" Delma stepped into the hallway.

"Head and neck." Phil followed Huddle into the hall.

"Say, fool," Delma waved at his blond girlfriend as he
and Phil walked out of the lobby toward the dining
commons. "Brenda says you been gettin' phone calls that
Clinton's been keeping from you. I can't be sure but
from what Brenda says, it sounds like the NBA," Delma
said. "Did you get drafted?"

"Yeh," Phil nodded. "Baltimore offered me eighty-
five hundred for the season and when I tried to play
Dallas off against them for more money, they hung up on
me."

"Well, I think they're trying to reach you again," Huddle said. "But since we're hardly ever in our rooms during
the day, they keep leaving you call-back messages and
Clinton keeps taking 'em and telling Brenda not to tell
you. So she tells me."

"Tell her thanks. I'm not sure I know what to do."

"You've got a home here, turkey. The NBA is a pig in
a poke."

"I wish I was as confident as you," Phil said. "I'm not sure *how* good I am."

"You're good, my man. Not nearly as good as me but then who is?" Delma laughed and opened the door to the dining hall. "Besides basketball is a black man's game."

"That's just because you guys work so cheap."

They were standing at the top of the stairs above the dining room. The veterans had two rookies from UCLA standing on chairs, hands over their hearts, singing the UCLA fight song.

"I hate this hazing shit," Elliott said. "Why do the veterans enjoy it? It's their psychotic black hole and it seems capable of swallowing us all in a split second. If their minds ever began collapsing in, one upon the other, the force of the insanity would be irresistible."

"You be the one got bonked on the head, turkey," Delma said. "You sound brain-damaged."

Delma was right. Phil Elliott *was* brain-damaged.

Joanne Remington-Hunter
—Now

Joanne Remington-Hunter was in the kitchen of her ranch house, reading the newspaper. Her dark hair pulled back hard and tied with a white ribbon, the ponytail hanging below her waist, she was sitting on a stool at the counter. She wore designer jeans and a white button-down shirt and her tired eyes scanned the headline of the financial page:

EMMETT HUNTER SELLS CRH BANK HOLDING COMPANY TO AUSBANC INC.

The Hunter Companies were going belly up. Ten-dollar-a-barrel oil, highly leveraged real estate deals, and bone cancer had already killed Conrad.

Joanne felt pity for Emmett, who was floundering helplessly without his brother to advise and guide him, but she was on her own again and had to look out for herself. Before Conrad was too sick, he had decided to sell the Dallas football club and, to Joanne, that had been the first clue and the last straw. Two weeks after the deal was made with the Denham-Laughlin Financial Group (who also owned Ausbanc Inc.) to buy the football team, Joanne had filed for divorce from Emmett.

Conrad died six months after the sale and for Emmett, who had spent most of his adult life learning how to drink, things turned from bad to worse. He had gone to Ross Denham and Bobby Laughlin, on the advice of

David Stein, with the idea of refinancing The CRH Companies, especially the electronics and oil companies. By the time Denham, Laughlin, and Stein were through with Emmett Hunter, he had sold out for fifty cents on the dollar, losing a financially shaky, but well-structured electronics company, all his real estate in southwest Texas, including the fifty thousand acres on the Purgatory Plateau, and over ten million barrels of oil production. They didn't even offer to buy the CHR Bank Holding Company, because they knew they had so destroyed Emmett's cash flow that the federal government would close it down in a matter of months. Denham and Laughlin were right; within six weeks Emmett was back begging them to take the Bank Holding Company off his hands, which they did for almost nothing.

Stein collected a finder's fee from Emmett for putting him in touch with Ross Denham and Bobby Laughlin. He never bothered to mention that his firm also happened to be corporate counsel for the D-L Financial Group.

But Joanne Remington-Hunter knew it, and she was pissed off; her divorce settlement was contingent on the financial performance of The CHR Companies, which, in just a matter of weeks, had for all intents and purposes ceased to exist. She was considering what sort of legal action she should take and against whom, as she read the latest bit of bad news in the paper. Her eyes slowed at the point where Bobby Laughlin discussed "the great trade potential in southwest Texas and along the Mexican border through participation in the Maquiladora Program, plus the great potential for tourism in the beautiful Purgatory River Country with the completion of D-L Financial's River Ranch Estates development."

The phone rang five times before Joanne could bring herself to lift her eyes from the bad news and pick up the receiver.

"Hunter Ranch." Joanne's voice turned soft and silky, as it always did on the telephone.

"Hello? Joanne? This is Phil Elliott." His voice was hesitant, distant. "I don't know if you remember me."

"Phillip," she gently interrupted. "How could you possibly think I wouldn't remember you? I think of you every day."

"Well, I had to leave Dallas kind of sudden and . . ."

"I know all about it, Phillip," Joanne cut in. "Emmett couldn't wait to tell me all about it."

"Well, all that was a long time ago, but I hope I never caused you any trouble."

"I can't remember any trouble you ever caused." Joanne laughed. "But then, it *was* a long time ago. The last time was when you and I went to that party in New York, the week before the commissioner suspended you."

"I violated the morals clause," Phil replied. "You're not allowed to have any morals in professional sports."

"So," Joanne asked, "to what do I owe this phone call? Did the fact I am out of the Hunter family have any effect on your decision?"

"That," Phil replied, "and the fact I am out of jail made it easier. I guess I would have gotten around to calling you sooner or later."

"So, why is it sooner?"

"I've been hired by Decker McShane at *Southwest View* to go back to Dallas and cover the team reunion this year."

"McShane? The little peckerhead who used to write sports?" Joanne did nothing to hide her distaste. "The little wimp that's married to State Senator Felice McShane?"

"That's him," Elliott replied. "And her. She represents the Lizzy Borden Wing of the women's movement."

"Doesn't your ex-wife run with that crowd?" Joanne asked. "I heard she was dating that slime David Stein."

"She was, the last I heard, which was just before he convinced the judge to put me in jail."

"That bastard Stein is the one who set Emmett up for Denham and Laughlin to just clean us out." Joanne's tone was venomous.

"I believe it's his special area of expertise," Phil replied. "Betrayal."

"Where's your son?"

"He's staying with John Wilson," Phil said. "He went up there when I checked into jail."

"You got custody of him?"

"She got everything else and didn't have any room for him," Phil said. "So? What have you been doing with yourself all these years?"

"The same thing as you, Phillip." Joanne sighed. "I

am growing old too fast, wise too late, and putting up a losing fight against bankruptcy."

"Lot of people in Texas in the same boat."

"Have you seen Seth Maxwell lately?" Joanne asked.

"He picked me up at the jail the other day, along with John Wilson," Phil said. "John's my attorney. Seth flew back to Los Angeles. He's doing a two-hour special for Mitch Simmons for the May sweeps. It's a TV movie version of his series, *Scout.*"

"The private detective show?"

"Yeh. It's in its eighth or ninth season now," Phil said. "He'll be back for the reunion, though. He's hosting the Seth Maxwell Special Olympics Celebrity Golf Tournament."

"Phillip, I just can't believe so much time has gone by." Joanne was sad. "Can you believe we've all gotten this old?"

"Yeh, Joanne, I can. The first thing every morning. I feel like someone wrapped me in a wet sheet and beat me with a garden hose."

"Oh, Phil, you always felt that way."

"Yeh, but now I feel like an *old man* who's been wrapped up in a wet sheet and beat with a garden hose. I'd sure like to see you again, Joanne." He blurted it out. "Are you coming to San Antonio anytime soon?"

"I can come to San Antonio anytime I like," Joanne replied. "I might as well come down there and do some shopping while my credit cards are still good."

"I have always had a deep personal affection for you, Joanne, that poverty, yours or mine, can never diminish."

Phil Elliott had dated Joanne Remington before she married Emmett Hunter and it was one of the contributing reasons he was thrown out of football. The reason officially listed in the Commissioner's Report was "the possession and use of illegal drugs."

"Poverty hit fast here," Joanne said. "I knew we were in trouble when Conrad got sick and I knew it was all over when he sold the club. I think that killed him faster than the cancer."

"I know the feeling; the old pro football postpartum blues. I missed it more than I thought I would," Phil said. "I know a lot of guys who said they missed the Vietnam War the same way."

"Sounds like you were all doing the same drugs."
Joanne chuckled. "I'm sorry Emmett and Conrad thought
it was so important to make you look like a drug addict.
If it's any consolation, the drug problem got a lot worse
after you left. These young kids using steroids and spend-
ing their bonus money to buy cocaine; a bunch of them
went totally nuts. We had two suicides and a rapist in two
years."

"What about Delma Huddle?" Phil asked. "Did he get
into coke? When I knew him, he didn't smoke grass. He
was a juicer. He liked his whiskey."

"Delma was set up by some guy named Jimmy Boxx
who wanted a job with the club," Joanne said. "He was
an ex-cop with big plans and schemes to clean up the
team. Emmett bought it and sold it to Conrad and the
next thing that happens is the motherfucker entraps Delma
with a gram and gets him fifteen years in Huntsville.
Goddamn! Fifteen years in Huntsville for a gram! Can
you believe that shit?"

"If Jimmy Boxx is who I think he is, I not only would
believe it, I would have expected it," Elliott said. "I met
a guy named Jimmy Boxx my rookie year. What happened to him?"

"He hung around for a few months after he busted
Delma, then went back to the West Coast, I think,"
Joanne answered. "Conrad found out later that Boxx had
been dealing steroids and cocaine, in the locker room."

"Boxx was a Hollywood drug dealer," Phil said. "Probably still is. He worked for Mitch Simmons Production, a
D-L Financial Company."

"Are they still making a movie of your book?" Joanne
asked.

"No. It's in *turnaround,*" Phil replied.

"What's turnaround?"

"That's where everybody in Hollywood takes a breather
before they start lying again."

Joanne laughed, hard. "Well, I loved the title *Famous
American Ducks*. I guess it's probably too late to start an
acting career."

"Joanne, I don't think you ever stopped acting."

"Very droll." Joanne cooled noticeably. "Phillip, I
have to ring off, my other line is blinking."

Elliott gave her the phone number to his apartment and she wrote it down on her notepad.

"Ciao." Joanne hung up and paused to doodle Phil's full name on her pad. Her other line *wasn't* blinking.

Poor Phil.

Poor dumb sumbitch.

Joanne could see him in that hot lonely apartment above the San Antonio River. Once she had considered marrying Phil Elliott but now she could see how impossible it would have been. He was always in such turmoil about the *meaning* of what he did.

The meaning of football?

Phil hadn't enjoyed being a professional football star enough to change his attitude toward the team and the league.

"I don't want *to be anything else* than me," he would tell her. "And I am *already* me and I won't change that just to play some game I got into by mistake in the first place. There aren't any sensible reasons for doing what I do beyond the struggle involved in doing it and what I become by virtue of that struggle. And I am not sure I like what I am becoming or what I am involved in anymore."

"You don't want to be successful?" Joanne couldn't believe what he told her.

"I want to have meaning and be *valuable,*" he had replied. "Having real human value, social value, and being successful are not the same. Success is a matter of opinion. Value, human social value, is real."

Phillip Elliott didn't understand then and he probably doesn't understand now, Joanne Remington-Hunter thought. *You have to want to be somebody to be successful. He just wanted to be Phil Elliott. I wonder how he feels about that now.*

She stroked her high cheekbone with her long slender fingers and drifted for a moment, lost in thoughts of the past. Her eyes focused on the notepad where she had written PHILLIP ELLIOTT five times in various hands. She picked up her pencil and carefully crossed out each one.

"The meaning of it all," she spoke softly, "is there's no meaning at all."

Joanne stepped outside onto the patio to the sounds of birds and a gentle wind in the oak trees. A dog howled from far off and other dogs, including her own, picked up and began to bark. A mockingbird leaped from the top of a live oak and stroked evenly through the cool evening air, his white wingbars flashing.

"Poor Phillip," Joanne said, "same bullshit, different day."

The mockingbird squawked and shook his head.

San Francisco—Then

They broke camp before taking the charter plane from LAX to San Francisco. The game was scheduled for Saturday afternoon in Kezar Stadium; it was the next-to-the-last exhibition game and Dallas had yet to be beaten. The training camp had been successful beyond B.A.'s wildest dreams. Dallas had the finest crop of rookies in the league and he had a solid team around a fine core of veterans. The offense was anchored around Maxwell, fullback Dave Purdue (a third-year man from New Mexico), running back Danny Raines, and five-year center Bill Schmidt. Delma Huddle at split end, O. W. Meadows and Jo Bob Williams at the guards, and Elliott at the flankerback; the rookies helped build a solid enough offense. Now B.A. could experiment at the remaining offensive positions until he found the right men, which he had by the fourth game of the regular season. It was to be Dallas's first winning season.

The buses were idling in the dormitory parking lot at the Assembly of God College, waiting to take the team to LAX for the flight to San Francisco. It was 9:00 A.M. Friday.

Phil Elliott cleaned out the last drawer and fastened his bag before he sat down on the bed. This tiny dormitory room had been his home for nine weeks and, in that short time, his life was changed permanently. It was a change he would spend much of his remaining life trying to understand and integrate into a world view.

Jimmy West was gone again, this time forever. He had

packed up and snuck off in the middle of the week after the second exhibition game. Jimmy had gotten all the way to Los Angeles. He had almost escaped, needing only one more ride to get him to LAX, and was standing thumb out beside the interstate, bag and baggage, when he was run down and killed by a hit-and-run driver.

Before he left the last time, Jimmy West had made Elliott promise he wouldn't tell anyone that he had gone.

"Please, Phil," West begged, "don't tell nobody. I gotta get out of here. There ain't nothing worse than this."

There ain't nothing worse than this.

Unfortunately, there were *lots* of things worse and poor Jimmy had barely gotten sixty miles before one ran smack over him.

"There are lots of things worse than this, Jimmy," Phil said to the ghost that had stayed in the room with him since his death. "There's a world of things worse than football."

Phil Elliott lived with those thoughts for his first years with Dallas. Finally, even that kind of mortal fear couldn't keep his whole life from slowly, but surely, unraveling.

There were lots of things worse in life but, after five or six years of professional football, Phil Elliott knew there also had to be lots of things better. What he didn't know was how to even begin his search for a better life. He wasn't ready to let go of what he had on the slim premise that there must be something better out there somewhere to grab hold of. The lesson of Jimmy West wasn't lost on Phil Elliott and no matter how beat up he got mentally and physically, he could never bring himself to quit. The one promise he had made to himself that rookie season— *never quit*—kept him in the game until the day the Hunters, B. A. Quinlan, League Security, and the commissioner himself, all combined to force Phil Elliott out of football.

The day Charlotte Caulder died.

"Let's go, turkey." Delma Huddle was at the door. "I already hauled my bags down. They're loading the buses."

Phil Elliott pushed himself up off the bed, grabbed his bag, and walked out, stopping only momentarily for a last look at this innocuous-looking cement block room in which so much had happened. It didn't seem possible.

Or even probable.

The plane was a PSA charter and when they landed in San Francisco, buses pulled out onto the runway apron and rolled up beside the plane. The players climbed off the aircraft and right onto the chartered buses. At the hotel, the room keys were spread out on a table near the registration desk and Elliott found he had a new room-mate: Seth Maxwell. The two men would be roommates the rest of their years together on the football club.

"First rule of the passing game, kid," Maxwell said, as he pulled the door to their room shut. "Always room with the quarterback. You get the bed closest to the door and I'll always answer the phone."

"I'm going to take a shower," Phil replied. He peeled off his coat and tossed it on the bed, loosening his tie and unbuttoning his shirt. "Goddamn, I'm tired."

"Pregame nerves," Maxwell said. "You need to go out with me and Mitch Simmons tonight. Have a few drinks and relax. You're too tense."

"Is Simmons bringing his eight-year-old daughter?" Elliott asked sarcastically. "Or just another starlet who *looks* like his daughter?"

"That's show business." Seth laughed. "And show business is my life."

Elliott pulled off his brown calfskin cowboy boots and lay back on the bed.

He was getting another headache. In three exhibition games, Phil Elliott had taken some vicious shots to the head.

Against Minnesota, the middle linebacker had caught Phil coming across the middle twice, and clotheslined him both times. Once in the face, bloodying Elliott's nose, and again, against the side of his head, knocking him dizzy and leaving his ears ringing for three days. Phil got a measure of revenge when he caught the linebacker from the blind side and cracked back on him, cut-blocking him at the knees. The Minnesota player left the game limping.

The Detroit secondary must have watched the Minnesota films and taken note of Elliott's crackback block, because they doubleteamed, clotheslined, forearmed, cut-blocked, and blindsided him all night. They beat him up, from the opening minutes to the final gun. The Detroit defensive backs played up close, bumping and running with Elliott constantly, sometimes bringing an outside linebacker wide in a walk-away position to help double him inside.

While Minnesota and Detroit spent their energy trying to knock Phil Elliott out of the game, Delma Huddle ran wild, scoring seven touchdowns in two games on a total of seventeen catches for almost four hundred yards.

In addition, despite the beatings, Elliott was able to score three times on nine catches for one hundred and seventy yards.

Unfortunately, none of that did anything to ease the headaches that were becoming an almost daily occurrence.

Elliott sat up and shucked his socks, then walked into the bathroom to turn on the shower. His head still throbbed.

"Did you see all them hippies and beatniks in the streets?" Maxwell yelled from the other room. "This town is full of homos and dopeheads."

"They're just people, doing what they want to do and trying not to hurt anybody else." Elliott walked out of the bathroom, steam billowing out behind him. "Don't tell me you don't believe in 'free love.' I know better. And all that shit they pump into us in the training room qualifies as 'dope' under any definition."

"You better never let B.A. or Conrad catch you talking like that." Maxwell had stripped down to his undershorts and was turning on the television.

"They don't care about drugs," Elliott said. "They just want us to take *their* drugs."

"As long as you ain't having fun, they call it medicine." Maxwell laughed and fondled himself through the fly of his boxers. "If you enjoy it, they call it 'dope' and pop your ass good for using it."

"What about all the amphetamines?"

"The jury is still out and as soon as somebody invents a drug that makes you a crazed, bloodthirsty killer without any accompanying euphoric side effects, speed will be history." Maxwell frowned. "I like speed myself, before, during, and after the game."

"It's too high amp for me," Elliott said. "I'm already pumping too much adrenaline. My prediction is that anabolic steroids will replace speed. I've seen guys in college change their shape like Plastic Man, taking that shit, with some pretty weird mental side effects, *none* of which I would describe as euphoria."

"Speaking of college." Maxwell leaned up to turn the TV channel tuner. He found a country-and-western show. "What are you doing about the draft?"

"I'm still listed as an on-campus student. So I still got a two S deferment. What about you?"

"Conrad pulled some strings in Washington and I'm an LB Three."

"What's an LB Three?" Elliott asked.

"That means, if war breaks out," Maxwell deadpanned, "I am the third one to go *after* Lady Bird."

Elliott laughed and finished undressing for the shower. "LB Three. Now *that's* funny." He turned toward the bathroom.

"Yeh, but the draft ain't," Maxwell warned. "When you get to Dallas, you make sure Clinton gets you into a National Guard unit. All the players are in the Guard. That way nobody gets drafted."

Phil Elliott remembered that advice. And his very first day in Dallas, he went to the club with his problem. Clinton's solution was to make a note reminding himself to draft three more wide receivers as soon as possible.

But in the San Francisco hotel, rookie sensation Phil Elliott wasn't too worried about the draft or anything else except maybe his headaches and the fact that he thought the world was falling apart. He let the hot water pound on him, loosening the general tightness and soreness that came of nine solid weeks of football, twice a day, five days a week, and at least once on Saturday in the last three weeks, exhibition games.

Tomorrow, it would be San Francisco in Kezar Stadium. San Francisco, a team Dallas had never beaten.

Phil was toweling himself off when he walked back into the bedroom. Maxwell was watching television, having to look past a giant erection to see the screen. He was watching Popeye cartoons.

"Listen, kid," Maxwell said, gripping his penis with

both hands. "The wind in Kezar can be tricky, so keep track of it. It can shift two or three times during the game and has a funny tail to it. Don't be surprised when the ball first leaves my hand, if the trajectory seems off, just keep running your route." He continued to fondle his erection.

Elliott rubbed the towel vigorously against his neck. "You gotta promise to wash your hands before the game."

Dreams—Now

They were riding the ridgeline on the far side of the Purgatory River, above River Ranch Estates. Ten-year-old Scott Elliott was riding the small paint pony next to Charlotte Caulder on her big gray quarterhorse. Phil Elliott rode about fifty yards behind, enjoying the view of the two people he loved walking their mounts along the rocky riding trail.

The sky was clear blue and the sun was high, painting their shadows hard against the cream limestone, yet it was neither hot nor cold. The temperature of the air was peculiar, almost nonexistent, and there was no wind, but the stunted oaks creaked and the branches swayed. Dust devils danced around them.

"You better be careful, stud. You're letting them get too far in front of you," a familiar voice spoke from behind and Phil turned in the saddle to see Seth Maxwell, astride a tall white horse, riding on his flank. He had two pearl-handled, nickel-plated revolvers strapped to his hips.

"What are you doing here?" Elliott looked at Maxwell, suited out in full Hollywood cowboy drag.

"Just looking after my favorite receiver." Maxwell grinned. "You're letting them get too far in front. This is dangerous country." Maxwell nodded upgrade toward Phil's son, Scott, and Charlotte Caulder, who were talking and laughing together, as their horses picked their way carefully through the rocks.

"Dangerous country?" Phil laughed. "This is a dude ranch, for chrissakes. What are you worried about—wild shots from the tennis courts?"

"You know, Phil, I get awful tired of warning you and watching you step right in the shit anyway." Maxwell took out one of the revolvers and began twirling it, finally slipping it easily back in its studded holster. "Now, look. They are completely out of sight around the bend. You don't know shit about traveling horseback in Texas. In fact, you didn't know shit about playing football in Texas, or writing in Texas, or just living in Texas."

"I know it can get to be a real pain in the ass, with people like you as my friends."

"Phil boy," Maxwell smiled, "I'm as good as it gets. You oughta know that by now, if you ain't learned nothing else, I'm as good as it gets."

Elliott tried to disagree, but found himself nodding instead.

"Yeh, Seth, I guess that's what scares me," Phil said. "I think you *are* as good as it gets."

"We're having fun now, ain't we, kid?" Maxwell laughed and his horse broke into a little sidestep canter. He was the beautiful white stallion that Maxwell kept on his ranch in his TV series *Scout*. The show was produced by Mitch Simmons and financed by Ross Denham and Bobby Laughlin through D-L Financial Group. The executive producer was Kennedy King Simmons, who had grown from a chubby eight-year-old hot fudge sundae freak to a beautiful young woman capable of knocking cars off Rodeo Drive just with her looks.

"I'm glad you didn't hold it against me, Phil," Maxwell said, reining in the big horse.

"Hold what against you?"

"Getting kicked out of football."

"You didn't kick me out, the Hunters and the commissioner did." Elliott was looking ahead, trying to catch sight of Charlotte and Scott.

"Did you realize you were the first man expelled or suspended from football for using drugs?" Seth asked. "I knew several guys they ran out of the game for *refusing* to use drugs, but you were the first they got for taking them."

"I just took the *wrong* drugs," Phil replied. They were approaching the bend in the trail.

"Well, things are a lot worse now." Maxwell looked ahead. "I don't see Scott or Charlotte. Do you?"

"No." Elliott stood in the stirrups, trying to see farther up the trail.

"I told you," Maxwell repeated. "You let them get too far ahead. This River Ranch Estates country is dangerous. You're on the Purgatory River, don't you . . ."

Maxwell was interrupted by the gunshots. They came from up ahead, exactly where Scott and Charlotte would be. Maxwell spurred his horse, Elliott's followed and, suddenly, they were there.

Charlotte Caulder lay on the ground; her face half blown away and her chest torn open from the bullets.

"Phillip, help me," she said, trying to rise. Blood poured out of her. "Please, help me."

Elliott just stared down at her, paralyzed.

"They got the kid." Maxwell sat with one leg across his saddle horn. "There they go." He pointed off toward the River Ranch Golf Course.

A golf cart careened down the hill with four people in it. Scott was tied up in the back.

"Dad! Help me!" Scott yelled, as he struggled with his mother and David Stein. Bob Beaudreau was driving.

"They've got me, Dad. You got to save me."

Courtnay Howard-Elliott, Phil's ex-wife, slapped her hand over Scott's mouth and tried to hold him still.

"You better go get them." Maxwell sat calmly on his horse. "I'd help, but this ain't my fight. Besides I'm on hiatus."

"Phillip, help me!" The rocks around Charlotte Caulder ran red with her blood. "Please, help me!"

"She just won't give it up. It's fucking up your life. Go get the boy." Maxwell began rolling a cigarette, his leg still hooked over his saddle horn. "She's dead, Phil. She's been dead for years. Let it go."

Elliott tried to get his horse moving after the golf cart that was speeding away toward the River Ranch Estates Golf Course. The horse wouldn't move.

"You know, once they get to the golf course, you can't touch them," Maxwell said. "It's out of your jurisdiction."

"Phillip, help me." Charlotte just bled and bled until the ridgeline flowed with her blood.

"Dad! Save me!" Scott yelled from the golf cart. "Save me, Dad!"

"How does this horse work?" Elliott asked Maxwell.

"Apparently, not too well." Maxwell laughed, then pulled his guns and pointed them at Elliott. "It's too late."

"I got to go after the boy," Elliott insisted.

"It's too late," Maxwell repeated, the pistols still pointed at Phil. "Look, they just crossed the eighteenth fairway. They're across the border. I gotta take you in for shooting this here gal." He looked down at the blood-soaked Charlotte Caulder. "You're gonna hang for this one."

The courtroom was small with just a high judge's bench and a witness chair. No jury. No spectators. Maxwell left Phil in front of the bench and disappeared.

The judge was David Stein. He sentenced Phil to hang for murder and failure to pay alimony and court costs.

The gallows were right behind him and the rope already around his neck. Stein followed Elliott up the stairs.

"You understand, Phil," Stein was explaining. "This is a *no-fault hanging*. You're not really guilty of anything, but the attorneys have agreed that to speed things up and help unclog the overloaded judicial system, you'll have to hang. But don't worry. Nobody blames you and this won't go on your record." David Stein tightened the noose and then reached for the spring lever. "Would you step over on the trapdoor, please, Phil?"

When he did, Stein pulled the lever and Elliott fell into eternity.

He woke up, soaked in sweat, in bed in his apartment above the San Antonio River.

He didn't know whether to feel good that he was still alive, or bad because he was awake.

He finally just got up and changed the sheets. Then got in a hot bath.

His back was killing him.

He missed Scott.

He missed Charlotte Caulder.

He was alone again.

And he was in pain.

Still.

Phil and Joanne—Now

The tall handsome woman stood at the curb outside the Alamo Bar and Grill, looking nervously up and down the street. Phil Elliott recognized Joanne Remington-Hunter as a victim of his enemy. She was still quite beautiful, an exquisite woman, expensively dressed with an air of purposely spare glamour. Joanne knew many of his enemies; she even married one. Her stunning beauty, grace, and sophistication were painfully familiar and slashed him like a knife.

Seeing Joanne renewed a burning pain that Phil had long ago reduced to a dull ache; an ancient dream disturbed his waking sleep. She was fantasy remembered: a face of prominent bone, casting angles and shadows on cream-soft skin surrounding deep, dark eyes. The unforgotten brown eyes turned to him, she smiled, and it was yesterday again. Joanne had quickly destroyed Phil's psychic defenses, years in the making.

"Hello, Phil." Her lips glistened, her teeth still perfect. "How nice to see you again."

"Mrs. Hunter." Phil gently gripped her hand in his. "The one person worth traveling across the Comancheria to see. You're more beautiful than ever."

"You remember the last time?" she asked, holding his hand in both of hers.

"I remember that day very well." Phil recited. "The Germans wore gray. You wore blue." He smiled. "Though very little of it, as I recall."

"Still quoting from *Casablanca,* I see."

159

"It comes over me in waves," Phil replied. "The doctor tells me it was all the hits of mescaline I took back in the sixties."

"Or all the hits in the head."

"Either. Whatever." Phil nodded and frowned. "The doctor also told me I picked a bad state to be in pain."

"Sounds more like a lawyer than a doctor," Joanne said. "He didn't recommend a *good state* by any chance?"

"I think to him a good state would be *unconscious*."

Phil stepped closer and pulled her to him. They hugged, kissing one another on the cheek.

"Well, Phillip." She stepped back and gripped both his shoulders. "You look much better than I expected. Of course, I expected you'd be dead by now."

"I'll have to get *better* to die."

"What do you do for exercise?" Joanne was looking over his long, slender frame. "You're so thin."

"I bitch a lot and don't eat much." He rubbed at his numb hands. "My neck, back and legs are too crippled to do anything more physical than short walks. I used to swim, but I lost the pool and the water in the divorce."

"Come on inside," Joanne said. "Poor baby. I'll buy you a glass of water."

"I'd rather have tequila. Lead the way."

Joanne went inside the Alamo Bar and Grill and Phil followed her to a small table by a back window overlooking the river. A fire crackled in the big stone fireplace; a long-barreled Kentucky rifle hung above the mantelpiece, below a four-color lithograph of the Battle of the Alamo. It was a popular subject.

"Well?" Joanne asked. "What shall we do?"

"How about a lot of drinks, then back to my place where you can watch me pass out." Phil lit a Marlboro and offered one to Joanne.

"No, thanks," she said. "When did you start smoking cigarettes?"

"I smoke when I'm in jail."

"You're out now."

"I'm expecting to go back." Phil let the cigarette hang from his lips. "A lot of bad-looking paper arrived today in the company of a man with a heavy-caliber weapon."

"You must have really pissed off your ex-wife." Joanne waved a waiter over. She ordered a margarita and

Phil asked for a triple Sausa Commemorativo on the rocks. "What was her name?"

"Howard," Phil replied. "Courtnay Howard. She's from Fort Worth."

"From near Diamond Oaks?" Joanne asked.

"Closer to the stockyards."

"Oh swell." She laughed. "You're lucky she didn't shoot you."

"I believe that is the premise she operates on."

"What is she after you now for?" Joanne glanced over at the waiter bringing the drinks from the bar. "Money?"

"She's already got it all."

"The boy?"

"Scott," Phil replied. "No. She isn't interested in the problems of single parenthood. I think she just wants revenge."

"Well, she better dig two graves."

"Three," Phil corrected. "I'm gonna kill her lawyer before she gets me." He picked up his glass and quickly drained it, setting it down and signaling the waiter for another.

"Are we binge-drinking to relieve ourself of life's little pressures?" Joanne asked, looking at the second triple tequila.

"Life's *big* pressures," Phil explained, holding the glass up. "I'm forty-seven and everything is falling apart at once; the economy, the social system, my life, and my body."

"Rebelling against the aging process is not healthy, Phillip."

"As near as I can tell, the goddamn aging process ain't too healthy itself."

"Everything is always a crisis with you," Joanne said. "And you always survive."

"That's just good crisis management." Phil smiled. "You can't fault me for that. Besides, I've got a ten-year-old boy to look out for and I can't figure out the math on our age and mileage differentials."

"Well." Joanne held up her margarita. "Here's looking at you, kid."

"I believe"—Phil smiled—"that is my line."

"This is a rewrite."

"So, we will live today as a blue page?"

"What's a blue page?"

"The color page they use when they rewrite movie scripts," Phil explained.

"Here's to a life of blue pages." Joanne took a long drink.

Phil followed suit, downing his second triple Commemorativo. He signaled the waiter for menus. "Promise you'll spend the night with me. I hate regaining consciousness alone."

"Yeh." Joanne picked up the menu. "You silver-tongued devil."

"I want you to share my nightsweats."

"You always knew how to romance a girl."

They ate dinner in the small fake adobe building above the river, alternately watching each other and the activity on the Riverwalk.

As the waiter cleared away the dishes, Joanne shrugged out of her light jacket and hung it behind her on the chair. Her V-neck silk pullover blouse matched the full skirt; the color was called Autumn Honey. Her high-top brown boots sagged in folds of rich French leather.

Phil struck a match to light another cigarette.

The tiny blue-white flame changed her face, finding new hollows and ridges, outlining her straight, thin nose, the high cheekbones, the straight jaw and slightly pointed chin. Her long hair was braided into a pigtail that was pulled up over her right ear and wrapped around her head; the different shades of brown formed a patchwork in the braid. Single hairs had worked loose and swung around her face like a halo, backlit by the lamplight.

"What are you staring at?" Joanne had noticed his stare. She smiled, her teeth white, glistening.

"You." Phil shook out the match, the cigarette still unlit. "You're too beautiful."

"*Too* beautiful?" She leaned forward, tugging at her boot tops. "Too beautiful for what?"

"To be a victim." Elliott rubbed his hands, trying to work out the cold numbness from his fingers.

"I didn't know they had rules and qualifying criteria for victims." She looked up as she continued to pull at her boots. The silk blouse hung loosely from her neck.

"They don't. *I* do." Phil was enjoying the view of her full breast, the nipple large and erect.

"Get your eyes full?" She had caught his glance and continued to hold her pose. Finally she leaned back, adjusting the neckline of her blouse, then smoothed her skirt. "Well, sometimes I feel like a victim."

"Feeling like a victim is politics," Phil said. *"Being* a victim is drama."

"And it's drama you're after," Joanne said. "That and looking down my dress."

"Drama's the game, Pee Wee Herman's the name," Phil replied, smiling. "He's the Bogart of the eighties."

"You already know there's no basement in the Alamo?" Joanne asked.

"Yeh. I was just over there." Phil nodded and grimaced in mock seriousness. "And no back door."

"Poor baby." She teased. "A writer in need of a victim."

"I already have the victim, it's the fate I'm pondering now." Phil finally lit the cigarette. "Suitable fates are truly rare, possibly mythical." He exhaled a cloud of smoke. "Whereas victims . . ."

". . . just walk in off the street." Joanne finished the sentence for him. "So? Who is this victim?"

"A beautiful woman in her late thirties, early forties. I'm writing a book about the Comanche Indians. Or trying to. Their history, their myths. Their victims." Phil stood suddenly to stretch his back and leg muscles; the pain had slowly grown to unbearable proportions. He bent and twisted at the waist, slowly and carefully; the knots pulled tight in the hamstrings, damaged lumbar and thoracic vertebrae popped and snapped against the tension. "Whew! I hate that. Old war wound." He sat back down and picked up his tequila, draining the glass in one long gulp.

Joanne watched the gyrations. She had seen him in worse shape and had known him well during the time he was accumulating the impressive array of injuries. "Receivers always get it in the back or the head," he had told her then, "because you can't take your eyes off the ball and the best position to be in is between the defender and the ball. So, they try to ram their heads through your back and out your chest to get to the ball. They're *trying* to kill you on every play but they don't expect to," Phil had explained. "Every so often, one of them will *actually* kill somebody. For some strange reason, it comes as a big surprise to everyone."

"So?" Joanne asked, as Phil put down his glass and looked around for the waiter. "How old *is* this victim of yours? Is she late thirties or early forties?"

"I'm too polite to ask." Phil caught the waiter's attention. "I've already done some pretty terrible things to her and her family. First, I turn a band of Liver Eater Comanches loose on them and now I've decided to age her fifteen to twenty years before I let the Comanches rape and kill her."

"Jesus! Phillip, that's terrible."

"Don't tell me. Tell them goddamn Indians. They got her stripped naked and staked out on the banks of the upper Guadalupe."

"Is that up near the Y-O Ranch?" Joanne looked away, into the fireplace. One eye reflected a tiny flame.

"Yeh, I think so," Phil replied. "Gillespie County, I think."

"Oh, Phillip!" She turned back smiling. "They had the best party at the Y-O, a few years back when they celebrated their Centennial. It was great! Champagne and all sorts of exotic foods. There's only about fifty thousand acres left of the original five hundred thousand but that was plenty. It was black tie and cowboy boots. It was outside and there must have been a thousand people there." She laughed at her recollection. "About halfway through the party, a norther hit with about a thirty-mile-an-hour wind and rain and hail. It was so funny. Emmett cussing and swearing, slopping around in five-thousand-dollar boots in ankle-deep caliche mud. You should have been there."

"I'll bet." Phil watched her face beam with good humor. She always had humor. "I'm sure this girl the Liver Eaters got would be glad to know that a hundred years later the weather fucked up Emmett Hunter's fun."

"You're the bastard that's slapping twenty years' age on her," Joanne shot back. "If she knew that, she'd hate *you* worse than the Indians."

"You think so?"

"I know so, honey."

They both laughed and then fell silent, gazing at one

another, trying to comprehend the meanings of all the time that had passed between them.

The waiter arrived with another round of drinks.

"Why are you writing about Comanches?" Joanne asked, finally.

"They were an interesting people who were technologically superior to anyone in their known universe and acted accordingly." Phil lit another cigarette. "For awhile. And then, in a very few years, they were wiped away."

"Is that all?"

"No, but it was a start." Phil exhaled and coughed. "They didn't consider any other people even human. They called themselves the True People and they were bizarre, bloodthirsty, brave, and frightened. There were never very many of them and their wars were very personal; they did what they wanted, to whom they wanted, how they wanted. It was a simple Us versus Them world view."

"What happened to them?"

"The Texas Revolution and annexation to the United States," Phil said. "The Comanches could not comprehend an enemy that just kept coming and coming. They had to reproduce lost warriors the old-fashioned way, by conceiving, nurturing, and raising them to fighting age and size. The Texans and the U.S. Army just got more troops from the East, mostly black men; the Buffalo Soldiers."

"So?" Joanne took a sip of her drink. "What is this woman's fate going to be?"

"What woman?"

"The one you just aged twenty years and the Liver Eaters have taken prisoner in her birthday suit."

"I haven't decided yet," Phil said. "Something in the realm of bloodlust, I'm afraid."

"She could use her feminine wiles. A little bear grease in the right places and she might deal with the Hell's Angels of the High Plains." Joanne wanted the girl to escape. "I'm talking the New Woman of the Frontier. Her struggle for political consciousness; fighting male chauvinism, sex discrimination, and a small band of Liver Eater Comanches." Joanne pressed enthusiastically. "Don't go laying the same old stereotypical role on her. We could be talking miniseries here."

"Think of Comanche sex and Comanche death as options. Which would you choose?"

"How about a new subject." Joanne drew back. "This is getting sick."

"I think that's my publisher's position, too." Phil stood again to stretch his back and legs. The feeling still had not returned to the tips of his fingers. "What about Delma Huddle? Decker McShane wants me to do a story about his drug bust."

"Why? That was years ago."

"It's supposed to have something to do with the upcoming reunion," Phil replied. "I will admit I haven't found the hook yet but maybe you can supply it."

"I only know what Emmett told me about that guy Jimmy Boxx," Joanne said. "You're the one who told me that he worked for Denham and Laughlin."

"He worked for Mitch Simmons, Seth's producer," Phil corrected. "Simmons is financed by D-L Financial which is Denham and Laughlin. That's how I made the connection. I don't know what he's doing now."

"Emmett was involved with the Southwest Conservative Trust," Joanne explained. "It was some sort of private deal involved in fighting communism. Denham and Laughlin donated money to Conrad back in the early seventies when he was trying to fly all those Christmas presents to the POWs in North Vietnam. That's where Emmett met Colonel William Glanton. He was involved later in some plans to rescue MIAs after the war ended. I remember Emmett flying down to Panama and to Costa Rica. Boxx claimed to be an ex-Navy pilot, but I think he just watched *Top Gun* too many times."

"Could he fly a plane?"

"Apparently," Joanne replied. "He showed up once in a uniform to pick up Emmett. I always figured he just bought the damn thing."

"He used to be a Los Angeles cop."

"No. This was a military uniform." Joanne paused, as the waiter approached.

"Mr. Elliott, you have a phone call," the waiter said. "You can take it in that booth over there."

It was John Wilson.

"I figured you would either be at Andy Crawford's

place or the Alamo Bar and Grill," Wilson explained. "First, Scott wants to say hello before he takes his bath."

"Hey! Dad!" The voice sounded small and distant, slightly frightened. "How ya' doin'?"

"I'm fine, boy." Elliott struggled to keep the quiver out of his voice. "I'm doing real fine. How do you like John's ranch?"

"Oh, it's okay." His voice dropped perceptibly. "When are you coming here?"

"Soon. In a few days." Phil nearly choked on the lump in his throat, tears welled in his eyes. "I wrote you a letter today. Have you ridden any horses?"

"Yeh. And I fell off and hurt myself." The pain in the little boy's words grew. "When are you coming up here?"

"I'll be there before you know it." Sadness enveloped him like a cloud and he struggled to keep the cheerful tone in his conversation.

"I know it already, Dad." He was tired and the loneliness was overwhelming him. "I miss you."

"I miss you too, and I love you." Phil stiffened against the awful pain of separation and fear. "Now, you take your bath and get into bed. John said he put a television and a VCR in your room, so you can watch a movie while you go to sleep."

"Yeh." The little boy was not enthused. "When are you coming?"

"In a couple days, Scott, that's the best I can tell you now." Phil spoke softly. "You get some sleep now."

"Okay. I love you." The boy spoke reluctantly. "I guess this is goodbye."

"So long, boy, just so long," Phil spoke, as he heard the rattle at the other end and the phone changed hands.

"He'll be okay." Wilson came back on the line. "He's tired and he gets scared."

"He's got every right," Phil said. "Thanks for calling. I've been sitting feeling sorry for myself and forgot all about calling him. What a guy I am."

"Just take it easy. He's fine." John Wilson tried to calm Elliott. He changed the subject. "I called for two reasons. The Dallas ball club is suing Delma for fraud."

"Fraud? For what?"

"They owe him eight hundred thousand dollars in deferred payments and are claiming that during those con-

tract years, he was under the influence of drugs and
therefore not performing up to his contractual obligations."

"How are they going to prove that even if it was true,
which I don't believe?"

"They're squeezing him with a grand jury," Wilson
explained. "They're threatening to immunize him and
make him name names or go to jail for contempt. If he
cooperates, they have offered to reduce his sentence to
time served. They got him between a rock and a hard
place."

"What names?"

"Who knows?" Wilson said. "But the new owners,
Mr. Denham and Mr. Laughlin, want to create a new
role model: the professional football player as informer.
Everyone is presumed guilty and innocence must be proved
over and over. They stand to save a lot of money in
deferred salaries if they get the right names and win their
fraud suit."

"Jesus!" Phil said. "This is amazing. Governor B. A.
Quinlan's War on Drugs is the hottest thing since red-
baiting. Everybody gets dirty and nobody stays innocent
for long without proof that they're not guilty."

"No one wants to stand up and be counted on this
one," Wilson replied. "So you be careful until you can
get up here."

"Sure, count on it." Phil paused. "John, have you ever
heard of the Southwest Conservative Trust?"

"Yeh. I don't know much about it."

"Well, find out for me. I'll talk to you later. Kiss that
boy for me and, if you can, stay in the room with him
until he falls asleep. He likes that."

"Hell." Wilson laughed. "I like it, too."

"John," Phil added, "Courtnay filed some more paper
on me today."

"What was it?"

"I never looked. A Bexar County deputy brought it by
this morning."

"That goddamn Stein." Wilson was angry. "I told him
I would accept service for you. They're just trying to piss
you off."

"I think they're succeeding."

"If I don't have copies of the filings in my office

tomorrow, I'll call the courthouse. Don't worry about it. If it's important I'll call you back."

"How about one more drink?" Phil asked, as he sat back down at the table. Joanne had watched him talk on the phone but did not inquire about the call.

"Then what?" Joanne glanced out the window at the Riverwalk, then back at Elliott. "Safe sex?"

"I don't think I've ever had safe sex."

"I'm not sure it exists," Joanne added.

"Do you ever see any of the old players?" Phil signaled the waiter for another round of drinks.

"Some." Joanne thought a moment. "Saw Alan Claridge a lot. He got pretty high profile as a congressman. He was in town raising money when they hospitalized him. I guess you heard about that?"

"AIDS?"

"That's the rumor." Joanne nodded. "God, it seems so awful."

"It probably *is* awful."

"Anyway," Joanne continued, "Art Hartman went to work for Denham-Laughlin Financial when he retired. He's done quite well. Lots of ex-players went to work for them in some sort of work training program that Denham set up after they took over the club. They place guys all over the country in all sorts of jobs. I understand that Monroe White works for them in Oak Cliff."

"It figures." Phil smirked. "He's in *black* real estate?"

Joanne nodded. "You know Thomas Richardson moved to Washington, D.C., and is number two man in the player's union. He's quite popular with the owner's council. I know Clinton Foote considers Thomas one of his greatest achievements."

"Things certainly have changed," Phil said. "I figured Richardson would give them nothing but fits. Instead, Thomas threatens to beat the shit out of me over a story I was writing about the strike a couple years ago."

"Everybody wants to come in out of the cold," Joanne pointed out. "Everyone except you."

"I want to, they just won't let me," Phil replied. "So, Thomas is helping Upton Gray run the union to everyone's benefit but the players. I never cease to be amazed by my misconception about my old teammates."

"I suppose you think Danny Raines should have turned down Clinton's offer to replace B.A.?"

"No," Phil replied. "That was one that made sense. Nobody understood the game like Danny. He's the perfect choice as head coach and I couldn't be happier for him. He loves the job and the game. He always did."

"Have you seen Seth lately?" Joanne asked. "Oh, I'm sorry, I asked you that before didn't I?"

"Yeh. He and John Wilson came down and got me out of jail." Phil watched the waiter approach and leave the fresh drinks, picking up the old glasses and emptying the ashtray. "You know, John's my lawyer. He's the only one I can afford."

"Where's Seth now?"

"Back in Los Angeles, making a fortune with his charm."

"The King always landed on his feet," Joanne said with obvious distaste.

"You dislike him that much?"

"I just never liked him as much as you did," Joanne replied. "You thought he walked on water. I just saw him as another football player with a good line."

"He was more than that," Phil argued. "He still is something special."

"Listen to you, after what he did."

"He did what he had to do," Phil protested. "It wouldn't have mattered what he did, they still would have thrown me out of football. I've had a lot worse happen."

"Yeh. I guess you're right. Who am I to talk?" Joanne sighed. "I married Emmett."

"Nobody wanted to fight with the Hunters any more than they want to fight with Ross Denham and Bobby Laughlin now," Phil said.

"Let's get out of here." Joanne stood suddenly, pulling her jacket over her shoulders.

"Might as well run, even if we can't hide."

San Francisco—*Then*

Maxwell went out to meet Mitch Simmons, the producer, and his two Texas money men, Ross Denham and Bobby Laughlin, for dinner at Fisherman's Wharf. Phil Elliott declined the invitation to join them when he learned that Simmons's gofer, Jimmy Boxx, would also be there. Phil had survived to the tender age of twenty-two partially due to an acute sense for character.

He had gone through the meat grinder of major college recruiting and chose Michigan State University, not because they made him the best offer and romanced him with coaches and alumni, but because they didn't. Other colleges and universities had wanted Phil Elliott's athletic talents a lot more than Michigan State and made the mistake of trying to impress that on him by any and all means at their disposal, with total disregard for the NCAA rules.

Michigan State wasn't that enthusiastic about procuring Elliott's skills and simply offered him an athletic scholarship. They even required him to play two sports to earn it. It was not a rich deal, but he took it. Because once he signed, entered school, and reported properly to practices, all he had to do to keep his contract and the vital control of his life was to practice and attend class and maintain a two-point average.

Had Phil Elliott taken any of the other deals, which included free cars, cash payments, clothes, and do-nothing jobs, the college would have owned him. The fear of breaking the rules of the game was strong enough in

Phil's character, but what was totally repulsive to him was the act of conspiring with an institution of higher education to violate the rules of the game.

Even at eighteen years of age, Phil Elliott knew that if you had no rules, you had no game. And playing the game was the single most rewarding experience in his life. It was a guiding force his whole life.

Phil stayed in the hotel, ordered room service, and studied the game plan for San Francisco. He marveled at the flexibility of B.A.'s offensive system to react instantaneously to any defensive set. He studied his routes and their adjustments against the various blitzes, man to man and secondary zone looks.

B.A. had been impressed with Elliott's size and speed, plus his ability to catch in a crowd and take a beating. So the head coach had put in running plays that allowed Phil the opportunity to deliver some blows to his antagonists.

As the flankerback, Elliott played either side of the field, depending on the formation. B.A. had put in power sweeps left and right, similar to the famous Green Bay sweeps with the guards pulling and leading; the exception was that B.A. always ran the sweeps toward Elliott's side and assigned him the job of cracking back on either the force men or the linebacker, whoever showed up first.

The crackback block was a vicious weapon; Elliott could split out fifteen to twenty yards and, on the snap, start down the line of scrimmage on his target's blindside. Because the force man, either the safety or the cornerback, and the linebacker were watching the guards and the ball, they seldom if ever saw Elliott coming fast and hard.

Over the years, before the crackback block was made illegal, Phil Elliott had taken out several knees, ankles, and twice had broken whole legs. It wasn't a one-way street; Phil had suffered three shoulder separations, cervical vertebrae damage that would eventually cripple his hands, broken ribs, and uncounted concussions.

As he studied the San Francisco game plan, Phil fully expected that sometime the following day he would suffer an injury, possibly crippling, and he would certainly get *his bell rung* again.

"The Wonderful World of Euphemism," Phil thought, as he thumbed back in his playbook to the glossary where he reread the definitions for clothesline, crackback, blindside, head slap, and cross-body block. Elliott couldn't help but wonder at B.A.'s ability to communicate the most violent acts in a manner that made them seem like harmless little parlor tricks.

"The man's a genius," Phil thought, reluctantly. "He must be—he realizes how great I am."

The television was on and Elliott leaned over to turn up the sound, as he tossed his playbook beside him on the bed. Humphrey Bogart was on the screen with Ingrid Bergman. They were somewhere in the middle of *Casablanca* and she was pointing a gun at him just after telling him how much she loved him in Paris.

"The heat must be affecting the bitch." Elliott tried to sound like Delma Huddle. "Either that, or they should rename this movie *Detroit*."

Phil drifted in and out of sleep, as Bogart and Bergman flickered on the screen. He dreamt of Jimmy West, lonesome for North Dakota and splattered all over the L.A. freeway. If he just could have gotten off the freeway. If he had just been drafted by Minnesota. If Phil had just gone ahead and turned him in again the moment he left the room.

Please, man, don't tell 'em I'm gone. There's nothing worse than this.

Phil jerked awake, as the car bore down on the hapless Jimmy West.

We will always have Paris.

All Jimmy West got was Oxnard.

Maxwell came in drunk, just before bedcheck. He staggered into the bathroom and Elliott could hear him pissing over the sound of the television.

" . . . *round up the usual suspects*."

Elliott pulled the covers over his head, as Maxwell came out of the bathroom. He flicked on the light with one hand while he shook his dick with the other.

"Hey, kid," Seth whispered, loudly. "Hey, kid. Are you awake?"

"Yeh." Elliott pulled the covers down and squinted against the light.

"You shoulda come." Maxwell finished shaking his dick and stuffed it back in his pants like he was bagging a rattlesnake. "We had a hell of a time. Went to some place where men dress up like women."

"Female impersonators?"

"Yeh." Maxwell nodded, his eyes red. "They had some of them, too." He laughed and began to undress. He fell backwards over the bed, trying to get his pants off over his cowboy boots, and passed out. Quarterback Seth Maxwell slept most of the night, crossways on the bed, stripped to the waist, his pants tangled down around his boots and his dick hanging out of the fly of the shorts.

He was definitely ready for the big game.

It was a cool, sunny day in San Francisco, as the buses made their way from the hotel to the football stadium. The incredible collection of people on the street was fascinating to Elliott. Flower children and Chinese, joggers and drunks, people of all colors, political and sexual persuasions; the sunny weather had filled the streets with the most cosmopolitan collection of people Phil Elliott had ever seen.

There was one block-long wall of posters advertising a Grateful Dead concert, and everywhere Phil looked were the words

PEACE AND LOVE

He was so taken by the atmosphere of the city that they were approaching the stadium and the gathering crowd before Elliott remembered he was on his way to play in a football game where behavior and appearance were strictly regulated, and a man with peace and love on his mind would get his ass kicked.

Maxwell was right about the wind in the stadium. It was tricky and dangerous, the kind that could leave a pass hanging in the air long enough to draw a crowd of defenders all bent on tearing the receiver in half. But Seth played the wind beautifully, and, since Frisco won the toss and took the ball, Maxwell put the wind at his back and came out gunning.

First, he hit Phil and Delma on short ins and outs, testing the defense while not giving them time to blitz. Then he changed up and caught the pass rush with a draw delay trap to Dave Purdue that went for eighteen yards. On the following first down, he called Phil on a play-action out and up. When Elliott lined up, he noticed the cornerback cheating up; after getting beat short and outside twice already, he wasn't giving Phil a third chance. The ball was snapped and Phil drove off the line. The route called for six steps, an outside move for three strides, then turn up the sideline and hope the ball was on its way. But, on his second step, Phil saw the cornerback coming right at him, his right fist clenched; he was headhunting. Quickly, Elliott altered his route slightly. He couldn't change it much because Maxwell would release the ball before Phil's final move. The quarterback was throwing for a spot and the receiver better be there. Phil had little choice, except to try to take the blow to the head in such a way so the force wouldn't knock him down. He broke outside two steps early and took the forearm smash on the side of the head. It staggered him, stars exploded in his head, but he didn't go down. The cornerman was committed and drove past Phil toward the sideline. He was beaten.

Now, all Elliott had to do was get upfield. He staggered slightly as he made his turn but quickly regained his stride. Maxwell had seen the hit and held up slightly on the throw, then laid it up gently into that Kezar tailwind. Elliott watched the ball floating slowly toward him out of the bright blue San Francisco sky. His legs were strong and the effects of the blow to his head did not break his concentration on the ball, although he saw spots and explosions of light he was fairly certain were not in the sky.

The ball settled into his hands at the eight and he was in the end zone immediately.

Now the pain and dizziness set in and he knew he would need some time to regain his senses.

Dallas beat San Francisco for the first time ever that Saturday afternoon.

Phil Elliott was but one of the reasons.

On defense, John Wilson picked off two passes from his strong safety spot, while the defensive line and linebackers shut down the Frisco running game completely. Tony Douglas, the middle linebacker, sacked the quarterback on the blitzes and Wilson got him once on a safety blitz. Defensive lineman Gino Machado made five unassisted tackles and nailed the quarterback once on a line stunt.

In the second quarter, with the wind in their faces, Maxwell cranked up the running game and Elliott was able to get a measure of revenge against the linebackers and defensive backs who had been pounding him unmercifully since his touchdown catch.

First, Maxwell called Danny Raines on a sweep right. They were running at the cornerback who had gone for Elliott's head. On the snap, Elliott took a couple of false steps downfield, looking into the defensive secondary for the force man. The first defender to show was the cornerback. He rushed toward the line of scrimmage, cutting inside Elliott, trying to meet the pulling guards and turn Raines inside where the pursuit could catch him; he never saw Elliott coming.

Phil dove headfirst at the man's outside knee and hit directly on the joint as the cornerback was planting his foot. He could hear the cartilage tear and the ligaments pop; the defender screamed and went down in a heap.

Jo Bob Williams, the first guard, turned inside and cut off the pursuit, while the second guard, O.W. Meadows, led Raines outside the pileup of Elliott and the screaming Frisco cornerback. Meadows knocked down the strong safetyman and Danny Raines cut inside the weak safety, running the rest of the way untouched; sixty-five yards for a touchdown.

It wasn't until Elliott began to untangle himself from the injured cornerback that he realized he was hurt himself. There was a grinding in his shoulder and a sharp pain up into his neck. He had torn his collarbone loose.

"You got a slight separation," Eddie Rand said. They were standing on the sideline and the trainer was pulling on the collarbone, watching the bone ends protrude into the skin. "I don't think it's too bad. It'll be sore for awhile, but you'll be ready for Green Bay next week. Come in Monday for treatment."

The San Francisco cornerback was taken off on a stretcher.

He never played again.

At the time, Phil Elliott didn't consider it his problem. It was several years before he understood. By then, Phil's personal body count included several more players, in-

cluding two from his own team he had taken out in
training camp scrimmages.

By the time Phil Elliott realized that every act of
violence had two victims, he had lost count of the acts of
violence and the number of victims.

But today in Kezar, Phil Elliott was excited, pumped
full of adrenaline, and suffering only slightly from a shoulder separation and his constant headache.

He watched the remainder of the game from the sideline with his shoulder packed in ice.

Emeliano and His Cousin

meliano sat back in the darkened bar, studying the
pool games under the small smoky spotlights. Shortly
he would have some money and could start betting
on his cousin who was winning steady. Maybe they would
buy some coke.

Everybody in the bar turned to the door when the
Anglo walked in and Emeliano felt a surge of sexual
pride. Emeliano didn't think the feeling strange. He enjoyed it. He reached into his shirt and adjusted the
nine-millimeter Browning tucked in the waist of his bright
green slacks.

Dressed in desert camouflage with his pants bloused
into shiny jump boots, Colonel William Glanton made
his way deliberately to the table where Emeliano sat.
Emeliano's brown Indian face was sullen, the pencil mus-
tache drooped slightly, the flat cheekbones were acne-
scarred, the thin neck disappeared into a flowered shirt
that seemed to hang from his collarbones.

Emeliano wasn't big but he had been taught that being
able to do something wasn't as important as being deter-
mined. Emeliano always wanted to be tough. He was
committed to being mean. He had the will to do evil.

The other brown men in the bar were agitated at the
Anglo's presence. Emeliano enjoyed the attention. The
Anglo ignored it; he sat erect, his confident military
bearing made Emeliano respect the man even as he hated
him. He knew the colonel was not only willing to be

tough, he had an expert's ability. The Anglo was a professional killer.

"What can I do for you, Colonel?" Emeliano leaned forward.

"I have work for you." The soldier's cold eyes looked through Emeliano.

Emeliano nodded. "What do I get?"

"Your name moved from the criminal element list to the protected list, a new identity if you need it."

"I got family in Costa Rica, they want to be Americans."

"Done."

"Okay. Who do I kill?"

"When you crossed the border into Texas, there was a Mexican-American traveling with you," Glanton began. "A big fella named Raul."

"He got left behind," Emeliano explained. "He hurt his ankle."

"We know that. He got picked up later by the sheriff and before we could kill him, he got away from our man."

"So what do you want us to do?"

"He's here in San Antonio. We don't want him talking."

"He can't talk if he's dead," Emeliano said.

LAX to Love—*Then*

After the San Francisco game, the team flew back to Los Angeles where a charter was waiting to take them to Dallas.

It was a long, noisy ride to Dallas, but Maxwell slept most of the way, waking as the plane encountered turbulence on its slow descent into Dallas.

"Looks hot down there." The quarterback looked at the plains below. The two cities of Dallas and Ft. Worth were set distinctly apart, separated by miles of flat empty land. He pointed off to the north. "You see that farmland up there?"

Elliott leaned toward the window and sighted down Maxwell's arm and extended finger. Phil nodded.

"That's where the new regional airport is going to be built. Conrad Hunter put a little deal together up there and I own almost five hundred acres of it."

"When are they building the airport?"

"In eight or ten years," Maxwell explained. "Whenever the time and the politics are right. I only paid two hundred and fifty dollars an acre for it, so I can just sit and wait. It'll be worth ten or twenty thousand an acre, when they announce the airport, and go nowhere but up."

"Sure. Sure. And Mitch Simmons is gonna put you in the movies and on television."

"And next Saturday night," Maxwell interrupted, "we will beat Green Bay for the first time in history and will be 5–0 at the end of exhibition season." He smiled, pleased with himself. "You got to think ahead, kid. You got to think ahead."

"I can't. I got a foreshortened sense of the future."

"You can't think ahead if you think *too much*," Maxwell said.

"Is that my problem, Seth?" Phil said. "Is that what's giving me headaches?"

Maxwell nodded and looked out the window as the plane banked hard and began its approach to Love Field in Dallas. "You have to look at life as a game and play the same way you play a game. You don't think too much on the field, but you think *ahead*, you're ready for things to happen before they happen. It's a necessary skill out there. Well, it ain't no different in life. Think ahead and nothing catches you by surprise; think too much and everything catches you by surprise."

Elliott frowned and shook his head, but he could find no argument in what Maxwell said.

"Look," Maxwell continued. "Conrad Hunter has put me into good land deals, oil and gas deals, a couple of apartment deals in Dallas and Fort Worth. They've all made money. I'm worth a million dollars on paper and it's because I think ahead."

"It may be because somebody thinks ahead, Seth." Phil finally found a loose end. "But I'm not too certain that it's you."

"What do you mean by that?"

"I don't think the Hunters are just being generous," Phil said. "It just happens that right now, you and Conrad are working toward the same end. What happens if you two ever go at cross purposes?"

"That's what I mean by *thinking ahead*." Maxwell smiled. "I will make certain that never happens."

"No matter what?"

"No matter what." Maxwell fixed Elliott with a stare. "And you can take *that* to the bank."

"I'd rather have cash, Seth." Phil smirked.

Bahia Massacre—Now

The wind was blowing hard above the canyon wall but the air on the valley floor was still and there was no sound but the splashing and gurgling of the river.

A small black dot circled in the hard cold blue of the sky.

A ground squirrel darted from beneath the cypress log torn and twisted by the last rise. He stopped at the edge of the gravel road, raised on his haunches and looked to the north and south as if checking for traffic.

He never looked up. Few animals look up.

Halfway across the road the eagle hit him.

The heavy razor-sharp talons sank deep hitting the spinal cord. The squirrel quivered once and was still.

The eagle ate the squirrel where it lay. He began by biting off the head. The eagle was pulling the intestines from the body cavity and bloody gut strings dangled from his beak when the Ford CrewCab pickup truck appeared up the valley.

A fifty-five-gallon gas drum was welded on the truck bed to augment the two saddle tanks, giving the truck almost one hundred gallons of gasoline and a range of one thousand miles between fillups. Gun racks were fastened behind the seat backs and above the windscreen. Two Model 94 lever-action Winchester rifles, a Browning .243 with a nine-power scope, a bolt-action .223 with another nine-power Redfield, two AR-15s, fully automatic with thirty-round clips, and two twelve-gauge automatics were stuffed into the leather-padded racks. The Blaines had customized this truck for the distances on the Plateau. There were no gas stations between the Blaine ranch house and Bahia, Mexico, the village closest to the Estrada Hacienda.

Jake Blaine, Judge Zack's son, was driving. Zack was in the back and L. Ray Prescott was riding shotgun. O. W. Meadows was in the truck bed, handcuffed to the rail. They were following the ridgelines and riverbed along the Plateau to Mexico, driving south on the apron of the mountain chain. Inaccessible, wild and dangerous country where anything might come out of the mountains and often did. They were delivering O. W. Meadows to Augustino Estrada to hold incommunicado until Jo Bob called from Dallas with instructions. They were taking Jake along because it seems he'd become friendly with a lawyer who'd been asking a lot of questions about the Blaines' finances. The lawyer had been taking Jake out, getting him drunk, which was not particularly difficult, and then pumping him for info. Jake was prime pumping material, so Zack decided it was time for his son to take a little vacation. He didn't much care for Jake's new friend, the lawyer, whose name was David Stein.

Augustino Estrada was the perfect host for this vacation. The Estradas had been friends and allies of the Blaines since the days of the French occupation of Mexico.

L. Ray was slouched down in the passenger seat, his wide-brim Stetson down over his eyes. Zack was lying down in the backseat, his battered hat on his chest. He was watching the floating ribbon of silent blue sky carved by the sharp red canyon walls while Jake watched the sky reflected in the white blue of the fast running water.

"Imagine how much power is laying around in Austin." Jake Blaine said. "It's lobbyists that run things. Oil and gas, construction and land developers, that's what used to run this state. Now, high-tech men like Ross Denham are going to get tougher to beat. We can't afford to hire a lobbyist to plead our cause to the legislature."

County Judge Zack Blaine shifted in the seat trying to ease the backache. The Judge said, "Well, we been running cows, sheep and goats a lot longer than they been drilling for oil or making computers in Texas. Always stay with sheep and goats."

They had been traveling since before sunup following the riverbed where the road had been graded and leveled. State money for county roads was one of the few sources of revenue and power still left to Zack Blaine in the Purgatory. He passed around the jobs to smooth out the rougher stretches of the Purgatory County roads in two-week shifts so that everyone got work. Zack's control of that money gave him power, which he used as wisely as he could. The Mexicans on both sides of the border liked the Blaines and all voted with the Blaine ticket for generations. Zack decided here and now he would teach Jake how to fight, how to survive, who to kill. It was time for him to learn.

He watched the eagle pass over. The sighting of an eagle always confused Zack. The eagles often fed on the Blaines' kid and lamb crop and cost the ranch money, but a voice long silent would speak as he considered the majestic freedom of eagles.

"Dad." Jake had spotted the eagle. He eased off the accelerator and reached for his Winchester above the windshield.

"Let him go," Zack said. "He's headed to Mexico with us."

We are all going to the same place, he thought. Me and Jake and the eagle. The pull on his backbone started in a new direction and he sat up and leaned forward in the seat. His eyes now lost in the floorboard shadows. That's what death is, he thought, the pull of gravity. The earth pulls you down, crumbles you like a mesquite fire that crumbles to red coals and then white ash. We'll all still be here in the end.

It was what Inez, his wife, always said, but to her it was a plea of anguish. *We'll all still be here in the end.* She took no peace from knowing that, but Zack did.

Zack Blaine, once tall and strong, was now thin, burnt and wrinkled, and bent at the fifth lumbar vertebra, crushed years ago in a fall during the Bandit Wars. The Blaines had come to aid Estrada when the PRI (The Institutional Revolutionary Party) encouraged land reform at Estrada's expense. Estrada and the Blaines won that one. Lately, though, they had lost a lot more than they'd won.

Although the life on the ranch was demanding, Zack Blaine's injury had taught him a lesson in human frailty. He worked Jake hard, but insisted on his education, making him read every night when at the ranch. While Jake read, the old man walked the floor, unable to rest for more than a couple of hours at a time, the pain in his back and creeping numbness in his legs prodding him constantly to his feet.

Jake had the Blaine nose, a large, long, thin, hooked affair that had a tendency after fifty or so years to start sliding down the high ridge of cartilage.

Jake had the mirror image of Zack's face, long-headed and sharp-featured. Zack's nose nearly reached his lip.

Jake was darker complected with black hair, more outgoing and friendly than Zack. He was also capable of greater rage. Jake had been bred into a clan of warriors all raised with killing and death in battle, but in his countenance one could see *murder*.

Zack Blaine was hoping for a warrior's strength to appear in Jake's personality. But something had to be done. Soon.

The truck climbed steadily out of the canyon and an ocean of grass rolled in all directions. The twenty-five-thousand-acre pasture of blue stem was irrigated from the aquifer.

"David Stein's daddy and the Laughlins bought that land and drilled the water wells with money they made running guns in Mexico during World War Two."

"Daddy, that was fifty years ago," Jake said.

"Mmm," Zack said, and that was all he said until dusk, when they reached Bahia.

Bahia was an adobe village of twenty structures built on a bluff above the river. The inhabitants worked in the fields about two miles south of town. It was a poor town but everyone had enough to eat. It had a small smuggling industry, mainly household appliances, optical lenses, and dollars. Guns and drugs were anathema, they brought the Terror.

As they drove through the village, Zack waved at several of the villagers he knew from years of visits. A cattle fence bounded the patio of the low adobe house that sat on the north edge of the dusty village square and served as Pablo Ocho's Cantina. A green Jeep with the top down was parked next to the low fence. The car had no plates.

Jake stopped in front of Ocho's. The Blaines and L. Ray Prescott stepped into the hot dusty street. L. Ray, ramrod straight and tall, his battered Stetson adding to his size, walked past the green Jeep through the stick gate and the low dark archway into the adobe cantina. Pablo, the owner, told L. Ray that the car belonged to a friend of his from San Antonio who was in town with his girlfriend. Zack and young Jake followed L. Ray inside.

Luisa, Pablo's oldest daughter entered the room. Short and stocky, her pretty Indian face surrounded by coarse black hair, cleaned and combed, flowing over the red-and-black-striped shoulder shawl. She smiled at Jake, who called her "a Meskin whore" and paid her after every visit. She had no other men but never told Jake.

"Okay," the old man said, "we'll stay here and wait for Estrada. L. Ray, grab the two ARs and the shotgun for me."

L. Ray turned and started out into the twilight. In a moment the foreman returned with the shotgun and assault rifles. He tossed one rifle to Jake and set the shotgun on the table in front of Zack.

"Truck's locked," L. Ray said. "O.W. is handcuffed to a post in the shade."

It was a small, dirt-floored, low-ceilinged room. The only light was the fast-darkening doorway and the kerosene lanterns that the old man had brought Pablo years ago as gifts and that Pablo was now lighting. Zack loved the yellow light on the mud walls and the urgent hissing and the smell of burning. He had warm memories of this place and liked it. He liked Luisa and Pablo, the gentle openness of village people who had known his father and his father's father. He enjoyed the village and its sense of self. They were a people together.

Pablo had just uncorked a gourd of pulque and was filling a glass for Zack when the American woman pushed aside the blanket that concealed the back room. She stepped through the low archway into the mysterious yellow light, her head down.

"Pablo, did that son of a bitch leave?" Courtnay

Howard-Elliott was hurriedly stuffing her hair up under a white wide-brimmed fedora. The rest of her outfit was brown riding boots, khaki jodhpurs, pants and shirt all draped in an ankle-length white duster. A pair of goggles dangled from the hand that was frantically jamming the loose strands of hair under the hat.

"Oh." She saw the men and stopped. "I thought I heard a car. Was it yours?"

Zack nodded. She seemed relieved. L. Ray kept his hand on his gun and his eyes on the door.

"I thought that somebody . . . or . . ." Courtnay stopped and looked around the room. "Is that green Jeep still out there?"

Zack nodded again.

"Good. Good." She took her hands down from her hair and stuffed the goggles in her duster pocket. "People have a habit of leaving me in out-of-the-way places."

"I can't imagine that, ma'am," Jake drawled heavily, an affectation he picked up and dropped depending on his reading of the situation.

"What can't you imagine?" Courtnay dug a cigarette case and a gold lighter out of the duster. Her hands were shaking.

"I can't imagine anybody forgetting you," Jake said.

"They *don't* forget, cowboy, they just *leave*." She drew on the cigarette and then squinted at him. "Are you sure that car's still there?" She stepped closer.

Jake nodded, then took off his hat and held it with both hands in front of his chest. The lack of a burn line on his forehead showed he wasn't a cowboy but she never noticed. She saw instead the good teeth, firm jaw, thick black hair.

L. Ray pulled Zack off to sit in the corner. Backs to the wall and eyes on both doors. His rifle leaned against the table.

"That's Elliott's ex-wife," he whispered to Zack. "She works for Laughlin. And runs with Stein."

"What's she doing here?" Zack studied her.

"I'm afraid we'll find out before the night's over."

Outside, the night quiet was broken with the arrival of Augustino Estrada and twenty of his men in a flatbed truck. The fine-boned, light-skinned Estrada leapt from the cab of the truck, excited, his dark eyes flaring. He stormed into the cantina.

Glancing at Jake and Courtnay at the bar, Estrada strode to the corner and sat with L. Ray and Zack.

"It's your old friend Denham again," Estrada whispered as he shook hands with Zack. "He has convinced Mexico City and Washington that there are communist drug smugglers all through this country. Trouble on the Mexican-U.S. border may bring the U.S. right into Mexico and Central America."

"Oh shit," Zack whispered.

"I used to be married," Courtnay was saying to Jake at the bar. "Never again. My ex was a lunatic. He definitely burned out some bearings and blew a head gasket." She took a long drink from the bottle of scotch that she had retrieved from the backseat of the green Jeep parked out in front. Jake gazed at the pretty face, oddly lit by the yellow light of the kerosene lamps.

"I have information that a gunrunner is due in Bahia," Estrada was now saying to Zack and L. Ray.

"Where you come from?" Jake was now asking Courtnay.

"Austin. I've been on my own since my divorce." She paused, then, "I think marriage is a trap."

"For who?"

"The woman. She has to take care of the house, raise the kids. I have bigger plans." Her eyes were glassy.

"What brought you clear down here?"

"This fellow I know." Courtnay's voice trembled. "He's a lawyer from San Antonio. We hauled some boxes of sewing machines down here. He says there's a big black market for them in Mexico." She suddenly noticed that Jake was holding her hand. "He's giving me five thousand dollars. I need the money." She withdrew, her eyes apologetic.

"Where is your friend now?" Jake reached for the retreating hand.

"I don't know. I guess he's looking for the people that want the sewing machines. They're still crated up in the back room."

"Let's take a look." Jake scraped his chair back and pushed upright and walked across the dirt floor. Sweeping the blanket that hung in the doorway aside, he stepped into the back room.

"Only pussy would get Jake off his ass," Zack whispered.

In a moment, Jake dragged the wooden crate out of the back room. He pried it open with the large bone-handled knife he carried in his gunbelt. Inside were twenty new AK-47 assault rifles, still packed in Cosmoline.

Zack looked at Pablo, whose eyes widened. Estrada shook his head. Courtnay gasped aloud.

"Exactly what kind of stitching did this friend of yours plan to do?"

Courtnay just stared.

"The Estradas shoot Americans who bring guns to Los Tecos," Jake said. "No trial. They just torture you, get what you know and shoot you full of holes with their brand new AR-15s."

"Goddamn. Goddamn." Courtnay spoke softly, beginning to shake. Jake closed the box, took her by the arm and led her back to the table.

"Somebody's outside," L. Ray said, lifting his rifle. He kept his eyes on the outside door.

"My men are hidden," Estrada replied as he pulled two fifteen-shot Smith and Wesson automatic pistols. "And well armed."

"Then we don't let nobody through that door," L. Ray said.

"Hey, gringo." A short, dark-complected man stood in the outside doorway, half hidden in shadows. "What are you doing with my woman?"

Zack knew him, Pepe Garza. Behind Garza were several uniformed Mexican DSID men, members of the Mexican secret police.

Garza saw the opened crate. "Mr. Blaine, what am I gonna do with you?" He looked at Jake, shrugged and pulled a .45 automatic from inside his coat.

All hell broke loose. Inside the cantina and outside.

Garza never got off a round as Milo and Zack cut him to pieces with the AR-15 and the shotgun.

Two men in the doorway got off about a half dozen shots before going down in the blizzard of fire.

Jake was hit twice in the chest and sprawled out backwards.

Miraculously, Courtnay had not been hit. She dropped quickly to her knees, covered her face and crawled out the backdoor. David Stein was waiting in the shadows.

He grabbed her and they ran for the plane hidden behind the village, about two miles through the brasada at the old airstrip.

The battle raged a moment longer then fell silent, except for the occasional gunshot as Estrada's men methodically executed the wounded. The street was littered with DISD men and weapons. The dead were being stripped. Estrada barked orders and soon Luisa and Pablo were on their knees in the street.

Inside, Jake died with a bubbling rattle at the same time Pablo and Luisa were executed.

Courtnay Howard-Elliott and David Stein climbed into the twin-engine King Air. David ran a quick check, then started the plane, taxied out and took off. They had been lucky; no one had seen or heard the plane when they arrived from PMI with the guns for Pepe Garza and his men.

In Bahia, they heard the plane taking off. Zack, L. Ray, and Tino Estrada were in Ocho's, standing over Jake's body.

"There goes the woman," L. Ray said. "I'll bet David Stein's on board too."

"He can't fly far enough or fast enough," Zack said. "He as good as killed my boy hisself. He is a dead man."

From the street came the sounds of an argument in Spanish punctuated by English.

"Goddamn you Mexican assholes, turn me loose!"

The sounds of struggle grew closer and suddenly a redheaded, skinny American came skidding through the door on his face. Estrada's men kept him on the floor. O. W. Meadows was led inside.

"Who's he?" Tino turned back to Zack. Zack turned to the handcuffed deputy and repeated the question.

"Jimmy Boxx," O.W. replied. "He works in Hollywood for Mitch Simmons Productions. D-L Financial owns Mitch Simmons. He produces Seth Maxwell's TV show *Scout*."

L. Ray nodded and glanced at Estrada and Zack Blaine. "We better leave O.W. down here and call Jo Bob from your place, Tino. He needs to know what happened."

Green Bay—*Then*

"This is the major test for us." B.A. was standing in front of the chalkboard in the locker room. It was hot and humid in Dallas. Green Bay had already taken the field but B.A. had purposely held them inside the sweltering room. "Green Bay has the simplest offensive and defensive philosophies in professional football. They just take you on man to man and beat you. Well, we're not only going to outplay them, we're going to outthink them. That's what we are all about, men. While they're still trying to figure out what we are doing, we'll be beating them at it."

And he was right. In all his years of playing for B. A. Quinlan, Phil Elliott never ceased to be surprised by the man's immense knowledge of football. It was rivaled only by his narrowmindedness about all other aspects of human endeavor. Phil had to admit, he was a worthy enemy. And it was several years before Phil even realized they *were* enemies.

By the fourth quarter, Dallas had a comfortable lead and both teams had begun to substitute freely, taking one final look at their players before the final cut.

There was less than five minutes to go in the game when the rookie middle linebacker clotheslined Elliott. Dallas had run a quick pitch away from Phil and he was taking it easy, just drifting downfield, in case the runner cut back toward him. It was a dumb move, but that did nothing to calm Elliott's fury when he caught the linebacker's forearm in the face and went down in a heap.

The next play was a strong side sweep and Elliott passed up the safety and the outside linebacker, intent only on revenge. They had already trapped the runner in the backfield when Elliott clipped the middle linebacker, purposely trying to break his leg. And, much to his surprise and the linebacker's dismay, that is exactly what he did. The bone snapped like a rifle shot, right next to Elliott's ear. He never forgot the sound or the sick sense of satisfaction it gave him.

Elliott was called for unsportsmanlike conduct and thrown out of the game.

When he reached the sideline, B.A. was waiting for him.

"That's the kind of hitting I like to see." B.A. had his arm around Phil's shoulder. "The shithead thought he could intimidate you and you made the little bastard pay the price. Let 'em all know that we are a force to be feared. Hurt 'em, cripple 'em, destroy the bastards."

Elliott always remembered those words. He also remembered that when he heard them, he was very proud of himself.

"We got a party to go to, Killer." Maxwell was already dressed and standing next to Elliott's locker, waiting for him to button his shirt. "Steve Peterson and Bob Beaudreau are throwing a little welcome home party for the team."

"The whole team?" Phil reached inside his locker for his jacket.

"The white players, the Hunters, and assorted groupies of all sizes and sexual persuasions." Seth smiled. "You really went after that guy out there tonight. What happened?"

"The asshole clotheslined me!"

"No!" Maxwell mocked. "The nerve of some people. He just hadn't heard about you being such a star and all."

"Fuck you." Elliott was suddenly furious. "I'm not afraid of any fucking cheap-shot linebacker."

"Hey! Hey! Kid. It's me, old Seth." Maxwell grinned. "Save the macho bullshit for the coaches. It's party time."

"Fuck!" Elliott began to feel nauseous. "I'm getting drunk."

"See? I told you that you would learn." Maxwell turned

and walked toward the door, a piece of dirty adhesive tape stuck to the heel of his shoe. Elliott threw his coat over his shoulder and followed his quarterback outside. He was already soaked with sweat by the time they reached Maxwell's Cadillac convertible.

Steve Peterson owned a sprawling house in Highland Park, an incorporated suburb near North Dallas. It was high-dollar country, long green and lily white.

The party was already going full blast when they arrived. The only blacks visible were in little red coats, waiting to park the guests' cars.

"You sure done a wonderful game, Mr. Maxwell," the black man in the red coat said, as he handed Seth a ticket stub and slid in behind the wheel of Maxwell's big Cadillac.

It was then that Elliott recalled that although the stadium was only three-quarters full, both end zones were packed with fans, all black and unconditionally enthusiastic in their support of the team.

"Praise from the cheap seats," Maxwell said to Elliott as they walked up the long walk to the front door of the Peterson house. "Now, for feedback from the wealthy."

At the door stood a stocky man with a craggy, corrugated face, narrow, furtive eyes, and thin close-cropped hair. A Dallas Police Department badge was hooked on his belt, almost hidden by his overhanging belly. In his thick, heavy hands he held a clipboard. He was hot and sweating, dressed uncomfortably in a brown-and-yellow-checked wool sport coat and black slacks.

GEORGE RINDQUIST was stenciled on the nameplate pinned to his coat.

"Go right on in, Seth." Rindquist grinned wickedly. "I'm sure this boy's okay, if he's with you."

Years later, George Rindquist would have a completely different opinion of Phil Elliott, all typed out and filed in triplicate with the Dallas football club and the League Security Office.

But at that moment, his job merely consisted of making sure nobody got inside Steve Peterson's house who wasn't rich, famous, or listed on his clipboard.

Things change.

"*Voilà*. The Beautiful People," Maxwell said, as he opened the door and led Elliott into a night, followed by years of such nights, that Elliott would barely survive, let alone ever forget.

Rock and roll was blasting from the expensive sound system and people were dancing, laughing, necking, and talking at the tops of their voices. It was like walking into the face of a blizzard and Elliott took an instinctive step back, before Seth grabbed his arm and led him head first into the turmoil that was *fame*.

"Come on, kid," Maxwell said. "There's Mary Jane and Joanne Remington. I told them we would be here."

Phil Elliott followed Maxwell's lead through the tumultuous crowd, as he shook hands and accepted congratulations, pats on the back from the men and kisses from the women.

Eventually, they reached the tall brunette and petite blonde, standing by the bar, talking to the Mexican bartender.

"Well, congratulations, boys," Mary Jane said, tiptoeing up to kiss Seth.

"We weren't sure you'd make it through the crowd," Joanne Remington said, offering Phil her hand.

"This boy needs a triple Commemorativo on the rocks," Seth told the bartender. "He's got places to go, illusions to see. I'll have a triple Cutty and water."

"You just missed Emmett," Joanne said, after they had their drinks. "B.A. said he would have the films on New York to show tonight."

"And Emmett *wanted* to see them?" Maxwell was surprised.

"Conrad wanted Emmett to see them," Joanne corrected. "He's already so drunk he'll be seeing them double."

"I wonder if that's anything like seeing them twice?" Phil asked.

"You'll know before the night's over," Maxwell said. "Drink up."

Elliott drained his glass.

"God! That's great!" Phil coughed. "Tastes just like gasoline."

"You keep drinking like that and you won't get any mileage at all out of me," Joanne snapped.

"What does *that* mean?" Phil turned to the tall, good-looking young woman.

"You're a big boy," Joanne replied. "Figure it out. I'm free for the evening but I don't want to spend it watching you throw up." She turned to Seth. "Did he get hit in the head again tonight?"

"He gets hit in the head every day," Maxwell replied. "It's his job."

"That's ridiculous."

"Better he than me." Maxwell drained his glass and ordered another.

Gunshots rang out on the patio by the pool.

"What the hell was that?" Elliott jumped. Nobody else seemed to notice.

"Beaudreau," Joanne said, sourly. "The fattest gun in town. He's nuts. He's just celebrating his release from Fairhaven, where the rich send their dopehead kids and alcoholic wives."

"He's second-generation oil money," Maxwell explained, as he took his drink from the Mexican bartender. "He's got his own insurance company."

"It sounds like he needs it." Elliott sipped on his second triple tequila. The taste was better.

"He and Steve Peterson are always trying to get the players to invest in their schemes," Maxwell continued. "Somehow the players end up broke and Peterson and Beaudreau just keep on throwing parties." Maxwell paused and lowered his voice. "I think those two boys that finance Mitch Simmons have some vested interest in both of them."

"Ross Denham and Bobby Laughlin?" Elliott asked.

Maxwell put a finger to his lips and didn't reply.

Joanne and Mary Jane acted as if they had heard nothing.

"Seth!" A middle-aged man in madras slacks and an open-collar shirt approached. He had a chubby bleached blonde on one arm and was holding the hand of a small boy who appeared to be about twelve. "Seth! You were great tonight." He grabbed Maxwell's hand and pumped it vigorously. "You remember my wife Martha and my boy Dickie. Dickie is going to be a ball boy for you guys this year. Conrad arranged it. Isn't that right, Dickie?"

The boy kept his eyes fixed on the floor and nodded his head.

"What the hell's the matter with you, Dickie?" The man jerked the chubby little hand.

"Dickie's fine, Louis." Martha spoke up. "Leave him be."

Louis turned furious eyes on his wife.

"Louis Lafler, Martha, Dickie." Maxwell quickly defused the situation. "I'd like you to meet some friends of mine."

After the introductions were made, Louis Lafler asked how Maxwell was going to do this year against Johnny Unitas. "Old Johnny wears those high-top shoes, like we used to in my day. I sure wish we'd had a pro team in Dallas when I was young." Louis Lafler paused, then changed direction. "How come we haven't seen you at a meeting lately? You come and bring that pretty wife of yours."

Elliott could see Mary Jane Woodley flinch at the mention of Maxwell's current wife.

"Well, we got to be going," Louis Lafler announced. "It's getting close to Dickie's bedtime. Say goodnight, Dickie." The man jerked his son's arm roughly again and the boy mumbled something, never taking his eyes from the floor.

"That boy will certainly grow up to be an axe murderer," Joanne said as soon as the Lafler family was out of earshot.

Actually, he grew up to be a gun and drug smuggler with the good fortune to have David Stein as his defense attorney. But Joanne wasn't far off.

"What did he mean about going to a meeting?" Phil asked Seth.

"He's president of the North Dallas Chapter of the John Birch Society," Maxwell replied.

"That explains the ugly madras slacks." Joanne laughed.

"Oh Christ!" Mary Jane was staring out the patio door. "Here comes trouble in duplicate."

Jo Bob Williams and O. W. Meadows marched in lockstep inside through the patio door. They were holding a small, prematurely balding blond man in a hot pink shirt and white slacks between them. His feet dangled uselessly as he protested just as vainly over being hauled around against his will.

"That's Steve Peterson," Joanne said to Phil. "The ever-obliging host."

Williams and Meadows marched right up to Maxwell and stopped.

"Present faggot!" Williams bellowed.

The two giant men thrust tiny Steve Peterson right up into Maxwell's face.

"Seth . . . ah . . . could you . . . ?" Peterson's face was flushed red.

"Put him down, boys," Maxwell said. "He's your host. Show some class."

"Release faggot!" Williams ordered and they dropped Peterson in a pile at Seth Maxwell's feet. "Attack bar!" The two big linemen pushed past Phil Elliott and stomped up to the bar.

"Two beers, greaser," O.W. spat. "Pronto, you pepperbelly, beaner sumbitch."

The Mexican was stunned to inaction.

O.W. reached across the bar and grabbed him by the lapels of his white jacket, dragging him halfway over the high table. Glasses and bottles scattered and broke on the floor. "I hate Meskins, specially slow Meskins."

Elliott looked at Maxwell who was helping Peterson to his feet.

O.W. pushed the bartender back across the bar and the Mexican hurried to find two beers, handing them quickly to Jo Bob and O.W. who turned and marched back out toward the patio.

"It's my turn to shoot the empties," Jo Bob said, as they strode away.

"Damn, I'm sorry, Steve." Maxwell brushed off the harried little stockbroker. Then the quarterback dug into his pocket and peeled a twenty off a thick roll of bills, handing it to the terrified Mexican. "Sorry, amigo."

The Mexican took the twenty, but the fear stayed fixed in his eyes.

"Mexicans generally get a bad deal in Texas," Joanne said to Phil.

"No shit!" Elliott replied. "Those two just wanted beer. What about all those sons-a-bitches down south that wanted their land?"

"At least Jo Bob comes by his love for guns legitimately," Maxwell said, as shots rang out again from the pool area. "His father is the sheriff of Purgatory County, just like his father before him. I imagine Jo Bob will eventually take over from his father."

"That's a pleasant thought," Phil said. The firing continued.

"The Williams family is very tight with the Blaines," Maxwell explained. "The Blaines have been running the Purgatory for a hundred years. It's beautiful out there. Jo Bob is going to take a bunch of guys hunting there after the season." Maxwell paused and then in a whisper to Phil he continued. "Bobby Laughlin has a big ranch out there. He's got it stocked with exotic game."

"Sounds like a good place to avoid," Phil said.

"What are you two whispering about?" Joanne was handing Mary Jane a glass of white wine.

"Seth is telling me who to avoid in this great state," Phil replied.

"Well," Joanne continued, "take a squint at that tub of shit standing by the pool. Avoid *him* at all costs. That is Bob Beaudreau."

Phil stepped over by Joanne and peered out the French doors. A fat man of about medium height, wearing a red sport coat and red slacks held up by a wide white belt, was standing spraddle-legged in white, tassled loafers. He was gripping a big blue steel .357 magnum in one hand and a bottle of beer in the other.

"Goddamn!" Phil stepped back. "He looks dangerous."

"You better believe it," Joanne said.

Steve Peterson wandered back out to the pool, as if he was drawn toward the humiliation that certainly waited there in the persons of Jo Bob Williams and O. W. Meadows.

A large man with slick black hair moved toward Seth Maxwell with his arms wide.

"Seth. Babe." He hugged the quarterback to him and Maxwell hugged him back. It looked to Phil like they were frisking each other. "Seth, Seth, Seth. Great game. I took you guys and the points and made a ton." He turned loose of Maxwell and stepped back.

"Tony Perelli." Seth made the introductions. "You know Mary Jane. This is her friend Joanne Remington."

Joanne carefully clasped the thick hand that Perelli extended.

"And this is Phil Elliott."

"Phil." Perelli gripped Elliott's hand tightly. "I feel like I already know you. You certainly have been a great help to my pocketbook." Perelli laughed and Maxwell, nervously, followed suit.

Phil smiled and worked his hand loose.

"Look, I got to go and make some collections." Perelli apologized. "But the first chance you get, Seth, we'll go back to Vegas. My treat. Bring your friends here." He turned and worked his way quickly through the crowd toward the door.

"Tony works for a couple of casinos in Las Vegas," Seth explained. "He likes to have ballplayers come out and stay as his guests. It's a good deal. Everything is on the house."

"What does he want in return?" Phil asked.

"Nothing," Seth said. "He's never asked me for a thing."

"He sure sounds like a bookie to me," Phil said.

"I don't ask him what he does."

"You don't have to," Joanne interjected, sourly. "Christ! He just yelled it at you. I thought you guys had rules against hanging around guys like him."

"We do," Phil said.

"Maybe guys *like* him." Maxwell laughed. "But not *him.*"

Phil was all set to argue, to say that Seth was cutting that line kind of fine, but Joanne Remington had unbuttoned the top button of her blouse and Phil got kind of distracted.

He decided to skip the argument with Seth Maxwell.

Joanne Remington and Phil Elliott left Steve Peterson's party together and returned to Phil's hotel room on Central Expressway.

Joanne's blouse was now completely open, and she wasn't wearing a bra. Her breasts were well shaped and firm. She unzipped and stepped out of her skirt, then looked herself over in the full-length mirror, inspecting her body as she thought a man would. She stretched toward the ceiling, stood on her toes wiggling her fingers, flexing and rolling her neck and shoulders, bringing her body awake. She definitely wanted to be here for this night. The muscles rippled up her calves, thighs, buttocks, and back, across her ribs and shoulders. Expertly, she aligned her spine and took the kinks out of her nervous system, building a high-speed sensual highway from her toes to her brain.

Confused and frightened by the conflicting signals he was sending to himself as his higher brain and lower brain battled for control of his emotions, Phil was nonetheless awed by her meticulous preparation.

Joanne's whole body was swaying and rippling, brown hair washing her shoulders, arms extended overhead, slender fingers wiggling and flexing. Licking her lips, her brown almond-shaped eyes seemed to pierce Phil.

Her whole ripe, rich body was surging. Joanne was swinging her upper torso in big circles. Her hair flew, her face in a dreamy smile. She stood erect, hands at her sides, with her eyes closed. Her body seemed to pulsate.

She focused her eyes. "You're still dressed?" She ran her fingertips across her lips and chin down through her cleavage, across her hard stomach. "I'm not going to miss this, Phillip." She pulled the covers back and stepped into the bed. "What about you?"

He stood fully dressed; he had taken root. His nerve was slipping fast. She was too beautiful, too much.

Don't flinch, Phil thought. Inadequacy began its distant drum. *Don't flinch.* That's what Seth Maxwell always said. Find a good woman or settle for a good game, but *don't flinch, man. Don't flinch.*

A good woman was already on the bed. Phil picked at the top button of his shirt as he looked at Joanne with one knee up, hands behind her head, her eyes wide.

Something was pulling on Elliott's shirttail telling him to run.

Joanne rolled over on her side. Cascades of dark hair ran down the delicately shaped hand cradling her beautiful face. Show him. Show him she was worth the risk. She would be generous and gentle to that pitiful little boy standing there, hoping and not hoping. She smiled at him and meant it. It was *all* worth the risk of *believing,* if only for as long as they took with each other.

Later, as they lay there listening to the night sounds, Phillip Elliott loosed a short laugh.

"What?" she said.

"Just thinking. I almost turned and ran when you lay down on the bed." He laughed again; it felt good. "I'm a compulsive paranoid. At airports I miss flights because of some compulsive feeling they were going to crash. I would wait for the news of the crash with no survivors."

"Except Phil Elliott." Joanne put her mouth against his neck, alternately chewing and licking.

"That's the story of my life," Phil said, becoming aware of the nibbling and rubbing and fingerwalking. "I've missed more planes that didn't crash."

"Maybe they would have crashed if you'd been on them." She licked on his jaw, enjoying the sensation of his whisker stubble against her tongue. "Maybe you're the victim affecting destiny. Think of all the lives you saved." She rubbed a hand across his chest and stomach.

"No. I'm just paranoid."

"Well, it adds an exquisite urgency to your lovemaking." She kissed his shoulder.

He was relieved when she complimented his lovemaking. *Who cares if she means it?*

She snuggled her face into the hollow below his jaw. "You are such a brave boy." She slid her hand down across his stomach, walking around softly with her fingertips. "I'm going to show you *how* brave."

"In for a dime, in for a dollar."

She collapsed on his chest after the ride to the finish, wheezing and gasping, their skin stuck together with sweat.

"That was great." She kissed him sloppily on the mouth, lost in the ozone. Whatever it was they had just finished doing to each other, she had *meant* it.

Joanne peeled herself off Phil's chest. As they came unjoined, he felt a sharp ache along his ribcage, under his right arm. She was aware of a deep cramp in her hip. She fell heavily beside him, rubbed her hip a moment and looked for the cigarettes. There were tears in her eyes. She lit up a short lethal unfiltered cigarette, inhaling deeply into her softest places. She held the smoke, letting it out slowly through her beautifully flared nostrils. She looked at Phil, her brown eyes wet.

"Life isn't all bad, Phil." She regained her composure.

"You know," he said, rubbing a hand along his side, "I think you tore one of my rib cartilages."

They were both right.

The phone rang at 9:00 A.M. and Phil grabbed it.

"Phil Elliott?"

"Speaking."

"This is Coach Quinlan's secretary. The coach would like you in his office at ten o'clock sharp." She paused. "And please bring your playbook."

She hung up without waiting for a reply.

"Who was that?" Joanne asked, stretching and rubbing her eyes.

"B.A.'s office." Phil hung up the phone. "I think I've just been cut."

The Unkindest Cut—*Then*

The team offices were in a small temporary building right next to the practice field and locker rooms. The whole complex was in the shadow of the new North Dallas Towers. As soon as the building was finished the team would move into and occupy the whole tenth floor.

At five minutes to ten, Phil Elliott arrived by cab in front of the temporary offices.

Inside, five other rookies, looking downcast as they clutched their playbooks, were waiting to be called into B. A. Quinlan's office. Phil had thought that the team only needed to cut five to make it under the roster limit, but apparently he was wrong.

Mac Kine must have finally signed, Elliott thought as he nodded at the other five and sat down to wait an eternity.

At least I didn't quit, he thought. *They couldn't make me quit.*

One by one, the others went inside and came out without their playbooks and with tears in their eyes. The last one, Satler Lomax from Cornell, winked and gave Phil a thumbs-up sign. Phil smiled and shrugged his shoulders.

The son of a bitch won't make me cry, Phil kept saying to himself, as he kept feeling the tears welling up in his eyes.

Finally, B.A.'s secretary, Ruth, came out and called his name. He followed her back through a maze of tiny cubicles to the head coach's office. Ruth knocked and opened the door, standing back to let Phil enter.

B. A. Quinlan sat stoically behind his desk. There were cans of film stacked everywhere. A projector sat on a table in the corner; the screen stood next to a two-sided portable chalkboard.

"Have a seat, Phil." B.A. did not look up. He was studying papers on the desk in front of him. He continued to shuffle papers and make marks while Elliott sat stiffly, soaked in perspiration.

Finally, B.A. put down the papers and leaned back, looking Phil right in the eye. The stern gaze caught Phil off balance and he quickly averted his eyes.

"So, Phil," B.A.'s tone matched his stare. "I'm sorry I had to call you here so early."

Elliott tried to collect himself for the coming shock. He was not going to flinch for B. A. Quinlan. He wasn't going to break, not after coming this far.

"But I prefer to have these meetings as soon as I can after I make a decision."

Phil nodded dumbly.

"And, since I really hadn't had a chance to go over your scores on the IQ and Multiphasic Personality Tests we gave you out in camp until last night . . ." He let his comment hang in the air.

Phil began to squirm uncomfortably on the hard wooden chair.

"I really wasn't ready to talk to you until this morning." B.A. glanced back down at the papers on his desk. "You scored *above* our preferable limits on the IQ test and your personality test showed some danger areas, concerning your response toward authority. The team psychologist believes you have pronounced anarchistic tendencies."

What the hell is all this? Phil thought. *Just get it over with.*

"Now." B.A. picked up the papers and sorted through them, pulling out five sheets already stapled together. "I've been going over your plus and minus scores for the exhibition season. I have to admit that I am impressed. You dropped only two passes in five games and you are an excellent blocker. As you know, football is based on the running game. The better a team runs, the tougher they are and the easier it is to then establish a passing game. Delma Huddle will remake the passing game in this league. His speed and quickness are so exceptional, he is a new dimension. *All* our opponents will have to adjust every defense just to deal with him."

Phil held his playbook tightly in his sweating palms.

Why was B.A. dragging this out?

The head coach seemed to be enjoying himself. He was certainly a cold fish.

"Let me have your playbook." B.A. finally seemed to be getting to the point of this exercise.

Phil handed the book over.

B.A. leafed casually through the pages.

"They're all there," Phil blurted out.

"What?" B.A. fixed his eyes on Elliott, who was ready this time and met the stare.

"The pages," Phil said. "I didn't take any."

"Nobody thought you did." B.A. reached the section he wanted and turned the book toward Phil so he could read it. "You see these?"

"Yes, sir. Those are the club's rules and regulations."

"That's right," B.A. snapped. "You're a smart boy, Phil. You picked up and learned the most complicated offense in football in a little over two months. You still don't run the best of routes but that's not your problem. Your problem is right here. You may be too smart for us and for your own good."

Elliott bit back a reply.

"If you are willing to learn these *and* accept the reasons behind them, I am willing to take a chance on you." B.A. never blinked. "My system tells me to get rid of you, in spite of your talent, because you'll just be trouble down the line. Football is war with soldiers and generals. The soldiers must take orders without question and without thinking. You're a soldier. You do what you are told. No arguments. No questions. Can you deal with that?"

"Yessir." Phil felt the giant hand that had been squeezing his heart all morning release its grip.

"Another thing, and I want a straight answer." B.A. closed the playbook. "You may be smart, but don't ever think you'll outsmart me." B.A. paused and let his gaze bore into Elliott. "The first two Sundays in training camp, you went to church and sat two rows in front of me.

Then, you never went to church again. I know because I check on things like that. Did you go just to impress me?"

"Yes, sir."

"Don't you believe in God?"

"I don't *not* believe in God, sir."

B. A. Quinlan considered the answer, dropping his gaze back to the pages on his desk. Finally, he tossed Elliott's playbook back to him.

"I guess that's between you and the Lord," B.A. said. "Get out of here and watch your step because it won't be just God watching you while you're a member of *my* football team."

Phil Elliott left the office without another word. He went directly to the rest room of the lobby and vomited.

When he left the building, he felt someone watching him.

Paranoia was life-enhancing in the business of professional football.

San Antonio—Now

It was dawn.

Joanne Remington-Hunter was still asleep on the couch.

Phil Elliott was at his desk thumbing through his notes, when he saw the roach on the windowsill. He carefully rolled the newspaper tightly and made a moral decision.

"The roach dies," Elliott whispered and smashed the bug flat.

The noise woke Joanne.

"There's one that *won't* survive the nuclear holocaust," Phil said.

"Oh, Jesus." Joanne moaned and held both her hands over her face. "Where are we?"

"My apartment." Phil watched another roach scuttle into a hole in the baseboard.

Joanne struggled to sit up, keeping her face shaded with one hand. "I thought you said it was fun to be a writer?"

"I lied." He was studying a third roach.

"Well," Joanne sighed and wrapped the sheet around her toga-style, then peeked over at Elliott through her fingers. The light from the window hurt her eyes. "I suppose I deserve to feel like this."

"Is that a question or an observation?" Phil leaned back and put his feet up on the desk.

"I'm not certain."

She pulled herself together enough to move off the couch. Still wrapped in the sheet, she padded toward the bathroom.

Phil spotted another roach and was stalking it, slowly raising his arm to strike a killing blow.

After several more roaches had escaped, Joanne returned, wiping her hand along the kitchen counter, making streaks in the dust. She wrinkled her nose at the sink full of dirty dishes.

"Judging by the kitchen," she said, watching Phil stalk another cockroach, "you're in a dirty business."

Phil carefully raised his arm, aiming at a roach next to his dictionary. He swung and the pain shot up his spine and exploded in his head, as a bit of bone seared into muscle and nerve tissue. His arm went numb. He dropped the paper.

"What's wrong?"

"Nothing." Phil grimaced and rubbed at the dead arm, working his fingers slowly into a fist and out to full extension.

"I know nothing when I see it," Joanne protested. "And that's not nothing. Look at you."

"Don't say anything." He slouched against the pain. "If they find out, I'm history."

"Who? Who is after you now?"

"Don't panic. Act natural. If you panic, we'll never make it to the door." Elliott rubbed at the back of his neck. "I can hear them massing in the baseboards, behind the counters."

"Cockroaches are a regular crusade with you, huh?" Joanne turned toward the back bedroom. "Well, you get on with your evolutionary engineering. I'm going to get dressed."

Phil watched the man paint the sign above the Del Rio Restaurant. It was pouring down rain. The man held an umbrella in one hand and a paintbrush in the other. He was thirty feet above the street on a ladder.

"He still working without a net?" Joanne walked in brushing her hair.

"He is working without, period."

"He still go in when the rain stops?"

"Yep."

Just as suddenly as it arrived, the thunder squall passed. The rain stopped and the sun came out. The painter slowly climbed down the ladder, the still-open umbrella and the paint bucket in his hands, while the brush was clamped tightly between his teeth. He reached the ground and quickly disappeared into the restaurant. He would reemerge when the rain began again. They had been watching him all afternoon.

"What the hell is he doing?" Joanne asked.

"Painting in the rain." Phil unraveled the newspaper he had been using to kill roaches and began reading. "Somebody snatched another DEA agent." He looked up. "That's three in a month in Mexico and Central America."

"Who is grabbing them?" Joanne tried to read over his shoulder.

"Other DEA agents," Phil said. "It makes it a lot easier to get promoted."

"Emmett calls that Executive Churn." Joanne smiled and kissed Phil on the cheek.

Phil turned the page to a story entitled A DAY ON THE BORDER. The accompanying pictures showed sophisticated sensors, deep radars, thermographs, laser illuminators, audio and video enhancing and infrared equipment that was intended "to stem the flood of illegal aliens."

Somebody has to do the shit work, Phil thought, as he studied a picture of the "operations room" in El Paso. It looked like a set from *Star Wars.*

"We still ain't stopping them," the acting Border Patrol chief was quoted as saying. "We even got us a Cobra assault chopper and an OV-1 with that penetrating radar and infrared that can pick up the body heat of a field mouse hiding in a cedar stump. We need men, money, and that real fancy high-tech super-secret gear that the drug cowboys get. We could use one of their mini-AWACs EC-2 surveillance planes but the drug war gets priority on the border. We're being invaded down here."

The aircraft mentioned were shown in pictures on the following page, along with a photo showing INS agents delivering captured aliens back into Mexico. They were caged in a converted step van.

The phone rang.

It was Andy Crawford. An ex-teammate and Rookie of the Year in Elliott's later years in Dallas, Crawford had helped Alan Claridge get elected and then bought into a bar with Dickie Lafler.

"Phil! There's a guy here at my bar looking for you." Crawford seemed slightly out of breath. "A big Mexican guy. He says he did some time with you out in Purgatory. I didn't want to bother you but this guy is drunk and crazy. And worst of all, he won't go away until he talks to you."

"Raul?"

"That's him." Andy sounded relieved. "What should I do?"

"Tell him I'll be right over." Phil paused. "You say he's drunk."

"Is a pig's ass pork?" Crawford whistled. "He's been knocking back cheap tequila for about two hours here. We're talking about one drunk Indian, my friend."

"Well, that means he and old Jesus have parted company," Phil said.

"He don't seem too happy," Crawford replied.

"Be there in half an hour."

Phil Elliott hung up the phone and turned to Joanne who was watching him and listening.

"Trouble?"

Phil nodded and frowned.

"You look for trouble, Phillip."

"I do not. Trouble looks for me, testing my thresholds."

"I enjoyed last night," Joanne said, as they made their way through the late afternoon San Antonio streets.

"I'll bet," Phil said. "Especially the sleeping."

"Okay." She laughed. "So you're not the American Gigolo, but I know you're tired. And the stress . . ."

"Please! Joanne!" Phil cut her off. "I'll make up my own excuses."

"Well? Let's hear one."

"Give me some time."

They weaved through the crowd, passing a shop window filled with piñatas: red burros, a multicolored variety of vegetables, and a red, white and blue Uncle Sam.

"Last night was hardly interstellar sex," Joanne began again.

"How would you know? You been fucking E.T.?"

"Phillip, don't get so defensive."

"I'll do better tonight," Elliott promised.

"Not with me."

"That's all right. I work better alone."

She shoved him toward the entrance to Andy Crawford's American Bar.

"Let's stay up here in the dining area." Phil led the way to a table by the stone fireplace. A mesquite fire crackled and smelled good. "Raul's in the back bar. I don't want to see him right away."

"What'll it be?" The waitress walked up.

Joanne ordered. "Two tequilas. Lemon and salt. Pronto."

"Make them doubles," Phil added. "And tell Mr. Crawford that Mr. Elliott is here."

"That'll mean something to him?" the waitress asked.

"Why don't you ask him and see, honey?" Joanne put a razor edge on her voice.

"And make those triples."

The waitress brought the drinks before going into the back to look for Crawford.

"You going to help this guy?" Joanne held her glass with both hands and sipped.

"As soon as I can figure out how to help myself," Phil replied, grimacing as he chewed on a lemon wedge, then licked salt from his thumb. "I just came here because I figured Crawford would send this guy to my apartment if I didn't."

"Would you have stayed out of trouble if I hadn't decided to marry Emmett?" Joanne watched him through the distortions of her tequila glass, causing his forehead to swell and his chin to recede. His eyes were unequal sizes and the lines around them deepened. "And married you?"

"No," Phil replied. "Besides, you didn't want me. You would have married some other rich guy in Dallas with his own football team and family cemetery."

"There were a lot more of them in those days."

"Things change."

She looked at him through the glass. "I still wonder. I wonder what you're thinking now."

"I'm thinking that the two thousand from *Southwest View* for the story about Delma Huddle will not cover my alimony, my rent, my ex-wife's house payment, and get me to Dallas and back," Phil said. "If not in one piece, at least with instructions for reassembly." Phil studied Joanne's eyes for any hint of the woman behind them. "And I wonder what you want from me."

"Your company." Joanne set down the glass. "I could always trust you."

"Can I trust you?"

"Do you see your ex-wife much?" Joanne didn't answer the question.

"Who? Courtnay?" Phil was confused by the sudden change in direction. "I have two."

"What?"

"Ex-wives."

"I mean your second," Joanne said. "The one you had the boy with." She made it sound like a criminal conspiracy. "Do you see her much?" She repeated the question.

"No, but she sues me pretty regular," Phil replied. "So we stay in touch."

"You still love her?"

"I don't know. This woman who is so actively engaged in being my *ex*-wife bears no resemblance to the woman I married."

"Things change," Joanne smirked. "Do you miss her?"

"Who she *was*, not who she is now." Phil shook his head. "Sometimes, I feel like she attempted some sort of psychological murder-suicide. She killed herself, but I survived with serious brain damage."

"Phillip! Joanne! Two of my favorite people." Andy Crawford walked out of the back room and moved toward their table. His six-foot-three-inch frame was still lean and well muscled, though his thick hair was tinged with gray. He was a handsome man, wearing a short brown leather flight jacket with a wool collar and a dark blue watch cap rolled and placed on the back of his head.

He shook Phil's hand and kissed Joanne's cheek, then quickly sat down.

"Your pal's still in back," he said to Phil. "The guy is a real piece of work."

The waitress walked up.

"I'll have what they're having, Mary." Crawford didn't look up, turning instead to Phil. "Damn, man, it's good to see you. How you been?"

"Fine. I saw Maxwell and John Wilson the other day."

"You saw Seth? How's he doing?"

"He's still rich and famous. He and Wilson got me out of jail."

"I heard about that, not just from your pal." Crawford nodded toward the back. "I see Wilson in here every now and then. I guess you both heard about Alan." It was a statement.

The waitress returned with Crawford's drink.

"Here's to us." Crawford picked up his glass, downing the tequila in two long gulps. He grabbed for the salt and lemon. "Whew! My first of the day. More, Mary," he said to the waitress.

Elliott looked at the empty glass. "You're still fast off the snap, Andy."

"That guy Raul has been driving me crazy, talking about killings, his wife and kids, and how he and Jesus don't hit it off so good anymore. Goddamn, he is one big Mexican."

"Yeh. He took up a lot of space in jail."

"Claims somebody tried to kill him," Crawford said.

"Who?"

"The guy he describes sounds an awful lot like O. W. Meadows," Crawford said.

"I wouldn't put it past O.W.," Elliott said. "I don't think Jo Bob realized exactly what he deputized.'

"If you can't trust an ex-teammate, who can you trust?" Crawford asked.

Phil and Joanne exchanged glances but neither said anything.

"That big Mexican is throwing up on the floor in the back bar," Mary, the waitress, announced. She set down their drinks.

"Goddamn it." Crawford looked at Elliott. "Take him outside, will you, Phil? Walk him around a little until he sobers up. The cold air will do him good. Joanne can wait here with me."

"I'll go with Phil, Andy," Joanne snapped. Her eyes narrowed; something about Andy Crawford's behavior puzzled her.

Phil walked into the back bar and quickly returned with Raul, who was very drunk.

"Amigo . . . amigo . . ." Raul mumbled, pathetically. *"Amigo? Qué pasó? Qué pasó?"*

"I don't know, Raul." Phil helped him into his coat. "Let's take a little walk and clear your head."

Joanne Remington-Hunter followed the two men out the front door.

"Damn!" Andy Crawford said, as they left. He drank his tequila and then looked around nervously. "Goddamn!" Crawford grabbed Elliott's drink and downed it.

"They coming back?" Mary asked.

"I wish I knew," Crawford said, reaching for Joanne's drink. "I wish I fucking knew."

Emeliano returned to the car parked outside the American Bar.

He had walked up the street to the liquor store for another bottle.

Striding straight and proud down the sidewalk, Emeliano enjoyed the surge of cocaine and alcohol. He felt the cold pistol against his belly, shoved in the waistband to keep him company on the walk to the liquor store and back.

"It's a good thing we drank the tequila." Emeliano believed what he was saying, as he opened the back door and slid into the seat behind his cousin. Both men wore full suits of desert camouflage and old-style Afrika Corps hats.

"You forgot to take this out of the window." Emeliano peeled the cardboard temporary license tag out of the rear window. He tossed it to the seat where it bounced off the short-barrel pump shotgun and knocked over the brown paper bag, spilling out the green plastic 000 buckshot shells. Emeliano picked up the cardboard license and set it behind him on the seat back ledge.

Colonel William Glanton had brought the pump gun this evening with the camouflage outfits. Emeliano had never fired a pump shotgun before and it took Glanton over an hour to familiarize the Costa Rican with the weapon; loading, firing, reloading, and the safety catches. Emeliano wondered if he would have to reload. He wasn't sure he remembered how. He worried about the safety catch and he worried about the shells being green plastic; they didn't seem deadly enough.

Cruz, Emeliano's cousin, switched off the ignition and the big racing cam chugged and rumbled to a halt. The car quit shaking.

"I'm low on gas," Cruz said. "This *chingasa* drinks it up."

It was getting late and the cold started to seep into the car. The windows began to fog. Emeliano began to think about putting this job off for a couple of days. He swigged on the new bottle of tequila and tried to make a plan. A long time passed. No plan came.

"There he is!" Cruz said.

Emeliano scrambled up in the backseat and saw nothing but fogged windows. He crabbed to his left and rolled down a window. He had trouble seeing; sitting up so fast had made him dizzy.

Emeliano's heart was pounding. He was sick to his stomach.

There were two men and a tall, brown-haired woman standing in front of the American Bar.

Emeliano recognized Raul. He didn't expect to have to deal with three people.

He still had no plan.

"There wasn't supposed to be three of them," Emeliano whined, as if betrayed.

"Let's kill them all." Cruz was drunk and enthusiastic. He turned the ignition key and began cranking over the cold, full-race engine. Using his free hand, Cruz began wiping the inside of the windshield, trying to clear himself a see-hole.

Emeliano wanted to put this off until another night, but he couldn't tell his cousin. Emeliano wished Cruz wasn't there. He was scared and forgot which way to push the safety catch; he had been flicking it absentmindedly with his finger and thumb and now didn't remember whether it was on or off.

Suddenly, the engine caught and the roar filled Emeliano's head with terror. His breath came in gasps. He flicked the safety catch back and forth indecisively, then he worked the pump action and ejected three shells.

He never knew he did it.

He guessed on the safety.

Phil Elliott and Joanne Remington-Hunter started down

the street, but Raul didn't move; he kept watching the smoking, rumbling car.

"Let's go, hombre!" Cruz yelled and stomped on the gas. The car lurched forward suddenly, about ten feet, and died.

Emeliano banged his head on the shotgun barrel.

Cruz ground the starter, leaving the standard transmission in gear with the clutch out; the car lurched and bucked up the street toward Raul, Joanne and Phil. As the car crawled closer, Elliott had a clear view of Emeliano in the backseat with the shotgun.

Emeliano pointed the shotgun at Raul. Wincing in anticipation of the recoil, he pulled the trigger.

Nothing happened.

Emeliano had guessed wrong on the safety catch. He pulled the gun back inside and pushed the safety catch without releasing the trigger, blowing out the back window.

Phil shoved Joanne into a doorway and covered her.

Raul turned and ran past them toward the river.

The engine caught again and the car lunged forward. Emeliano racked another shell into the chamber and took a quick shot at Raul, who was crouched and running awfully fast for such a big, drunk man. The range was a little far and the nine-pellet pattern splattered on the pavement and brick storefronts, sounding like someone had thrown a handful of rocks.

Emeliano had no idea where his shot went and was sure the green plastic shells were no good.

The car was quickly gaining on Raul and Emeliano shot again, shattering the window behind the running man.

"Shoot him!" Cruz was screaming. "Shoot him!"

Raul cut down an alley and Cruz slid the big car in behind him, slamming into the building with the right rear fender. The collision threw Emeliano into the window frame and split his forehead.

The car pulled alongside Raul and Cruz reached out, almost touching the big man.

"Shoot him! Shoot him!" Cruz screamed.

Emeliano shoved the gun out, the barrel scant inches from Raul's back, closed his eyes, and pulled the trigger.

There was a slight click as the firing pin slammed down on an empty chamber.

The shotgun was empty.

Emeliano was stunned.

When he opened his eyes, Raul was nowhere to be seen.

Phil Elliott and Joanne Remington-Hunter watched from the doorway as the big green Dodge backed out of the alley and raced off down the street.

A red and white piece of cardboard was sucked out the rear window and fluttered silently to the pavement. Phil ran quickly into the street and picked up the temporary license tag.

Joanne stepped out of the doorway when Phil returned with the tag in his hand.

"Come on," he said. "I've got some questions I've wanted to ask my old teammate Andy Crawford for a long time. I think tonight is the night."

"What the hell is going on out there?" Andy Crawford was still sitting at the table when they returned to the American Bar. "Where's your buddy?" A note of hesitancy crept into his voice.

"Oh, he sobered up once that cold air hit him." Phil sat down and placed the license tag on the table. He stared for a long moment at Crawford who dropped his eyes and began to study his shoes. "Where did our drinks go?" Phil said, finally. "Did you think we weren't coming back?"

"Hell no . . . I just . . . ah . . . I drank 'em," Crawford stammered. "Mary! Get us three more."

"That's fast drinking, even for you, Andy," Joanne said. "You got a problem?"

"No! Well, hell, we all got problems." Crawford stumbled on his words. The combination of alcohol and fear made his head swim. "I . . . I just haven't been myself since I heard about Alan having AIDS."

"How about when you heard those gunshots a moment ago?" Phil asked.

"What gunshots?"

"You got feathers on your lips, Andy," Phil said. "You want to try that again?"

"What?" Crawford twisted in his chair and shuffled his feet. "Try what again? I didn't have anything to do with that."

"With what, Andy?" Elliott watched the old running back's face as Mary put down the drinks. "You didn't have anything to do with what?"

"That!" Crawford pointed toward the door. "Out there. I didn't know they were going to do something like that." He grabbed his drink and took a deep swallow.

"Who?"

"I can't tell you who, for Christ sakes!" Crawford whined. "They'll do the same to me."

"If they use the same two guys, you got nothing to worry about," Phil said. "Now, tell me who you called when Raul showed up here?"

"I called you."

"Who did you call before you called me?"

"Jesus, Phil, they'll kill me."

"They'll probably kill you anyway, Andy." Elliott shook his head. "How could you get involved with people like that?"

"That's a silly question, coming from you." Crawford laughed, but he had tears in his eyes. "Have you forgotten about Bob Beaudreau?"

"A day doesn't get past me, I don't give a moment to Bob Beaudreau," Phil answered. "Are you telling me Beaudreau is involved in this?"

"In a way." Crawford shook his head; the tears were now running down his cheeks. He wiped them away and looked at his hand. "Look at me. I'm a mess. I just don't care anymore." Andy Crawford took a deep breath and sat back. "You got a cigarette?"

Elliott tossed the pack across the table and watched as Crawford lit the cigarette.

"First," Andy exhaled, "I tested positive for AIDS, but I can live with it. They told me there's a fifty-percent chance I won't actually develop the disease."

"Good for you," Joanne said. "But I think I'll have a fresh glass anyway."

"Very funny." Crawford smiled wryly.

"Those are better odds than we just had out there on the street, Andy," Phil said. "Who set that up?"

"I'm not sure, Phil," Crawford said. "I swear. Look, things got a lot different after you left Dallas. The money kept getting bigger and the people stranger. It is *real* big

business now. There are a lot of very bad people involved in football now.''

"There were a lot of bad people around then, Andy,''
Elliott replied. "Beaudreau murdered two people and
walked.''

"It's worse now. Believe me.'' Crawford paused. He
picked up his glass and drained it. The alcohol was affecting him. He *wanted* to tell Elliott what he knew. He *had*
to tell someone and he had always trusted Phil Elliott.
"When Ross Denham and Bobby Laughlin bought the
club, they offered a bunch of us players and ex-players a
chance to go to work for their companies. Phil, you
wouldn't believe how many different things these guys
are involved in.''

"Try me. I suspended disbelief a long time ago.''

"They are connected all the way from Washington,
D.C., to South America,'' Crawford said. "They have
these companies in Mexico and Central America.''

"I know all that, Andy.''

"Well, me, Tony Douglas, Thomas Richardson, and
O. W. Meadows used to work for them on a contract
basis,'' Crawford explained. "I first got involved through
the Southwest Conservative Trust. Their political action
committee practically financed Alan Claridge's first campaign for Congress. After that, they offered me a job
working with Dickie Lafler's group. That's where I got
the money to buy this bar.''

"Dickie Lafler's group?'' Phil was not surprised. "The
guys that got caught smuggling?''

"Yeh.'' Crawford nodded.

"How come you stayed in the clear when the operation
got rolled up?'' Phil asked.

"I was the snitch. Lafler and the others were stealing
from the D-L company. God, it was easy to do. There
was so much cash we carried it in big laundry bags,''
Crawford said. "Lafler and the others got greedy, so I
told my boss, Colonel Glanton.''

"William Glanton?''

"That is the man. He is very dangerous,'' Crawford
said. "Anyway, they just turned them over to Internal
Revenue and the FBI. They left me alone completely.
And they let Dickie Lafler cut a deal through his lawyer,
David Stein.''

"How much did Stein know?"

"He knew everything," Crawford answered. "He is *the* D-L Companies' attorney. He knows just about everything. At least, that's the way he acts."

"What exactly were you doing for Denham and Laughlin?"

"We would fly things in and out of Central America," Crawford explained. "Mostly through Panama and into Costa Rica. The boxes would be marked machinery or something for the D-L companies down there. They own a big English-language newspaper and several bottling plants. But I think the boxes were full of weapons. Hell, I *know* some of them were full of weapons because we looked. Sometimes we flew soldiers down there. Lafler had a deal with Laughlin to bring cocaine and cash back out."

"Where did these flights originate?"

"The Purgatory Military Institute," Crawford said. "That's normally where we returned except on a few occasions, when we came right back to Air Force bases. That would be the only time Colonel Glanton would wear his uniform."

"Who all made these flights?"

"Besides Lafler and his group?"

"Yeh." Elliott pressed. "What ex-players, guys that I would know?"

"Me and Tony Douglas made several together until B.A. got him that game warden's job in Purgatory." Crawford paused. "O.W. made a few. It was a good way to pick up extra cash."

"So is contract murder, if you don't have any qualms about it," Joanne spat.

"Delma Huddle made a couple, until he figured out what it was about." Crawford ignored Joanne's remark. "Thomas Richardson brought Delma in . . ."

"And Jimmy Boxx took him out," Phil finished the sentence.

"You knew about that?" Crawford was surprised.

"Not until this moment," Phil said. "Was it Glanton you called today?"

"Yeh." Crawford frowned. "He came by yesterday and told me to keep an eye out for this guy Raul. They knew he was in San Antonio somewhere. I had already called Glanton when the Mexican starts talking about you. It freaked me out. I had no idea you were involved. That's why I called you. I just didn't know what to do. Believe me, I didn't know they were going to kill him."

"They didn't."

"What?"

"They tried like hell, but he got away."

"I'm glad." Crawford sighed.

"That's big of you," Joanne said. "You motherfucker!"

"What happened to all the cash?" Phil asked.

"I'm not sure, but I think it all went to D-L Financial and they moved it to the various savings and loans they owned," Crawford said. "They had a lot of bad real estate paper is what I heard. Then the oil market went to hell and they had real cash flow problems. I know they were involved in some peculiar real estate deals because they would pay us all cash just to put our names on loan applications and land titles for that big River Ranch Estates development out in Purgatory."

"Was Jo Bob Williams involved?" Phil asked.

"Jesus! Absolutely not!" Crawford shot back.

"What were you thinking about, you asshole?" Joanne glared at Crawford.

"Let up on me, Joanne. The Hunter family was no home of love and charity." Andy Crawford turned and faced Joanne Hunter. "I'll tell you what I was thinking about. I was thinking about how I was an old man at thirty, and how people like you bought new fur coats with the money I made for you wrecking my body, and how there aren't many good-paying jobs for ex-pro ballplayers. I hurt every day, all day and all night long, and the goddamn Hunters sure never gave a shit about what was going to happen to me when I was fifty years old and couldn't walk."

"Nobody held a gun to your head," Joanne said.

"You women are all the same."

"Is that why you're a fag!" Joanne turned red, her face was cold and mean.

"I'm not ashamed of what I am." Crawford spoke softly. "Which is more than you can say. Nobody forced you to marry that slime Emmett Hunter."

"Kids." Elliott held up his hands. "I hate to break this up, just when you are both so wonderfully bitchy, but we have more serious problems than our sexual persuasions and mistakes we made in past lives. There are at least two crazy men with a shotgun running around trying to kill people that Colonel William Glanton doesn't like. Any one of us could be listed in that category."

"I don't care anymore. I'm going to die anyway." Crawford was resigned.

"We're *all* gonna die eventually, Andy. The idea is to prolong life and make it meaningful." Elliott finished his drink and signaled the waitress.

"Make sure we get clean glasses," Joanne said, as Mary moved back toward the bar. Crawford did not react.

"Look, Andy," Phil continued. "Football taught us commitment. It's up to us to find a new direction for that commitment now that we know professional football was fraud and deception. The fact that we were lied to and deceived does not take away or make useless some of the things we learned about life while we played the game. The commitment, as I understand it, should be to live a meaningful life. We have to use different yardsticks to measure our progress; yardage and money led us into this trap. We have to find something else worth living for, to get us on with living."

"Have you found the meaning?" Crawford asked.

"No." Phil smiled. "But I know my only hope is to keep looking and the more I look, the more convinced I am that what I seek is not out there in the world." Elliott pointed around the room, then pointed back at himself. "It is in here, in *me.*"

"Well, if it's in *you,*" Crawford said, "it's *broke.*"

The next morning, in San Antonio, in his apartment above the river, Phil Elliott hooked his TENS unit to his belt but was unable to reach the electrodes stuck on either side of his thoracic vertebrae. So he attached the cables to the electrodes glued to his cervical vertebrae and turned on the unit, adjusting the amperage and pulse rate of the electrical shocks running through the degenerating bone and muscle.

The doctors had been talking about drilling holes in his head and trying to short-circuit the pain with electrodes planted permanently in his brain.

"Sorry, doc," Phil had said. "Nobody gets inside the head. It is my last hiding place. My ex-wife's attorney has wanted in there for months."

"You know the pain is just going to get worse," the doctor had replied. "And with all this goddamn antidrug propaganda, the goddamn legislators keep restricting our ability to prescribe the really effective pain killers."

"If it gets to the point I can't stand it and the only solution is a bunch of holes drilled in my head, I'll do the drilling myself."

The doctor shook his head. "What caliber?"

"I'll surprise you."

"Quit talking like that."

"I'm *not* suicidal, doc. If I feel the need to put holes in somebody's head, I've got a list."

"Am I on it?"

"Not yet."

"That's reassuring."

"Then again, I haven't seen your bill yet."

"Just turn on your TENS unit and get out of here."

Phil was at his desk, thumbing through his notes on the events of the previous night at Andy Crawford's bar. He was puzzling over what Crawford had said about the flights from the Purgatory Military Institute into Central America when Joanne walked in from the bathroom. She had wrapped herself in a towel and was combing out her wet hair.

She glanced at the dirty dishes still in the sink.

"The maid hasn't come yet," Elliott said.

"You've got a maid?"

"No, but I keep hoping one will show up."

"What is that thing?" Joanne pointed at the TENS unit, the cables, and the electrodes. Phil wasn't wearing a shirt.

"It's a transubcutaneous nerve stimulator," Phil said. "It sends electric shock to those electrodes attached along my spine. It's supposed to reduce the pain from the fractured vertebrae."

"Does it?"

"Sort of, but then I usually end up turning it up so high, I burn the shit out of myself and have to stop using it until the burns heal. Say, could you give me a hand and

plug those two wires hanging down into those two electrodes? I couldn't reach them, my shoulders are too
stiff."

Joanne picked up the wires, handling them like they
were live rattlesnakes.

"Just plug them into the little holes."

She did as he instructed and the muscles along his
spine bulged.

"Aaaah!" Phil yelped.

Joanne jumped back, terrified.

"Goddammit, Phil!" Joanne yelled. "You told me to
do it."

"Shit, I'm sorry, Joanne." Phil was twisting the dials
on the unit attached to his belt. "I forgot and left the
damn things turned on." He adjusted the settings so the
muscles just twitched rhythmically.

"God! You scared the shit out of me." Joanne adjusted her towel. The aureoles of her magnificent breasts
were visible.

She walked to the window and looked down at the
gray-green San Antonio River.

Phil shuffled the pages, studying what he had typed.
Last night's events read like a bad detective story and
from all the early indications, Phil Elliott was not going
to like the ending. Assuming he was even *around* for the
ending.

Phil put Joanne on a flight to Dallas that afternoon.

"I'll see you at the reunion." Phil kissed her cheek.
"I'll be the one with the knife in his back."

"That's not funny."

"You can say that again."

He watched her disappear down the jetway. He felt
old and lonely.

Back in his apartment, he packed a bag.

He would stop in Austin, see his ex-wife about all the
court papers she was filing on him, and drop by *Southwest View* to pick up the two thousand from Decker
McShane.

Elliott was heading for the door when the phone rang.

It was Sheriff Jo Bob Williams.

With some bad news.

*   *   *

Courtnay came to the door in white deck pants rolled up halfway to the knee and a man's open-collar white shirt. Her dark hair was twisted up in a loose bun on the back of her head, a few loose wisps dancing around her collar. Her fresh washed face was shiny and pretty, the brown eyes crinkled with premature lines.

"What do you want?" she asked. Courtnay looked tired, leaning on the door, frowning.

"How about a little relief from your lawyer?" Phil asked.

She never gave an inch, and now was certainly no exception. "Why are you here?"

"I'm in town to pick up an advance from Decker McShane. I just stopped to tell you I'll be late on the alimony."

"Late! You already owe me for six months. That's forty-eight hundred dollars. I could sue you."

"You'll have to get in line." Elliott had six more years of contractual alimony at eight hundred dollars a month. "Can I come in? I like to visit my money every now and then."

"Well . . . okay." Courtnay was reluctant but relented.

He entered, trying not to feel the loss of being a stranger in the house that was once his home. A brown leather briefcase sat on the dining room table. "Nice case for the model career woman."

"It's not mine." She took the briefcase and put it in the hall closet.

"What are you doing with it, muling dope to Stein or corruption money for D-L Financial to the governor?" He grinned.

"Fuck you."

"You speak of love like a praying mantis."

Phil struck a match, lit a cigarette, handed it to Courtnay and lit himself another, pulling the cigarette from his lips. "I can see by the look on your face you are more danger-ous than ever." Phil smiled. "Of course, that was what I liked most about you."

"I thought you gave up smoking."

"I started again in jail," Phil said. "It's important to have something to trade besides sexual favors."

Courtnay sucked deeply on the cigarette, her cheeks

caved in, suddenly lost in her mood. The lines deepened around her mouth and eyes.

It was obvious to Phil, being so closely acquainted with her many moods, that Courtnay was in the throes of depression. He didn't know why. He just didn't want her to suddenly blame him simply because he was there.

"I'll make us some coffee." She walked into the kitchen.

Phil checked quickly through the papers on her desk, searching for clues to just what was happening in her life that might confirm his suspicions about her depression. Making him coffee was a certain tip-off that Courtnay's life was akilter. She didn't make him coffee when they were married.

The desk was littered with the usual bills and invitations to political fund-raisers. Phil lifted the desk pad. Underneath was a single folded letter-sized piece of paper. He opened the paper. All that was listed was a name, phone number and address of a man named Tom Reece. Elliott quickly copied the information and was looking out the window when she returned with the coffee.

"How is Scott?" Courtnay asked.

"He's doing as well as can be expected. I talked to him the other day."

"Did he ask about me?"

"Yes," Elliott lied. "I told him you were doing fine and missed him."

"Well, that is the truth." Her tone was accusatory.

"What is? That you miss him very much? Or that you are doing well?"

"Both!"

"Well, if you love him so much why don't you write him a letter or call him on the phone?"

"Because I've been busy working," she snapped. "Unlike you."

"What is your *work?*"

"I coordinate Mr. Laughlin's daily routine." Courtnay was defensive. "I meet interesting, exciting people who make things happen."

"Like human suffering on a monumental scale?"

"Very droll." She shook her head. "Still the same contrary asshole."

"And shit still runs downhill," Phil replied. "How's Felice?"

"Just fine. She'll get reelected . . ."

"As soon as she puts together a coalition to repeal the law of gravity." Phil was expressionless. "Still sleeping with Stein?" He knew the answer. The betrayals in his life astounded him.

"Yes. I respect his idealism, his intelligence, his commitment."

"Being young and rich, not to mention all the cocaine, adds a certain zing to all that idealism, intelligence and commitment."

"You hate everybody."

"I haven't met everybody yet," Phil laughed. "Lay down with dogs, you get up with lawyers and politicians. But power *is* the ultimate aphrodisiac. I might sleep with the governor, if he asked. So, now that we're finished with the polite small talk, listen to me. Your crowd is involved in some very bad things, with some very bad people."

"Like who? And what?"

"Like murder, for starters."

"That's your typical paranoid bullshit," she said.

"Look, I know D-L doesn't want me trying to stop development in the Purgatory. But that's starting to feel like small potatoes. There's a lot of other shit going down. Which is why I think this whole reunion story they want me to do is a trap." He paused. "Is it?"

"You're just paranoid." Courtnay walked to the liquor cabinet and poured two water glasses half full of whiskey.

"I'll drink to that," Phil said, picking up the glass. "Or, maybe I'm just terminally crazy from watching you change again and again, waiting for the day you would love me but not want to live with me. It had to come, 'cause when you lived with me you didn't love me."

"How could you ever say that?"

"I watched you look at yourself in the mirror every morning. It was only a matter of time."

"I got tired of arguing with you."

"About what?"

"Everything."

"Pretty nonspecific." Phil sighed. "Goddamn I'm tired of being nuts, trying to deal with ignorance."

"It was a no-fault divorce."

"The perfect end to a no-fault marriage?" Phil asked.

"Is that it? You'll go to church on Sunday in clean underwear with a clean conscience? And you believe it? That's perfect. What a goddamn society. The Constitution says that no one is all powerful, instead no one is responsible. Now I've got to go to the reunion and find out what the bastards *think* they're doing, what they *say* they're doing, and if I live long enough, what they *really are* doing."

"There are still some decent men around," she protested.

"If there are, they're on your menu," Phil said. "David Stein may be your oyster on the half shell right now, but one day you'll be so busy changing clothes and personalities and makeup, you'll forget to check the calendar to see if you're dining during an 'R' month."

"Marvelous simile," Courtnay said. "At least when you were writing I didn't have to hear it."

"You *never* hear the one that gets you."

"Arguing about everything again, are we?" she said. "You argue that nobody is in charge, then you get mad at Governor Quinlan and Colonel Glanton for trying to plan and bring a little discipline to life."

"Yeh!" Phil shot back. "That's not order, that's their own *logical* crime called justice."

"I miss Scott," she said suddenly. "I miss him every day." Her eyes filled with confused tears. "I guess I believed you'd both be around after the divorce."

"You jerked the world out from under the boy." Phil looked around. "What the hell. I guess against all evidence, *I thought you would be around forever, too.*"

He finished his third drink. Then his fourth. Then he poured his fifth.

"Can I stay the night in the guest room?" Phil asked. "I've had too much to drink to drive back down the hill."

"Yeh, I guess so." She had turned to stare out the window, and now waved him away without looking back.

"You know what I miss the most sometimes?" Phil leaned against the doorjamb and looked at the floor. "All those people I thought were my friends. They just seemed to disappear when the going was really crazy and tough, and I was running out of money."

"Oh, they're still around." Courtnay smiled lazily. "They're *my* friends now."

"I knew a lot of them before I met you."

"I'm sure it was a tough choice for them," Courtnay said. "But, you know what they say: winner takes all."

Phil laughed. "Now that is funny."

In the bedroom, he pulled off his shirt and started unhooking the TENS unit. He had trouble again with the two electrodes between his shoulder blades and thought, for a moment, about asking Courtnay to help.

He decided against it.

Never let them know how bad you're hurt.

B. A. Quinlan taught him that.

A long time ago.

During the night, Courtnay slipped up to the guest room door and watched Phil sleep. She saw how he had the pillows arranged to ease the pain of his smashed body.

Lately, sleep was coming hard for Courtnay and when she slept she had dreams that made her cry. She would just wake up crying, with no memory of the dream.

She blamed it on Elliott.

Feeling uneasy, she stared angrily at him for a few more moments and then returned to her own bed.

Courtnay Howard-Elliott finally fell asleep around 5:00 A.M., just as the pain in Phil's back was becoming unbearable. It had wakened him earlier but he stayed in bed for a few more minutes.

He dreaded this part of the day—getting out of bed. He always woke up scared because he knew how painful the next hour would be, until he could get the scar tissue and calcified joints working again.

He dragged himself out of bed and onto the floor, where he began his ritual of stretching exercises. When he was finished stretching, he stood and began walking, slowly, unsteadily, back and forth across the room. He held on to the bedposts, then balanced himself with a hand against the wall until he could walk unassisted.

After about five minutes of walking and stretching, Phil pulled on his clothes and hooked up his TENS unit. He detached the two cables that would run to the electrodes stuck beside his thoracic vertebrae and stuck them in his shirt pocket. He would find somebody to help with them later.

Elliott crept uneasily down the hall to Courtnay's bedroom. She was sprawled across her bed in a deep sleep.

Back in the foyer, Phil retrieved the brown briefcase
from the closet where Courtnay had placed it the night
before. He placed the case on the dinette table and
studied the combination lock. Phil knew Stein's home
and office addresses by heart; he had received so many
insulting letters from the attorney over the past year.

Elliott began to try the obvious combinations: the first
three numbers of his phones, frontwards and backwards,
the last three numbers, again in both sequences.

It took him ten minutes before he popped open the
case, using the three numbers in his home address.

He began to dig through and read the papers inside the
case. Phil found nothing interesting until he found a large
brown envelope addressed to Ross Denham at his office
in the Southwestern Conservative Trust Building (which
used to be the North Dallas National Bank Building, a
small two-story antebellum-style structure that was pur-
chased by the Southwest Conservative Trust with the
vaults intact).

Inside the envelope were several folders.

The first folder was entitled THE GOLDEN EAGLE PARK.

It was a presentation to the secretary of the interior.

The cover letter was an enthusiastic approval of a plan
to create a park to protect the golden eagle by condemning certain properties in the Purgatory and putting them
under the management of the National Wildlife Refuge
System. It was no coincidence that the land to be con-
demned was the entire Blaine Ranch and a few smaller
ranches that were contiguous to the Blaines'.

The letter was signed by both Governor B. A. Quinlan
and the chairman of the Parks and Wildlife Commission,
Louis Lafler.

The presentation to the secretary of the interior, which
would, if approved, destroy in the strokes of a pen the
Blaine Ranch and, also, increase the value of River Ranch
Estates, Governor Quinlan's Pigskin Ranch, and the
Denham-Laughlin Exotic Game Ranch tenfold, was pure
genius. The argument for the golden eagle park was
classic doublespeak. Obviously written by David Stein,
the document pointed out that the rapid development of
the area (all being done by D-L Financial) made the
interior secretary's decision all the more urgent. It was

brilliant and disastrous for everyone but the very people who were doing all the damage.

Underneath the golden eagle park presentation were several letters, the first a copy of a letter from Tony Perelli, Seth Maxwell's gambler friend from Las Vegas, to David Stein. There was a handwritten notation across the top from Stein: "Thought you should see this. DS." The letterhead read:

TONY'S CASINO
ON-THE-STRIP
LAS VEGAS, NEVADA

Phil scanned the letter.

Dear David,
    Our friends in New Jersey just sent their accountant out to look at the books. I gave them the second set, but I am afraid he didn't like what he saw. He wanted to talk to our accountant. I said he was up at the new place in Reno. He flew back to Jersey last night. Then, first thing this morning, I got a call from Smashie who said he would be here in a week and wasn't going to leave until he saw the accountant or $2 million in cash. They know we've been skimming. The upside is they don't know how much. If they talk to the accountant they will. So, our only choice is to give them the $2 million. Sorry.

                    Sincerely,
                    Tony

David Stein had clipped a note to the letter:

RD, I don't know if this sleazy fuck is jerking us off or not. But, there is no way I can find out in a week without talking to the boys in Jersey. I think we better pay and then take our time and carefully find out. If this asshole is fucking us, I'll turn him over to the Colonel. I know the tough nut will be digging up the $2 million with our cash flow problems. That'll have to be your decision. Going to one of

our banks could be dicey with the Feds everywhere.
I know we have a flight to Panama out this week
and Beaudreau's people could accept that big a
shipment at short notice. I've had our accountants
going over the football team's books and it is
worse than we thought. That goddamn Conrad
Hunter hid a bunch of debt on us. I have run down
all those companies that he claimed would pay
in full for their luxury boxes in October and they're
all bogus. The old bastard set us up on all the
deferred money to players too. He cashed in all the
annuities that were to provide the money to pay
those salaries. As soon as we finish sorting out the
football club and the stadium's books, I think we
should meet at your offices up there. I should be
done in time to make the reunion.

Incidently, speaking of the reunion, I am working with the Colonel on a plan to remove Phil
Elliott as an obstacle to our acquiring his thousand
acres that cut through River Ranch. The problem
should be solved by the time the reunion is over.

Phil Elliott found nothing more of interest in the briefcase and returned it to the closet, went into the kitchen
and made a pot of coffee.

He took his coffee out on the deck and watched the
sunrise, while he thought through what he had just read.
A plan to remove Phil Elliott. Well, it wouldn't be the
first time someone tried to remove him. It seemed like
people had been trying to remove him his whole life.

Phil was drinking his second cup of coffee when
Courtnay joined him. He had been thinking about Scott.

The sun began to heat the deck where they were sitting. It was still cool. Phil was sweating. It wasn't from
the sun.

Courtnay had been up about an hour before she made
her appearance. She had spent most of the hour at her
vanity, studying her face in the mirror and putting on her
mask for the day.

She looked great.

They sat for about ten minutes without saying a word.

Finally, Courtnay spoke.

"Don't mistake my hospitality," she said. "I was just too tired and drunk to throw you out last night."

"There is truth in wine, my dear."

"Fuck you!" She was suddenly angry. His presence had become offensive.

"Thanks for the offer." Phil pushed himself to his feet. "But I have to be off. Take good care of my house."

"It's not your house and if you don't get the hell out right now, I will call David and have him file on you for breaking and entering."

"I guess this means a blow job is out of the question?"

"Goddamn you! I'll make you pay for saying that!"

"Ah," Phil said and smiled sadly. "For revenge is always the delight of the mean spirit, of a weak or petty mind! You may draw proof of this in that no one rejoices more in revenge than a *woman*." Phil limped slowly toward the door. "I was quoting one of your Roman philosophers there, I think."

The gray Ford was waiting up the road as Phil pulled out of Courtnay's driveway and headed downhill on his way to the offices of *Southwest View* magazine. The gray Ford fell in behind him at a respectable distance.

There was only one man in the car and he wasn't trying very hard not to be seen. Phil took that as a good sign. The car was so plain, obviously chosen *not* to draw attention, which was exactly the reason it caught Elliott's attention in the first place. Phil assumed it was the law and not a hitman or some other thug type sent to make his life miserable or over.

The gray Ford followed him right into the underground parking garage, driving past Phil's chosen slot and parking about ten spaces away. The driver backed into his spot, so he could watch Elliott's car easily.

A plan to remove Phil Elliott.

"You say, 'How are you? Good luck,' " Phil sang, as he walked to the elevator. "But, you don't mean it." The elevator door opened. A woman in a business suit was already on board. Phil pushed the street-level button and kept singing. "You know, as well as me, you'd rather see me paralyzed. Why don't you just come out once and *scream* it?"

The woman sidled by him as the door opened.

Phil walked out into the sunlight and headed toward the *Southwest View* offices.

Playing the Game

"Mr. McShane will see you now," the receptionist said.

Phil Elliott limped through the big hand-carved door.

Behind the big hand-carved desk sat Decker McShane, editor of *Southwest View* magazine and husband of State Senator Felice McShane.

"Hidy, Phillip. Have a seat?" Decker leaned back in his chair.

"No thanks," Phil said. "I haven't got a place to put it."

"God! You must have had a terrible night."

"Seven of them a week," Phil said. He would say nothing about being at Courtnay's. "Decker, why the story on Delma Huddle? He's an old friend. There is no way I can ask him the stuff your readers want and you won't print the stuff I want to write about it."

"Like what?"

"That he was framed by a guy named Jimmy Boxx and that Denham and Laughlin were behind it, because they wanted to force Conrad Hunter to sell the club."

"Hey! Take it easy." Decker held a finger to his lips. "D-L Financial owns this magazine."

"I know it," Phil said. "So you won't want to hear that they also lured Seth Maxwell into retirement with offers of a big Hollywood career and did the same to B.A. with the promise of being governor."

"You're right. I don't want to hear it." Decker stood

up behind his massive desk, his hand outstretched. "So, I guess you better try and figure out a way to write a story I'll be able to publish."

"It don't matter how hard I try, there's no guarantee you'll publish," Phil said. "So I better get my money now. Where's the two grand?"

"The check's being cut." Decker walked over to his big telescope by the window. He spied on the city from his office. The building was set on a hill.

"Show me something different, Phil." He looked into the eyepiece. "Give me something I can sink my teeth into."

"Let me do the next *'Search for Texas' Best Chicken-fried Steak.'* "

"Funny." Decker turned from the scope. "Show me another way besides dodging bullets with you. I notice that *whatever* it is you're doing, you're doing it alone."

"If it was easy, little old ladies in wheelchairs could do it."

"From the look of your walk, there's a wheelchair in your future."

"Naw. I've got a sedan chair and four Pakistanis in your lobby."

"Felice called, just before you got here," Decker said. "You spent last night at Courtnay's?"

"What's keeping the check?" Elliott dodged.

Decker ignored the question. "I'm going to do a series of stories for the magazine analyzing the frontier spirit of the Jews and Arabs, compared to the spirit of early southwestern Americans," he said. "I figure to stay a month, travel around and get to know the Middle Eastern mind. Then hole up on the coast of Spain and do the series of stories."

"Gonna spend a *whole month* on the Middle Eastern mind?" Phil said. "That ought to cover it all."

"Want a drink?" Decker took a key from his vest pocket and unlocked his desk drawer, then punched a hidden button. There was a buzz and a secret bar swung out of the wall.

Phil cast a questioning glance at Decker and then at the bar.

Decker shrugged. "The nigger maids were stealing my scotch."

Phil nodded and began rummaging through the bottles, looking for the expensive tequila he knew Decker kept. He found the bottle and poured the tequila over the ice in a tall glass.

"You know, Decker, you're so rich, you think you must be right." Phil took a long drink. "You sell your opinion like you're selling beer. You put everything in the marketplace, including your immortal soul. If I'm right about your owners, you done sold your soul to the Devil. Not that I believe in the Devil. But I do believe in evil and you have sold out."

"That's a cruel thing to say, I've always been a friend to you."

"As *my* friends go, that's true. I apologize. But for Christ sakes, you're tough to work with. You change your mind more often than you change your socks."

"You don't change your socks at all." Decker laughed.

"I can't afford new ones, but I won't sell my mind for a new wardrobe."

Decker looked up from his telescope and frowned. "I believe you are the one here begging an advance. Now go back, find out and write what you think you know and get everyone mad at you. It sells magazines."

"Decker, my story will begin with the rise of an obscure university math major to computer salesman whose genius quickly brought him through the tangled web of microchip fast-lane high-tech corporate politics. At twenty-six he engineered the takeover of the company he had joined out of college. That company quickly grew into a billion-dollar company handling information processing for government agencies. Information became his currency; with it he bought power. Using his wealth of information and bottomless checkbook, Ross Denham pyramided his holdings into a giant financial conglomerate which allowed him unlimited access to capital and he began developing real estate by loaning money from *his* banks to people to buy *his* properties. Finally, he bought gambling casinos and film companies. But, like all crazy men with real money, he wouldn't find true happiness until he owned his own professional football team. He chose to steal the Dallas team from Conrad Hunter who was dying of cancer. He had to hurry because Conrad had a clause in his will dividing the team among his kids.

Somehow, in the course of the hurried negotiations, dying all the way, Conrad Hunter plotted his revenge against the man who had his star receiver framed on a cocaine charge, lured his star quarterback to Hollywood, and talked B. A. Quinlan into running for governor of Texas." Elliott paused, for effect. "As we speak, I can hear that sorry bastard's cackling laugh from the grave. I don't know what he did, but D-L Financial's ass is in a crack. So I'm going to that reunion and find out how and why." Phil laughed. "And I can start with Delma Huddle's dope bust. Now, I want my check and, believe me, I'm cashing it quick."

The door to Decker's office opened and in walked a tall, handsome woman with a check in her hand.

"That's for him." Decker pointed toward Phil.

"That check doesn't feel a bit warm, does it, ma'am?" Phil smiled.

"No, sir." The woman was puzzled and looked back at Decker.

"Just a little joke, Mary," Decker said. "He's a writer."

"Oh, that explains it." She handed Phil the check, then turned back to Decker. "The cheese fall off his cracker?"

"His lunch bucket's empty," Decker replied. Mary laughed.

"They laughed at Tolstoy," Phil said with a smile, folding the check into his shirt pocket.

"Only when he was telling jokes," Mary said. She left the office laughing.

"You don't expect me to publish . . ."

"You will, Decker, or someone else will get the credit."

"Goddammit, why do you insist on looking for the worst?"

"My own peculiar personality dysfunction," Phil replied. "I always try to understand the differences between right and wrong, true and false."

"You *would* say 'credit.' " Decker looked out at the city, then down at the river. "Did I ever tell you that my mother worked at a department store, on the first floor? I didn't even know there were any more floors. My mother would put money or sales tickets into these little pneumatic tubes and shoot them across the store where the tube would disappear through a hole in the ceiling.

After awhile, something would come shooting back down
the tube to my mother and she would conclude the transaction on the basis of what came back." Decker turned
away from the window, lit a cigarette and puffed deeply
on it. "It was funny. I never thought about what happened at the other end of the tube. I quit going to the
store and never went back until after I had graduated
from high school. By that time, she was working upstairs
in the credit department. I remember the first time I
went to her office. They hadn't remodeled the store yet,
and the pneumatic tubes still snaked along the ceiling. It
was the first time I had been above the first floor. It was
quite a shock to me to see that old pneumatic tube ended
right there in her office. Quite a shock." Decker shook
his head. "I tell you, I just thought it would end in some
place a little more magical than the credit department. I
guess I just never thought, until that moment . . ."

"I guess not," Phil interrupted. "Or since. Where did
you think the tube ended? Heaven?"

"It would've been a little nicer." He fingered his solid
gold cross. "I guess I never really considered the second
floor at all. Or the third . . ." Decker talked slowly,
vacantly. " . . . or . . . fourth . . . I kept sitting at her desk
that day and staring at the tube and it was like my whole
life was rearranged."

"Well, you added another story."

"That's funny." Decker frowned. Phil shrugged and
nodded his head. It was a mutual gesture they had created over the years to short-circuit the ritual of apology
that was always necessary between two friends.

"Life is like that," Phil said. "Every time you think
you've succeeded, you find out that you've just gone up
another flight of stairs. There is still something going on
up above, 'cause you can hear the footsteps. Then, after
years, you discover the elevator, and you think now
you'll ride to the top, but all you learn is that all floors
look about the same and in the elevator you can't tell
whether you're going up or down. If, by some insane
fluke, you reach the top of the building, you will walk
into the CEO suite and find a little wizened-up guy over
on the couch hanging up the phone. 'It's for you,' he will
say. 'They want to see you back down on one.' "

"That's pretty cynical."

"That's easy for you to say," Phil laughed. "You never got past the credit department on two."

"Write your story," Decker said. "But it's a goddamn cynical view. If all businessmen are thieves and crooks, then who cares?"

Phil didn't argue. He *couldn't* argue.

"I didn't say *all* and I believe there are lots of people who do still care. I also believe that some day someone will speak and be heard. Then watch out."

"He better have a loud voice and a long memory."

The Latin station Decker was playing suddenly began playing polka music. Phil felt a slight disconnection as if he had stood up too fast.

"Oh yeh," Phil said. "Historical perspective is your bag. You should call this magazine *The Long View.*"

"The test of time," Decker said. "Just how much shit runs downhill."

"Hell, Decker, if you wait long enough, downhill ain't downhill no more."

The Action

The gray Ford followed Elliott out of Austin, as he headed north toward Wilson's ranch. Phil thought about trying to lose him, but he wanted to know who this guy was and what he wanted.

His knees ached and he still hadn't hooked up the two TENS electrodes between his shoulder blades. He thought for a moment about asking the guy in the gray Ford for some help, but instead he drove out to the I-35 and headed north.

He turned on the cruise control, then twisted in the seat and straightened his legs slightly. It lessened the pain in his knees and right ankle, where a compound break and dislocation had improperly healed.

The gray Ford was about a quarter mile back and stayed there.

Phil Elliott had been driving about an hour when he had to take a piss. He also needed to get out of the car and walk around. His hands and right leg had lost all feeling.

After he parked, Phil crawled slowly out of the car and held on to the open door, working his dead leg until the feeling began to return.

The gray Ford had pulled in and parked about fifty yards short of Elliott.

There was one other car and an eighteen-wheeler in the rest area.

Phil staggered awkwardly into the bathroom. He had just finished and was zipping up his pants when he heard the door open. Phil watched the man from the gray Ford move into the room and stop.

"Come on, Phil. Let's go to my car and talk."

"Who the hell are you?" Phil demanded.

The man looked hurt. He sucked in his gut and smoothed back his hair. "Don't tell me you don't remember the guy who stole your college girlfriend away from you!"

Phil Elliott's mouth did its best to drop all the way to the floor.

"Holy shit!" He looked into the middle-aged eyes of his onetime best friend and college basketball teammate. "Gates Ford!"

"Are you still with the malting company?" Phil wanted to know, sitting in Gates's car.

Gates Ford looked at him in amazement. "Don't you read the papers?"

"Only when I'm in jail and starved for entertainment."

"I was *only* front-page news a few years ago. International Malting turned out to be a front for the CIA. I wrote an exposé about it—*Inside Out*. Made the *Times* best-seller list for six weeks."

"Never heard of it," Phil apologized.

"You writers are all the same," Gates said. "Only looking out for yourselves. One critic even went so far as to call me a good writer for a lousy communist double agent."

"A money review if I ever heard one," Phil said. Then he looked at his old friend and said, "This reminiscing has been a lot of fun. But why the hell are you following me?"

"Because you are running with some major bad guys, my friend. And I thought you could use a hand."

Gates Ford stuck his hand out. After a moment's hesitation, Phil shook it.

He had a feeling he was making a mistake but he figured, *What the hell. If you can't trust an old teammate, who can you trust?*

Gates Ford had joined International Malting as he did many things in his life. By accident, blind and backwards. He was embarrassed by how easy he had been to recruit. The interviewer was a tall, distinguished gray-haired man who talked about how International Malting was looking for one "special man" who understood commitment and dedication. They met in one of those cubbyhole offices at the University Placement Bureau. Ford had been called to the interview by the university placement director.

The job offered was assistant to the president, at $1,250 a month with an automatic $500-a-month raise after the first six months. After one year, an evaluation session with the executive committee would decide Ford's future in the malting business. If he stayed with the company, his salary would be three thousand dollars a month, with merit raises.

Ford's few questions about the malting business and his specific responsibilities were deflected.

The tall gray-haired man gazed at Ford's transcript with apparent approval and said, "We would like for you to come to San Antonio and visit the plant and offices of International Malting. We're out by the Air Force base."

Ford went. The business had something to do with the brewing of beer but he was never quite sure what. They didn't need salesmen because they sold all the malt they could produce, and they didn't need buyers because they had guaranteed long-term supplies. International Malting *did* need an assistant to the president and Gates Ford "was just the man to fill the bill" because of his "unique qualities as an All-American basketball player." Ford's open agnosticism did not go down well with IMC, but they never let him know that. Ford was always encouraged to be "open and honest," which he was until he found out who really paid his salary.

At lunch in the teakwood-paneled executive dining room, Dillingham Butts, the president of International Malting, told Ford, "I like you. We all like you and want you to take this job. Do you like to travel? We have international accounts."

"What would I do?"

"Don't worry about the details," the president reassured. "You can learn those as you go along. Mainly it involves traveling in foreign countries as our . . . er . . . *my* representative." Dillingham Butts read the confusion in Ford's face as cunning. "Isn't the money enough?"

Ford couldn't figure out what the fuck this job entailed but the money was certainly enough. He said nothing, only because he didn't know what to say.

"How does fifteen hundred a month sound?" the president asked, upping the offer. As a starting salary for a twenty-two-year-old man with a degree in history and journalism, it sounded like a fortune. Ford nodded his acceptance, knowing his voice would fail him, break or quiver, and they would take back their offer.

"Congratulations." Dillingham Butts stood; lunch was suddenly over. "Let's go up and see your new office."

The spacious corner office had reflection glass outside walls and teakwood inner walls. The desk was massive and the recruiter—the small man with his gray flattop haircut—looked like a small boy as he sat behind it. Heavy leather sofas faced each other across a glass table in the center of the room, on top of a Persian rug. At the far end was a long conference table. Ford thought it looked like an office out of *Town and Country* magazine.

"The first thing you'll have to do is go to language school, because of all of our international accounts," Butts said. "We have a contract with the government school to train our people. Get the papers, Rupert." The recruiter left for a moment and returned with a legal-sized document one hundred pages thick.

"It's just routine. Since you'll be taught on a government installation we have to observe certain bureaucratic niceties." Butts spoke gently, studying the look in Ford's eyes. "Don't worry," he laughed. "We won't make you *read* it. Just sign where Rupert's got the X's."

And Ford did.

Gates Ford never saw the recruiter, Dillingham Butts, or the office again.

But he did go to Armed Forces Language School in California for ten months, where he studied ten hours a day for five days a week and five hours on Saturday. The whole class went crazy. Half were washed out in the first six months while the rest became alkies, dopeheads, or functionally insane.

Ford did as many drugs, drank as much alcohol and went as crazy as possible. But he finished the school. Two months later, the executive board of International

Malting Company interviewed him and declared him excellent material. The following day he flew to Panama
and visited with the head of the Latin American division.

When he signed the paper in his elegant new office,
Ford unknowingly agreed to do everything and anything,
including obeying the National Secrets Act. They never
told him what branch of the service he was in and,
eventually, when he got to Ethiopia, gave him uniforms
and badges for all ranks, from all branches.

First they sent him to a secret listening post in the
mountains of Ethiopia to intercept Russian radio and
television transmissions. The Ethiopian natives hated the
Americans and tried to kill them, if they could catch one
or two isolated. Guns were not allowed to be carried off
the base because they were afraid the men would start
killing Ethiopians. They were right about that. Ford wanted
to kill Ethiopians real bad after they stoned Bill Jones
from Cincinnati to death in the village square.

The Ethiopians caught him when he stopped to take a
piss and the three other guys with him walked on out of
sight. They stoned and stomped him to red mush.

Bill Jones from Cincinnati was regular army, and was
there when Ford arrived. Jones taught him how to throw
rocks at the Ethiopians to keep them away. He taught
Ford which rocks had the best trajectory, which were
good for distance, which rocks had real "stopping power"
but were light and small enough to carry in your pockets.

They sent Bill Jones home through Vietnam and told
his parents a truck he was riding in struck a mine just
outside of Saigon. His letters had all been censored so his
family never knew he wasn't in Vietnam. They never knew
he had been smashed to death somewhere in the Stone Age.

After they shipped the body bag to Vietnam, Ford
broke into the post armory and stole an M1911 .45 automatic and two hundred rounds of ammunition.

Ford was carrying it two days later when the same
Ethiopians followed him as he walked alone through the
village square. He let them get real close and then killed
all six of them. The neolithic savages were too surprised
to run. They knew that American policy prohibited guns.

"They were stunned, standing there with their mouths
open," Gates Ford told Elliott, as they sat in the car. "I

watched them try to understand." His face flushed and
Ford laughed. "All I did was revoke their diplomatic
immunity. A minor change in U.S. policy seemed to
make a big difference to them."

"Do me a favor, Gates," Phil said when his old friend
had finished telling his story. He pulled the two cables
for his TENS unit from his shirt pocket. "Help me hook
these up. My fucking back is killing me."

Gates plugged the cables into the electrodes. "Do you
feel as bad as you look?" Ford asked.

"Worse."

"Maybe this'll help."

Ford unlocked his briefcase and pulled out a thick
manila envelope. "Show these to Wilson and nobody
else. He'll tell you it's all inadmissible in court, but now
you'll know what you're up against. It's always good to
understand what motivates your enemies."

When Phil took the envelope, Gates said, "Now what
do you got for me?"

Operating on the theory that you have to trust somebody or go completely crazy, Phil Elliott told Gates Ford
everything he knew about Ross Denham and Bobby
Laughlin, D-L Financial and the various enterprises they
were involved in from Central America and Mexico to
Nevada and Texas.

When Phil was done, Gates stared at him in surprise,
but said nothing. He extended his hand one more time
and again Phil shook it. Ford started the car and opened
the door on Elliott's side.

Phil stepped out, Gates backed up the gray car and
drove off, leaving Elliott standing on the pavement with
the envelope in his hand.

Scott

Elliott turned in through the gate to John Wilson's place. It was not quite dark and Phil could see them all sitting on the front porch watching the last of the sunset.

A small figure burst off the porch and came running down the drive. It was Scott. Phil immediately recognized his son. The way he ran, his head up and his arms flailing wildly. Scott ran with joyous abandon. The sight brought tears to Elliott's eyes, as the sight of his boy always did, since the day he was born.

Phil stopped the car and got out, waiting to scoop the boy up and hold the little body to his.

"Dad!" Scott seemed to fly through the air. Phil caught him and hugged him, feeling the little arms around him, the small hands on his back. He kissed the boy on the neck.

"Squeeze me tighter, Dad!" The voice seemed so familiar, yet so different, as did everything about him. He had changed so much. Could it have only been two weeks? It seemed like forever.

Phil hugged the delicate body tighter, afraid to squeeze as hard as he wanted.

Scott started kissing him all over the face. It was a tickling sensation and felt wonderful. Then they hugged each other again.

"It took you so long to get here." Scott started talking, rapidly, as he crawled into the car and scrambled across the seat, pulling down the middle armrest to sit on. Scott

246

always sat on the armrest, right next to Phil. "Where have you *been?* I've been waiting and waiting. We rode horses today and then went swimming. Wait'll you see the swimming pool. Are we going fishing tonight? Remember, you promised. They got a whole bunch of baby cats, I mean, kittens in the barn. I'll show you. . . ."

He kept on as Phil eased in behind him and closed the door. He slipped the car into gear and continued up the drive.

" . . . and then Johnnie fell off the horse into these bushes and got stuck. I had to go get his mom to get him out and he cried and cried but I didn't cry at all. Yesterday, we chased the ducks on the pond with golf clubs until Johnnie's dad caught us. He got pretty mad, they were his brand new clubs, but we didn't hurt 'em or anything, we just hit the water and mud. We didn't hit the ducks. We *did* hit some frogs with 'em but we didn't tell. You won't tell, will you, Dad? It would get Johnnie's dad *real* mad and we already hit the frogs so there isn't nothin' we could do to make it better. Oh, Dad!" The little arms went around Phil's neck. "I missed you sooo much. I'm so glad you're here."

Phil patted the little arms and said nothing. Then, he wiped the tears from his cheeks with the backs of his hands.

"What's the matter, Dad?"

"My cheeks itch."

"Oh, I'll scratch 'em for you." The little fingers were all over his face rubbing and scratching. "Your face is wet."

"I got sweaty on the drive up. It was hot."

"Gosh, no kidding? It's been cold here."

Phil parked the car on the apron of the driveway.

They walked hand in hand to the front porch.

In his free hand, Phil carried the envelope from Gates Ford.

"Whattaya got in the envelope, Dad? Did you bring me a surprise?"

Phil's heart sank. He had completely forgotten to bring a present.

"Yeh, I brought you a surprise," Phil lied. "But you don't get it until tomorrow."

"My dad brought me a surprise!" his son said, proudly,

as Phil followed him shamefaced onto the porch. "But I can't open it until tomorrow."

John Wilson was at the head of the steps with his hand out.

"Good to see you made it," Wilson said.

"This is *your* surprise." Elliott slapped the envelope into his hand. "We can talk about it later. Hi, Jane." Phil spoke to Wilson's wife who was sitting on the swing. Both of her children were asleep on either side with their heads resting in her lap.

"Johnnie and June fell asleep, Dad. They couldn't wait up for you. But *I* did." The boy was so proud.

"I'm glad you did, Son." Phil bent down awkwardly, painfully, and gave Scott a big kiss on the lips.

"Scott, you know what?" Jane spoke in a whisper. "I'll bet if you go get dressed for bed, your dad will let you open your present tonight. Then, tomorrow bright and early, you two can go fishing."

"All riiight!" Scott headed into the house on a dead run. As soon as the boy was out of sight, Phil turned to Jane with a look of distress.

"Don't you say a word, Phillip Elliott," Jane said. "You think I don't know you well enough to know how you are about remembering to give gifts? His present is already wrapped and in the front closet. So get that dumbass look off your face and go bring it out here. It's a Nintendo entertainment system. That's all he's been talking about. That and how he hoped his dad would remember that he wanted one."

Shame and embarrassment, sadness and pain, love and gratitude washed over Phil, all at once.

"Now don't fall all to pieces on me. We've been friends a long time." Jane smiled. "You can just add it to John's fee."

"Where's Delma?" Phil regained some control.

"He couldn't wait up either," John said. "He's still on penitentiary time."

By the time the boy was back, all washed, teeth brushed and dressed in his Michigan State pajamas, the packages were stacked on the porch table. Phil and John had carried Johnnie and June into bed.

Scott tore into the wrapping and paper ripped and tore and flew everywhere, as the little boy dug for the prizes hidden inside.

"A Nintendo! Dad! You remembered!" He rushed over to where Phil was sitting, holding a glass of tequila, and jumped in his lap. Again the little arms and small hands went around Phil's neck and this time squeezed so hard they hurt his neck. Phil didn't mind.

In fact, he hugged the little body even closer to him and hung on for dear life.

You've Got to Change Your Evil Ways—*Then*

Satler Lomax was on time for his meeting with Head Coach B. A. Quinlan. He brought his playbook and his searing disappointment with him and was sitting with the other four players in the team office lobby when Phil Elliott walked in carrying *his* playbook.

Satler Lomax was surprised. He was unhappy about the fact he was going to be released by Dallas but he wasn't surprised. They had picked him up on waivers from Chicago and then just used him to hold dummies. He had less than three minutes of total playing time and he was a rookie. Rookies didn't have much chance of making it. And worse, he was a free agent. No one had thought enough of him to draft.

But Phil Elliott getting cut was a surprise. Satler Lomax couldn't believe it, but here was Elliott, looking just as disappointed as the rest of them.

Elliott had played in every game and, combined with Delma Huddle, they had turned the passing game around. Seth Maxwell finally had someone to throw to who could catch and run.

Just goes to show me that my old man was right, Lomax thought. Satler Lomax was the son of a wealthy Houston oil man who had sent him off to Cornell. Satler had wanted to play football at A&M. But his old man made him settle for the Ivy League.

"I've got connections in the East, boy, and you're gonna be a politician or a diplomat, if it kills us both," the Old Man had said.

Now Satler Lomax was sitting in the team offices, realizing how smart his father really had been. By donating huge sums of money to the party in power, the Old Man had secured the promise of a job at the State Department for Satler.

The job didn't start until November, which had given Satler his chance to take a shot at big-time football. He had failed and this morning he would turn in his playbook. He wasn't sorry. He hadn't quit. He just didn't have the talent. It was apparent to him and he was proud to have lasted until the final cut.

But Phil Elliott being cut, that didn't make any sense at all.

Satler Lomax was still thinking about Elliott when he sat down in front of Coach Quinlan. He was so preoccupied that he didn't hear much of B.A.'s standard waiver speech, except for the obviously special parts thrown in just for him.

"You have great character, Satler, and I'm sure it will take you far in politics. I wish we had a spot for you because of the real special nature of your character." B.A. paused. Satler suddenly realized that his father had *arranged* for him to be picked up by Dallas, a sort of extended summer camp on toughing the old character. "In fact, it makes me doubly sad to have to let you go, when right after you leave I'm going to have to call in a player whose talent is forcing me to go against my better instincts about his character. I brought him in this morning with his playbook to teach him a little lesson in who runs the world. But I'm going to keep him because of his talent. He needs your character, because you understand how the world runs and who runs it. This guy. . . ."

Phil Elliott! Satler Lomax thought, smiling to himself. *He's keeping Elliott and it's killing him. Yeh, you dumbass, I know how the world runs and who runs it. I learned it from my dad, not from you. My dad is one of the men with real power in this world.* And, suddenly, it was all right not to be playing football for this clown. *My old man buys and sells guys like you every day and I'm going to play the games my dad plays,* Satler Lomax was thinking, as he realized the speech was over and the room was silent. He stood and walked out, leaving B.A. standing there with his hand outstretched.

As Satler Lomax passed Phil Elliott in the lobby, he winked and gave him the thumbs up sign, but Elliott was too devastated to catch the real meaning. He just smiled back wanly and shrugged his shoulders.

From that day on, Satler Lomax always felt that he and Phil Elliott shared a special bond.

So as Satler Lomax sat in his hotel room in Dallas, waiting for Gates Ford to report on his meet with Phil Elliott, he pondered all this past history.

It was as if he was organizing a little reunion of his own.

Fishing Expeditions

"I got one, Dad!" Scott yelled, as his pole bent. The fish was trying to make a run for the weeds. The boy's face beamed, as he wrestled with the rod and reel.

"Okay. You've got him," Phil said, calmly, as he reached up and grabbed the belt of the boy's pants. Scott had jumped to his feet in the boat at the first tug on his line, and Phil didn't want him to fall in the pond.

"He's a big one, Dad!" The little hands clutched the rod and he tried to yank the fish clear out of the water and into the boat with one pull.

"Great. Great. Now, just start reeling him in." Phil held tightly to the belt, as the boat rocked. "You've got a big one, all right."

Slowly, but surely, Scott tugged and reeled, dragging the reluctant fish toward the boat. Phil caught sight of the bass, just before it broke the surface of the water. It *was* a big fish, three or four pounds, and he wasn't going to get into the boat quietly.

The fish leaped out of the pond, shaking its head, trying to throw the hook. Scott's eyes doubled in size.

"Holy shit!" the little boy said and redoubled his efforts.

Phil had to strain to keep from laughing. He didn't want this fish to get away. He didn't want his boy to be disappointed. His heart was hammering as the fish made another spectacular jump and headed back toward the weeds.

"Don't let him get into the weeds." Phil couldn't keep his mouth shut.

"I won't!" Scott was irritated at the interruption. "I *know* what I'm doing." He pulled back on the rod and dropped it forward, quickly reeling in the slack line, keeping the hook tightly embedded in the big bass's mouth.

It took about five minutes, but to Phil it seemed like an eternity, before the boy had tired the fish and brought him alongside the boat. Elliott dipped the net under him and lifted the big bass into the boat.

"That's a big one, isn't it, Dad?"

"That's a huge one."

"Let's put him back."

"You want to throw him *back?*"

"Sure." Scott smiled, proudly. "I've caught bigger ones. If I put him back, I can catch him again. John makes me clean all the fish I keep."

"Well," Phil looked into the live basket trailing behind the boat. "We have plenty of bluegills and sunfish to clean."

"Good. Let's quit. I want to go play with my Nintendo."

As Phil rowed back to the shore, Scott suddenly asked, "Why doesn't Mom ever call me?"

"I don't know that, son." Phil paused. "One thing you should always remember is that your mother and I always love you. What went wrong between your mother and I was *not your fault.* I'm sorry that you are the one who has to be unhappy because your mother and I made mistakes with our lives."

"I must have done something wrong."

"No! You have to promise me that you will always remember that you *never* did anything wrong. When you feel unhappy, don't ever think it's your fault that you're unhappy. Try, instead, to just think about things that make you happy. You're a little boy. You're supposed to have fun and not worry about things."

The boat settled into shore and they climbed out.

"All right, Dad. I'll try." They walked along together in silence. Phil frantically searched his mind for something to say, some way to ease the boy's obvious pain. But if he found something, it would just be another artfully concocted deceit.

"Listen," Phil said, finally. "Why don't you run on up and wash? Then you play with your Nintendo and I'll get Delma to help me clean the fish."

"You sure, Dad?"

"I'm sure." Phil bent awkwardly and kissed his son, then gave him a pat on the bottom, sending him on his way up the hill to the house. He watched the little boy run, looking for signs of himself.

All he saw were reminders of her.

"Nigger work," Delma said, as he grabbed the last fish and ran the fillet knife along its spine. Delma Huddle's face was lean but deeply lined. Phil hardly recognized him when he came in that morning and woke them to go fishing. He still had the well-muscled body that had propelled him down a football field like a rocket but he was completely bald.

"It fell out by the handsful," Delma said, catching Phil's gaze. "During the trial and my first few months in prison, my hair *just fell* off my head. I was totally bald by the end of the first year."

John Wilson walked in and sat down at the kitchen table with Delma and Phil.

"Jo Bob's here. Helene and Jane are going to take the kids to Six Flags," Wilson announced. "Maxwell is due any minute."

"Well, I'll be a motherfucker!" Jo Bob Williams walked into the kitchen, his huge frame filled the doorway. "A lawman's wet dream, a kitchen full of convicts."

"I don't see you wearing no piece, Sheriff." Delma twirled the fillet knife. "I could have you looking like one of these here fish in no time."

"Why don't you just come here and give us a kiss." Jo Bob laughed and lumbered over to Delma who stood up. They hugged. "Goddamn, I am sorry, Delma."

"Ain't nothing you coulda done, Jo Bob. They set me up and took me off."

"Well, the hunt ain't over until I piss on the fire." Jo Bob released Delma and clamped his huge hand onto Wilson's shoulder. "Between us and the legal eagle, we'll get you out of that place."

"We already got him out," Elliott said. "Let's work on *keeping* him out."

"You better work on keeping yourself out," Jo Bob said. "I'm tired of taking care of your narrow ass."

"Before I forget." Wilson turned to Elliott. "I talked to Stein this morning and your wife is willing to consider dropping the receivership action, if you'll take out a two-hundred-and-fifty-thousand-dollar insurance policy with her as beneficiary."

"That's kinda like painting a target on his back, ain't it, counselor?" Jo Bob asked.

"Otherwise, we got more problems." Wilson did not respond to Jo Bob. "Courtnay's filed more paper today, claiming you broke into her house and tried to strangle her."

"Fuck!" Phil yelled. "Why would she do that?"

"Because her lawyer told her to," Wilson said. "Clients often do what their lawyers tell them. I know *you* find that hard to believe. Stein says they'll drop that too, if you agree to the insurance policy."

"Stein claimed he had a plan to eliminate me in that letter to Denham I found in his briefcase," Elliott said. "It's like they're trying to drive me to killing her."

Delma finished cleaning the fish and said, "I had a cellmate. He was in on murder two and always swore to me that he was framed. His wife kept screaming that he was trying to kill her. Finally, somebody *did* kill her and they didn't look no farther than that poor motherfucker. He said her lawyer ended up with everything they owned, just showed up in probate court after the murder trial with a general power of attorney signed by the dead woman and walked out with it all."

Phil was suddenly very frightened. He got up and went into the guest bedroom. Momentarily, he returned with the notes he had taken at Courtnay Howard-Elliott's house, including the name he found under the desk pad and the information from Stein's briefcase. "Find out who this guy is and what he has to do with Courtnay." Phil handed the name to Wilson.

"Tom Reece?" Wilson read the name. "This shouldn't take long." He left the room to make a phone call and returned shortly. "I have a private detective I use in El Paso. I told him it was hot and to go see this guy. But right now, we need to hear Delma's story."

"My story is simple." Delma began pacing the kitchen.

"They pulled me in front of a grand jury and immunized me. They want names, mostly ex-players. If I say these guys used drugs, I'm out in six months. If I don't give them names, I do the whole sentence." Delma stopped pacing and looked at his ex-teammates. "I don't mind telling you, being a stand-up guy is not very appealing right now."

"What names?"

"It's a strange list," Delma said. "It's not who you would think. Elliott's not on it."

"So many people got him by the balls," Jo Bob said, "they probably don't figure they can even get a handhold."

"Maxwell's on the list," Delma blurted out. "Guys like that. The big money players. The stars."

"Any active players?"

"Some."

"Have you gotten any help from the union?" Phil asked. "You and Thomas Richardson were good friends from our rookie year on."

"I ain't heard shit from the union," Delma said. "It's funny you should mention Thomas. You guys remember when Conrad was dying and Denham and Laughlin were in the process of buying him out?"

Everybody nodded.

"It was just before Richardson went to work full-time for the union," Delma continued. "Thomas was trying to be a player's agent at the time. Well, not many people know this. Thomas told me one night, when we were both pretty drunk. It was after I got busted. Anyway, Conrad called Thomas up to the hospital for a meeting. When he got there, Conrad had ten new contracts drawn up for players who were already signed. The money was huge, but the base salaries were exactly the same. Conrad had given them millions of dollars in deferred money. He asked Thomas if he thought he was a good enough agent to get these guys to sign the new contracts and then keep their mouths shut. Thomas did it."

Delma stopped talking, but continued pacing.

"And?" Wilson finally asked.

"All ten of those guys are on the list."

"I don't get it," Jo Bob said.

"I do." Elliott stood up suddenly. "Don't you see? D-L Financial has money problems. I know that somehow Conrad sold them a bill of goods and this deferred money is some of it. They've got Delma in civil court suing him for fraud. D-L Financial is claiming that Delma used drugs when he was a player and violated the clause about keeping yourself in the proper physical condition to play football. If they win against Delma, they'll refuse to pay him the deferred money due on his contracts. If Delma names these names to the grand jury, D-L Financial will go to them with the grand jury testimony and suggest they forget their deferred money and trust in God and good fortune to keep them out of the criminal courts. If they refuse, they'll haul them into civil court and start screaming about drug use."

"But grand jury testimony is supposed to be secret," Jo Bob said.

"Where the hell have you been?" Wilson said.

"I stand corrected. You fucking jail-house lawyers."

"We need to find a way to look at more of D-L Financial's books," Elliott said. "Just what I saw in that briefcase tells me they got more money problems than deferred contracts to football players."

"Why don't we just call 'em up, asshole?" Jo Bob said. "Maybe they'll have somebody run 'em on over here to us, just before they kill us all. You do understand these people are tangled up in murder?"

"Is that what O.W. told you?"

"After awhile."

"We may not have to *ask* anybody for that kind of information," Wilson said. "There is some guy going around handing it out in envelopes in roadside restrooms."

"No!" Elliott spun and looked at Wilson.

"Yes." Wilson nodded his head, slowly. "It isn't a complete set of books or anything like that, just some photocopies of ledger entries and incorporation papers. But it's more than enough to start. D-L Financial has their fingers in a lot of pies. Some of the pies don't belong to them and others may well be illegal."

"We've got a decision to make in a hurry," Delma said.

"What's that?"

"What do we tell Maxwell?"

Wet Work

"I say we kill her now and have the son of a bitch arrested in front of everybody at the reunion." Colonel Glanton grinned, showing his oversized teeth. "That ought to make the papers."

"Hold on, Colonel." David Stein held up both hands. "That's only a contingency plan. I won't allow you to make some idiotic unilateral decision here."

"I'd like to see you stop me, you little Jew fuck."

"I don't have to sit here and take this abuse," Stein protested.

"How about *this* abuse?" Colonel Glanton reached across the desk in Stein's office and slapped him across the face. The force of the blow knocked the small man against the back of his chair.

"Christ! You're crazy!"

"Fuck you! I'm a military man and I take action when my men are threatened. This asshole is going around asking questions about our operations. Deputy Meadows has disappeared and Douglas, the game warden, is deader than JFK. So don't try laying any of your legal double-talk. You're either a soldier or a straw man in this operation. You better decide which, pronto!" Glanton glared at Stein. "Because the straw men are going to get lit up real soon."

"All right, calm down," Stein said as he carefully pulled the bottom drawer of his desk open with his foot. Inside, within easy reach, was a stainless steel .357 revolver. "I called you here about something else entirely. You have a flight into Panama scheduled for this week and you're going to come back with a full load."

"I thought we had decided it was too hot to be bringing back full planes."

"This order comes from the top," Stein went on. "We have to have two million dollars cash next week, minimum. We need operating funds, so pack that plane full. I've already made arrangements at both ends. The Panamanians will wait for their end, but Beaudreau will be at the Purgatory Military Institute with the cash on delivery."

"Why don't they just take it out of one of the goddamn banks they own?" Glanton didn't like this end of the work. "What the hell is the use of owning all those banks if you can't take the money when you want it?"

"You may not have noticed the state of the economy, but currently the banks and savings and loans are tapped out," Stein told him as condescendingly as he could manage. "We could do some juggling but with the feds all over the banks, now is not the best time to do that. Hell, the paperwork alone would take more time than we have. The people in New Jersey want the money."

"I'm not scared of those flat-nosed hoodlums," Glanton said. "If they want to go to war, I'll show them what the hell war is all about."

"I'm sure you would, Colonel," Stein said. "But keep in mind, when they fight a war, they kill the officers first. Unless you want to spend the rest of your life having your wife start your car for you in the morning, I would do what I was told."

"I'm going on the record now against this operation."

"It is duly noted, Colonel." Stein smiled. "Now, if you don't mind, I have other business to attend."

Colonel William Glanton left, as David Stein dialed Ross Denham's private line, bypassing the switchboard at D-L Financial Group.

"Denham."

"This is David. I filed the papers on Elliott and made the offer to his lawyer this morning. Wilson said he'd get back to me after he talked to Elliott."

"What if he agrees?"

"I'll tell him we've changed our minds and we're considering filing more complaints to the court," Stein replied. "If he's smart, he'll give us the Purgatory land and go back to Michigan where he belongs. He should have stayed there when I had him run out before Bob Beaudreau's murder trial."

"We own the judge," Denham said, "so the receivership suit is a certain lock. Elliott hasn't any choice but to do what we tell him now."

"It's just that the son of a bitch *never* does what he's supposed to do."

"He will this time."

"I'm not so sure," Stein said. "Courtnay's been a real pain in the ass lately. It worries me. I'm afraid she might have run off at the mouth to Elliott about Tom Reece."

"So? What's the big deal?" Denham asked. "She was married before."

"She never divorced him."

"You've got to be kidding me." Denham's voice went soft, a sure sign that he was angry. "She's a bigamist?"

"Yeh." Stein was nervous. Denham would hold this problem against him personally.

"If she's a bigamist, that would make all her claims against Elliott groundless." Denham's voice was barely audible. Stein knew he was in big trouble.

"I've been thinking about a new course of action," Stein said.

"Colonel Glanton has a plan he thinks is foolproof. I'm beginning to think he may be right," Denham whispered. "You've got her power of attorney?"

"Yes," Stein replied. Sweat beads had broken out on his forehead. "But I think that is very drastic and should only be used as our final fallback. It puts me way out on a limb."

"You're already way out on a limb, buster." Denham spoke softly, slowly. "I could always give you to the boys from New Jersey. You're the straw man in the Nevada operations. I could save myself two million dollars and be rid of you and them."

"Hold on a minute, Mr. Denham. You need me."

"I don't *need* anybody, pal," Denham shot back. His voice raised only slightly. "I *use* people. I don't ever *need* them. I bought a whole football team just to *use* them."

"If you will recall," Stein said, regaining his composure, "I warned you that you were going too fast on that deal and time has proven me right. We wouldn't have cash flow problems if you'd let me take more time to look over those books. Conrad Hunter hid a ton of debt in the stadium lease, he renegotiated ten contracts with millions in deferred money that wasn't funded and then he cashed in the annuities on all the past deferred contracts."

"He committed a major fraud," Denham said.

"So what are you gonna do?" Stein began to take command. "Dig him up and sue him?"

"The football team is *not* the issue here!" Denham finally blew. "The issue is that we have a big exposure on your latest girlfriend and you failed to ever mention it."

"I thought it was under control," Stein said. "I had paid off Reece, as soon as I learned about him and the two daughters . . ."

"Two daughters!" Denham was furious. "She and Reece have two kids?"

"Listen to me," Stein said. He stood up and walked to the window of his top-floor office. "Reece is no problem. He's married again and got more kids." Looking out his window, across San Antonio, Stein's eyes fixed on the top floor above the coin shop at Commerce Street and the river. It was Elliott's apartment. "I called this morning and she hasn't contacted him or the girls. I'll handle her. Don't worry."

"You *better* handle her." Denham's voice had again dropped to a whisper. "Or I'll have the colonel do it."

"Fine, Mr. Denham. Consider it done." Stein heard the click as Denham hung up. He was feeling better. It was just a little glitch.

Everybody settles, eventually, even Elliott. Stein smiled to himself. *Settling is what lawsuits are about. At some point, everybody quits.*

At that moment, Colonel Glanton was answering his car phone. It was Ross Denham.

"Get over here. We got a people problem," Denham said.

Glanton grinned as he recradled the phone and made a left turn.

"People problem?" he said to himself. It was a personal code between him and Denham.

Colonel Glanton had some wet work to do.

The King—*Now*

"I brought the Purgatory tax rolls, like you asked." Jo Bob Williams returned to the kitchen with an armful of ledgers. He stacked them in front of Elliott.

Phil tapped the top ledger. "These have the names of the people who bought property in River Ranch Estates?"

"Everybody who owns or bought property in the county up to the first of last month," Jo Bob replied. "Going back fifteen years."

"How did you get them?" John Wilson wanted to know.

"Purgatory County's sheriff is also the tax assessor," Jo Bob explained.

"What are we looking for?" Delma asked.

"Names," Phil replied.

"Well, you got the right books." Delma flipped one open. "This one is full of names."

"We're looking for familiar names, or a pattern of names," Phil said. "Something like that. I'm guessing that one of D-L Financial Group's schemes was to loan money to anybody to buy land in River Ranch Estates without any expectation that the money would ever be paid back. Then, once they had filled up one of their savings and loans with bad paper, they would sell it off, buy another, or get a new S&L charter and do the same thing again."

"The classic land flip bust-out scheme," Wilson said, and then left the room. He returned shortly with the envelope Gates Ford had given Elliott. "Here are some partial loan records of a Dallas S&L that D-L Financial owns. You guys will be interested in the names." Wilson pulled the sheets from the envelope.

All four men gathered around the copies of the savings and loan company records.

"It's almost all ballplayers and coaches," Delma said. "All Dallas players."

"And all nonperforming," Wilson added. "Look who else is there."

"The King? Maxwell?" Delma shook his head in astonishment. "And B.A.!"

"Goddamn! Here's James High. He's the state banking commissioner."

"But these aren't real estate loans," Elliott pointed out. "These are personal notes, unsecured."

"Look at this! David Stein for two hundred thousand dollars, unsecured." Jo Bob ran a thick finger down the list of names. "O. W. Meadows for twenty five thousand dollars and Tony Douglas for the same, both unsecured."

"And never paid back, would be my guess," Phil said grimly. "All right, let's see if any of the same names show up on the Purgatory tax rolls."

The names were all there as purchasers of River Ranch Estates properties. The first liens on all the properties were held by other D-L Financial Group S&Ls.

"They're using these S&Ls like their personal little piggy banks."

"Look back at the other names on the Dallas S&L," Wilson said. "There's Louis Lafler, chairman of parks and wildlife."

"Which explains his enthusiastic support for condemning the Blaine Ranch and turning it into a golden eagle refuge."

"These people here," Wilson checked off several names with large cash loans, "are state legislators. They're responsible for pushing through the municipal utility district that D-L Development needs to make River Ranch Estates even possible."

"Look at the babe that got one of the biggest loans of all." Jo Bob pointed at the list.

"Felice McShane," Phil said. "Like I couldn't have guessed."

"We need to get down to the hospital and see Alan Claridge," Wilson decided.

"How's he doing?" Jo Bob asked.

"Not good. Yesterday, we got to talking about Denham and Laughlin. He told me that they had an incredible amount of influence in D.C. He didn't say any more, but he wanted to. I think if Phil and I go see him, tell him what we know and show him these documents, he might open up to us."

"What do the sheriff and I do?" Delma asked.

"You keep Maxwell company," Wilson ordered. "Tell him we're at the hospital with Alan, but don't tell him anything about what we know."

"What we *think* we know," Phil added. "If I know Maxwell, he won't be too anxious to visit the AIDS ward."

"Speak of the King . . ." Jo Bob was looking out the kitchen door, through the living room picture window.

A white stretch Cadillac limo was making the turn into Wilson's driveway.

"I figured he'd show up riding that big white horse from his TV show," Delma said.

"It's probably inside the limo," Elliott told him. "Serving drinks and watching the stock market tape for him."

"So what *do* we tell him?" Jo Bob asked.

"That he's great," Delma said. "He'll take it from there."

The Congressman

Alan Claridge was hardly recognizable. His athlete's body was withered and covered with open, running sores, and his mouth and lips were a mass of canker and cold sores.

"So?" Claridge kept his eyes on the television but he seemed to be staring through the screen. His eyes sunk deep in the sockets. "What do you guys really want?"

"What do you mean, Alan?" Wilson protested feebly. "We came by to see how you're feeling."

"B.A. called me today." Claridge's dead eyes never moved. "He told me Elliott might show up here and be careful what I said."

"Are you being careful?" Elliott asked.

"It's way too late to be careful." Claridge glanced slowly at Elliott, then moved his eyes back to the television. "Are you writing another book or just out looking for trouble, like the old days?"

"A little of both, I guess."

Claridge tried to smile, but it was too painful. The attempt broke open several scabs on his lips. They began to bleed.

"What did Andy Crawford tell you?" Claridge closed his eyes against the pain.

"That he met Ross Denham and Bobby Laughlin through the Southwest Conservative Trust when he was raising money for your first campaign for Congress," Phil began. "And later, Denham and Laughlin pulled him into a smuggling scheme with Dickie Lafler. Arms and men into Central America and cocaine and cash back out to the Purgatory."

"That's about all he really knew." Alan Claridge opened his eyes and tears ran down his cheeks. "As soon as I got to D.C., they put me on the House Banking, Finance, and Urban Affairs Committee. They wanted me to learn the art of the pork barrel."

"Who is 'they'?" Wilson asked.

"All the politicians that D-L Financial own. There are a lot of them and most of 'em are silent partners in D-L Financial. They raised millions for B.A. when he ran for governor. They funnel the money through the Southwest Conservative Trust's political action committee and through the individual members, plus other PACs they have set up in Texas, Virginia, and Maryland. D-L Financial collected a lot of chits and so far the guys in their pockets have been able to stop any investigations of D-L Financial's savings and loans."

"I heard that D-L had cash flow problems," Elliott prodded.

"They do, but they're short-term problems. It's only because the federal money they were expecting got held up on a legislative technicality." Claridge's lips barely moved. He just lay motionless in the bed, as the information poured from his brain. It was a frightening sight. "Right now, in Washington, there is twenty-five million dollars for the Purgatory Military Institute's airport. It's part of an emergency funding for the drug war. It only cost D-L twelve million dollars to build the airport. The theory is that the airstrip will allow the drug warriors another base from which to operate aircraft to patrol the border. What isn't mentioned is that a fully operational airport makes the River Ranch Estates Industrial and Office Park viable. They can jump right into the Maquiladora Program with a fully operational airport."

"But Crawford said they are using that airstrip to *smuggle* drugs!" Wilson said.

"Well, that's actually something that falls in Phil's area of expertise," Alan replied. "What would you call that, Phil?"

"Ironic," Elliott replied.

"See." Claridge's voice rose slightly. "The boy knows it when he sees it."

"Is there more?" Wilson asked, his legal mind whirring, searching for a handhold.

"Lots. And not just D-L Financial." Claridge felt the blood running from the open cold sores down onto his chin. "Hand me that gauze pad, John. Be careful, don't touch any blood. I'm one poisonous son-of-a-bitch."

Wilson handed Claridge a clean gauze pad from the pile on the bedside table. Alan moved slowly, taking the pad and blotting up the blood on his face.

"Did I get it all?" Claridge never moved his eyes from the television screen. The six o'clock news was just beginning.

"Yeh. You got it," Wilson said, absently reaching for the bloody pad.

"Hey!" Claridge quickly pulled the pad out of reach. It was the only movement he had made with any authority. "Don't touch the blood, dumbass!" He pushed the blood-soaked gauze into a plastic bag that hung on the far side of his bed. Claridge groaned as he moved. The pain was intense.

Nobody spoke.

B. A. Quinlan's face filled the TV screen.

"He's going to announce another new anticrime plan," Claridge said softly. "There's big money in crime, no matter what side you're on. The coach is on both sides and don't even know it. He thinks he got elected because he won a lot of football games and showed a lot of character."

"You mean he doesn't know what D-L Financial is all about?" Wilson asked.

"Well, let me put it this way." Claridge began to rasp, his throat filling with phlegm. "You two played many years for the man. What would you do? Tell him the truth or just fool him?"

"Fool him." Elliott and Wilson spoke in unison.

"He may know some things, but what he knows he don't really *know*." Claridge coughed. "If you get my drift."

Wilson and Elliott both nodded.

"He has appointed a new crime commission." Claridge's voice was getting weaker. "Felice McShane is the chairman. Steve Peterson, Art Hartman, and Bobby Laughlin are members. They've installed toll-free eight-hundred numbers so people can call long distance and snitch for free. They're offering rewards. B.A. said he wants to make the job of enforcing the law easier."

"Police work is only easy in a police state," Elliott mumbled.

"No shit, Sherlock." Claridge started to laugh but it quickly degenerated into a deep, hacking cough. When he stopped coughing, Claridge began talking again, hurriedly. Time was his enemy; nothing else scared him anymore. "In a few weeks, River Ranch Estates will get fourteen million dollars in Economic Development Administration grants, courtesy of a whole bunch of politicians, including myself. Plus, the Defense Department is granting five million dollars to the Purgatory Military Institute for the study of 'the border problem.' "

"Well, I guess my source on D-L Financial's money problems was wrong," Elliott said.

"Yes and no," Claridge replied. "The short-term cash problem is their most urgent and, as I have just explained, we have taken care of that. But the House Ethics Committee is about to start an investigation of me. My friends will stall it as long as possible, but eventually they will get to me. I am the cut-out man. I'll take the fall. That is one downside. The upside of the investigation is that by the time they get enough evidence, I'll be dead."

"*That's* the upside?" Elliott said. "You'll take the fall for a bunch of crooked politicians and D-L Financial and the Southwest Conservative Trust then fool everybody by *dying.*"

"Every cloud has a silver lining," Claridge said without emotion. "Now, long term, D-L Financial's oil operation, D-L Oilco, has some problems. They spun off into nuclear energy and began financing and building nuke plants. Now, it looks like a disaster. The costs skyrocketed and unless Washington orders the taxpayers and utilities to bail them out, the ripple effect could destroy them. We're talking billions of dollars here."

"Well, they covered themselves well in the Purgatory," Elliott said. "They're getting municipal utility district legislation that will allow them to own four coal-powered electrical plants and tax everybody in the district to pay for them, as well as their sewer and water facilities."

"Yeh, I know. Nobody said those boys were dumb. I'm just pointing out a *potential* problem. It is almost certain the federal government will order someone to bail them out." Claridge paused. "Unless . . . everything I just told you, plus what I'll bet you already know, was to become public information."

"Is this supposed to be the silver lining in *my* dark cloud?" Elliott asked.

"One of them," Claridge replied. "The other issue that B.A. suggested I avoid is letting you speculate on the potential problems of AIDS and professional football. Can you imagine how fast this disease would spread through a locker room?"

"Jesus! Do you think you were infected while you were playing?" Elliott asked.

"They don't know," Claridge said. "But Crawford has the antibodies in his blood and nobody is certain how long the incubation period might last. Some say as long as fifteen years."

"You and Crawford were both playing fifteen years ago," Elliott said. "In a locker room full of guys with open cuts and turf burns. The whole goddamn *team* could be infected!"

"I believe that is the kind of speculation the league is trying to avoid," Claridge said. "And I am not the only player to be diagnosed with AIDS. There is at least one other one who has died from it. And there are several other player deaths that are, at best, suspicious. The commissioner has ordered all team doctors to refuse to even comment on the possibility of AIDS in the locker room. They're not even supposed to test for it."

"Well, at least they're consistent in their head-in-the-sand approach," Elliott said grimly.

"Just remember," Claridge said. "You didn't hear any of this from me. At least, not while I'm still alive. Now you two get out of here. I'm tired."

The King's New Clothes

It was getting dark as John Wilson stopped his car in his driveway next to Maxwell's white limousine.

Delma Huddle, Jo Bob Williams, and Seth Maxwell were sitting on the front porch working their way through a bottle of one-hundred-proof Absolut vodka.

Maxwell's driver was asleep in the back of the limo. The women and kids had not returned from Six Flags.

"Drinks for my men." Maxwell staggered to his feet, as Elliott and Wilson stepped onto the porch. "And water for their horses." Seth was dressed in a western outfit he had taken from the wardrobe of his television series. "How's my boy Alan doing?"

"Not bad," Elliott said, taking the glass that Delma had filled and offered him, "for a dead man."

"Christ, Phil!" Wilson said. "Claridge is doing all right." He followed suit and took a full glass from Delma, then flopped down, exhausted, on a chaise lounge.

"Seth was just telling us about the politics of movies and television." Jo Bob changed the subject. "It all sounds real similar to professional football."

"The fucking network canceled me." Maxwell slumped down. "I was doing great and then some New York executive decides to put *The Scout* up against NBC's number one show. The Nielsen ratings killed me. That and Mitch Simmons Productions suddenly has a cash flow problem. I may have to sue them to get my syndication money. Goddamn Mitch won't even return my calls."

Seth Maxwell was extremely drunk. The other four men exchanged glances.

"Well, if you want to sue somebody," Phil offered, "feel free to use my lawyer. He works cheap."

"Thanks but no thanks," Wilson said. "One client like Elliott is enough. How bad is it, Seth?"

"I am flat busted," Maxwell slurred, trying to focus his eyes on John Wilson. "The goddamn football team owes me a shitload of deferred money but they ain't paid it and don't plan to pay it. They say I may have violated my contract when I was playing."

"Didn't you have any money saved or invested?" Wilson asked, shocked.

"Yeh. I had over a million dollars in CRH Bancshares," Maxwell replied. "I tried to unload them before Emmett ran the bank holding company into the ground, but it was like trying to sell swampland in Florida. Now the FDIC has stepped in and declared the holding company insolvent. D-L Financial bought all the banks for a song and my Bancshares stock is worthless."

"Seth, didn't Denham or Laughlin tell you what they were doing?" Phil asked.

Maxwell shook his head, then drained his glass and held it out for Delma to refill. "I never should have let those guys get me away from Conrad Hunter. Conrad wouldn't have done this to me."

"Conrad is dead, Seth," Elliott said. "Besides, you told me once, a long time ago, that you would never cross Conrad and then you went and left him for Denham and Laughlin, and Mitch Simmons' Hollywood Dream. Did you think Conrad would let you get away with that?"

"I didn't see how Conrad could do anything to hurt me."

"Well, he did," Wilson said. "My guess is he cashed in the annuities that were to fund your deferred payments. How much were you supposed to get?"

"Two hundred thousand dollars a year for twenty years," Maxwell said. "Starting this year."

Delma said, "Four million dollars! Fuck me!"

"They already fucked you, Delma," Maxwell observed.

"Well, turkey, they about to start fucking *you*."

"No sense confusing him with any of that now, Delma,"

Wilson said. "He looks confused enough for one night. What *are* you going to do, Seth?"

"I hired that hotshot attorney out of San Antonio." Maxwell turned his bleary eyes on John Wilson. "He says I'll have no problem getting my money."

"What hotshot attorney?" Wilson asked. His voice betrayed a note of worry.

"Who else," Elliott interrupted. "David Stein."

"How did you know?" Maxwell looked at Elliott.

"Just a lucky guess," Phil replied. "How much did he want in advance?"

"A hundred thousand," Maxwell said. "I'm going to have to sell my house to raise it."

"I wouldn't do that, Seth," Wilson advised.

"Why not?"

"Because David Stein is Denham and Laughlin's attorney," Elliott said. "He'll defend you to your last dime."

"He never said anything to me." Maxwell's voice turned small. "What's he talking about, John?"

"Stein is *their* attorney, Seth," Wilson explained. "And since D-L Financial bought the football team, *they* are the ones responsible for paying your deferred money. You're not the only player having trouble getting your deferred money. It is too complicated to go into tonight, but I wouldn't retain Stein if I were you."

"What should I do?"

"Right now, keep on getting drunk," Jo Bob suggested. "That's what I'm going to do."

"I'll drink to that," Delma said.

The ex-teammates sat on the porch and drank until the women and kids returned from Six Flags. Then Maxwell crawled back into his limo and headed for his penthouse in the hotel that was set up as headquarters for the reunion.

Jo Bob and Helene Williams left with their kids for Helene's parents' house where they would stay.

Phil Elliott put Scott to bed and sat with him until he fell asleep while describing how much fun he had on the latest terror ride at Six Flags.

When Phil came out of Scott's bedroom, only John Wilson and Delma were still awake. It was a little after 10:00 P.M.

"Jesus!" Elliott said, flopping on the floor in the living room. "What a day!"

"Do you remember when every day was like this?" Wilson asked. "Did you realize you were young then?"

"I do now," Elliott said. "God! I feel old."

"The idea now is that we *all* get older," Delma said, grinning. "And that ain't going to be as easy as it sounds."

"It was all so simple then," John Wilson said. "All we had to do was win on Sunday and the rest of the week took care of itself."

"It was like somebody else lived that life," Phil replied. "Phil Elliott, the football player, was a guy I knew but it sure doesn't seem like he was me."

"You realize the kids that are playing now weren't even born when we started playing?" Wilson asked. "It was all so long ago."

"All we got are memories and injuries," Delma said. "Sometimes, I don't know which hurts the most. I look in the mirror sometimes and just can't believe that's me, an old bald-headed ex-player. It's tough to get on with living."

"Sometimes I wish I could go back." Wilson was gazing at the carpet.

"I don't want to go back," Elliott said. "But I sure wish I felt like I was moving forward in some positive manner."

"Well, John," Delma asked, "any ideas on how I should handle myself in front of the grand jury? It's pretty obvious, after what Maxwell said tonight, what they're after. If I don't give it to them, somebody else will."

"Probably Maxwell." Elliott sighed.

"When do you have to appear?" John asked.

"Next week."

"What about your old college friend, Phil?" Wilson asked. "Do you think he has the clout to help us?"

"Probably," Phil replied. "The question is, *will* he?"

The phone rang. Wilson snatched it up, listened for a moment, then handed the receiver to Elliott.

Phil Elliott said, "Hello," listened for a few moments, then hung up.

"That was him," Elliott announced. "He wants me to meet him downtown. Now."

"Do you want me to go with you?" Wilson asked.

"No. He said to come alone. I'll listen for awhile and then ask what he can do about the grand jury. He says he has an old friend of mine with him." Elliott shook his head. "I can't wait to see who *that's* going to be."

"Are you carrying a gun?" Wilson asked.

"No." Elliott grinned. "I wouldn't know who to shoot at this point, anyway."

The Company Men

The address Gates Ford had given Phil Elliott over the phone was in a run-down warehouse district south of downtown.

The number was painted neatly on the blue door of the old brick warehouse. Elliott turned off the ignition and the headlights, then sat for a moment in the car, considering where he was and wondering why.

Finally, Phil stepped out of the car and walked to the door, trying the lock. The blue door swung open into a dimly lit, large storage room. Just inside the doorway to his right was a staircase.

"We're up here, Phil." Gates Ford's voice floated down to him.

The second floor was well lighted and completely furnished like an office. There was a bank of computers along one wall and several desks scattered around the large, open room. A partition cut off the back wall and the space was divided up into several offices.

Gates Ford and Satler Lomax were waiting at the head of the stairs.

"Phil, glad you could come," Ford said, then pointed to the man at his side. "You remember Satler Lomax."

Elliott stared at the man blankly. "To tell you the truth, I don't."

"We met years ago." Lomax smiled and extended his hand, trying to mask his disappointment. "I spent part of training camp with Dallas when you were a rookie."

"Sorry." Elliott shook Lomax's hand.

"I was cut the day B.A. brought you in to tell you he was going to keep you even though you had a bad attitude." Lomax laughed.

"Well," Elliott replied. "It never improved and he was finally able to get rid of me."

"You two will have to discuss old times later," Gates interrupted. "Phil, you went to see Alan Claridge at the hospital. What did he tell you?"

Phil frowned at Ford. "I don't remember agreeing to be a snitch for you."

"You're right. I'm sorry," Ford said. "He told you that the plan was for him to take the fall for D-L Financial and then die before they could get his testimony. He also told you that D-L Financial's money troubles were short-term and there would soon be a ton of federal money on the way to bail them out. And he told you that D-L Financial's involvement in nuclear power was causing them the most trouble." Ford smiled at Elliott. "Correct me if I'm wrong."

Elliott said nothing but he did look impressed.

"Well, here's what he doesn't know," Ford continued. "The federal money will never show up and D-L Financial could possibly collapse. Denham and Laughlin are in deep shit, along with their paramilitary pal, Colonel William Glanton. They just cowboyed it up too much out in the Purgatory country. Glanton headed up a little program they called the Picketline, you ever heard of it?"

"It sounds familiar." Elliott was expressionless.

"They put together a special unit of ex-military men, law officers, border patrolmen and customs agents," Ford explained. "Do you know what these guys did?"

Elliott shook his head.

"Under the overall command of Colonel Glanton, who took his orders from Denham, these assholes went out and patrolled the border, looking for wetbacks," Ford continued explaining. "And when they found them, they killed them—men, women, children. Your old teammates Tony Douglas and O. W. Meadows were involved."

"Why would they do that?" Elliott tried to betray no emotion. His stomach churned.

"A couple reasons," Ford replied. "First, Denham is your major right-wing anticommunist. He sees commies behind every bush. His theory was that at least half of the wets coming into this country were secretly communist terrorists."

"Bullshit!" Elliott said.

"That is exactly what we told him, when he came to the Agency with this theory five years ago," Satler Lomax interjected.

"Our mistake," Gates Ford continued, "was thinking that he was just making this argument so the federal government would finance the security of his River Ranch Estates Maquiladora Program. We figured he just wanted federal guarantees of security to take to potential participants in his industrial and office park. Big companies would feel safer about building plants and investing in property out there if there was some sort of military presence. When he created the Purgatory Military Institute, it seemed like the same kind of logic."

"We learned too late that we were wrong," Satler Lomax added. "The jerkoff *really* believed all those poor souls were part of a Soviet-Cuban-Nicaraguan plan to infiltrate southwest Texas. We figure he has killed hundreds, maybe thousands, of illegals."

"Why the hell didn't you stop him?" Elliott was frightened. It all made too much sense.

"We weren't really certain, and besides . . ." Ford hesitated.

"You were in business with the son of a bitch in Central America!" Elliott finished the sentence. "So as long as he was killing people nobody cared about, you didn't look too close."

"Phil, you're trying to make a very fluid, gray situation into solid black and white." Lomax picked up the conversation. "We weren't certain of anything, until your pal Sheriff Williams found that abandoned truck full of dead wetbacks and arrested a witness named Raul, who you met in jail."

"Who has conveniently disappeared," Phil added, "after they tried to kill him. He's probably dead now, or still running."

"We'll get to him in a minute," Gates Ford said. "As you told me when I first talked to you at the roadside park, Williams thinks Raul saw who put those people in the truck and left them to die. One of those involved was another ex-teammate of yours, Tony Douglas. And, as I understand it, Sheriff Williams has a witness who saw Raul kill Game Warden Douglas. Am I right so far?"

Phil Elliott nodded his head. His mind was racing. He was afraid for his son. He was afraid for everyone.

"Furthermore," Ford continued, "Sheriff Williams took another of your teammates and his deputy into custody, because he thought he was involved. That was O. W. Meadows. He sent Meadows into Mexico to be held by Augustino Estrada near Bahia. The Estrada family and the Blaines, who are Sheriff Williams' political allies, have been friends for years. The situation becomes very dicey at this point. We certainly want these killings stopped and the killers brought to justice but, even in a best-case scenario, you'll only get as far as Colonel Glanton before the unbroken chain of evidence ends."

"That'll do for starters," Phil said.

"Unfortunately, it's not good enough for us," Lomax replied. "We're talking about international borders and sovereign countries who must never learn of the Agency's participation in Denham and Laughlin's operations, including their companies in Central America."

"If you write about it," Gates Ford said, "we'll just deny it and sue you."

"Then what the hell am I doing here?"

"We're trying to help you," Lomax answered. "But you've got to help us."

"D-L Financial Group has serious cash flow problems." Gates picked up. "Some of them they don't even know about yet. Eventually, they are going to come to us to bail them out and we are going to refuse. At that point, they will really panic and begin to make big mistakes. They're already having trouble meeting the financial obligations incurred by their football team. Now, *there* is where you can write anything you want. We aren't involved in that and most people pay closer attention to football than they do to international politics. For instance, Denham has convinced your ex-coach and current governor that unless state and local tax funds are made available to the team, they're going to move the franchise."

"Governor Quinlan is going to start the ball rolling in the speech he's scheduled to give at the reunion dinner," Satler added. "We'll keep feeding you information about the franchise as we get it. In return . . ."

"In return," Phil cut him off, "you keep Delma Huddle out of Huntsville. *And* find a way to shut down the grand jury that Denham got empaneled to force *somebody* to name football players as drug users so D-L Financial doesn't have to pay these players their deferred salaries."

"Now, Phil," Gates hesitated, "that's a state grand jury. We don't have the right to operate in the United States."

"That's never stopped you before."

"Well," Lomax said, "we'll see what we can do."

"You better do it soon," Elliott said. "Because if you can't protect Delma in Texas, it means you can't protect me and I've got lots of trouble with a certain judge that Denham controls and I'll be back in jail before I can type my first sentence."

"I guess we could get these guys federal jobs," Ford said. "Then they'll be out of your hair and we'll have their dicks in *our* pocket."

"Fair enough?" Lomax asked Elliott, who shrugged. "Good!" Lomax went on, "Come here, I want you to say hello to somebody."

Satler Lomax led Elliott back to one of the offices and opened the door. Sitting on a wooden chair with his feet up on the steel desk was Raul. He was smoking a big cigar. When he saw Phil, Raul's eyes lit up.

"Hey, *amigo*." Raul grinned. *"Qué pasa?"*

"Where did you find him?" Elliott turned back to Gates Ford.

"He was hiding at his mother's house in Las Cruces City," Ford replied. "We picked him up just in time."

"What do you mean?" Elliott looked from Gates back to the grinning Raul, puffing mindlessly on his cigar.

"Come here." Gates motioned Phil toward another door. "Satler, you keep Raul company, while I show Phillip who we found outside Raul's mother's house."

Ford opened the door and Elliott entered the darkened office first. Gates followed and closed the door, leaving the room in darkness. He walked over to a set of drapes that ran along one side wall and pulled them open, revealing a large window into the next cubicle space. "It's one-way glass," Gates explained. "You recognize those two guys?"

Emeliano and Cruz Rivera sat shackled to a long wooden

bench. They were still dressed in their desert camouflage.

"Raul has already identified them as two of the men who crossed the border with him," Gates said. "He says they are also the two who tried to shoot him outside Andy Crawford's American Bar in San Antonio. My guess is they work for Colonel Glanton."

"What do they say?"

"Nothing yet, but that will change. They were driving the same green Dodge you described to me. They had new plates, stolen in San Antonio. You'll be interested in what we found in the car." Ford picked up a brown envelope and dumped the contents on the desk. He pulled the drapes closed and turned on the desk lamp.

Phil Elliott dug through the wallets, key chains, knives, and pieces of paper, until he found a photograph. He froze when he saw the picture.

"Recognize her?" Gates Ford asked.

"Goddamn! That's my ex-wife." Elliott turned the photo over. Someone had scrawled Courtnay's Austin address on the back in pencil. "What are they doing . . . ?" Phil didn't finish the sentence. He looked up wide-eyed at Gates Ford.

"Yeh," Ford said. "That's what we think too."

"They were supposed to *kill* her?"

"Right after they finished off Raul, would be my guess." Ford picked up a scrap of paper and handed it to Elliott. "Look at this phone number. Do you recognize it?"

"It's mine." Elliott stared at the numbers scribbled in pencil. "I don't get it."

"You would have," Ford said. "These guys would have killed your ex-wife, then a couple of Austin cops, friendly with Colonel Glanton, would have arrived at the scene just in time to kill the two Costa Ricans. They would have found the picture and your phone number on one of them. You go down on murder one for hiring your ex-wife's murderers."

"Where is she?"

"We've got her in a safe house," Gates said. "When we explained to her what was going down, she came all apart. She's cooperating with us and will be a big help in tying Denham and Laughlin to Glanton. David Stein was careless around her. She knows a lot."

"She can have that effect on men," Phil said. "She makes them careless."

"I think Stein felt she was acting too unstable and mentioned it to Denham who decided to turn her over to Glanton. They could kill two birds with one stone. She had filed enough charges against you, claiming you were trying to kill her. Combined with the evidence planted on the two Costa Ricans, your trial would have lasted about ten minutes," Gates explained. "My guess is that Stein is holding her power of attorney and would have ended up with control of everything, including your boy."

"I'll kill that fucking lawyer," Elliott whispered.

"You've got to stop saying stuff like that in public," Lomax advised.

First Light

"Jo Bob is on his way back over here," John Wilson said. He had been reading through the documents that Gates Ford had passed Phil at the roadside park and was still up when Elliott returned from his meeting with Ford and Lomax. "Maybe you ought to get a little sleep."

"I can't sleep," Elliott said.

"You look exhausted."

"I am. But even if I could sleep, I'd still wake up exhausted," Phil explained. "I go to sleep tired and wake up tired."

Elliott yawned and stretched. His spine popped and snapped so he readjusted the dials on his TENS unit, increasing the width, time, and intensity of the electric shocks running through the damaged muscles and nerves along his backbone and neck.

"So, what is your pal Ford gonna do?"

"According to him and Lomax, D-L Financial is in deep shit," Phil explained. "The FBI is heading up a big investigation."

"Who is this guy Lomax?" Wilson asked. "The name sounds familiar."

"He said he was with the football team during camp our rookie year. Claims he got cut the day B.A. had me bring my playbook in and gave me the lecture about my lack of character."

Wilson frowned, lost in thought for a moment, then spoke. "I remember him. Good-sized guy with dark hair?"

Phil nodded.

"We picked him up from Chicago about halfway through camp," Wilson said. "His dad was a big shooter out of Houston."

"If you say so."

"I do," Wilson said. "After B.A. cut him he went to work for the State Department."

It was beginning to get light outside. A car pulled into the driveway and its headlights swept across the front of Wilson's house.

"That'll be Jo Bob," Wilson said. "Incidentally, my man in El Paso called about Tom Reece. He was married to your ex-wife about twenty-three years ago. They had two daughters. She left him and the kids when the youngest was about a year old. She just disappeared."

"Sounds true to form," Elliott said.

"With one exception," Wilson continued. "There's no record of a divorce."

"She didn't bother to divorce him?" Elliott was stunned.

"Apparently not. They were living in a trailer house and he was working at a gas station. There wasn't any property, so she just walked."

"I wonder if Stein knows?"

The car pulled up to the house and its headlights shut off.

"I'll bet he does," Wilson said. "It may be why she's become a liability to them. If she's still married, she has no claim on any of your property, especially the thousand acres out in the Purgatory that Denham and Laughlin want so bad."

"Is that worth killing her for?" Elliott was confounded.

"Apparently so," Wilson replied.

The front door opened and Jo Bob Williams walked inside.

"It's first light," Jo Bob said. "The best part of the day." He looked from Wilson to Elliott. "Didn't you guys go to bed?"

Wilson brought Jo Bob up to date while Elliott went to the bathroom and splashed water on his face and the back of his neck.

"Goddamn, I'm sore," Phil said, when he returned to the living room. He lay flat on his back and closed his eyes, listening to Wilson explain to Jo Bob what they had learned from their various sources. When John finished talking, Elliott sat up and pulled the business cards from his shirt pocket.

"You need to call Ford," Phil said to Jo Bob. "He told me they plan to make a cocaine bust at the Purgatory Military Institute. Ford wants to talk to you about it."

"Should I call him now?" Jo Bob asked.

"No reason that son of a bitch should be sleeping when we're not."

Jo Bob went into the kitchen to use the phone. Elliott lay back down. John Wilson continued to look over the documents Phil had gotten from Gates Ford at the roadside park.

Shortly, Jo Bob Williams returned from the kitchen. "Looks like I'll have to go back to Purgatory right after the game," he said.

"At least you won't miss the Seth Maxwell Celebrity Golf Tourney and the Welcome Back Cocktail Party tonight," Elliott said. "I know how you hate to pass up a free drink."

"It's you that wouldn't pass up a free drink if the bar was on fire," Jo Bob replied.

"You better smile when you say that, Sheriff." Phil stayed flat on his back with his eyes closed. The TENS unit sent long, hard, electric pulses along his spine, making his body twitch.

"I am smiling," Jo Bob said. "What the fuck is the matter with you?"

"It's been a long day," Phil sighed. "Why do the days and nights seem so long and my life seems so short?"

"You're just an old outlaw," Jo Bob said. "You've outlived your time."

"Bullshit, Sheriff," Elliott said. "I was an old man at twenty-seven. A young man trapped in an old man's body."

"Why don't you send that idea to your agent?" Jo Bob laughed. "I think there's an idea for a George Burns movie in there somewhere."

"We *did* spend our youth awfully fast," Wilson said. "It was a pretty quick fall from the grace of good health."

"Nothing lasts forever," Jo Bob said as he sat down. "Your body is a temple."

"Our bodies were the temples only if you worshiped money," Phil said. "B.A. and the Hunters were the high priests and we were the human sacrifices. It'll be interesting to see what these new kids are like."

"They have an unreal world view of basic economics," Jo Bob told him.

"And we didn't?" Phil asked sarcastically.

"We never dealt in such awesome sums of money," Jo Bob said. "They are driven by a desire for things, unearned things. They get bonus payments to just show up every year. They defer their pain the way we deferred money and they swing between greed and fear. You don't realize how lucky you are."

"You got that right," Phil said. "Somehow my good fortune has escaped my perception."

"Phil," Jo Bob continued, "I learned most of this from you, knowing you and watching you. You aren't greedy and you don't expect to get paid for work you didn't do. You don't fear the future because you've already been to the edge and looked into the abyss. Sure, you got maimed in the process but you *really* understand life, whether you admit it or not. What's important to you is the work. Hell, that's why you loved and hated football at the same time. Playing the game was pure, it was your work and you did it well. That B.A. and the Hunters were corrupt and exploited the players was a separate issue altogether. You would have played until you dropped if *they* hadn't finally boxed you into an unbearable dilemma. They finally made you choose between your beliefs and the work. You kept the faith and walked."

"They fired me," Phil said.

"You *made* them fire you," Jo Bob said. "You could have backed off and changed what B.A. called 'your attitude.' But it wasn't just your attitude. It was your character. They wanted you to stop being you and Phil Elliott refused. These new players will do anything the owners tell them, including change their state of mind. As long as the insult is cash, they'll piss in a bottle and let sportscasters talk about the state of their urine. Can you *ever* imagine doing that?"

"Not and stay sane," Phil replied. "The moment you let them inside your head, you're lost."

Jane Wilson walked into the living room.

"You boys want breakfast before the kids get up?" she asked. "You've got to be at the golf course by ten."

"Phil and I will have bread and water." Delma Huddle walked into the living room, grinning and scratching his bald head. "No sense spoiling us." Delma looked at Elliott. "You gonna play golf, turkey?"

"No," Phil said. "I'm going straight to the clubhouse bar and practice my drinking for the Welcome Back Cocktail Party. If I get enough vodka in me, maybe I'll actually *feel* welcome."

The Golf Tourney

"**P**hil!" John Wilson was holding the phone. The kids were all in the kitchen eating breakfast. "It's your agent in New York."

"Grant?" Phil had grabbed the receiver.

"*Sports Illustrated* will buy a story on Dickie Blades, Dallas' number one rookie." Grant Grinnell spoke in his even, measured way. "It pays five thousand dollars plus expenses."

"You know *SI* doesn't want to hear what I'll have to say."

"There's a kill fee," Grinnell added.

"I'll take it," Phil said immediately.

"Okay," Grinnell replied. "I'll get a deal memo out and lock it up. Good luck."

"Thanks, Grant, I'll need it," Phil said. "We're on our way to Maxwell's golf tourney right now."

"Good news?" Wilson asked, as Phil hung up the phone.

"A magazine job," Phil replied. "A story on Dickie Blades."

"Bill Mays is his agent," Wilson said. "I'll have my secretary call him and set up an appointment for you."

"Thanks, John."

"I'm just trying to get paid."

"No chance of that."

"I know, but I've got to keep hoping."

Phil went into the kitchen and kissed Scott goodbye between bites of Frosted Flakes.

Helene Williams arrived with their kids. All the children were going to stay at the ranch while the men went into Winwood Hills and the Seth Maxwell Celebrity Golf Tourney.

Jo Bob and Phil rode there with John Wilson. Andy Crawford was just getting out of his car in the already crowded parking lot as they pulled up.

"I just came from seeing Alan in the hospital," Crawford told them, after they had all said hello. "He's not doing well. He said you guys came by the other day, told me to give everybody his regards. Does anybody know where we sign up for this thing?"

"The headquarters are in the clubhouse," Wilson explained. "They held an auction for partners with the proceeds going to the United Fund. Each of us gets to play with a rich businessman. The spoils of fame."

"I'll just go straight to the bar," Elliott said. "I couldn't swing a golf club without about twelve shots of novocaine. I'll have about twelve shots of vodka instead. Maybe I'll be able to talk to some of these assholes then."

Phil sat in the bar at a window table overlooking the first tee. Except for Elliott and the bartender, the room was empty. Phil nursed a double Stolichnaya on the rocks and watched each foursome tee off.

Seth Maxwell was the first up and the local news cameras crowded around as Seth joked and kidded with the other members of his foursome. Art Hartman, Seth's backup quarterback when Phil played, was now president of D-L Savings and Loan, Dallas, the flagship S&L of D-L Financial's 85 thrift institutions in Texas. The other members of the foursome were Art's bosses—Ross Denham and Bobby Laughlin.

Phil got a measure of enjoyment when both Laughlin and Denham shot poorly off the tee. Laughlin missed the ball completely on his first swing.

"I hope that makes the six o'clock news," Phil said to himself, as the foursome moved off the tee and a large contingent of the press went with them.

In the second foursome, Phil recognized only Louis Lafler, an old crony of Conrad Hunter's, now safely tucked away in the Denham-Laughlin camp as chairman of the Parks and Wildlife Commission, which had recently recommended the acquisition of the Blaine Ranch (and most other properties not owned by D-L Financial in the Purgatory) for a golden eagle refuge and national park.

Elliott recognized no one in the next several foursomes, although he was certain they were ex-Dallas players. A lot of them had come and gone in the years since he had been exiled from the locker room.

Then, the crowd around the tee parted and the next foursome took their places for the publicity photo opportunities. Phil Elliott knew every member and took a quick drink. The sting of vodka choked back the anger, rising uncontrollably in his throat, as Bob Beaudreau, dressed completely in red, smiled and laughed with his three companions: Steve Peterson, Tony Perelli from Las Vegas, and Phil's old teammate Thomas Richardson, now assistant executive director of the player's union.

Bob Beaudreau, the stuff of Phil's nightmares, the murderer of his dreams, the man who had shot and killed Charlotte Caulder and David Clarke. His glass was suddenly empty; Phil waved it blindly. The room had gone red. The rage was like a knife in his chest.

There the murderer stood, grinning and waving. He had snuffed out two lives and left Phil's a smoldering ruin, then he hired David Stein to defend him and walked on an insanity plea. The case made Stein's career and everyone thought Beaudreau a remarkable, clever and wealthy man to be able to beat a double murder rap in Texas, a state that usually had more people on Death Row than any other.

"Phillip? Phillip?" The voice seemed to come from a distance, down the long, dark hallway of the past. "Phillip?"

Elliott was startled from his furious thoughts.

Joanne Remington-Hunter stood next to Phil's table. Her classic face was spoiled slightly by a frown. "Phillip! What *is* the matter with you? You can't be drunk already?"

"It's not because I'm not trying." Phil stood up quickly, then glanced out at the tee. Beaudreau and the others were gone. Four strangers now stood in their place.

"What is the matter with you?" Joanne was insistent.

"Nothing." Phil shook his head, trying to clear his

thoughts. "Nothing. And you are the perfect cure for it. What brought you out here?"

"I had to talk to Emmett." Joanne sat down and looked at the empty glasses in front of Phil. "John Wilson told me you were in here getting an early start. He wasn't exaggerating."

"You want something?" Phil sat down. The bartender approached.

"I'll have a bloody Mary," Joanne said. "I don't want you to get a reputation for drinking alone."

"I'm never alone." Phil watched the retreating bartender. "I've always got a complement of ghosts, live and dead."

"You saw Bob Beaudreau," Joanne guessed. "I'm sorry."

"I guess I should have been ready, but I never am."

They both gazed out at the golf course and the crowds until the drinks arrived.

"I told Emmett I was going to have to file suit against him for mismanagement of CRH Inc.," Joanne said. "According to my lawyer, it's the only chance I have. He says eventually I'll have to sue D-L Financial and David Stein, but I have to sue Emmett first. He wasn't pleased."

"Nobody enjoys lawsuits but lawyers," Phil said. "At least you could go out and get yourself a new wardrobe for the courtroom. My ex-wife did and charged it to me."

"Are you still doing the story on Delma and the reunion for *Southwest View*?"

"I'm not sure what I'm doing," Phil said. "I've got to try and do a story on Dickie Blades first."

"You look tired." Joanne sipped her Bloody Mary. "When did you last get a good night's sleep?"

"Nineteen-sixty-five." Phil smiled. "Spring, I think. I got hold of a lot of Seconal."

"I'm sorry, Phil. I've been wrong about you so many times." Joanne reached across the table and touched her finger to the back of his hand. "I mistook your courage and compassion for stupidity and your honesty for weakness."

"Don't be too quick to judge yourself," Phil told her. "When I was younger, I had dreams that helped me deal with all this shit. Now I'm running out of time and hope."

"But now you've got that beautiful boy," Joanne interrupted. "He loves you without expectation. God, I wish somebody loved me like that. I didn't want stretch marks, so I got crow's-feet instead."

"It's not easy to grow your own friend," Phil laughed. "But you're right. I wouldn't change anything if it meant losing him."

"I always gambled on my looks," Joanne said. "The odds have turned against me."

"You'll always be beautiful, Joanne. It comes from inside you."

"I believe the saying is, 'Beauty is only skin deep, but ugly goes all the way to the bone.' " Joanne laughed and she radiated. "We ought to try and pick up the pieces together."

"You don't need my problems," Phil cautioned. "You married into respectability and that's worth something. You don't need to squander that by hooking up with me, especially if you expect to have to confront Denham and Laughlin in the future."

"Soft people have to court the favor of hard people," Joanne said. "I've always relied on the kindness of strangers."

"Blanche DuBois," Phil said. *"A Streetcar Named Desire."*

Joanne smiled and nodded. "I've decided to let you have *Casablanca* back."

"Well," Phil smiled back. "Louie, this could be the beginning of a beautiful friendship. Or something like that. I haven't seen the movie in awhile."

"Well, I have to go." Joanne stood and came around the table next to Elliott. She leaned down and kissed him long and hard on the lips. She held his face in her hands. The kiss ended and she leaned back to look at the face she cradled in her soft hands. "Goodbye, Phillip." She released him and turned in one fluid movement. He watched her, as she moved gracefully and quickly out of the bar, disappearing into the light.

One Step Up and Two Steps Back

Phil Elliott stayed at his table in the bar and watched the last several foursomes tee off. He recognized Gino Machado, an old teammate, who now had a Lincoln-Mercury dealership. Gino, a raging wild man on the football field, had turned into a quiet, acute, and successful businessman. Machado had saved money when he played and returned to his hometown with his fair share of fame and fortune. He went into the car business with a high school classmate and channeled all that energy he spent on the football field into selling cars. A heavy amphetamine user in football, he never took another pill and his rise in the world of automobiles and finance was meteoric.

Machado had written Phil after the publication of *Famous American Ducks* to congratulate him on the book, saying he looked forward to many more. Still married to his first wife, his high school sweetheart, he had five children. The eldest boy was in Harvard Medical School.

The next ex-teammate Phil recognized was Dave Purdue, a fullback from New Mexico and a five-time All-Pro. Purdue had retired back to New Mexico and got his law degree. His practice consisted of defending the rights of the poor and fighting big land developers who preyed on the indigenous Hispanics and Indians. David became an expert in property rights and water law, once arguing a case in front of the Supreme Court of the United States.

Elliott ordered another drink and made a note to himself to make certain that he and Wilson spent some time

talking to the old fullback about the situation in the
Purgatory.

David Purdue hit a perfect tee shot, straight down the
middle of the fairway. There was a smattering of applause among the few spectators still at the first tee. The
oldest of them had been in first grade when Purdue
played and had no idea or much appreciation of just how
great the man once was on a football field.

Except for his gray hair, Purdue looked younger than
when he played. He had lost forty pounds and not one of
his teeth.

"Lean and mean, David." Phil smiled, pleased by the
evidence that at least *some* of his ex-teammates appeared
to have emerged unscathed from professional football
and had gone on to live useful and productive lives.

As Purdue disappeared down the fairway, Phil turned
to the door. Some thing, some feeling, had dragged his
attention away from the golf course.

A familiar figure stood, slightly stooped, silhouetted by
the back-light in the doorway to the bar. The man entered
the bar tentatively, almost a wandering kind of gait, as if
he was lost or confused. Maybe he was both. He stopped
near the bar and looked around the empty room, finally
fixing his attention on Elliott.

Phil squinted, staring back at the familiar man.

After a moment, the man started toward Elliott, paused
and then continued toward Phil. He straightened his shoulders and his walk was quicker, more purposeful. As he
drew nearer and the light from the window illuminated
his face, Phil Elliott found himself looking into the eyes
of his old coach, Governor B.A. Quinlan.

Elliott stood up, quickly, as if some invisible puppeteer
had pulled all his strings at once.

"Hello, Mr. Elliott." B.A. extended an open hand. "I
thought that was you."

"You surprised me, Coach . . . ah . . . I mean Governor." Phil clasped his hand. In spite of everything, Phil
was inexplicably pleased to see his old coach. "You never
called me Mr. Elliott before."

"You're one of my constituents now." B. A. Quinlan
smiled, but the look in his eyes was melancholy.

"What are you doing here?" Phil asked. "Alone, I

mean. I thought governors were always surrounded by aides and bodyguards?"

"My aide is on the phone, trying to find Danny Raines. We're supposed to meet today. Seth was just coming in off the first nine when we arrived, and he has charmed my bodyguard into a state that might be called 'dereliction of duty.' " B.A. smiled again, sadly. His face was flushed, there were dark circles under his eyes and he smelled of gin.

They were both still standing.

"You look like you could use a drink, Coach." Phil indicated the chair across from him, as he sat down. "Please, join me."

B.A. looked around behind him and then back at Elliott. He was weighing variables Phil could only guess at.

"Why not?" B.A. sat. "We shared something very important, even if we seldom agreed on what it was we were sharing. I'm glad to see you, Phil. I don't know why."

"I hear you." Phil loosed a short laugh just as the bartender arrived.

B.A. ordered a very dry martini with two olives. Phil stayed with double vodka on the rocks.

"So. How do you like being the governor?"

"It is not what I expected," B.A. replied to Elliott's surprise. "But by the time I realized my miscalculation, it was too late. I was already elected." The drinks arrived. "I had expected the campaign to be a difficult and trying time, making speeches and promises on issues I felt very strongly about. But I had assumed that, if I was elected, the opportunity to do good things would ease the sting. Like football, I assumed that if I approached the governor's job with discipline, dedication, self-sacrifice, hard work, and character, eventually I would achieve my goals. I also prayed for guidance."

"And you discovered that politics was *not* like football?"

"Politics is only about one thing." B.A. took a long drink of his martini. "Power. Who has it. Who doesn't. And who wants it. The battle for control of the power is carried on by only a few hundred people and they all know each other. While the truly powerless are the anonymous masses of people, millions of them."

"You need their votes," Phil said. "That gives them some power."

"At election time, it entitles them to be deceived into thinking they are exercising power," B.A. said. "I got them to exercise it in my favor. Then, as governor, I would be able to act on the important social issues that I campaigned on and fulfill some of the promises I made. I was quickly disabused of that notion. As governor, I found myself being forced to help the already powerful, other politicians, rich contributors . . ."

"D-L Financial Group and all that it encompasses?" Phil interrupted.

"Is this an interview?" B.A. stiffened.

"Absolutely not, Coach," Phil said. "We're just two old football players swapping stories."

"I know you're in town to write a magazine story," B.A. said.

"I know that you know," Phil said. "Alan Claridge told me you called him at the hospital and warned him to be careful what he told me. I'm not writing anything about you. More than likely, I won't write anything at all. Believe me." Phil held up his glass, then took a drink. "You were telling me how you got sidetracked in office. You did understand when you ran for the job that governor is a relatively weak office, constitutionally, in Texas."

"I knew, but I felt that it was a high-profile position and I could exert a positive influence." Governor Quinlan's face was slightly bloated. B.A. drank when he was a player but quit when he became a coach. It was obvious to Phil that the strain of politics had driven the governor back to the bottle with a vengeance. Governor B.A. Quinlan was not a happy man.

"Do you miss football?" Phil asked, watching B.A. finish his martini.

"Yes, I do. Things were much clearer then. What about you?"

"I missed it more than I thought I would, but I left under peculiar circumstances. We *all* loved the game. That's why we put up with you and the Hunter family."

B.A. laughed. "I'm sorry your career ended the way it did, Phil. I never thought you were a dopehead. Christ! You should have seen the kinds of players that went through Dallas when they could afford cocaine." B.A. began to relax and ordered another drink. "You were a good receiver, Phil. But you didn't help your career by running around with Emmett Hunter's fiancée."

"Touché." Phil smiled. "It was not a good career move, I'll admit that."

"You were never a team player, as I recall," B.A. continued.

"Are you *still* trying to sell me that team bullshit?" Phil asked. "The *Hunters* were the team, we were just the equipment. That's one point of interface between professional football and politics. You, with the help of Denham and Laughlin, convinced a majority of the voters to join your team and elect you governor, because as members of the team they would benefit from this team spirit."

"I believe the citizen is responsible for the state of his society," B.A. said, without much conviction.

"Have you been able to deliver any of the things you promised your new teammates, the voters?"

"Not yet." B.A. avoided Phil's gaze. "But my people tell me that in my second term I'll be able to do much more, because my support will have solidified."

"And you buy that?" Phil shook his head. "Would you accept that kind of excuse from a football player?"

B.A. turned his melancholy eyes on Phil and shook his head. He picked up his fresh martini and downed half of it.

"Aw shit, enough shop talk," Phil said. "How's your family?"

B.A. paused and looked out onto the golf course.

"Come on, B.A.," Phil said. "One father to another, forget football and politics."

"You got kids?" The governor's face brightened. "I didn't know you married. I thought after that horrible murder of your lady friend . . . I just assumed . . . well, you know. I was truly sorry to hear about that."

"That's a nice thing to say, Coach. I appreciate it." Phil realized, at that moment, just how much of a tool of Denham and Laughlin B.A. really was. "I've got a boy, ten years old. I'm divorced, but I'm raising him myself."

"Well." B.A.'s face split into a wide smile; the sadness left his eyes, a new energy inhabited him. "My girls are all married and doing fine. I've got five grandchildren and one great-grandson."

"You're a *great*-grandfather?" Phil laughed, feeling suddenly very giddy. It was not the alcohol. For the first time in all the years they had known one another, Phil Elliott and B. A. Quinlan were communicating on real, human terms of the most meaningful nature. They were talking about their kids. B.A. and Phil were drinking together and pondering their own mortality. It was like a great knot had suddenly come untied deep in Phil's gut, in his soul.

"You gonna let your boy play football?" B.A. asked, his face bright with interest.

"So he can grow up and be like his dad? Are you nuts?"

"You can't stop him," B.A. said, smirking. "I know that much about kids and I know quite a bit about you. You'll give in."

"I already have, but I told him he had to wait until high school. In the meantime, I'll try and brainwash him with tennis and golf. Have you had a chance to see any of the old guys?"

"I see a few of the players that stayed in Texas from time to time. But you're the first of the *real old* guys who moved away that I've seen," B.A. replied. "I was really sorry to hear about Alan Claridge, struck down in the prime of his life by such a horrible disease."

"How come Alan is in 'the prime of his life' and I'm a 'real old guy'?"

"Did you two play together?"

Phil nodded.

"Gosh, there were so many players and time seems to fly by," B.A. said. "I thought you played with Bill Schmidt."

"Yeh. Our careers overlapped," Phil said. "It was the same with Claridge."

"Schmidt was a real tragedy," B.A. said. "I always wondered if there wasn't something I could have done. But by the time I wondered, it was too late."

"What happened?"

"You know Bill went to work for Conrad Hunter as a rookie and had moved up to vice president of CRH Inc. He was very successful." B.A. spoke slowly. His face tightened with pain, the sadness crept back in his eyes. "Then Conrad sold the football team and the bone cancer killed him. Emmett ran CRH Inc. into the ground. Bill Schmidt lost everything."

"Jesus! That's terrible, I know how much he loved that job. He worked hard. Hell, Coach, you're governor. Can't you get him something?"

"I wish I could." B.A. looked into his drink, he seemed to be studying the olives. "He took an overdose of sleeping pills."

"Why?" Phil felt like someone had hit him in the chest. "When?"

"Who knows why, except he had a big insurance policy that even paid off on suicide." B.A. had tears in his eyes. "He did it last July. I thought you would have heard about it."

"I was off-planet in July."

"What?"

"I was in jail in the Purgatory."

"That's where Denham and Laughlin are building. I had to call this special session of the legislature for them to push through MUD legislation for their River Ranch Estates." B.A. seemed irritated at having to do Denham and Laughlin's bidding. "Why were you in jail?"

"You just discussed it. River Ranch Estates. My boy, Scott, and I own a thousand acres right in the middle of it. I put it in trust for his education."

"It ought to be worth a pretty penny when that boy reaches college age."

"Ah," Phil said, "there's the rub. Denham wants the land now and is trying to force me to sell it. They're using my ex-wife and a judge they own down there."

A frown pressed the governor's lips together. His forehead wrinkled.

"Everytime I refuse to sell, David Stein has my ex-wife file a charge against me and, at some time during the trial, I offend the judge and he throws me in jail."

"Are you telling me the truth?" B.A. had chilled, slightly. "You are a man who tends to anarchism."

"Oh, I probably was in contempt a couple times," Phil replied. "But this has been going on for over a year and, after each time in jail, Stein immediately threatens more trouble if I don't sell the boy's land."

"This has to be some sort of misunderstanding." B.A. was searching for a hold. "I know David Stein. He's a well-respected lawyer. He handles a lot of work for the party and he's corporate counsel for D-L Financial Group."

"Bingo!"

"I can't believe Denham or Laughlin know anything about this."

"They know, Coach," Phil said. "I'm sorry you count on them for support. They are not nice people, but politics make strange bedfellows."

"Well, I'm going to look into this." B.A. seemed concerned, maybe angry. "Does Jo Bob know the details?"

"Jo Bob knows. So does John Wilson," Phil said. "John's *my* attorney. B.A., I am flattered and surprised that you would concern yourself with my problems, but I must warn you to be careful. D-L Financial Group is a very powerful and highly connected company. You *can't* trust them, so be careful who you discuss this with. Please believe me, if you cross them you can kiss the governor's chair goodbye."

"First, Phillip, I'm *not* doing this for you," B.A. replied. "You're a big boy, you can take care of yourself. In fact, I believe I had a hand in teaching you how. I'm doing this for a ten-year-old boy. Secondly, if you think I'm afraid of Denham, Laughlin, David Stein, or that idiot Colonel Glanton that they scammed me into putting in charge of the military units of the drug war, you don't know me as well as you think." B.A.'s lips were a thin line, his eyes sparkled. "Finally, I still have a great faith in God and believe that the Good Guys win, especially when I'm involved. I still have people around me I trust and have known all my life. Remember, I have one great advantage over you—I am a Texan born and bred."

Phil considered for a moment whether he should mention Gates Ford and Satler Lomax, and all that their presence in Texas inferred. He dismissed the idea, when he saw what could only be the governor's aide and bodyguard stride through the door and look frantically around the room.

The two men spotted B.A. and Phil.

"Governor," the aide said, as the bodyguard looked Phil over. "It's time for you to meet with the press. Coach Raines will meet us at the Welcome Back Cocktail

Party." The aide barely glanced at Phil. "You'll excuse us, sir."

B.A. stood and shook hands with Phil. "I enjoyed our conversation," he said, then pulled his shoulders back and strode purposefully out of the room, looking every bit the governor of Texas.

Phil sat and enjoyed the view, until the three men disappeared.

Somewhere beyond the door, a general clamor began. The press and the governor had met.

Phil Elliott sipped his drink, listened to the noise of the press conference, looked out at the peaceful green of the Winwood Hills Golf Club and tried to absorb what had just happened.

It had been all too surreal. He found it hard to comprehend.

What did it mean?

What should he do?

Whom should he tell?

What should he believe?

He was lost in thought, as he stared out the window, and had no idea how long he sat there. Slowly, Phil was aware that the bar was filling with people. The golfers were coming in off the course.

Elliott looked around the room for familiar faces, then decided that Wilson would find him.

"A man's got to believe in something," Phil said to himself. "And I believe I'll have another drink."

The Welcome Back Cocktail Party

"I don't know *what* to tell you." Phil Elliott sat in the backseat as John Wilson drove. Jo Bob Williams sat next to Wilson.

"B.A. just sat there and drank martinis while we talked about everything from our kids and the good old days in football, his disillusionment with politics, Alan Claridge and Bill Schmidt, to D-L Financial, David Stein, and their attempts to force me to sell Scott's land."

"What did he say about D-L and Stein?" Wilson wanted to know.

"He had a hard time comprehending that they would swindle a ten-year-old boy to the benefit of River Ranch Estates," Phil said, "but he acted like he planned to find out. He'll contact you two, I think."

"My God!" Jo Bob sat up in the car awed. "There it is. Look at that place!"

Directly ahead was the B. A. Quinlan Dallas Football Complex. Wilson turned into the entrance and passed the crowded miniature golf course. Vendors sold pennants, hats, shirts, and personalized football jerseys, as well as food and drinks. A schedule was posted next to an enclosed gift shop that carried a much larger inventory of Dallas football memorabilia and a designer clothing store. The schedule listed the times of guided tours at five dollars a person through the complete practice complex.

Somewhere behind the twelve-foot fence, the team was practicing on one of the two complete football fields. One field was natural grass, the other was artificial turf.

The cocktail party was being held in the Room of Champions, built specifically for the purpose of entertaining VIPs, team parties and reunions.

"They got two tennis courts and eight racketball courts here," Jo Bob said. "Indoor! The whirlpool is twenty-five feet square, the pool's Olympic-size and there's a weight room with every kind of weight machine made in the Western world. Did you see *Rocky,* the one where he fought the giant Russian? They got all that stuff that Russian had."

"Who lost?" Phil asked. "Rocky or the Russian?"

"The Russian," Jo Bob admitted.

"I rest my case."

"Look at the Players' Parking Lot." Wilson pointed. "There's nothing there but Porsches, BMWs, Mercedes, Maseratis . . ."

"That's Dickie Blades's Rolls Corniche," Phil observed.

"Bill Mays said that Blades wanted to meet you after he finished practice," John Wilson explained. "You can do the interview then. Who's that behind us?" Wilson was leaning up looking in the rearview mirror.

Phil turned and saw the yellow Lincoln Town Car. "That's Gino Machado. God! Look at that car. It's a '77 Lincoln, one of the biggest production cars made. He's turning into *the players' lot.*"

"Ohhh shit," Wilson said.

Jo Bob started laughing, then twisted in his seat to get a better view. "He's gonna show these new kids that they shoulda bought Detroit Iron."

Gino Machado drove through the players' lot carefully, slowly and methodically. He drove the big Lincoln up one row of exotic imported cars and down another, making certain that he put a fair-sized dent or scrape in every single car in the lot. He saved Dickie Blades's Rolls for last. Using the full front bumper and grill of the Lincoln, he banged a good-sized dent in the driver's door.

Wilson parked his car and the three of them waited for Gino Machado to finish his rounds and pull across the street to the Visitors' Parking Lot. Since they had all played together and Gino was still married to his first wife, Susan, there was no need for introductions. Instead, they all just hugged and laughed at the marks that Gino had left on the foreign cars.

"Let 'em know that Gino's been in town." Machado laughed and opened the door for Susan. He, Elliott, Jo Bob, and Wilson followed Gino's wife into the Room of Champions.

The far wall was completely covered with a blown-up photo of The First Championship Team. All four men had played important parts during that championship season but their pictures looked like strangers. It wasn't just that youth had flown from each countenance; their faces now had a certain tension, a kind of subcutaneous expression that never left, whether they were smiling, frowning, laughing, crying, or raging.

David Purdue was already there. He had come with an Indian boy from Taos who was a big Dallas fan. The two of them were talking to Art Hartman. Susan Machado led Gino, Phil, Jo Bob, and John over to Purdue. She gave David a hug and a kiss, then everybody said hello to the Indian boy. Finally, they got around to Art Hartman.

"So, Art," Jo Bob said, "how long before the public figures out your savings and loan doesn't have enough cash to finance a used car?"

Hartman winced, noticeably.

When Elliott shook Art's hand, it was cold and clammy.

"Jesus, Art," Phil wiped his hand on his pants. "Don't take it all so seriously. It was other people's money you guys lost."

"All right, you guys," Susan said. "No more bank jokes."

"Jo Bob, where's O.W.?" Gino asked. "I heard he went to work as your deputy after he busted out in Houston real estate. When we played, it was like you two were joined at the hip."

"When they got out in the real world," Phil interjected quickly, "they had to have surgery." Phil watched Jo Bob struggle to control the expression on his face, which had turned pale at the mention of O. W. Meadows.

"Well, where is he?" Gino persisted.

"I had to leave somebody on duty in the Purgatory." Jo Bob had regained his composure.

"What the hell is there to do out there besides hunt and watch people get haircuts?" Gino laughed at his own joke. Nobody else did. "I remember when Seth took us out there, back in the old days, to hunt on Laughlin's exotic game ranch. It was pretty wild country."

"It's all changed," Jo Bob said. "D-L Financial Group, the same guys that bought the team from the Hunters, are developing all that country. They've built a big resort area."

"No kidding?" Gino turned to Art Hartman. "You gonna make a lot of money out of this, Art?"

"Your wife said no more bank jokes, Gino." Phil grinned and watched Maxwell's one-time backup quarterback twist his face up into a semblance of a grin. "Sorry, Art. These linemen never know when to quit."

"Which was damn fortunate for Hartman during his quarterbacking days," Jo Bob said.

"You especially, Jo Bob," quarterback-cum savings and loan president Art Hartman said. "You *never* stopped—talking in the huddle."

David Purdue, gray and lean, grinned. "Well, Art, it wasn't like *you* ever had that much to say."

Purdue was a man of few words and very dry humor. The quiet, sly remark made everybody laugh, including Hartman. Art was the youngest among them and therefore, according to locker room tradition, had been the first target for jokes since his rookie year.

Hartman usually took the ribbing as part of the turf. But today his laughter was nervous and too loud, almost maniacal. He was obviously under a lot of pressure.

"Is Tony Douglas coming?" Hartman asked. He had stopped laughing suddenly and fixed his eyes accusingly on Jo Bob. "Didn't B.A. get him a game warden's job out in Purgatory?"

Jo Bob continued to laugh as he cut his eyes quickly from Elliott to Wilson and then back to Hartman.

"Tony's probably in town," Wilson offered quickly. "But I'll bet he's stalking his favorite bars, using his job training to track down a couple of women."

"I thought he was married." Hartman continued to press the subject. He seemed to know *something*.

"Phil, how come you don't chase a few girls while you're in town?" Hartman changed the subject. There was a palpable sense of relief.

"I caught one a while back," Phil replied. "It's still a

toss-up whether I'll survive it. A truck doesn't have to hit me to get the idea."

"I heard the truck hit you anyway," Hartman said.

Elliott was angered by the remark, but just smiled thinly and nodded.

At that moment, Seth Maxwell and a large entourage of press, fans, women of dubious virtue, and hangers-on of no virtue at all burst into the room with all the style and decorum of a race riot.

The women in the group weren't old but they weren't young either. They appeared as delicate flowers just past full blossom, still pretty but beginning to droop, their brilliant colors fading, the petals curling and turning brown at the edges.

The men were all manner of personality and form, although excess flesh was preponderant and the common state of mind hovered near the far reaches of desperation.

The press corps were the dregs. The top television, radio, and print people were long gone, having been catered to immediately by Seth's publicity man and the PR people from the golf tourney. They had easily met their deadlines; good video footage made the six o'clock news. One station even got a network feed out of Seth's comments about "the mind-dead programmers," referring to the rival network that had carried Maxwell's series and had then made the decision to cancel *Scout*.

Maxwell was drunk and his publicist was doing his best to contain the damage this might cause to Seth's image. The flack was fighting a losing battle.

"The King has seen better days," Susan observed. She was the first to comment on what they all were thinking.

The Room of Champions was filling quickly, as more ex-players, guests, and press continued to arrive. Elliott searched in vain for a familiar face. It had all been *so long ago*. He struggled to recall the pleasant memories, while repressing the painful.

An open bar was set up in the corner farthest from the door, creating a traffic flow that eliminated congestion at the entrance to the room.

Seth Maxwell led his horde to the bar. He had yet to notice Gino and Susan Machado, John Wilson, Jo Bob, Hartman, and Elliott.

They had sure noticed him, though.

Maxwell was aberrant in a way none of them had ever witnessed before. It wasn't that he was just drunk and schizoid; they were all familiar with the many faces of Seth Maxwell—it was part of his legendary charm. But *this* behavior bordered on the grotesque. His efforts to be enchanting were painful.

"What is the matter with Seth?" Gino Machado picked up his wife's observation. Maxwell poured a drink on Steve Peterson who had just arrived and walked over to say hello. "He's acting like Jo Bob and O.W. at a postgame party," Gino said.

"He's become a field study in the science of teratology," Phil said.

"What's teratology?" Hartman asked.

"The study of freaks," Susan answered. "Hollywood is not the best place for a guy like Seth. He never had a firm grip on his identity when he played football, but football was *real*. When he played a great game, it was a reaffirmation of his self. In ten years of living out in fantasyland, he's lost all track of the real Seth Maxwell."

Susan Machado was approximately right. Age and anxiety had taken a terrible toll on the ex-quarterback's self-esteem and sense of identity. He looked exhausted and on the edge of losing control.

"He used to be able to shift from old Seth to The King and back again like he was double-clutching a dragster," Gino said.

"I'm afraid his clutch is gone," Elliott said. "I can hear the gears grinding clear over here. The network canceling his show didn't help his mental state."

"Neither did the team refusing to pay his deferred money," Wilson added.

"What?" Gino Machado snapped. "He had four million in deferred payments set up! What the hell happened?"

"It's a long story," Wilson told him.

Phil Elliott watched Art Hartman's face as John Wilson repeated what Maxwell had told them, leaving out the information involving Delma Huddle and the grand jury's demand for the names of drug users.

Hartman's eyes darted around the room as he feigned

ignorance and lack of interest. Sweat had beaded on
Art's upper lip; he chewed nervously on his thumbnail.

"Didn't they give Seth any reason for refusing to pay?"
Susan Machado glanced at her husband, then looked
back at John Wilson.

John Wilson just shrugged and looked at Art Hartman.
"Have you heard anything, Art?" Wilson's eyes were
wide with innocence, his jaw slightly slack.

"No!" Hartman jumped and answered too quickly.

"I wonder if this has anything to do with that lawsuit
these new owners filed against Delma?" Gino said. "Aren't
they refusing to pay *his* deferred money?"

"I don't know." Hartman denied what they knew he
knew. "Why are you all looking at me? I'm just an
employee of D-L Financial. They don't tell me about their
corporate plans."

"Where is Delma?" Susan asked.

"He'll be here," Wilson said. "He skipped the golf
tourney because of all the press. He's coming with Jane,
Helene, and the kids."

"Good!" Dave Purdue said, returning from the bar
with a root beer for the Indian boy he had brought with
him from Taos. He handed the boy the drink. "Jesus will
have somebody to play with."

"How old are you, Jesus?" Phil asked.

"I am almost twelve."

"You're older than our children," Phil said. "My boy
is only ten."

"Did you ever defer money in your contracts, Dave?"
Gino Machado's voice betrayed concern.

"Not me." Purdue smiled. "I didn't trust those guys
outta my sight. I wasn't accepting any promise to pay me
money ten or fifteen years after I last laid eyes on Clinton Foote."

Everybody laughed but Hartman, who tried to smear a
sickly grin across his sweaty face.

"Gino's got money due next year." Susan grimaced. "I
don't like the sound of this. Thank God, Gino has been
so successful in business. We don't *need* the money,
but . . ."

"I'll be goddamned if I'm gonna let those bastards
keep my money!" Gino swore. "They owe me fifty grand

a year for ten years and I'll get it, if I have to take it out of Clinton Foote's personal bank account. That asshole got an account at your bank, Art? We'll go get it right now."

"No. No!" Hartman was close to panic.

Just then, Monroe White walked into the room. He was accompanied by Griffith Lee, a wide receiver from Grambling, who had backed up Delma at the split end position.

Both men looked prosperous and happy. Monroe saw Elliott and the others and waved, his face splitting into a wide grin.

The two men made their way through the increasingly crowded room toward Elliott.

"Monroe!" Gino's face lit up. He and White had played in the same defensive line. Machado hugged the giant black man, while Griffith Lee shook hands with the other men and kissed Susan on the cheek. David Purdue introduced both his ex-teammates to Jesus.

"So?" Machado asked. "What are you two outlaws doing?"

"We both took advantage of the Player Vocational Program that the union set up with D-L Financial," Griffith Lee said. "Monroe got his real estate license and I'm working for ICC here in Dallas."

"I didn't know ICC had an office here," Phil said. Wilson and Jo Bob had concerned looks on their faces. "I thought they were strictly an Austin operation."

"That's the corporate headquarters," Griffith Lee explained. "That's where I went for training. Thomas Richardson set it up. He's in charge of the union's vocational program. I trained in Austin for ten weeks on computers and learned how to gather information. The office here in Dallas does deep background checks on job applicants for nuclear plants. We have contracts with nuclear power plants and utilities all over the country."

"It looks like it pays good," Machado said. Gino always judged the man by his wardrobe. "That's a five-hundred-dollar suit."

Lee smiled and nodded. "It's an interesting job. You can't imagine how much information ICC has on people in their computer banks in Austin. We can access them from our office in Dallas."

"That's good news," Phil said sarcastically.

"I don't have a top clearance," Lee continued. "But, I can still get info through Austin from the FBI, the IRS, Social Security, and the Department of Defense. But the thing that always amazes me is how much info I can get on someone just over the phone. I'll call some applicant's friends or neighbors and they'll tell me anything I want to know. People are just natural stool pigeons. They *want* to snitch on other people. It's incredible."

"And you got this job through the union?" Dave Purdue asked. His eyes were wide. His lips curled down in a frown.

"We both got jobs through the union," Monroe White interrupted. "Upton Gray and Richardson went to D-L and asked them to help set up this Vocational Training Program for ex-players from all over, young and old. It's a great deal. They offer training in computer programming and operation, real estate, banking and finance. Steve Peterson teaches a course on the financial markets and the stock exchange. At least, he did until the SEC went after him for insider trading. John Gauthier is taking over from Peterson."

"They've even started law enforcement classes out at the Purgatory Military Institute," Griffith Lee added. "They've expanded the program to include ex-military personnel. Colonel Glanton and Mr. Denham have plans to make PMI the Citadel of the Southwest."

"Upton and Richardson have done a great job putting this program together," Monroe enthused.

"Well, that's great news, guys," Elliott said bitterly. Monroe and White looked at him, surprised at the tone of his voice. But Jo Bob jabbed Phil, hard, in the ribs before he could say anything more.

"It *is* great," Monroe explained, still looking at Elliott, puzzled. "They paid us while we learned. Andy Crawford was in my classes for a while, but he dropped out."

"He's got himself a bar in San Antonio," Wilson cut in. "He's doing real well."

"Is he coming today?" Lee asked.

"He and Delma both should be here any minute," Jo Bob said. Then, to Jo Bob's great relief, the door banged open and in scrambled Scott Elliott, June and Johnnie

Wilson, Jane Wilson, and Helene, his wife. The Williams kids had decided to stay with Helene's folks.

Bringing up the rear was Delma Huddle. He slid through the door, during the general commotion caused by the wives and kids, and tried to sidle unnoticed along the wall over to where Jo Bob, Phil, John, and the rest were grouped.

While David Purdue, Monroe, Griffith Lee, and Hartman were greeting the wives and meeting the children, Wilson pulled Elliott off to the side.

"This ain't the place to cause trouble," Wilson told him. "So try to shut the fuck up."

Phil was trying to think of a rejoinder, then decided he'd go for an apology, but he was interrupted by a loud crash over by the bar. Seth Maxwell had passed out and fallen into a table and several metal folding chairs, sending them clattering across the tile floor.

Scott Elliott ran up and jumped into Phil's arms. "What happened to Mr. Maxwell?" he asked.

"He must have slipped and fallen, Scott." Phil kissed the boy on the cheek, as he held him in his arms.

"Looks to me like he got drunk and passed out," Scott said, slipping his arms around his father's neck. He stared over at Seth. "Yeh, he's drunk as a skunk."

"I'm going outside to get some air," Phil said to the boy. "You want to come?"

"Naw. I want to stay here and play with that new kid, Jesus." Scott wriggled out of his father's grasp and scooted off in search of Jesus and the other kids.

John Wilson shook his head and walked back to join the group, which had slowly surrounded Delma, shaking his hand and patting his back and shoulders.

Phil pushed outside through a fire exit and walked to the Visitors' Parking Lot. He was sitting on the hood of Wilson's car when Danny Raines walked around the corner of the building. Raines had been a running back when Phil played and was now Dallas's head coach.

"Hey, Phil." Danny walked over and the two ex-teammates shook hands.

"Practice over?" Phil asked, lighting another cigarette and offering one to Raines, who accepted. Elliott used his lighter to fire up both cigarettes. Raines took a deep drag and exhaled slowly, with obvious pleasure.

"Practice over?"

"No. I just couldn't stand the sons-a-bitches anymore."
Raines laughed and coughed. "These kids get weirder
and weirder every year."

"Worse than us?"

"You couldn't hold a candle to these kids," Raines
said. "By the time they reach us, these kids have
come up through high school and college systems that
are so corrupt that they have to be sociopaths to
survive."

Phil Elliott laughed. "The University of the Living
Dead."

"Don't get me wrong, in case you're writing something," Raines said. "There are a lot of great kids, but
the bad ones are *so* bad you keep forgetting all about the
good ones. So many colleges send us kids who are not
just poorly educated, but greedy, selfish, lacking any
grace or style, and with no sense of *real world* responsibility. Christ! The agents are getting to these kids in high
school, buying them off by the time they've reached
college. The big schools send us players with immense
talents, but they're usually creations of the latest chemical-
technological advances that leave them emotional and
spiritual cripples with all sorts of long-term physical and
psychological problems. Athletes from Hell with agents
from Hollywood." Danny Raines took a long drag on his
cigarette. "I'm sick of it. Every three or four years,
Upton Gray and the union take them out on a strike that
hurts everybody but Upton Gray."

"He operates on the theory that there is no such thing
as bad publicity," Phil said. "As long as they spell his
name right and put it in the lead paragraph."

"I'm just pissed off today," Raines explained. "There
really are a lot of good kids in the game, but they always
seem to end up as the victims. I don't know what to do.
How do you reach kids today?"

"Why don't you give me a high-dollar job, trying to
communicate with them?" Phil suggested.

"I'm serious, Phil," Raines said. "Even the most successful of these players are suffering from all sorts of
immense, unconscious stress. The money has gotten too
big. It's out of control. It has almost reached the point
where the agents are picking the kids who get drafted.

Then they turn around and sell them out to the clubs because they know the clubs'll be around long after any one player is gone."

"Meanwhile, Upton Gray goes on strike for free agency," Phil said.

"You got it."

"What's Dickie Blades like?" Phil asked.

"He's a great talent and he's a smart kid," Danny Raines said. "He's unusual. You doing a story on him?"

"I'm supposed to."

"You'll like him."

"Are you going into the cocktail party?"

"Not today," the coach said. "I'm in a miserable mood. I'd like to see Seth, though."

"Too late. He already passed out."

"What happened?"

"Too much bad news and scotch."

"I heard about his TV show."

"He also lost everything in the collapse of CRH Inc. and Clinton Foote told him that he'd have to sue if he ever hoped to get his deferred money."

"What the hell is all that about?" Raines was angry. "Clinton's trying to do the same thing to Delma."

Phil nodded. "You don't have any inside information about it?"

"I work on game plans and schedule practice," Raines said. "They don't even ask my opinion about a player's dollar value."

"It was good to see you, Danny. Good luck against . . ." Phil paused. "I don't even know who you're playing. You can see that I'm out of touch."

"New York. We should beat 'em. I'll see you at the dinner after the game, Phil." Danny Raines turned and walked toward the coaches' lot while Elliott returned to the cocktail party.

"Let's go." John Wilson opened the fire door, just as Phil was about to knock on it. "Crawford never showed. We're heading back to the house."

"I've got to interview Blades," Phil said.

"Shit! I forgot. Helene and Jane have already gone with the kids back to my place," Wilson said. "They got Maxwell in the training room on oxygen."

"It ain't the fall from grace that gets you," Phil said. "It's the sudden stop."

"Call me if you can't get a ride back to my place."

"I'll get him to bring me out there in that slightly dented Rolls."

The Number One Pick

"Hey, man," Dickie Blades said, as he and Phil Elliott walked to the Players' Parking Lot. "I read your books. You really stuck it to them dudes. I loved it."

"Thanks." Phil noticed that Blades was the only player leaving the building. "Is practice over?"

"For me," Blades grinned. "I told 'em I had an appointment. The other guys are still out running wind sprints."

"Will we be able to talk before your appointment?"

"*You're* my appointment," Blades said. His brow wrinkled and he looked from side to side as they walked onto the lot. He noticed the damage to the players' cars. "What the fuck . . . ?"

Dickie Blades stopped and surveyed the whole lot.

"Look at that, man. Somebody dented up every car in the lot." Blades continued walking until they reached his Rolls. "Awww man." He looked at the dented door on his Corniche, then he began to laugh. "I guess we must have done something to piss off a very compulsive dude." He climbed into his car. Phil got in on the passenger side.

"Well," Blades said, as he started the Rolls-Royce, "that's why God gave us full-coverage insurance." He backed out of his space and pulled out of the lot onto the road.

Soon they were cruising down the interstate toward Blades's high-rise penthouse in North Dallas. When Phil played, blacks couldn't live in North Dallas. This one had a four-thousand-square-foot penthouse.

Things change.

Blades pulled a gadget about the size of a cigarette lighter out of his coat pocket. He stuck one end of the rig in a nostril and sniffed, then he clicked a small lever on the side and repeated the process with his other nostril.

Blades sniffed a couple of times and rubbed his nose, then he handed the little machine to Elliott.

"Want some coke?" Blades offered. "Just pull that lever down and snort. It's pure pharmaceutical."

"No thanks, Dickie," Phil said. "But let me explain something. I'm raising a ten-year-old kid by myself, so I can't fool with drugs and take the risk of losing my kid. Now, if I was a *regular* writer or if I *really* wanted to get published with this story, I'd make note of your coke machine, pretend to be your pal, do up a bunch of your coke, then write up everything sordid I could find, excluding my own behavior. But the *realpolitik* is simpler. I don't expect they'll publish what I'll write. The popular image of you is a greedy nigger who took money from his college and his agent, getting yourself declared ineligible your sophomore year and forcing the league to draft you under threat of a lawsuit, then signing for more money than ninety-nine percent of the people in this country will ever see, which is obviously much too much money for you. The magazine expects me to write something within these parameters. But if they want that they'll have to get somebody else." Phil paused and looked at Blades. "All I plan to do is hang around you for a couple of hours and hope to see the person that no one else has written about. So far, I find you really likeable with a good sense of humor and want to see in you what *only I am able to see and write about*. If my uniqueness cannot connect with what is unique and unappreciated in you, then I'll take the kill fee from the magazine."

"Kill fee?"

"Write a story they don't publish and I still get one third of my fee."

"I trust you, man," Blades said.

"You'll trust others in your career," Phil warned, "and you'll get burned. I'm just offering some advice from an old player. Be careful, chill out. Be careful, Dickie, because someday another writer will come along and he'll seem just like me. And if you do what you just did with me, the guy will smile, nod, and swear he's your friend, then he'll kiss your ass and tell you to trust him for some more juicy bits of gossip. When he finally leaves and gets to his typewriter, he'll put your offer of cocaine in the lead paragraph. Believe me, this game gets a lot tougher. It don't ever get easier. The stakes just get higher."

"I know what you mean, man." Blades steered the car off the interstate and pointed it toward the tall apartment building in the distance.

"Look," Phil continued as Dickie pulled into his garage. "In my case, the stakes are a few grand for publication versus a couple of grand less as a kill fee. If I write that you offered me cocaine, no matter what the rest of the piece is about, I'll get published and make five thousand, which is big money to me right now. Hell, I could probably renegotiate my fee up to ten-K if you had a nude white woman in your apartment."

Dickie Blades broke out into an uncontrollable laughter. He fell against the side of the elevator and tears ran down his cheeks. Phil smiled at Blades's hysterical laughter.

The elevator stopped and the doors slid open.

Standing just inside the penthouse, obviously posed and waiting for Dickie Blades to come home, her arms wide open, her long hair flowing over her shoulders and full breasts, was the best-looking blonde Phil Elliott had ever seen.

She was stark naked.

Phil Elliott's mouth hung open. His feet were stuck to the floor.

Dickie Blades continued to howl with laughter as he staggered past Phil and the nude blonde, finally collapsing on a huge leather couch.

"Well, Dickie," Elliott said, finally, "you are doing your damnedest to get me published."

The blonde fled to the back of the penthouse to dress.

Phil and Dickie sat in the living room, looking south toward the skyline of Dallas.

"You know," Dickie began. "They told me if I went to the university, my dad would have a thirty-five-thousand-dollar-a-year job and a new house for him and my mom. I would get a new car of my choice, a thousand a month in cash, plus a forty-five-thousand-dollar bonus for signing the NCAA letter of intent, a Visa card with a five-thousand-dollar limit, and, of course, my scholarship and a rent-free apartment."

"Who told you that?"

"The governor of Texas."

"B. A. Quinlan?"

"No. The one before him. He was on the University Board of Regents. He told me, on the other hand, if I went to Oklahoma, I could never come back to Texas again. And I would be smart to get my family out of the state before something happened to them."

"He made you an offer you couldn't refuse."

"Hell, would you have refused it?"

"He didn't make it to me," Phil said. "He made it to you."

"What the hell is that supposed to mean?" Blades turned angry. He stood and paced the room. His six-four, 225-pound frame was intimidating. "You think I was scared? Or stupid?"

"I didn't say that." Phil shifted slightly on the couch.

"What the fuck!" Blades was angry. "They drafted me number one and I'm making more money than any running back in the league."

"You think."

"You callin' me a liar?" Blades turned on Phil, his fists clenched.

"No. I'm calling *them* liars," Phil explained. "Nobody knows what anybody *really* makes in this business. It's a basic rule of football finance. Clinton Foote would never let anybody know what you're making or let you know what anybody else is making."

"My agent knows. He told me."

"Did you understand what he was saying?"

"Yes!" Blades snapped.

"Dickie?" Phil said. "Your agent has other clients and his biggest client is the league. The second biggest is the union, since they've got the right to approve agents. At best, you are third on his list of folks he has *got* to please. And if he don't please you, there's more players. There is only one league and one union. Think about it. He *has* to please the owners, the union, and, more and more, even the press, before he concerns himself with you."

"You're talking trash, man."

"You got a copy of your contract here?"

"Yeh, I do."

"Would you let me see it?"

The blonde returned to the room and curled up in a big leather chair where the glass wall joined the aquarium wall. Blades had an aquarium, fourteen feet high by thirty feet long. It was filled with scores of exotic fish. Blades stared at his fish for a long time. Finally, he turned and walked into the back of the penthouse. Phil waited, looking out over the Dallas skyline that had changed so radically since the last time he had viewed it from this perspective that he had no sense of familiarity or nostalgia. It was a strange city, inhabited by strangers who got stranger all the time.

If you wait long enough, downhill ain't downhill no more.

"Here it is." Dickie Blades strode into the room. He moved like a cat. He was a pleasure to watch. His movements were like brush strokes. He thrust a five-page document at Elliott.

"Is this all?" Elliott said, as he took the pages from Blades's long-fingered hand. "You've got beautiful hands," Phil added, as he dropped his gaze to the paper.

"Jeez man!" Blades slip-stepped away. "You some kind of fag?"

Phil smirked but kept his eyes on the pages. He read carefully, noting several ambiguous passages. Finally, he put the document down and shook his head. "Is this all?" he repeated.

Blades bobbed his head and shoulders. "Yes."

"This is an outline . . . ah . . . lemme try and explain . . ." Phil fumbled. "This is what we would call a deal memo. It's not a contract."

"All the numbers are there, everything we agreed on."

"This is like one step above a handshake," Phil said. "Do you know if Bill Mays might possibly have the real contract and just gave you this as sort of a simpler breakdown?"

"I've never seen anything but this." He snatched the document from the table and ruffled angrily through the pages. "See? Here? That's my signature and that's Clinton Foote's."

"Dickie, does Bill Mays know you do cocaine?" Phil asked.

"Sure. He was the first person to ever give me any," Blades replied. "He would bring it to me at the university when I was a freshman and he was trying to convince me to sign with him to represent me. Mays gave me money, plane tickets to Jamaica, and introduced me to the two finest white ladies I ever knew—Honey over there in the chair and cocaine."

"You're taking a terrible chance," Phil said. "Random drug testing is high on the commissioner's list of public relations programs."

"No sweat." Blades moved around the room like a cat. "Mays has a deal with Clinton Foote that I will never be tested for drugs."

"My God, man." Phil watched the big running back prowl the room. "Do you believe that? The cocaine will give Clinton the perfect way to bust your balls when the time comes for him to put you in your place. And you don't even have a legally binding contract." Phil wrote down John Wilson's name and phone number on a piece of paper from his memo book. He tore out the page and handed it to Blades when he slinked past on his way to study his fish.

"What's this?" Blades's gaze followed an angelfish.

"He's an ex-player and a good lawyer. He was an officer in the union but he resigned when Upton Gray couldn't account for $500,000 in union funds. He's negotiated lots of players' contracts."

"I've *got* an agent and a contract." Blades turned from the huge aquarium and looked at Phil.

"No, you don't." Phil was exasperated. "Mays is setting you up for a royal screwing. You still have time to turn it around on them, but you got to get off your butt and do something. This is the kind of player swindle I could write a good story about with a happy ending. You would come off as a sympathetic character and I could show explicitly what these rats do for money."

"Dickie, honey," the blonde said. "Bill called. He said he would be over to take you to that place." She was a bad liar.

"What you want, bitch?"

"She is trying to tell you, without my catching on, that

your agent will arrive shortly with a totally fraudulent reason for us to end the interview," Phil said.

Blades's silence was deafening.

"Look, Dickie, the league is a government-protected monopoly," Phil explained further. "What happened to the main character in *Famous American Ducks can* happen to a star of your caliber. There is a Standard Player Contract that *every* player has to sign. You haven't signed it. You don't even know about it. Somebody's lying to you."

"Why would Bill Mays lie to me?"

"Why would he tell you the truth?"

The blonde disappeared into the back of the penthouse again. Phil and Dickie exchanged glances. Phil pointed at the speaker phone. Dickie slumped his shoulders and looked sadly at Elliott. He reached out to push the button on the speaker, then changed his mind, gently lifted the receiver and listened.

Elliott watched Dickie Blades's proud face go soft and shift. The flesh seemed to come loose from the facial bones, sliding into an expression of shock and disappointment.

Dickie Blades hung up the phone. "She's talking to Mays on his car phone." Blades looked down at Phil. "She's telling him you're over here causing trouble."

"Did Clinton Foote pay you according to the schedule set out in this deal memo?" Phil asked. "You should have gotten ninety-six thousand a game."

"No." Blades's voice dropped. "I wanted to buy this penthouse and furnish it. Bill got Clinton to loan me the money against my contract, so I could pay cash. I didn't want to borrow the money and pay the interest."

"Why not?" Elliott said. "Interest on a residence mortgage is deductible."

"Well, Bill arranged for a no-interest loan through Clinton Foote."

"According to this deal memo, you're owed a 1.5 million-dollar signing bonus," Phil said. "You could have used that to buy this place and had money left over."

"Bill Mays suggested I defer that money until after I'm through playing."

"Dickie, that is cash money," Phil said as calmly as he

could. "Demand it now. Are they paying you interest on
the 1.5 million?"

"Bill is still negotiating that with Clinton."

"While you lose five hundred dollars a day in interest!
They are fucking the shit out of you and Mays is helping
them. He's gonna be here any minute and I don't want to
discuss this with him. Put this thing away and let's convince the blonde we're off the subject."

Bill Mays stepped off the elevator into the penthouse.
Phil Elliott was taking notes and drinking wine while
Blades ambled around the penthouse and explained why he
thought the Dallas offense was perfect for his style of
running.

"And you've been taking martial arts training since the
start of training camp?" Phil asked with artificial interest.

Blades went through a short karate routine. "I've also
been working with the New Dallas Ballet."

"You should see him, Phil." Mays picked up the thread
of conversation as if he and Phil were old friends. "He
could be a black Baryshnikov."

The blonde was snaked out on the floor, drinking from
a long-stemmed goblet.

"Well, Dickie," Mays clapped his hands. "We got to
get going." He turned to Phil. "You understand. Dickie's
a busy, busy boy."

"So are you, Bill," Phil smiled. "So are you."

"You can call a cab from downstairs," Bill Mays said.
"We have to leave, okay?"

"Bullshit, Bill. He can wait here," Blades argued. "I
trust him."

Catching a Cab

After they had gone, Phil wandered around Dickie's sumptuous penthouse, reading and rereading the memo that Bill Mays had sold to Blades as a contract. Once they had Blades convinced he had a valid contract for long-term big money, guaranteed for years and years, Mays and Clinton Foote were nailing him to a cross of immense debt.

Phil walked back into Blades's bedroom, snooping around. Elliott suspected that the robbing and swindling of Dickie Blades was connected to Delma Huddle's grand jury subpoena and upcoming deferred-payment suits.

The suspicion was confirmed when he found David Stein's business card on Dickie Blades's bedside table.

On the card back was a phone number and the name *Harvey*. Phil picked up Blades's bedroom phone and dialed the number. It was a familiar number, Phil had dialed the number before.

Elliott admired Blades's black silk sheets and specially made ten-by-ten-foot bed, as the phone rang.

"Hidy. This is Harvey. I'm not here. Please leave your name, number, and measurements. I'll get back to you."

Phil hung up.

It was unmistakeable. Phil recognized the voice and remembered whose phone number he had often called, *so many years ago*. In a world where nothing changes but the changes and the increasingly rapid rate of change, Harvey Belding, ex-professor, goofy sixties radical of sorts, and sometime drug dealer, *would,* ironically, be the only apparent constant.

Phil turned the business card over and over in his hand. David Stein on one side and Harvey Belding on the other.

Phil picked up the phone again to call John Wilson and say he would be on his way as soon as he called a cab.

Seth Maxwell's face filled the big-screen television in Blades's bedroom. The network was running a repeat episode of *Scout.* Seth looked young and vibrant, a sad contrast with the man who had passed out at the Welcome Back Cocktail Party.

Elliott held the telephone in his hand as he walked up close to the TV, trying to decide if the difference in Maxwell's television appearance was makeup or age; meaning, was this a rerun from the early years of Maxwell's career?

As Phil approached, the picture turned fuzzy and a sharp buzzing noise cut up Seth's dialogue. Phil instinctively stepped back from the television. As soon as he did, the picture distortion and the buzzing sound stopped.

"Hello?" Phil could hear Delma on the other end of the line.

"Hold on, Delma," Phil said. He moved the telephone toward the TV; the buzzing and video distortion returned. He pulled the phone away; the audio and video cleared up again. "I'll call you back!"

Elliott hung up Dickie Blades's phone, then unscrewed the mouthpiece. Inside, Phil found a tiny gold-colored transmitter. He decided to leave it in place.

He continued his wanderings through the large penthouse. All the phones had transmitters installed. They were all the same. Phil made an overscale drawing of the transmitter to show to Gates Ford.

A small transmitter would require a receiver, somewhere relatively close. Since there was only the one penthouse, the next floor down offered the best options. Elliott figured it was probably Clinton Foote and League Security keeping track of Dickie Blades, but the connections with Stein and Harvey Belding had him wondering.

The phone rang. It was the doorman.

"Your cab is here, Mr. Elliott."

Phil got off the elevator on the floor below the penthouse and checked the apartments. The residents' names were embossed below the doorbell. He had walked to the north end of the hallway, directly beneath Blades's bedroom. A set of double doors cut off the last three apartments, 1034, 1035, and 1036. There were no names on the double door and it was locked.

The elevator reached the ground floor. Phil could see the taxi waiting in the circular drive. By the way the doorman treated Elliott, it was obvious that Dickie Blades was the most important tenant in the building.

"Jonah?" Phil read the doorman's name tag as he put his arm around him. "When Mr. Blades returns would you tell him I had to go?" Phil frowned. "I promised I would wait and we would go down and meet his friends on the tenth floor, but maybe I can meet him later. He gave me the names of the people in 1035 but they slipped my mind."

"I'll look the names up for you, Mr. Elliott," the ancient doorman said. Phil followed him around behind his desk into his little cubicle of an office. "You probably don't remember me, but I'm a big fan of yours."

"You're old enough to be." Phil smiled.

The doorman laughed. "I'm Jonah Jones. I was the doorman at the Twin Towers. They're in bankruptcy now. But back when you was playin', I used to see you a lot when you came to the Twin Towers to see Miss Remington. She was a real nice person." Jonah Jones was digging through his card file.

"She's still a real nice person, Mr. Jones," Phil said. "I just spoke to her earlier in the day."

"Well, now, ain't that a coincidence." Jones kept digging. "Here they are." He pulled three index cards from his file. "All three of those north end apartments were rented by a George Rindquist. I remember now, Mr. Rindquist is a retired Dallas policeman."

"He sure retired in style, too," Phil said, his mind racing. George Rindquist had been the local vice cop that Ray March, head of League Security, had hired to tail Phil and collect evidence to prove Elliott had violated the morals clause of his player's contract. Rindquist had testified against him the day he was suspended from football.

The day Bob Beaudreau murdered Charlotte Caulder and David Clarke.

The day Phil's life had taken a nose dive into lunacy.

Help me, Phil. Please help me. Blood poured from her wounds, as he held her head in his lap. His hands and clothes were covered with blood.

". . . Mr. Stein was . . ." Jonah Jones was talking, when he noticed the look on Phil's face. "Mr. Elliott? Mr. Elliott?"

"What? Huh?" Jonah's voice pulled him back to the present and Phil's hands and clothes were no longer soaked red with blood. "I'm sorry, Mr. Jones. I lost it there for a minute."

"I know what you mean," the old doorman said. "Sometimes, I can remember things that happened fifty years ago better than I can remember what happened yesterday."

"What were you saying about Mr. Stein?" Phil asked. "Is that David Stein, the attorney?"

"Yes. I was saying that Mr. Rindquist does a lot of entertaining. He knows some important people including Mr. Stein and Miss Joanne's ex-husband."

"Emmett Hunter?" Phil asked. He began to sweat. "Anybody else?"

"Mr. Maxwell," the doorman said. "He's up there now with Mr. Stein and Mr. Hartman. He seemed sick or something. They had to help him to the elevator."

"Is Rindquist in now?"

"I haven't seen him leave, since Mr. Denham and Mr. Laughlin arrived."

"They're up there, too?"

"It must be some party," Jonah Jones winked and laughed. "You oughta go on up and join them boys."

"We'd have us a *real* party then, Mr. Jones. I've got to go." Phil looked out at the cab waiting in the driveway. He dug in his pocket and pulled out two dollar bills, handing them to the doorman. "Thank you for calling me the cab, Mr. Jones."

The doorman took the bills and pocketed them. "Thanks, but I didn't call that cab. It just showed up and the driver came in, asking for you. He said you were up in Mr. Blades's penthouse."

"You know what, Mr. Jones? I think I might just as well wait for Dickie Blades to return." Phil was now soaked with sweat. He kept one eye on the mysterious cab. "Do you have a pass key to Dickie's place? I'll just wait up there and watch TV until he returns."

"I don't know . . ." The doorman paused, then smiled. "What the hell, he left you up there alone."

"Mr. Jones, you've known me longer than most people," Phil said. "If you can't trust me, I guess I'm in pretty bad shape." Elliott kept glancing, nervously, at the cab.

"Here." Jones dug through a cabinet below the desk. "This is an extra key I always keep for Mr. Blades for when he forgets his. Just make sure I get it back."

Phil handed him a five. "When I'm in the elevator and gone, please go out and tell the cab driver that I have already left the building through the back door."

The doorman's eyes widened.

"I didn't call that cab either, Mr. Jones." Phil took the key. "And my momma told me a long time ago, 'Never get into a car with a stranger.' If I took that cab she'd tan my hide."

Back inside Blades's penthouse, Phil searched and found a fourteen-shot Smith & Wesson nine-millimeter automatic in the drawer of a bedside table. He checked the chamber. The gun was loaded with hollow points.

Jo Bob answered the phone at Wilson's.

"Come and get me, Sheriff," Phil said, giving directions to the penthouse. "I'm being held prisoner in the lifestyle of the rich and famous."

"Are you safe?"

"Dickie Blades owns a very nice Smith fourteen-shot nine-millimeter. I'll be fine. You be careful getting here." Elliott had mentioned the automatic for the benefit of whoever was listening downstairs.

Outside, the wind was picking up. Gusts were hitting twenty-five to thirty miles an hour, as air masses moved rapidly out of the southwest to fill a low-pressure area somewhere near Oklahoma City.

In the South Atlantic, tropical storm Ida had been upgraded to a hurricane and continued on its heading toward the Gulf of Mexico.

And, as a cold front moved down slowly from Canada, Phil Elliott sat on Dickie Blades's couch and began to shape a story about Delma Huddle's drug bust. It wasn't going to be the story that Decker McShane was hoping to publish in *Southwest View*, but it could just possibly be one hell of a story.

Harvey Belding just might be an important piece to this incredible puzzle, especially if Delma confirmed that Dickie Blades was one of the names on the grand jury list.

The grand jury was District Attorney Wade Hampton's witch hunt, and Hampton was expecting to ride to reelection on the publicity generated by his public crucifixion of ten or twelve Dallas professional football stars.

The district attorney took his orders from the Denham-Laughlin Machine and would destroy anybody on their orders. Anybody, that is, except himself.

And years ago, when Phil Elliott was still playing ball, a struggling young lawyer named Wade Hampton used to stop by Harvey Belding's from time to time to score a little cocaine. He was the first person Elliott ever met who had a coke habit and, if Wade Hampton still had his habit and Harvey Belding was still his connection, a whole new deck of cards was just shuffled and set for dealing.

All that remained was to name the game and choose the dealer.

Phil would make damn sure he kept track of the wild cards.

Harvey—Then

Harvey Le Roi Belding invited Phil Elliott to speak to his sports psychology class at Southern Methodist University. The two men had met at the Fair Park Band Shell where the Students for a Democratic Society chapter from Michigan State University was holding a rally protesting the Southwest Conference's refusal to allow blacks to compete in intercollegiate sports.

The Fair Park Band Shell was in the shadow of the Cotton Bowl and the participants felt that added impact to the protest.

It was also in South Dallas, where a wandering group of angry blacks would make sausage out of the protesters, black and white. As well as the swarm of FBI agents, wearing aviator sunglasses and toting 35mm cameras with zoom telephoto lenses.

Harvey Belding had taken his Social Issues in Psychology class to Fair Park to witness the demonstration. It was a change from his usual lesson plan, which was taking turns reading aloud in class from *Ramparts* and *Rolling Stone.*

Phil Elliott had gone to the demonstration because several of his classmates and teammates from Michigan State University were members of the MSU chapter of the SDS. Phil was hoping Gates Ford would be among them. He wasn't. Gates had taken the job with International Malting that Phil had turned down.

Phil stood outside the fence, to the side of the band shell, and looked for familiar faces among the MSU delegation. He didn't see any of his friends and had difficulty listening to the program, because the incredible number of FBI agents on the scene kept talking among themselves and squeezing in front of Phil to take pictures of the speakers and the audience.

Harvey Belding sat with the fifteen members of his class in the front row. Each member of his class, which was completely Caucasian, had been given a class assignment to ask and be prepared to discuss, pro and con, the merits of all sides of the problem. Several of the students felt that it would be all right for blacks to play football for SMU, as long as they didn't attend school there.

Excluding FBI agents and Harvey's class, the crowd numbered around ten to fifteen people, and four of those were derelicts, who hung out at the band shell and drank wine every day, anyway.

The FBI agents seemed especially interested in the derelicts.

"These radicals are masters of disguise," the special agent in charge told one of his younger agents.

Phil overheard the remark and laughed out loud.

In an instant, the agents surrounded him with cameras and photographed him from every angle possible.

"That won't do you any good," Phil told them. "I'm in my disguise. In reality, I'm a Zulu prince. Booga! Booga! Booga!"

A couple of the younger agents were infuriated by the remark. Grabbing Phil by the arms, they tried to push his face into the cyclone fence. But they couldn't move him. One of the advantages of being an athlete.

The tussle drew the attention of the SDS people and they began hurling insults at the FBI.

"Fascists! Nazis! Pigs!" A heavy-set woman stood at the podium, pointing toward Elliott and the agents.

Then the derelicts took up the chant, as best they could. "Flashists! Nasels!" yelled a tall man in a dirty overcoat, waving a bottle of Mad Dog 20/20.

The FBI agents looked bewildered and huddled together.

"Come on, you guys," Phil said, looking around at the confused, nervous FBI men. "You don't have to take that shit. You got guns and you outnumber them two to one."

"You!" The agent in charge yelled at Phil. "Shut the fuck up or I'll arrest you for inciting a riot."

In a few minutes, the derelicts went back to wrestling over the bottle of Mad Dog and Harvey Belding dismissed his class. The FBI agents released Elliott and the Great Band Shell Commie Insurrection was over.

Phil was walking back toward the Cotton Bowl when Harvey Belding overtook him and invited him to speak to his class on sports psychology.

"These are rich kids," Harvey said. "They don't understand the importance of anything but new cars and high fashion. They don't understand poverty or the due process of law. They all assumed immediately that you were guilty of something or the FBI wouldn't have treated you that way. Come to my class and give them some insight into violence and the working class."

"I'm not too good at that kind of stuff," Phil said. "I'm afraid I would scare those little shavers."

"Come on and follow me to Gordo's across from the campus," Harvey said. "I'll buy you a beer."

"Any good-looking women in your class?"

"There are some knock-out chicks," Harvey said, "but no women."

Harvey and Phil went to Gordo's and then on to the Blue Chip Private Club and got knee-walking, commode-hugging drunk. Phil liked Harvey's intelligence and quick wit. They became good friends.

The next day, Phil Elliott spoke to Harvey Belding's sports psychology class.

Harvey and Phil stayed friends and stayed in touch, until George Rindquist was assigned by Ray March of League Security, with the approval of Conrad and Emmett Hunter, to follow Phil Elliott until he found or manufactured enough evidence to have Phil suspended from football for violations of the morals clause.

During the years he and Harvey were friends, Phil Elliott met lots of young, radically ambitious people at Harvey's house, smoking grass and doing drugs.

A young Wade Hampton, attorney at law, was the first man Phil knew with a cocaine habit.

Wade Hampton was at Harvey's house the day Harvey and Phil returned from the SDS rally at the Fair Park Band Shell. Hampton was on his way to the courthouse to defend a client on a DWI. It wasn't difficult to get the charges reduced, in those days. Texas law allowed a person to drink alcohol *while* driving a motor vehicle.

"Harvey, I need help," Wade Hampton said. He was lying on Harvey's couch when Belding and Phil Elliott walked through the door. "I've got to be at the courthouse in an hour. I got drunk and stayed out all night. We're talking a world-class hangover here."

"What do you want?"

"Something for my nose." Hampton glanced suspiciously at Elliott. "I need two. I made a deal with the assistant prosecutor to reduce a DWI to careless driving and I need some for him. It was part of the deal."

Harvey went upstairs and left Phil and Wade Hampton alone.

"This is a big case for me." Hampton sat up, his hands were shaking. "Bobby Laughlin is my client. It's the first time I've represented him. He's a big shot from Purgatory County. I'm considering politics and it would be nice to have a chit from Laughlin, he owns some banks and savings and loans. You ever hear of D-L Financial Group?"

Phil shook his head, feigning ignorance. He had known about Denham and Laughlin since his rookie year when Seth Maxwell took him to the Polo Lounge after the L.A. game.

"It's a big venture capital outfit. They own real estate development companies and the real estate to develop. Laughlin and Denham are among the largest land owners in Texas." Wade Hampton licked his lips. "They're in the oil business and film production for television and the big screen." Hampton stood up, unsteadily. "Ohhh, my head. I got to have a beer." He stumbled off toward Harvey Belding's kitchen.

Harvey returned downstairs, just as Wade Hampton emerged from the kitchen, sweating, with a Pearl beer in his hand. Harvey handed the future Dallas D.A. two small, folded packets of white paper.

Hampton immediately disappeared into the bathroom. They could hear him snorting through the closed door.

"He *is* in bad shape," Harvey said.

"What is that?"

"Cocaine."

"And he's gonna give some to the assistant D.A.?" Phil looked back at the bathroom door.

"Yeh. Only stockbrokers, lawyers and rich kids can afford coke," Harvey said. "I am an expert at the demographics of drugs. I consider what I'm doing as a field study."

Wade Hampton finished snorting the coke, took out his Visine, put two drops in each bloodshot eye, then splashed water on his face. He walked out of the bathroom, as he dried his face on Harvey's towel. "Thanks Harvey, I'm ready to face the Supreme Court."

"You'll need eight more packets to pass out," Phil said, "if you want a unanimous decision."

Harvey—Now

"Head for the Oaklawn District," Phil told Jo Bob, as they pulled away from Dickie Blades's building.

"Are we going cruising for fags?" Jo Bob's coat hung open and Phil could see the revolver snugged into his shoulder holster.

"We're going to visit an old friend," Phil said. "You remember Harvey Belding?"

Jo Bob's brow wrinkled, as he rummaged around in his head for the name from his past. Finally, he nodded his head. From the way he nodded, his remembrances were not as friendly as Elliott's.

Phil looked out the side window. They were driving on the LBJ Freeway and the traffic was heavy. When Phil was a rookie, the area was all open country; small farms and ranches, two-lane highways and little towns. The city of Dallas had seemed a long way off to the south. Now, there were high-rise buildings, shopping centers and housing developments. Dallas's northern metropolitan limits stretched out even farther. Slowly but surely, the city had grown like The Blob, absorbing everything in its path.

And to the northwest, just as Seth Maxwell had predicted so many years ago, sat the Dallas-Fort Worth Metropolitan Airport, mile upon square mile of concrete and buildings squatting on what was once $250-an-acre farmland.

"I wonder if we've changed as much as Dallas has?" Phil asked.

"People don't change, Phil. Things do."

"You've changed, Jo Bob. I like to think that I've changed." Phil paused and thought for a moment. "Maybe you're right. I don't know anymore."

"I mean, deep down," Jo Bob said, as he steered onto I-35 and headed toward downtown Dallas. "Sure, we've grown old and changed on the outside. Age has forced certain changes in our outlooks and lifestyles. Even though I'm a sheriff sworn to uphold the law and I carry a gun, I'm a much quieter, gentler, more thoughtful man than I was when I was a football player. But it was the change in jobs, forced on me by age and injury, that initiated the change in me."

"Whatever caused it," Phil argued, "it's still change."

"Environment and circumstances. Got to adapt. If we don't, then we die," Jo Bob said. "Literally, like Tony Douglas and, very possibly, O. W. Meadows. Or figuratively, like Maxwell."

"What if the man decides *against* adapting to circumstances? What about the man who disagrees? The man who looks in the mirror and doesn't like what he sees and wants to change? Or looks out the window and wants to change what he sees?"

"That has always been your problem, Phil," Jo Bob said. "You're always looking for the bad in everything and everybody, yourself included. You know what I like most about being a sheriff? The laws are black and white and written down in books. I can see what the rules are, then I enforce them."

"What about people like Denham and Laughlin? If a law gets in their way, they just have it changed. Where is justice? What happened to truth?"

"That's not my problem."

"The hell it ain't," Phil shot back. "You've got a serious mess on your hands, waiting back in the Purgatory. You didn't bring me those tax rolls because you really believed that justice was going to triumph in your jurisdiction. Deep down, you are already preparing yourself to make a serious moral decision. You put it on hold when you left for the reunion, but O.W. is still being held incommunicado by the Estradas on your orders and Tony Douglas is still dead."

"And . . ." Jo Bob was gripping the steering wheel so

tight his knuckles had turned white. ". . . somebody stuffed a bunch of women and kids into a trailer truck and left them to suffocate." Jo Bob's voice was almost a whisper. "The motherfuckers! I'll kill them myself. I don't care if I have to shoot Denham himself."

"We got to catch them first, Jo Bob," Phil said. "And we've also got to figure a way to keep Delma out of Huntsville and clear of that grand jury. Harvey Belding is going to help us."

"I don't think I'll ask how."

Jo Bob pulled up in front of Harvey Belding's house.

The old two-story house had been completely redone and painted white with a light yellow trim. The grass in the front yard looked like a golf green. The large front porch had been completely rebuilt and screened in with expensive hand-made swings at each end.

The glass in the front door had been removed and replaced with custom-built, leaded stained-glass windows.

Jo Bob followed Phil onto the porch and up to the front door. Elliott pressed the doorbell.

"Hidy." Harvey's familiar voice crackled from the small speaker mounted in the doorframe. "Can I help you?"

"I'm certain you can, Harvey," Phil replied, "if you try *real* hard."

Shortly, the door opened and Harvey stood in the doorway, wearing an expensive silk dressing gown, matching pajamas and mink slippers with the fur on the inside. He was grinning from ear to ear, his smile enhanced tremendously by his new set of capped teeth.

"Phil and . . ." He paused only a split second. ". . . Jo Bob. Come on in, come on in. It's been what? . . . Fifteen . . . twenty years?" Harvey stepped away from the door and motioned the two men inside.

"That's approximate enough," Phil said, shaking his hand and moving on into the designer-decorated house. "I see you made a few changes in the old place."

"I decided the sixties were over and flaunting it was back in." Harvey was shaking Jo Bob's hand. "Whether you had it or not. I decided to take a little better care of myself too. I've got Nautilus gear in the back room and a heated pool in the backyard. I built a greenhouse over it, so I can swim every day, year-round."

"Well, you look great," Phil said.

"Thanks, Phil. You look a little tired, yourself," Harvey said. "I've been keeping up with your adventures out in the Purgatory. I'm sorry that they've been sticking it to you."

"How do you know so much?" Jo Bob asked straight out. He was irritated that the business of his county was gossip for a bunch of Dallas yuppies.

"Sheriff, it is frightening what people tell their drug dealer." Harvey walked over to his fireplace. He was burning mesquite wood. The flames danced in yellows, blues, and greens. Mesquite made a beautiful fire and the sweet aroma filtered through the room. "The only thing more frightening than what my customers tell me is who they are." Harvey picked up the autographed football that Phil had given him years ago.

"That's what we need to talk about," Phil said.

"It was maybe six months after you left town, Phil." Harvey spoke as if he hadn't heard what Elliott had said. "But I think your getting fucked over and run out of Texas was what *really* blew the cobwebs out of my brain. You're run out of football and Beaudreau blows away your girl and that other guy. You're history and nothing happens to Beaudreau 'cause he has the money to hire Stein. Anyway, I sort of let that shit simmer in what was left of my brain for about six months. Then, I took a sabbatical and traveled. I tried to find you in Michigan, but you were well hid and you'd covered your trail well. I went to Santa Fe and stayed at a friend's place for eight months, drove to the hot springs at Ojo Caliente and spent the time getting my mind and body back in shape. When I finally came back here, the property values were changing and the young and greedy were moving in. I went back into business but I selected my clientele pretty carefully. I already had *some* high-class customers."

"Like Wade Hampton and David Stein?" Phil asked.

"I just told the others I was out of the business," Harvey said, nodding his head in answer to Elliott's question. "I never did drugs again. It was an important decision in weighing the pros and cons of getting back into sales. Most of my customers are of the same demographical group you just named. I'm talking legislators, judges, lawyers, bankers, brokers, and some *really*

important people that I would prefer you not ask me to
be more specific about."

"I only ask if absolutely necessary."

"And I only tell under the same circumstances." Harvey smiled. "As you can probably infer, I have more
money than I have time to spend it. So, the last few years
I've been collecting information, hoping to invest it in
power."

"Stein isn't the only person bringing you information
from the Purgatory, is he?"

Harvey shook his head. He walked to the woodbox
and picked up a pair of white cotton gloves, putting them
on and reaching into the box for two sticks of mesquite.
Placing the wood on the fire, Harvey removed the gloves.

"Would you fellows like a snifter of brandy?" Harvey
smiled. "It's expensive as hell and tastes wonderful."

"We'd love that, Harvey." Phil walked over and looked
at a small drawing.

Harvey was at the bar pouring the brandy into extra
large snifters.

"That's a Picasso." Harvey handed Jo Bob his brandy
first, then walked over to Phil. "I've got Renoir, Warhol,
Monet, a Matisse, and a Van Gogh that I'm sure is
stolen, but don't know who to ask and not lose the
painting."

"Years ago, when we used to sit around and get high,
you predicted it would all turn out like this," Phil said.
"Not *your* obvious success and lifestyle, but you predicted that all those kids who acted out their rebellion
against their parents by raising hell with the system would
themselves become exactly like their parents or worse.
They'd get tired of trying to effect real change in society
and ultimately decide to try and make a profit out of
their knowledge of the deep inequity in the society. You
told me that few, if any, of these middle-class revolution-
aries would stay the course. And that the direction of
society was set in stone. The really rich control society
and their children weren't going to turn their back on
privilege and self-indulgence for long."

"Social change and revolution must answer to the bottom line," Harvey said. "I believe what I told you was,
'You would die a poor man if you lived according to your
conscience.' "

"Well, you've convinced me," Phil said.

"Say, fellas." Jo Bob was looking at his watch. "It's getting late. I like my existential philosophy in the morning with my coffee and a donut."

"Harvey." Phil changed his tone. "I need information on some people."

"Will you give me power in return?" Harvey asked.

"It's possible, if I survive," Phil said. "We're going up against some very powerful people."

Harvey turned to Jo Bob. "You wearing a wire?"

Jo Bob shook his head.

"I need to know about David Stein and Wade Hampton."

"They've been here."

"Together?"

Harvey nodded. "Hampton's a regular customer. He's got a three-hundred-dollar-a-day coke habit."

"Does D-L Financial control him?"

Harvey nodded. "Him and several others in his office. Denham told him to empanel this grand jury that wants Delma Huddle to name names. He and Stein were here talking about it one night. Somehow, Hampton was able to rig the jury and stack it with people controlled by Denham. He and Stein thought it was pretty funny. It doesn't matter to them *what* Delma says. They've already got a list of names and they'll subpoena those people after they're through with Delma."

"Do you know who's on the list?"

"I got the idea they were all ballplayers that had big contracts with the football team," Harvey said. "The grand jury'll tell them they've been named as drug *dealers*. David Stein will represent them and convince them Denham can get them off, but it will cost a huge sum of money."

"Exactly the amount of money deferred in their contracts," Phil said.

Harvey nodded.

"But if Delma refuses to name anybody," Jo Bob said, "what's to keep him from saying that?"

"Bobby 'Boxcar' Jones," Harvey said.

"I remember reading about him, a few years back," Jo Bob said. "He played a couple years of ball, when Conrad owned the team. He was seven foot tall and weighed close to four hundred pounds."

"Big as a boxcar," Harvey said.

"What happened to him?"

"PCP and shooting speed. B.A. traded him to Houston where he damn near beat the defensive coach to death with his bare hands. Houston hushed it up, hoping to trade him off and get back the number one draft pick they gave Dallas. He went to Oakland and disappeared. He showed up back in town about a year ago with a lot of cash, close to a million. He hooked up with Bob Beaudreau. He met him when he was a player. Beaudreau sent him to San Antonio and David Stein."

"Where is he now?" Phil asked.

"In the Dallas County Jail," Harvey said. "The story I got was that Beaudreau swindled him out of his money, then Stein got Hampton to arrest him on drug charges, before he discovered he'd been robbed. Boxcar still thinks Stein and Beaudreau are his friends. He expects to be out any day."

"What does this have to do with Delma?" Jo Bob asked.

"After the grand jury finishes with Delma, he'll be taken to the Dallas County Jail to await transport back to Huntsville," Harvey explained.

"And Boxcar Jones will be his cellmate," Phil added.

"Stein will have already told Boxcar that Delma named him to the grand jury," Harvey said. "End of story."

"End of Delma!" Jo Bob started pacing back and forth in front of the fire.

"We're going to have to do something fast," Phil said.

"You always told me, 'the best defense is a good offense,' " Harvey said. "Hampton's been taking money for years from D-L Financial for his reelection campaigns. They get around the election laws by setting up phony political action committees and making some of their employees contribute to his campaign as individuals, then pay them back with 'special bonuses.' He's got hundreds of thousands left over from past campaigns. The money's in a secret account and a couple of safe deposit boxes at D-L Savings and Loan, Dallas."

"Art Hartman's president of that bank," Phil said. "Art's gonna have to help us whether he wants to or not."

"He might as well." Harvey shrugged. "According to

Stein, D-L Financial has filled that bank with bad loans to finance sales of houses and lots in their developments."

"Including River Ranch Estates?" Phil wanted to know.

"I would assume. I know that Hampton has property out there," Harvey said. "Although, they've got an S&L in San Antonio and one in El Paso that they're using for the same thing. They got ex-ballplayers running those institutions, too."

"That's what their Vocational Training Program is all about," Phil exclaimed. "They get the cooperation of the union to help them pick out ex-players and then they teach them just enough to be fall guys. The ex-players are so thrilled with their success, they don't realize what's happening until they're in so deep, it's too late. If they realize it at all."

"The way Hartman looked at the cocktail party," Jo Bob said, "he knows he's in deep shit. He went back to Wilson's with us afterwards. Maybe he's still there."

"Go call him," Phil practically shouted. Jo Bob went to use the kitchen phone. "Anybody else ever come here with Hampton or Stein?"

"Sometimes Bobby Laughlin and that guy out of *Soldier of Fortune* magazine," Harvey answered. "They'd be in town for meetings of the Southwest Conservative Trust, asking for more money for their antiterrorist program at Purgatory Military Institute. They'd stop by here and get drunk or high, then start running their mouths about all their schemes, how smart they were, and how they were the first line of defense at the Mexican border. They really seem to believe what they say. That guy Glanton is a real nut case."

"Did they ever talk about the Picketline?" Phil asked.

"The gang that goes out and kills wetbacks, because Denham and Glanton think they are commie terrorists? All the time."

"Shit! We've got to find a way to prove it."

"That's easy, but I've got to have some time to consider the ramifications."

"What are you talking about?"

"This whole house is wired for video and audio tape recording." Harvey pointed at a large stereo speaker mounted high on the wall. "There's a video camera in there and in every room in the house, including the bathroom. Microphones too. The recording equipment is hidden downstairs. If it happened in this house, I've got it on tape."

"Who else out of that crowd has been here?"

"O. W. Meadows and Tony Douglas came by one night with Stein and Glanton," Harvey said. "They talked about killing you and Jo Bob. Tony and O.W. volunteered to kill you, gladly. They didn't want to kill Jo Bob, but agreed they'd do it if Glanton ordered them."

"What about PMI?"

"It seems to be, among other things, some kind of paramilitary operation," Harvey said. "The drug war is a cover for some kind of terrorist or counterterrorist training. They talked about hitting the Blaine Ranch and going into Mexico after the Estradas. Also, they have plans to hit the sanctuary church in Purgatory and make it look like terrorists."

"How did they plan to do that?"

"They've got Costa Ricans, Nicaraguans, and El Salvadorans at PMI," Harvey explained. "They take a couple with them when they hit the church, then kill 'em and leave the dead bodies as evidence."

"What about B.A.?"

"The governor? He gives them some problems because he's not a rubber stamp and they've got to keep lots of this stuff secret from him."

"Does he know about the flights out of PMI?"

"Yeh. He just doesn't know anything about what they bring back."

"You mean, the cocaine?"

"And men," Harvey explained. "That's how the Costa Ricans and the others got there. They're mercenaries, over twenty-five hundred of them: Mexicans, Nicaraguans, El Salvadorans. Glanton says he trains them for urban warfare with mock-ups of Purgatory. Of course, Glanton's a stark, raving lunatic."

"If I need them, would you let me have the tapes?"

"I could make you copies." Harvey was hesitant. "We're fooling with dynamite here. Who would you give them to?"

"I'm not sure." Phil paused. "There's a couple of guys in town from Langley investigating Denham and Laughlin's crowd."

"Gates Ford and Satler Lomax?" Harvey frowned. "They were here the other day with Stein. David said it was just a social call and they were friends of his from Washington."

Elliott's mouth gaped open. His heart sank and a wave of nausea swept over him, leaving him soaked with sweat.

"Hartman's still there." Jo Bob walked in from the kitchen. "Let's go."

Phil nodded, dumbly.

"Be careful, men." Harvey smiled and grasped Phil's shoulder affectionately. "It's a jungle out there."

Phil Elliott followed Jo Bob Williams out to the car.

He didn't know what to do. The more he learned, the less he knew.

Teammates—*Then*

"Mitch Simmons said he'd send a limo to pick us up and take us out to Oxnard." Seth Maxwell snatched his suitcase up and slid his arm through the strap of his soft leather shoulder bag. "We'll meet Jo Bob and the others at the Rodeo Bar."

Phil Elliott sat on his suitcase, watching the other passengers scramble after their luggage. The baggage claim area was crowded. The energy in the room was palpable, as the travelers' autonomic nervous systems caused all sorts of confusion; the repressed fear of flying had begun to spill out.

Seth and Phil had flown from Love Field in Dallas to Los Angeles in the first-class section of a new 747. Despite the fact that he was thirty-five thousand feet off the ground, Phil had enjoyed the flight immensely. He and Seth had climbed up to the lounge above first class as soon as the seat belt sign was turned off. They were the only first-class passengers, so they had a stewardess apiece to wait on them.

After a few drinks, the deep, agonizing pain in Phil's back, caused by the fractured vertebrae, torn muscles and nerves, began to ease. In the years between his first flight to training camp and this one, Phil Elliott's body had been shattered beyond repair: fractures in his lumbar, thoracic, and cervical vertebrae; a splintered leg and dislocated ankle; uncounted concussions; broken and dislocated fingers; numerous breaks and tear-dislocations of his nose; torn cartilage and ligaments in his knees. Several surgical interventions had already been necessary to repair his knees, his broken leg, and his dislocated ankle.

Pain was Elliott's constant companion and drugs had become a food group in Phil's diet. During the last two seasons, Phil was taking injections of novocaine and cortisone before every game. The cortisone was used to reduce inflammation and pain in his badly damaged right knee. Unfortunately and unknown to Elliott, the powerful steroid was causing the knee joint to dissolve.

As he sat in the upper-deck lounge of the 747, drinking to dull the pain, Phil reflected on his career and life. His career could be defined as highly successful, having been the starting flanker, since his rookie year, on what had become one of the best teams in the league. They had won the championship the last two seasons.

But beneath that veneer of triumph, many of Phil Elliott's victories had been Pyrrhic. The sacrifices he made to win had left him battered and bloody, inside and out. His first marriage failed quickly under the stress of life in professional football, but he took some solace in the fact that he and his first wife remained friends, forgiving each other for the emotional wounds they had inflicted on each other. She remarried within a year and had taken a job in the advertising business where she was now a senior creative director on the agency's biggest account, making in salary and bonuses nearly twice what Phil earned as a professional football player.

Each injury to his body and indignity that ravaged his soul left him less and less complete as a person. The joy of victory no longer replaced what was lost in the agony of defeat; bit by bit he was destroying his physical body and his spiritual self.

Sleep no longer came easy, if at all. And waking in the morning was a torturous process, a miserable struggle to restore movement in his broken body and motivation in his savaged psyche.

"Would you like another drink, Mr. Elliott?" The beautiful young stewardess hovered beside him. Maxwell and the other hostess were molesting each other on the small couch. Her blouse was open and Seth had his face buried between her breasts.

"Yes," Phil said. "But don't think you can get me drunk and start demanding sexual favors. I am deep into an existential funk which always heightens my moral code."

"A couple more triple tequilas"—the girl flashed a dazzling smile—"and it will be your *area* code that we'll have to change."

"I look that bad?"

"Let me put it this way," the girl replied. "When we reach L.A. I will recommend that you be taken out of the plane with the luggage." She laughed and took Phil's glass to refill it with Sausa Commemorativo.

"So, are you a football player?" The girl set the tequila down and took the seat next to Phil. "Like Attila the Hun over there?"

"Yes and no," Phil said. "I am a football player, but I'm not like him. Football players come in all sizes and shapes, suffering from a wide variety of existential dilemmas."

"So what's your problem?"

"I'm a young man trapped in an old man's body." Phil took a drink of tequila and grimaced. "And I'm lonely." He felt like an idiot, the moment he said it.

"The whole world is lonely." She meant what she said, he could see it in her eyes.

"Even you? You're too beautiful to be lonely long."

"That's a laugh." She flashed that beautiful smile again. "A beautiful woman can be just as lonely as a famous football player. And for approximately the same reasons."

"People don't look past the surface. Fame and beauty are only skin deep."

"You're very perceptive," she said, "for a football player." She reached into her jacket pocket, pulled out a card and handed it to Phil. "It's got my home number and a number at LAX where you can leave a message. Call me sometime." She kissed his cheek, lightly. "For luck." Standing up, she walked to the stairs leading down to the lower cabin. She was smiling as she disappeared below.

Elliott touched the spot on his cheek where she had kissed him as he read the card: *Beatrix Robertson*. He looked at the two phone numbers. There was no address.

"Trixie, I'll bet they call you Trixie," Phil thought, knowing there was little chance they would ever meet again. He had liked her, but something told him that his life was out of control. "Nice to meet you, Trixie." He put the card in his shirt pocket and Beatrix Robertson out of his mind. "See you in another life, babe."

"Hey! Phil!" Maxwell stood over him, bags in hand. "Get your ass off your suitcase and your head outta your ass. The limo's waiting."

It was a gray Rolls-Royce. The driver was Korean.

Maxwell and Elliott continued their drinking in the rear seat, while the driver drove them up Interstate 405 north toward Oxnard and the Rodeo Bar.

Training camp began in two days at the Oxnard Assembly of God College.

Several of their teammates were waiting at the bar. They had planned one last big party before training camp started.

Phil didn't always get along with some of his teammates and, lately, his changing moods about life in general and football in particular had exacerbated his personal conflicts with other players. But *they were still his teammates*. There was a nebulous kinship between them. They had become kindred spirits over the years, bonded by the pain, fear and joy of a hundred battles. They were an exceptional community bound together by blood spilled and tears shed over many seasons of warfare.

They had won and lost *together*.

They had *endured* together.

They had *survived* together.

They were artists and warrior-philosophers.

Their universe was the stadium, their battleground one hundred yards long.

They were *teammates*.

"As the cowboy said to his horse," Maxwell spoke to Elliott, "why the long face?"

"I seem to be losing my taste for the life."

"You're kidding?" Maxwell poured himself another scotch. "You *really* don't like this?"

"I love the Rolls. It's what I've been doing to get the ride that's confusing me." Phil looked out the window at the familiar brown hills. "I mean, I love catching a football. I love playing the game. It's everything else. My life off the field has no direction, no meaning. I feel like I'm treading water from game day to game day."

"What would you do if you didn't play football?" Seth argued. "Who would you be?"

"I'm not sure I know who I am *now.*"

"Quitting football isn't going to help you find an identity."

"I know." Phil shook his head. "Football has probably done more to make me really look at who I am than anything else. But the only way I'll know for sure is to quit."

"The struggle, Phil," Maxwell said. "It's the struggle that makes us who we are. As B.A. says every year, 'adversity makes you stronger.' "

"My grandmother used to say, 'what don't kill, fattens.' " Elliott frowned. "And, I think, she stole that from Nietzsche. I'm *sure* B.A. did. The man is one hell of a reader. I have to give him credit. He's one book-smart guy."

"He was a fighter pilot in the Big War," Maxwell said. "An ace."

The Rolls limo turned off at the Oxnard exit. In two minutes, they pulled up in front of the Rodeo Bar.

"Now, don't start right off fighting with Jo Bob and O.W.," Maxwell instructed Phil. "Remember, they're your teammates. Tony Douglas might be here, too. So just chill out, keep drinking and talk to Delma and Wilson, or Claridge and Crawford. Think good thoughts and, for Christ's sake, lose this goddamn depression you've been hauling on your back since we flew out of Love."

"Mr. Maxwell?" The driver spoke. "I'm going to go get something to eat, then I'll be back here to wait for you."

"Terrific." Maxwell handed the driver a fifty. "Let's go, Droopy."

O. W. Meadows, Jo Bob Williams, Tony Douglas, Alan Claridge, Dave Purdue, Delma Huddle, Gino Machado, Thomas Richardson, and Andy Crawford were sitting at the long table at the back of the bar, near the jukebox.

A long, rectangular shaft of light split the darkness of the bar as Phil opened the door and Seth walked inside ahead of him.

Everyone turned toward the door, including the two customers at the bar and the bartender.

"The King! The King is here!" O.W. yelled from the back of the darkened room.

"Whiskey for my men!" Seth hollered. "Water for their horses!" It was one of his standard entry lines. Maxwell and Elliott squinted in the darkness, their eyes unadjusted to the dim light.

"Over here!" Jo Bob yelled. "Head for the jukebox."

Seth stumbled on the edge of the dance floor, then quickly turned his misstep into a series of dance moves.

"All right!" Tony Douglas howled. "Fred Astaire and Ginger Rogers!" He began to applaud. Jo Bob and O.W. followed suit, then Crawford and Claridge added their applause. Delma Huddle and Dave Purdue continued talking about the problem of finding decent housing in Dallas. Richardson brought up the subject, because his unfair housing suit was still in the courts. The fact he had filed it had put Thomas in deep shit with Clinton Foote. Foote had reprimanded Richardson for filing the suit against an apartment developer who refused to rent him an apartment in a North Dallas complex with an occupancy rate of under 60 percent.

The black players had been forced to live in South Dallas, almost twenty miles from the practice field.

Richardson's suit would change that, rapidly.

"We don't like our players involving themselves in social issues," B.A. had told Richardson. "It can be a distraction when you should be concentrating on the game."

"You ought to try sleeping with scorpions in your bed," Richardson had replied. "It *really* breaks the concentration."

"The judge will have ruled on the realtor's appeal by the time we're back from camp," Richardson interrupted Delma, who had the facts wrong. "We already won the suit in federal court. Any North Dallas apartment building manager or owner who refuses to rent a vacant apartment to a black man is in clear violation of the Fair Housing Act. The appeal is just for reduction of punitive damages the judge already awarded," Thomas explained. "The realtor has already accepted the ruling that blacks *cannot* be kept from living in North Dallas."

"It's not *just* blacks." Dave Purdue clarified what Richardson said. "It's anybody, regardless of race, religion,

national origin, and all those other labels people use."
Purdue grabbed a pitcher of beer and refilled his glass.
"Hell, before long, they'll let *defensive linemen* move
into decent neighborhoods."

"I'll drink to that," Alan Claridge said, as Maxwell
reached the table and began shaking hands with his
teammates.

"You'll drink to what?" Seth asked Claridge. Maxwell
had his free arm around O.W.'s shoulder and was shaking hands with Tony Douglas.

"Letting defensive linemen live in decent neighborhoods." Delma laughed.

"Damn straight," Maxwell said. "This is goddamn America. Tony! You buy the drinks, since you're the only
defensive player here."

"Naw, come on, let's wait a minute," Douglas protested. "John Wilson and Hartman are gonna be here in
a minute. Wilson can afford to buy a round. He's a
lawyer now."

"Great," Maxwell announced. "We'll drink two rounds."
Elliott slid into a chair next to Dave Purdue. "What
are we drinking to?"

"The American Way of Life," Purdue replied.

"Which one?"

"That's why we're drinking two rounds," Claridge said.
"How you doing, Phil?"

"I'm still sore from the championship game," Phil said.

"I see you're still bitching, motherfucker," Jo Bob
replied.

"Freedom of speech, Jo Bob," Crawford interrupted.
"The American Way."

"Let's drink to that on Elliott," Meadows suggested.
"Then maybe Art and John will be here."

So Phil Elliott bought a round of drinks to celebrate
freedom of speech. Everybody ordered double shots of
tequila.

"Men!" Maxwell stood when the drinks arrived. "Raise
your glasses."

Suddenly, light sliced through the room. Art Hartman
and John Wilson had arrived. Maxwell kept standing and
ordered two more tequilas, handing them to Wilson and
Hartman after they found their seats.

"Men! And you too, Art." Maxwell never let up on

Hartman, drafted the year before as Seth's eventual replacement. Seth was trying to make certain that, should the eventuality arise, it would be on his terms. "I want you all to raise your glasses high and look around this table. We are the heart of this team, a championship team. That makes each and every one of us *champions*. Even Art." Maxwell grinned. "We are about to begin another season. I know B. A. Quinlan better than any of you and he will expect us to be better this year than last year. So, look around at the guy on either side of you and across the table from you and remember, you guys *need* each other. I need all of you. We are *teammates* on the best team in football. You'll never share any experience with another group of men that approaches what we will experience this year."

"What we experienced the last couple of years was pretty fucking amazing," Delma Huddle said. "Here's to all of . . ."

"Wait a fucking minute!" A voice boomed out of the darkness. "You assholes are drinking toasts to each other as *teammates* and you already forgot all about me!" Out of the dark hallway that led to the bathrooms and a side entrance to the bar, a misshapen apparition moved ponderously toward the table. In the dim light of the bar, it seemed as if a giant insect was clawing across the floor. Slowly, scuttling on what appeared to be several legs of different size and shape, the figure moved closer and closer into the eerie light of the jukebox.

No one moved. They watched the hobgoblin draw closer until they finally made out the shattered remains of Danny Raines. The running back's smashed body hung on a specially built metal frame. His ruined knees were encased in plaster from his toes to his hips.

Full of novocaine for his bad back, cortisone for his knees, and dexadrine for his game face, Danny Raines had then suffered a thermonuclear injury in the fourth quarter of the championship game. Making a cutback from the sideline and stepping over a downed defender at the same time, Raines's foot stuck suddenly in the artificial turf.

Three defenders hit him from different directions at full speed. His leg was still in the air, trying to make the stepover, when he was hit. Both his knees blew out completely, one ankle was dislocated and the foot turned 180 degrees. His hip was out of joint and three discs in his spine were ruptured.

"Danny," Maxwell's voice was soothing. "Danny. How could we forget about you?"

"Nobody could forget you, Danny," Elliott said. "I will certainly remember you, forever. You look like an absolute piece of shit. They ought to hang your ass up in the Museum of Modern Art. Is that thing welded?"

"Get this cyborg a drink!" David Purdue, Raines's partner in the backfield for years, yelled at the bartender. "And a can of thirty-weight!"

The drink arrived.

"Teammates!" Maxwell lifted his glass toward Raines. "Past, present and future. May we never forget what being *teammates* means." He slugged down the double tequila and everyone followed suit.

Elliott wondered if he was the only one who noticed that Seth *never* defined what the term *meant* to him.

Before the training camp ended, David Purdue would be gone.

And before the season ended, Phil Elliott was betrayed by Maxwell and suspended forever by the commissioner.

Teammates.

Then.

Teammates—*Now*

Wilson's house was lit up inside and out when Jo Bob and Phil arrived after their visit with Delma Huddle. The driveway was lined with cars.

"It looks like the cocktail party moved out here," Jo Bob said, pulling his car up behind Gino Machado's Lincoln.

Elliott could see, through the picture window, people standing around in small groups and filling the sofa and chairs in the living room.

"Phil! Jo Bob! Come over here." John Wilson was sitting on the porch with Delma Huddle. "Did you learn anything worth writing from Dickie Blades?"

"The usual stuff," Phil said, and filled them in on everything from Dickie Blades's finances to Harvey's various clients to Boxcar Jones.

It was the part about Boxcar Jones that made Delma run his hands over his bald head. "What a sorry world this has become."

"Don't give up, yet," Phil told him. "Harvey gave us some names and information. And he has a couple of smoking guns he will give us.

"What's he got?"

"I can't tell you. Not yet."

"What's going on here?" Jo Bob asked.

"Just after you left to get Phil, Crawford showed up," Wilson explained. "He missed us at the cocktail party, so he came out here and brought some of the other guys."

"Who'd he bring?" Phil asked, peering inside through the window. "The Russian Army?"

"Just teammates," Wilson said. "Gino and Sue, Purdue and his faithful Indian companion, Jesus; he's back in the pool with the other kids. Art Hartman even came."

"How about Maxwell?" Phil asked. "Did he ever regain consciousness?"

"He's here somewhere," Wilson said. "We had to wait around for him to come around the second time."

"What?" Phil scowled in confusion.

"Didn't you tell him, Jo Bob?" Wilson began laughing. Delma loosed a small giggle.

"I forgot," Jo Bob said. He turned to Phil. "After you took off in Blades's Rolls, we went in to check on Seth, before we left. He was drunk but conscious. So we were walking back into the party, when this tall, slightly heavy brunette walks up to Seth and says, 'Do you remember me?' Maxwell is weaving and trying to focus his eyes on this woman. 'I was Percy Walker's wife,' she told him."

"Percy Walker, the quarterback they drafted the year after I was fired?" Phil asked.

"The same one," Wilson added.

"Maxwell don't recall her or the name," Jo Bob continued, "but, never one to miss a chance to make a pass, Seth mumbles something about her 'bein' the prettiest little heifer in the room.' She smiles and said she was glad he thought so, but she was at the party to settle an old account. Then this big babe draws back her fist and hits Seth right in the face, knocking him flat on his back."

"You're joking!" Phil smiled and then began to laugh.

"Maxwell is spread-eagled on the floor, nearly unconscious." Jo Bob started laughing and it interfered with his ability to finish the story. "The babe . . . leans down into his face . . . and says . . . 'That's for taking my husband out drinking and chasing women. We had two kids and you nearly wrecked our marriage!' Then she spits on him and walks out." Jo Bob could no longer control his laughter and doubled over in hysterics.

The four men laughed long and loud out into the dark north Texas night.

"I gave Blades your name and phone number, John," Phil said, finally. "I told him he could trust you. We didn't get too deep into his situation before Mays showed up. He's got a pneumatic blonde working as a deep penetration spy, excuse the pun." Phil took a deep breath. "By the way, was Seth with you the whole night?"

"He just got here about half an hour ahead of you two," Delma said. "He told us at the cocktail party he had to stop by his hotel room and would catch up with us later. Why? Where was he really?"

"George Rindquist has moved in right below Blades. The doorman said he had a lot of visitors tonight: Stein, Denham, Laughlin, and Maxwell."

"You think they got something planned?" Delma began rubbing his bald head again.

"I'm sure they got a plan, but not for tonight," John said. "Seth is still trying to work both sides of the street. He needs the money."

"Hi, Dad!" Scott ran out on the porch, wrapped in a beach towel. He crawled up in Phil's lap. "Hug me, I'm cold." Elliott hugged the wet body to him and began blotting Scott dry. He was shivering, his little body covered with chill bumps. "Hug me harder."

Phil squeezed the boy against his chest and kissed the top of his head.

"I'm going to take a bath." Scott jumped to the floor and padded barefoot into the house.

"God!" Delma said. "The dreams I had when I was his age. The ability to dream is a great gift from God. Think how awful life would be if the extent of our dreams never exceeded what life finally makes us settle for. He's a great kid, Phil."

"Thanks, Delma," Phil said. "Have you guys given much thought to what we are celebrating this weekend? And I don't mean the first championship."

"Yeh." Jo Bob spoke slowly, thoughtfully. "That once we were young and we were good. We counted for something. Now, we are closer to the end than the beginning. But we left our marks."

"Yeh," Delma said, "mostly on each other."

"We were *teammates* on the best football team in the world," Jo Bob continued. "In a game that only fifteen hundred men are good enough to play, at any one mo-

ment in time, in the whole universe. We were *the best*.
It's funny how much more it means to me now than it did
then. Christ! I've grown to like Elliott for a lot of different reasons, but our friendship took root because once
we were teammates."

"Like Delma said, Jo Bob." Phil shoved his hands in
his hip pockets. "When you're young your dreams are
limitless. Now that you're old, you have to settle for a
friend like me."

"I used to think that my talent, work, and sacrifices
would always be appreciated," John Wilson said. "But,
as time passed, the memories dimmed and the appreciation vanished altogether. I've settled for being a good
attorney. I dreamed of being Perry Mason."

"I still hang on to some of my dreams," Phil said. "I
still believe in good guys and bad guys. John, you've had
to learn to live in the gray areas, because you fight your
battles in the courthouse. You have to know when you've
won as much as you can, when you've gotten as close to
the Truth as the system will allow. When you started
handling my legal problems, you gave me some advice
and I knew it was true."

"What did I tell you?"

"You warned me that I'd find myself in lots of trouble
if I walked into the courthouse and thought in terms of
winning and losing," Phil said. "You were absolutely
right."

"Then *why* didn't you listen?" Wilson wanted to know.

"Because I still have dreams," Phil said. "And those
dreams are about winning. I just don't know how to
quit."

"What are you talking about?" Art Hartman shuffled
drunkenly out of the house and onto the porch.

"Winning, Art. And quitting. And teammates."

Wilson picked up Elliott's lead. They had to make
their move soon. It might as well be now. "We were just
recalling how important being teammates was to us when
we played and how it may be even more important now."

Hartman stopped walking and looked from Wilson to
Delma Huddle, then to Jo Bob and, finally, back to
Elliott.

"We've seen the books, Art."

"What books?"

"Your savings and loan books," Wilson said. "D-L Financial have it packed with bad paper to finance their development schemes, and you're going to take the fall."

"That's a lie."

"Art, we got the copies of your ledgers from the feds," Phil said. "You're our teammate. That's why they gave us the documents. They don't want you. They want Denham, Laughlin, Stein, and Glanton. If you help nail them, we'll keep you out of the shit."

"Why would you help me?"

"Because we're teammates," Jo Bob said. "And when somebody fucks over your teammate, you're supposed to do something about it."

Phil smiled. Jo Bob was paraphrasing lines from *The Maltese Falcon*.

Tears began to trickle down Hartman's cheeks. "I'm scared. I've got to talk to somebody."

"I would suggest the first man you talk to be your lawyer," John Wilson stood up.

"Will you . . . ?" Hartman was about to crack like an egg.

"Of course, Art." Wilson put his arm around Hartman's shoulder and led him inside into his office. "I want to help you. We're *teammates*."

Kill Fee

"**M**r. McShane? Mr. Denham is calling." Decker McShane recognized the secretary's voice. "Certainly." The editor/publisher of *Southwest View* magazine didn't hold for many people, but his magazine's owner was one he did.

As he waited, Decker thought about Phil Elliott. Something told him that Denham was calling about Elliott. Phil had been in Dallas just long enough to have had time to do something that would infuriate Denham. Decker wondered what it was. His stomach was uneasy. Decker liked Elliott.

Decker remembered one night at the Chambers, when Phil and Courtnay were still married and living in Austin. David Stein had said to Phil, "You must really like that new house in West Lake. What a perfect place to write in peace."

Elliott had turned, slowly, and stared at Stein.

"Nobody," Phil said, finally, "*nobody* writes in peace."

Decker had loved the look of embarrassment on Stein's face.

"Decker?" Denham's voice drew McShane back to the present.

"Yes, sir." Decker gripped the phone tightly.

"Decker, I'm busier than a one-legged man in an ass-kicking contest." Denham spoke rapidly. "So, let's stick this hog. I got every little pissant dictator south of the Rio Grande waiting to talk to me."

"What can I do for you, Mr. Denham?"

"You can begin by telling me why the hell you hired Phil Elliott to write a story on the reunion up here in Dallas?"

"I thought he might give us a good angle on the misfortunes of Delma Huddle," Decker replied. "They were teammates."

"I *know* they were teammates, you damn fool. We own the goddamn club!" Denham said. "We want this guy broken and you give him a job . . . I suppose you already paid him?"

"I'm afraid so, sir." Decker repressed the urge to talk back to this self-styled little Napoleon. But not only did D-L Financial own *Southwest View,* they also comprised the majority of his wife's political campaign money through their various illegal deliveries of large amounts of cash. Decker would have quit the magazine long ago, but Felice would have divorced him for ruining her political career.

"We got enough trouble with Elliott without you paying him to come up to Dallas and dig around our football franchise, looking to make more trouble for us," Denham said. "Yesterday, the guy has drinks with the governor and now Quinlan has one of his hometown boys asking all sorts of questions about River Ranch Estates and why David Stein and our judge in Purgatory would try to force a ten-year-old boy to sell his property by continually filing charges against the boy's father!"

"I'm sorry, Mr. Denham." Decker was smiling from ear to ear.

"We don't need Governor Quinlan starting to ask questions about what's going on in the Purgatory, right now. We need him in our pocket! He has to take the lead in pushing the Border Control Acts. We got everybody and everything lined up to *follow him* and now your pal's got him wriggling around! If he asks the wrong people about what we're doing, we can kiss River Ranch Estates *goodbye!*"

Not to mention all the other seriously illegal shit going on, Decker thought.

"So just fire the bastard," Denham said.

"That'll make him suspicious," Decker replied. "I think, if I just leave him alone, he'll . . ."

"I don't care *what* you think," Denham cut him off. "Fire him!"

"You're the boss."

"And don't you *ever* forget it, asshole." Denham hung up.

Decker heard the click. "Nice talking to you, too."

Walking over to his telescope, Decker laughed. "Goddamn, if he ain't doing it again!"

Decker tracked Phil down at Wilson's.

"Denham wants the reunion story dropped," he began. "Which means you already have or are about to uncover what is really happening with the football team and D-L Financial Group. I'd advise you to stop whatever you're doing."

"Is that advice, or have you just kicked me off my story?"

"Think of Felice."

"I'm doin' it now!" And Elliott hung up the phone.

Decker paced for about five minutes, then picked the phone back up.

"All right, all right," Decker said as soon as Phil lifted the receiver. "How can I make this up to you?"

Phil laughed. "See if you can get Denham and Felice to reverse the space/time continuum. There are people now dead who were alive when I started." Elliott continued: "But if you really want to help, send me the magazine file information on the Blaines, River Ranch Estates, Bobby Laughlin, Denham, the Estrada family, anything on the Combined Border Interdiction Unit, David Stein, the eagle park, and the Purgatory Military Institute."

"Shit. Don't do this to me."

"I'm not doin' anything," Phil said. "It's only that with what I already got and what you could send me, we could bring down the whole lot of ugly fuckers." When Decker still said nothing, Phil added, "And probably win a Pulitzer Prize, to boot."

That did it.

"I'll send you what I've got, but if you tell anybody . . ."

"I know. You'll deny it."

"So where are we?"

"On what?"

NORTH DALLAS AFTER FORTY 361

"On my goddamn Pulitzer Prize-winning story!"

"I thought I was fired."

"Well, you're hired again, goddammit. Go get the fuckers."

The Bodyguard

They were driving past the waving crowds. The heat of the blazing sun reflected off the gold and silver glass towers and cubes. Department of Public Safety Special Agent Bob Tracy, Governor Quinlan's security chief, liked the new glass buildings when choosing a route for a motorcade, because few of them had windows that opened.

The Reunion Parade was a milk run for the gun man with the HK-91 watching for snipers in the upper-floor windows from his position in the rear of the follow-up station wagon.

It was a standard car formation. Bob Tracy had set up dozens of them as Governor Quinlan's head of security.

The five-minute car went out ahead with the bomb squad. Following them came the marked Dallas Police Unit, then the muscle car, carrying the Special Weapons Team with heavy assault capability. The spare limousine driven by Walsh Creed, Tracy's assistant, would follow the SWAT car and carry Billy Benson, Governor Quinlan's aide.

Governor Quinlan sat in the elevated seat and waved at the crowds. Bob Tracy sat in front and lower than the governor. He had ridden shotgun for Governor B. A. Quinlan ever since his lifelong friend had decided to run for governor. Quinlan and Tracy had flown P-51s together in WWII.

B. A. Quinlan went on to a successful career in football and now politics. Bob Tracy had returned to college after the war and earned his law degree, then joined the FBI. Tracy had just retired from the Bureau when B.A. talked him into becoming his director of security and personal bodyguard.

"What has Billy Benson found out about D-L Financial?" the governor asked Tracy. "Are they really harrassing Elliott, trying to force him to sell his kid's land to River Ranch Estates?"

"Billy says there is no doubt that Stein has gotten some rulings out of that Purgatory judge that are in contradiction with the law," Tracy replied, his eyes scanning the crowd. "The question is whether the judge knowingly contravened the law for Stein or is just another dumbass hillbilly judge that made a mistake."

"The choice is stupid or on the take?" the governor asked, as he smiled and waved. "What do you think, Bob?"

The rest of the parade was strung out behind the governor's limousine, including two follow-up cars, the staff and press cars, and an intelligence car filled with plainclothes cops.

"It's an awful lot of coincidence," Tracy said. "I'd put some more men on it."

"I already have," B.A. said. "Mr. Denham got wind of it and took it as a direct insult. Which, I suppose, it may be."

As they swung down around the sloping curve toward the overpass, Bob Tracy caught sight of movement in the shrubs lining the sidewalk. It was the quality of the movement that caught Tracy's attention—furiously spare and efficient. A section of the hedgerow swiftly parted and the barrel of a scoped, silenced H&K special-order sniper rifle slid into view. The rifle was in the hands of an Hispanic and, as Bob Tracy looked at him, the Hispanic's face seemed five times normal size and Tracy recognized him as someone he'd seen before.

All movement had turned to slow-motion and people changed proportions. The gunman was moving very slowly and Tracy studied the face at the same time he was grabbing the governor's lapel. The Hispanic had thick eyebrows, a knobby forehead, and was three-quarters bald.

"Gun! Gun!" Tracy yelled, pulling himself upright and

shielding the Governor with his body. Tracy felt the impact of the slugs before he heard the muffled shots.

"Go! Jimmy! Go!" Bob Tracy yelled at the driver. The first two shots seemed painless, but Tracy could feel his legs go slack. "Go! Jimmy! GUN! GUN! GUN!"

The driver floored the accelerator and the limousine surged ahead as the last two shots tore into Bob Tracy's side, blasting through his ribs, missing all the soft organs, knocking two chunks off his thoracic vertebrae, and shattering three ribs as they exited.

The governor finally realized what was happening and fell to the floor of the limousine with Bob Tracy on top of him.

The limousine swerved out of line and sped through the parade, heading for the hospital. One follow-up car chased the governor's limo to the hospital. The second follow-up car and the intelligence car stopped and the doors flew open, spilling cops in plain clothes with guns drawn into the street. The lawmen hadn't seen or heard the shooting, so they spread out in a wide sweep toward the overpass and the hedgerow.

The Hispanic had a car and driver waiting on the other side of the overpass. The pedestrian walkway under the overpass was hidden from view by the hedgerow and the cement pilasters. By the time the lawmen reached the spot the gunman had fired from, he was in the car, cruising at 55 mph, five miles from the scene of the crime.

Bob Tracy felt the pain. His insides were burning. He could feel the exact places the first two slugs had lodged because the lead was still hot and scorching his flesh. The pain washed over him in waves as he fought to keep from blacking out. He had to stay conscious. He had to protect the governor.

He reached inside his coat for the automatic pistol he carried in a shoulder holster; the movement caused searing pain. His head spun and he missed the grip of his pistol, shoving his hand into something warm and wet. He pulled his hand back. It was crimson to the wrist with Tracy's own blood.

"Well, I'll be damned, Governor." Tracy held his blood-soaked hand up. "Will you take a fucking look at that?" The bodyguard's eyes rolled back in his head and he passed out.

Ain't Gonna Study War

Phil Elliott had stayed home from the Reunion Parade to do some work on his notes and watch the kids. The parade was scheduled for 8:00 A.M., which meant the others had to be up by six and leave by seven to arrive on time. The children were still asleep when they left.

Phil was reading through his notebook when his favorite drug dealer, Harvey Belding, called.

"I'll be there in an hour," Harvey said. "I've got something for you."

Elliott went back to work.

Scott was the first one up. Phil fixed him pancakes for breakfast.

"Thanks, Dad," Scott said, getting up from the table and taking his empty plate to the sink. He gave Phil a kiss and disappeared into the playroom.

Phil heard a car pull up in front of the house and he went to the window to see Harvey Belding get out of a blue Mercedes. Phil unlocked and opened the front door.

"Somebody tried to shoot the governor during the parade!" Harvey's eyes were wide. There was a slight tremble in his voice. "They missed Quinlan but hit his bodyguard."

"Jesus! Did they catch the shooters?"

"I don't know. I just heard the first report on the radio, when I was about a mile from here." Harvey had a package wrapped in brown paper under his arm. "Turn on the television."

Phil went to the television and turned it on. Harvey walked inside. They both watched the screen. The *Donahue* show was on.

Phil picked up the remote control and ran through the channels. He finally found a special report. They were just finishing up. The newscaster was standing at the hospital emergency entrance.

". . . repeating once again. The governor was not injured, saved by the fast action of his bodyguard, Bob Tracy, who covered the governor with his own body. Tracy was shot four times and is listed in critical condition. Stay tuned and we will bring you updates as soon as more information is available. Once more, an assassination attempt against Governor B. A. Quinlan, while he was riding in the Reunion Parade honoring him and the members of Dallas' first championship team, was foiled by the fast-thinking heroics of Bob Tracy, Governor Quinlan's bodyguard and security director, who threw himself on top of the governor, getting hit four times by bullets meant for Quinlan. There have been no arrests at this time. Back to you, Don."

The station cut back to the studio and their anchorman.

"We'll have more on the attempted assassination of Governor Quinlan, but first this word." The newsman looked down and began to shuffle papers on the desk in front of him. The station segued to a laxative commercial.

Elliott flicked to another station.

The screen was instantly filled with the angry face of Colonel William Glanton. He was being interviewed live outside the hospital.

". . . and there is no doubt in my mind . . ." Glanton's face was red, his lips flecked white with spittle. ". . . that this barbaric act was an attempt by the South American drug lords and the drug kingpins in this country to strike down a great American who has the courage to take the lead in declaring war against them and the insidious threat they pose to the very heart of this country."

"Do you have any proof that this assassination attempt was related to the governor's war on drugs?" the newsman asked. His hair, stiff with spray, stayed unruffled in the gusting wind.

"Proof!" Glanton roared. "What more proof do you need? There is a very brave man inside that hospital, his life hanging by a thread, that's all the proof I need!"

"Yes, but . . ." The newsman was frightened by Glanton's outburst. He was afraid to ask his follow-up question.

"Do you have any suspects?" The newsman winced as he asked. "Have there been any arrests?"

"Believe me, sonny"—Glanton scowled—"there will be arrests. You can bank on it."

"There's my exit line," Harvey Belding said. He handed Elliott the brown package. "These are copies of the tapes. I'm packed and leaving town for parts unknown."

"It seems like a good time to make yourself scarce." Phil took the package. It was heavy. "What about your house?"

"I sold the house and the business."

"The business?" Phil was surprised. "What are you doing, franchising?"

"I sold it all to a stockbroker who's trying to recover from the crash in the fall of '87," Harvey said, smiling. "He incorporated and everything. Now he's recommending the corporation stock to his clients."

"He's selling stock in a drug dealership?"

Harvey nodded, a wry smile twisted his face. "I *love* this country."

They both turned and looked again at Colonel William Glanton's face on the television.

"If I was looking for a suspect in this assassination attempt," Harvey said, "I'd start with that asshole right there. He's got the expertise, the equipment, and the men. All he needs is a motive."

"I may have given him that," Phil said. "Apparently, B.A. was investigating the legal troubles I've been having out in the Purgatory. I mentioned to him the other day that D-L Financial was trying to steal Scott's land from him, then Decker McShane called to tell me that Denham was furious about B.A.'s office asking questions about the behavior of David Stein and the Purgatory judge."

"Well, I'm outta here," Harvey said. "Be careful who you show those tapes to. It's hard to tell the good guys from the bad guys."

The Governor

B. A. Quinlan was sitting next to Bob Tracy's bed. He had never felt so confused, frightened, and sick to his very soul. He frantically searched his heart and mind for a fragment of peace. He recited Bible verses to himself and prayed for guidance and strength.

What was he to do?

The chaos that began with Bob shielding him from the gunman had carried him stoically through all the gunfire, the blood, the high-speed race to the hospital, the doctors working desperately to save Bob Tracy's life, nurses and orderlies running in and out of the operating room, the screaming and yelling, the tears and sorrow of his staff, the utter befuddlement of the Dallas police. The complete pandemonium had seemed to fill him with strength and a sense of cool command.

But, finally, all the confusion ended.

The doctors had saved Bob Tracy's life with their unflappable skills and dexterity.

Bob was moved to a quiet room in the intensive care unit and B.A. had stayed with him. Two DPS officers were guarding the door. And suddenly it was quiet, giving B. A. Quinlan an opportunity to reflect on what had happened.

Someone had tried to kill *him*. The intensity of that realization made his head swim and he vomited in the waste can next to his chair. That person was still out there. What had he done to anger someone so much?

The world was turned upside down. There must be some mistake. He was a good man. He didn't deserve to have his body shredded by hot pieces of metal.

B. A. Quinlan could not integrate this experience into his life. He understood killing. He had done it himself, shooting German planes out of the sky. But that was different. He didn't *hate* the men he killed. It was a job that had to be done. It was war. He was serving his country with honor. They gave him medals for bravery and promotions because he had shot down so many planes.

But none of it was personal. It was done for a good cause.

The realization that he was frightened, no, not frightened, he was *terrified*, slowly dawned on him. The terror grew like a cancer. The governor began to tremble, tears welled up in his eyes, and he began to shake violently.

He began to recite the Psalms and, slowly but surely, he regained a parcel of composure. But it was a delicate composure with a very thin skin. He had no confidence in himself at all.

The door opened and the two FBI men walked into the room. The governor did not even try to rise. He just nodded at them, acknowledging their presence. The chief surgeon walked in behind them.

"Just a few minutes, gentlemen," the doctor said. "He's still not out of danger."

The FBI men nodded and opened a ring binder. It had pages and pages of pictures.

"Mr. Tracy, can you hear me?"

The wounded man grunted.

"We got your description of the man who shot you. Do you still stand by it?"

Bob Tracy nodded his head. "Seen him before, somewhere."

"We have some pictures. Would you please look and see if the man is among them?"

Tracy nodded his head again.

The doctor adjusted the bed slightly, raising Tracy's head.

The taller agent quickly shuffled through the pages of the book until he found the one he wanted. He showed the page to Tracy.

Bob Tracy couldn't lift his arm. The agent laid the

book next to his hand. Tracy's finger crawled slowly across the page, then stopped and tapped one photo.

"Him," the bodyguard said. "It was him."

Governor Quinlan got shakily out of his chair and walked over to look at the photo.

The face seemed to leap off the page at him.

B. A. Quinlan recognized the man immediately. Pete Ruiz. He had met him several times with Colonel Glanton. The man was an employee of Denham's, an advisor on Latin American affairs. He often spoke at fund-raisers held by the Southwest Conservative Trust.

The governor was paralyzed with fear.

The FBI men left and B. A. Quinlan never said a word. He no longer trusted himself. His mind and body were beyond his control, confusion and terror made oatmeal of his brain.

The only man he trusted enough to tell what he knew lay shot to pieces on the bed beside him.

He sat back in his chair and began to cry.

Sexual Politics

Felice McShane watched David Stein fondle himself. She loved his thick curly black hair and dark eyes, dimpled chin and good teeth, his smile. Their affair began during their activist days; they would spend themselves sexually with the same fanatical frenzy and endurance that powered their politics. Felice McShane and David Stein had been lovers since the old Power Now coalition days. After exhausting hours in bed they would laugh and sing their favorite double-entendre song, "We Shall Overcome."

"I've missed you." Felice dabbed perfume behind her ears, on her wrists, backs of knees. "The campaign's been hell. I've been meditating a lot lately, trying to keep myself together."

"I'm glad you decided to meet me, Felice. I was afraid there might be hard feelings."

"There are. You dropped me for Courtnay without even a goodbye." Felice's eyes filled with tears. "It hurt terribly. It still does. But I love you. She doesn't."

"My relationship with Courtnay was never more than attorney-client in her divorce action. *You brought her to me* and asked *me* to handle her case as a favor to you. I don't handle divorce cases, but you wanted Elliott's head on a plate."

"That didn't mean you were supposed to start fucking Courtnay, and drop me like a bad habit."

"Well, all that's in the past. I'm not seeing Courtnay."

"Where's she been?" Felice was suddenly cheerful and

interested. "I haven't seen her in a couple of days."

"She's off on a trip somewhere," Stein lied. He didn't know where the hell Courtnay was, which was part of the problem. "Elliott came by the other day and upset her."

"I hope somebody's got a death list and Elliott's on it," Felice said. She rubbed her naked legs together, feeling a definite sexual glow.

"Somebody does and he *is* on it." Stein blurted out the secret information in a desperate and dangerous way to try and quickly win back Felice's sexual and political loyalty.

"Really? A death list?" Felice was genuinely startled.

He turned to her. She kissed him, then ran her lips down his neck into the hollow of his prominent collarbone.

"You're serious?" Felice was kissing him on the stomach and looked up at him, her breasts against his bare thighs. "And Elliott?"

"Yeh." He sighed.

Felice looked into his face; her skin was soft and smooth, free of tension. She seemed blissfully at peace with the world. Nothing pulled or clawed lines of care around her eyes and mouth. A beatific face of almost pure innocence. Almost.

"I hope Elliott gets blown away." Felice smiled, an effortless smile; her eyes glowed and sparkled. "See if you can get him moved up near the top of the list." She pressed her lips wetly against his stomach, then ran her tongue over his skin, pushing the tip into his navel.

"Keep going," Stein clenched his jaws, "and I'll get him to number one on the chart."

Later, Felice's mood was even better. "Tonight has been marvelous, like the old times. My whole body was just floating." Felice touched her skin, soft and smelling slightly of soap and sweat. "I feel like we've never been apart, David. I missed you so much for so long when you were with her, I thought I'd go mad. But tonight has been so incredible. It was almost worth the wait."

"Just almost?"

"We're not through, are we?"

He leaned over State Senator Felice McShane and pressed the strong washboard musculature of his deeply tanned stomach against her thin willowy body and tangled himself up into her long hair and slim legs, slowly pressing her back on the bed.

"Jeesus Gawd Almighty." Felice tossed from side to side. Stein held on tight. "Jesus . . . Jesus . . . Jesus . . . Jesus." She kept on thrashing and clawing. "Oh my God . . . oh my God. . . ."

David leaned over and kissed Felice on the lips. "We've discussed enough religion for tonight," he said, cupping her breasts and kissing them both softly. "I demand more sex, Senator." Felice looked into the hard dark eyes and face above her, so unlike Decker's face, corroded, creased, frightened, mad, and careworn. She closed her eyes and raked him across the back.

A two-and-one-half-ton truck rumbled by the hotel; the windows vibrated. The driver downshifted the big truck and Stein heard it roar up the street.

"When is our next state affair?" He was dressed. The big truck rumbled by again. "I'll work my schedule around the business of government."

"What about tomorrow?" Felice suggested. "Decker's gone all week."

"It's a date." Stein kissed her and was out the door. The big two-and-one-half-ton truck was rumbling by for the third time.

David Stein had a bounce in his step as he walked to his car parked in the street. He glanced over his shoulder toward the rumble of the truck, then stepped to the curb giving the big army transport truck plenty of room.

"Hey, fella!" The big truck slowed and a sergeant in camouflage and a red beret called to Stein. "Say, pardner, can you tell us how the hell to get back on the interstate? We been going in circles the last hour."

"I know." Stein laughed. "I kept hearing you. All right, go straight through the next three lights . . ." He pointed up the street and walked up to the truck cab. ". . . then take a left at the muffler shop . . ."

The sergeant was listening intently, his brow furrowed.

". . . and go all the way to the—" Stein heard a noise behind him and turned, catching movement from the corner of his eye, just as the rifle butt slammed his head into the basic black zone.

The Last Team Meeting

Phil and Scott Elliott were walking back to Wilson's house from the pond. They had caught several fish, but Scott decided he didn't want to keep them.

John Wilson was waiting at the top of the hill with a newspaper in his hand.

"How did you do this morning?" John asked the boy.

"We caught twelve or fifteen fish, but I threw them all back."

"Was it fun?"

The boy nodded.

"I need to talk to your dad. Why don't you run up to the house and see what the other kids are doing?"

"All right." Phil leaned down and Scott hugged his neck, then ran off toward the house.

"Alan Claridge died last night of a heart attack," Wilson announced. "And Art Hartman left here last night, went home and blew his own brains out. He was afraid of going to prison."

Phil shook his head. "I wish we had given him a little more support. He *was* our teammate. Who else knows?"

"Just you, Delma, Jane, and me," Wilson said. "But it'll be in the afternoon paper. I called around and everybody is coming over here this morning. We're going to have a meeting and discuss where this leaves us all."

"What the hell else can happen?"

"This." John opened the morning paper. The headline read: ATTORNEY MURDERED.

"They found David Stein's body near Fair Park," Wilson said. "He was bound head and foot, his throat was cut."

"That'll limit his effectiveness in front of a jury," Elliott said. "Now what do we do?"

"Keep going," Wilson told him. "I got through to B.A. at the hospital this morning. He sounds pretty shaky but he agreed to meet with a few of us to hear what we had to say. Before he does anything drastic."

"What do you mean, *drastic?*" Elliott asked.

"District Attorney Wade Hampton made an announcement this morning that he considered the attempt on B.A.'s life a 'drug-related crime' and was urging B.A. to enact a state of emergency and activate the special drug and border forces and call for martial law, until the perpetrators are brought to justice. I'm paraphrasing, but that is approximately what he said. If B.A. does what Hampton requests, the military, and especially the Border Interdiction Forces, will have police powers. They'll have the right of search and seizure without going to a judge for warrants, suspects can be held incommunicado for up to forty-eight hours without the right of legal representation or the necessity of having any charges filed against them. All this is legal under the new drug war legislative package. We've got to convince B.A. to stop this," Wilson said. "The lieutenant governor has already said he would enact the state of emergency if B.A. doesn't make some kind of public appearance by this afternoon."

"Is B.A. going to allow it to happen?"

"He didn't sound too good on the phone," Wilson said. "Our meeting is scheduled for this afternoon at the hospital. I would say that the lieutenant governor will have a free hand unless we can convince B.A. differently."

"That won't be easy," Phil murmured. "I've never known anyone to convince B.A. of anything. Except . . ." Phil stopped.

"Exactly," John Wilson nodded. "Except Seth Maxwell."

"All right, you guys, settle down."

Delma Huddle and Phil Elliott were staying at the house. The others arrived throughout the morning: Jo Bob and Helene Williams, Dave Purdue and Jesus, Andy Crawford, Gino Machado and Susan. Seth Maxwell had been the last to arrive, pulling up in his limousine and stumbling drunk out of the backseat.

Now, Wilson was trying to organize the pitiful remnants of what was once the best football team in the world.

"All right, settle down." John was standing by the television set. "For those of you who haven't heard, Alan Claridge died of a heart attack last night in his hospital bed."

The reaction of the others was predictable. The men talked about what a great guy and player he had been while the women stayed in the kitchen and cried. Some of the men had tears in their eyes also.

The next announcement hit like a bombshell.

Art Hartman had killed himself and, in a roundabout way, it was connected to the attempt to kill B. A. Quinlan yesterday morning, as well as the execution-style murder of attorney David Stein.

Wilson gave them all a moment to digest that information, then he hit them again.

Tony Douglas had been murdered and O. W. Meadows had been arrested by Jo Bob on an open charge of murder. And those events, too, were connected with the attempt to kill their old head coach.

Wilson proceeded, methodically and logically, to lay out the suspicions that D-L Financial was linked to all of the crimes and Colonel William Glanton was the likely suspect behind the actual murders, acting on the orders of Denham and Laughlin.

"Our job today is to figure a way to get B.A. to listen to our theory and convince him that it's true," Wilson said. "The floor is open."

"The first thing you gotta do is convince *me* that it's true." Maxwell slurred his words. He was still drunk.

"Sober up first, Seth," Wilson said. "We haven't got time to listen to you babble drunkenly here all morning. You are either with us or against us. Don't think that Denham and Laughlin are going to do you any favors, Seth. They don't need you anymore. Remember, they got you to betray B.A. and the Hunters to go to Hollywood. Now they're betraying you. They have a grand jury empaneled to investigate drug use in sports. Delma was the first witness and they gave him a list of names."

"And you're on it, turkey," Delma said. "If I name you as a cokehead, I don't have to go back to the joint.

"We're pretty certain that Denham and Laughlin compiled the list for Wade Hampton, the D.A.," Wilson said. "All the names Delma saw were players with large amounts of money deferred from their contracts. If they get you nailed on Delma's or anybody else's testimony, they take you aside and suggest you forget about collecting your deferred money or face a criminal charge and *still* lose your deferred money, based on the ruling they expect to get in the civil case of fraud they've got going against Delma, claiming he violated his contract by using drugs."

"Those motherfuckers." Maxwell stood, shakily. "They promised me. . . ." He suddenly stopped talking.

"What did they promise you, Seth?" Phil asked. "You'd get your deferred money, if you just kept them informed on the rest of us?"

"Somethin' like that." Maxwell slumped back in his chair.

"I wouldn't take that promise to the bank," Wilson warned. "These guys have gone way past swindling. They are into murder on a large scale. They're probably responsible for the killing of scores of wetbacks out in the Purgatory. That's why Jo Bob arrested O. W. Meadows and it's how Tony Douglas got himself killed. We're pretty sure they were working a Denham-Laughlin operation called the Picketline under the command of Colonel Glanton. It's all part of the drug war which was B.A.'s big political issue during the campaign."

"If we can't convince B.A. of the conspiracy," Phil added, "we can expect a real shit storm."

"Are we doing this on our own?" Gino Machado asked.

"At this point, yes," Phil replied. "But, if we can convince B.A., he'll intervene with the law enforcement agencies, both local and federal. His position will be the official one—that's why they tried to assassinate him."

"Look, you guys," Dave Purdue spoke. "I believe *you* believe what you say, but I'm not sure *I* believe what you say."

"Jo Bob, you show them the videos and other bits of evidence we have," Phil said. "John, you show them Alan's and Art's depositions. If that don't convince them, fuck 'em." He turned to the players, his ex-teammates.

"You either *will* do the right thing and then with B.A.'s help we'll come out all right at the end, or you *won't* do the right thing," Phil said. "In either case, I'm leaving. I've always hated team meetings."

SWCT—*The Agenda*

"So? We make do with the situation as it lays out now?" Ross Denham asked, only it wasn't really a question. When no one answered, he went on. "We are all horrified by the events of the last couple of days, but we must continue with business as usual. Personally, I felt that Mr. Stein *and* Mr. Hartman were losing that hard edge that our business requires. We're a multinational firm and cannot let ourselves be constrained by conventional moralities. We must always focus on the end results of our various operations and develop our means as required to achieve those results. Bill Mays will be brought up to speed to take over as counsel to replace the late Mr. Stein, and Steve Peterson has agreed to take over as president of D-L Savings and Loan, Dallas."

"What's our position with the governor?" Bobby Laughlin asked. "Has anybody talked to him since the shooting?"

"I did. Over the phone," Denham replied. "But I'm not sure he was listening. He said nothing and has left us with a vacuum to fill, but fortunately Wade Hampton used all the power of the district attorney's office and the lieutenant governor was only too happy to declare a state of emergency, which has basically put law enforcement in our pocket. Colonel Glanton is already positioned. I think it's safe to say that the governor is no longer a factor, one way or the other."

It was a long oval conference table in the executive

meeting room of the Southwest Conservative Trust Building. Denham sat at one end and Laughlin was placed at the other. Between them sat the other members of the SWCT Executive Board: James High, the state banking commissioner; Louis Lafler, the commissioner of parks and wildlife; Steve Peterson, stockbroker and newly named president of D-L S&L Dallas; Bob Beaudreau, president of Beaudreau Insurance Co.; and George Rindquist, a retired Dallas cop, now head of security for SWCT.

"So," Denham asked. "What's on today's agenda?"

"The North Texas Savings and Loan Holding Company is about to be declared insolvent," the banking commissioner said. "I have been assured by the FSLIC *and* the comptroller of currency that our rescue plan will be accepted over all others, as long as we have two hundred million dollars in cash to pump into the member S&Ls. The holding company will be dissolved and we will end up with the S&Ls and all of the real estate paper they hold. It's high-quality stuff. They just flew too high, too long. The FSLIC will let us spin off the bad paper into a separate bank and if that bank fails, the taxpayers and the FSLIC pick up the tab. It's a no-lose situation."

"How much do we have to pay?" Denham asked. "Besides the two hundred million?"

"Five percent to the comptroller," James High answered. "And five percent to our people in the FSLIC. It has to be cash and untraceable. The usual deal."

"This isn't *exactly* the same deal as we had on the other banks," Denham said. "The comptroller and the FSLIC used to split the five percent. Now they want five apiece. Why?"

"Because this is a no-risk operation," High replied. "D-L Financial will get to move in immediately and look over all the books. After a six-month period, *you* will get to choose what loans and collateral you keep and what you spin off."

Denham nodded. "Now, since Mr. Stein and Mr. Perelli met such untimely deaths, we have more time to go over the books of our operations in Nevada. I have sent word to Las Vegas for the accountant to come here immediately and bring the books. Once we are able to spend some time on the books, I am certain we will be able to create satisfactory responses for any questions our New Jersey partners may have."

"It is important we keep our Nevada operations running smoothly," Laughlin added. "They're an important part of our money-laundering operation. I suggest that if our New Jersey partners ask for a larger fee, we give it serious consideration. The important thing is that the bookkeeping is done well so we can continue to run money through the casinos."

"You'll find on the third page of your folders the stocks I recommend be bought over the next three weeks," Steve Peterson said. "My sources have reported major defense contracts will be let to these firms, causing the stocks to take a considerable jump. We should drop the stocks listed on page four because the DOE is going to refuse licenses for their nuclear plants."

"Excuse me." George Rindquist raised his hand. "I don't know if now is the time for my report . . ." He looked at Denham, who nodded his head. "I've had Dickie Blades under constant surveillance and the other players on Mr. Hampton's list on limited surveillance. I believe I have enough to support any charges we can get Mr. Hampton to force out of Delma Huddle in front of Mr. Hampton's grand jury."

"Good, George," Denham said. "That will be invaluable when we begin to restructure the salaries of the football team. It's information that should be passed on to Clinton Foote."

"I'll get it done right away, sir," Rindquist replied.

"Anybody else with a report on expenses and costs, before we discuss sources of income?" Denham asked.

The commissioner of parks and wildlife, Louis Lafler, stood.

"The secretary of the interior has given tentative approval of our plan for a National Golden Eagle Park out in Purgatory country," Lafler said. "As you know, the secretary will shortly resign to become chairman of the Committee to Re-Elect the President. He can guarantee us the park for a twenty-million-dollar cash donation to the committee's slush fund."

"Twenty million!" Denham howled. "He's just electing a president, for Christ's sake. It ain't like he's running a college football program."

"Speaking of football," Bobby Laughlin said. "The Japs have upped their offer to one-hundred-seventy-five million to buy the franchise, the stadium, and all contiguous real estate. It would be a straight cash transaction. That would help us keep our banking and savings and loan operations liquid."

"I don't think now would be the time to make that transaction public," Denham pointed out. "It is my sincere hope that Governor Quinlan has not lost his grip on reality to the point that we would regret having informed him of the pending transaction with the Japanese. He wasn't too pleased about it when we first informed him of the preliminary talks. Now, if he is really shocked by the assassination attempt and the wounding of his friend, Mr. Tracy, we can't be certain *what* he'll do. Hopefully, he will have forgotten it."

"Mr. Beaudreau, can you update us on your transactions with our friends in Central and South America?" Laughlin asked. "We need to schedule our cash flows, if we are to take advantage of the Golden Eagle Park and the collapse of the North Texas Savings and Loan Holding Company."

"The shipments will arrive at Purgatory Military Institute throughout the day on Tuesday," Beaudreau began. "Allowing an extra day to our distribution and collection schedule, we should have received by the following Tuesday, 1.7 billion dollars from our clients. How you plan to redistribute that into your financial institutions will determine when that money can be laundered and appear on D-L Financial Group Institutions books."

"The money washing and depositing should take another week," Denham said. "So we can safely say that three weeks from Tuesday our books will be ready and we can then make our bid for the North Texas Savings and Loan Holding Company."

"Any other business?" Denham looked at the men around the table.

"The speaker is concerned about the death of Congressman Claridge," Laughlin said. "The congressman was his cut-out man between him and the ethics committee investigation. He fears that Claridge may have decided to make a clean break on his deathbed. Our sources have reported that John Wilson and Phil Elliott visited with him this week and Wilson went back for a second visit with his legal secretary the next day. The visit lasted most of the afternoon. It is possible that he gave Wilson a statement."

"Make a note to have that information passed on to Colonel Glanton," Denham said. "Under the current state of emergency, he can order Wilson's office and house searched and can hold Wilson himself for up to forty-eight hours. That'll be more than enough time to find out anything Claridge may have told Wilson."

"Is there anything else?" Denham asked. "If not, I will entertain a motion that this meeting of the Executive Board of the Southwest Conservative Trust be ended."

The proper motions and seconds were made. A vote was taken. The meeting was adjourned.

The Game

The meeting had gone as well as could be expected. Phil did most of the talking, with Wilson and Jo Bob chipping in where appropriate. Tapes were played, documents were shown, depositions were read. And when it was all over, B. A. Quinlan leaned back, face impassive, and glanced at Seth Maxwell.

Maxwell, who hadn't said one word, not even "hello," looked up at his ex-coach and nodded. It was only the slightest hint of a motion, a disconsolate bob of the head. But it was enough to get the governor to stare deeply into Seth's bloodshot eyes and make his decision.

Before long, Elliott and Jo Bob were in a room with Governor Quinlan, his aide, Benson, FBI agents, investigators for the state attorney general, the attorney general himself—Bigfoot Walton—and the U.S. attorney for the Northern District of Texas.

John Wilson was on his way southwest with his wife, Helene Williams, and all the children. They would stay on a friend's ranch until things sorted themselves out.

Seth Maxwell had had enough of meetings. He was already well on his way to getting as drunk as possible back at his hotel bar.

The governor was going over the various legal and military options that faced them.

"We know we can push Glanton and his men into Oklahoma, but that is not the most desirable scenario. It could easily result in a large number of civilian casualties. I prefer to go to the game and participate in the reunion

384

ceremonies, then at that time make my statement. We can send Glanton and his men back to the Purgatory Military Institute. Once that danger is dealt with, then we can begin to prosecute Denham and Laughlin and that whole bunch."

"Begging your pardon, Governor," one of the FBI men said. "But there is a possibility that they will try and have you killed at the game or on the way there."

"Yes, that's possible," B.A. said. "But I can't stay holed up forever and I think this reunion offers a perfect forum. The game is the second of a network double-header, which will give me nationwide coverage. I *have* to do it."

"Governor?" Benson was at the door. "The motor-cade is ready. We need to leave now. This is timed down to the last second. Once in the limousine, you stay inside, until we pull through the stadium tunnel and up onto the field. Elliott and Williams will ride with you in the back. The FBI is providing a driver and a gunman for the front seat. The cars in front and back will carry FBI men with assault rifles. There will be three limousines in the mo-torcade and all three will have darkened windows, mak-ing it impossible to see inside. So, if there is a gunman waiting, he won't have a shot at you inside the limo."

"Fine, Benson." B.A. stood up. "I'm going in to talk a minute with Bob Tracy, see if he's got any ideas."

"This was *his* plan, Governor," Benson said. "Please hurry. We're on a tight schedule. The limousines are parked in the underground entrance to the emergency room."

Governor B. A. Quinlan walked into the adjoining room to spend a moment with his wounded friend Bob Tracy.

Jo Bob Williams looked at Phil Elliott. "I'm glad we only have *this* kind of reunion every twenty years. Any more than that, I couldn't stand."

Phil turned to the television mounted on the wall. It was tuned to the weather channel. Hurricane Ida was zigzagging across the Gulf of Mexico, keeping everyone along the coast on their toes. It would make landfall sometime today or tomorrow. The question was *where?* The rains preceding the hurricane had already started to fall in northern Mexico and south Texas. The rain was heavy all the way west to the Purgatory.

"Let's go, boys." B.A. strode out of Tracy's room and into the hall. "We got a game to win."

The scene at the stadium looked like highlights of the Third Reich. There were soldiers in camouflage everywhere, stopping people randomly, demanding identification, conducting searches of cars *and* people. There were machine gun emplacements at the entrances to the parking lot.

The motorcade swung into the parking lot without stopping. That was the first gamble of the plan; they would not stop or obey any commands issued by this paramilitary group, still under the command of the lieutenant governor, still acting as if it were a case of statewide emergency.

Driving through the lot, making for the underground entrance to the stadium, the caravan passed some of the most bizarre and frightening scenes Elliott had ever seen.

The men in camouflage had people at gunpoint leaning against cars with their hands behind their heads while the soldiers searched them. Along one cement wall, at least twenty men were lined up, hands behind their heads, while the five soldiers who had put them there were laughing and arguing about who got the next drink of tequila from the canteen.

"This is horrible!" Quinlan said. "Horrible! This must be stopped at once. We can't allow this. What's frightening is the people seem to be willing to let these criminals get away with this illegal behavior. My God! Look at that." The governor pointed toward a big deuce-and-a-half truck. The soldiers were loading civilians into the back of the truck at gunpoint.

"It is amazing how quickly people become docile and work hard to please their oppressors. I oughta know. I've done it lots of times," Phil said. "Is it independence or teamwork that builds the kind of character necessary to resist the natural inclination to give in to fascism? What do *you* say, Coach? Is it the team man or the individual who will rebel against this?"

"I wish I knew the answer, Phil," Governor Quinlan said.

"I wish you did too, B.A.," Phil replied. "Because you've sure as hell had plenty of opportunities to make that decision. You're going to *have* to make it *today*, Coach. Or we all go to hell in a handbasket."

The motorcade drove down under the stadium and, very shortly, back up onto the field. The stadium, three-quarters full of people, was 100 percent filled with a roar of approval. The ceremony had already begun and the last of the players were being introduced. The FBI man on the passenger side jumped out and opened the door for B.A. Jo Bob and Elliott walked on either side of the governor to the center of the field where the old-time players were lined on each side of the small podium.

"Did you notice how many of those soldiers were Meskins?" Jo Bob asked.

"I think they're the mercenaries that Harvey Belding said had moved into the PMI," Elliott replied. Then, all he had to say after that was "Shit!"

Elliott and Jo Bob stood fidgeting. Dave Purdue stared at Clinton Foote, never taking his eyes off the general manager's face. Gino Machado gave the thumbs-up sign to Phil. Seth Maxwell just stared at the ground, never looking up.

Elliott was vaguely aware of applause, whistles, yells, and foot stomping.

Clinton Foote had just introduced Governor B. A. Quinlan, the coach of that championship team. B.A. mounted the stairs to the deafening applause and roar of the crowd. He stood by the microphone for a full five minutes, until the applause finally subsided.

"The proudest moment and sweetest memory of my long life is the day these boys won the championship," B.A. began, his eyes glistening with tears. "The boys who are here today, the boys who weren't able to make it because of other commitments, and those boys who have passed on to meet the Lord. These are disciplined and dedicated people and this world needs more of them. It is up to us, me and you, here in the stadium, and those of you watching at home. These are perilous times and there are many politicians and businessmen demanding some sort of quick fix. For a long time, I went along with this kind of thinking." B.A. was speaking without notes and he kept his eyes moving across the crowd. "As you all probably know, I had a brush with death the other day. Only the quick and selfless actions of my lifetime

friend, Bob Tracy, saved me. Sadly, the bullets meant for
me hit Mr. Tracy." B.A. paused to wipe tears from his
eyes. "I have stayed with Mr. Tracy until today, when I
decided to come here and share some of the thoughts
that I continued to contemplate during my bedside vigil.
I wanted a quick fix. It would make me look good as
governor, but then I remembered the reunion and *these
boys* and *the struggle* we endured to win.

"It reminded me, there are no quick fixes," B.A.
continued. "It took years for the problem of drugs to
reach the current state, and it will take years and much
disciplined and dedicated effort to reduce the problem of
drug and alcohol abuse, and the damage caused." He
spoke with force and true emotion. "The drug war will
never be over and we were foolish to ever believe that to
put ourselves on a war footing would give us that quick
fix." B.A. stopped and turned to look at Elliot and Jo
Bob.

"The first casualty of war is truth," B.A. said. "And I
can tell you, from my own personal observations, truth is
dead and the drug war has adopted a strategy of scorched
earth. You people had to pass through military forces to
attend this game. Some of you were hassled and insulted,
others were searched without any probable cause, which
is a right guaranteed you by the Fourth Amendment in
the Bill of Rights. Some people didn't make it here, at
all. They were arrested without cause and can be held
incommunicado up to forty-eight hours without right to
counsel, or bond, or even be told why they are being
held." B. A. Quinlan had fixed the crowd with his cold
steel stare. The stadium noise had quickly died and the
people listened intently.

"The United States of America is not just a geographi-
cal area, it is also a game," B.A. said. "It is a game of
morals and laws, played out in each citizen's mind and
soul. The morals and laws are the rules in the Game of
Life in America. Life in other countries has different
rules. Now we are under martial law, which is one of the
alternatives allowed by these new drug and terror laws.
The men who pushed these laws through the Congress
are honorable men, for the most part, but it is just that
which makes it so desperately important that we return
power to the duly elected and appointed officials. Today,

you people were forced to submit to invasions of your privacy and approached by soldiers who know nothing about the due process of law. While I was in the hospital waiting for my friend to regain consciousness, I recalled that we had fought in World War II because the Nazis and the Japanese wanted to rule great parts of the world and, in order to achieve that role, they had destroyed the human rights of millions of people. Hell, they destroyed millions of people." B.A. again paused to wipe his eyes. "Bob Tracy and I, as young men, fought for the democratic way of life, the Constitution and the Bill of Rights and all that's included. We were young and not very sophisticated, but we went up every day and fought the Nazis in the sky. We won that war because it was a true war. The drug war is not a war, or even a quick fix, it is a political scheme to change the rules of the game called America for the specific advantage of a rather small group of wealthy men in Texas, California, Nevada, Arizona, New Mexico, Washington, D.C., and Mexico.

"The idea is to get the population so worked up about drugs that the quick fix would meet with such enthusiastic approval that to stand against it would be fatal to the person's career, life, and family. There is nothing more dangerous in politics than to be declared 'soft on drugs.' " B.A. paused and took a long look at the crowd and the remnants of the championship team.

"Well, I am here to tell you, I am now against the drug war and all that it entails," B.A. said. "Because its basic premise is to deny the due process of the law to specified people. If they can deprive drug kingpins, low as they are, of their rights today, and not only get away with it, but be praised for their dedication to the American Way of Life, it is a very short jump to depriving *everybody* of their rights. They have broken the rules of the game called America. No rules means no game. I will not be a part of a plot to dismantle the intricate web of laws that protect us from those in power, for that is what America is about: laws and morals." B.A. wiped his brow. He stopped and studied the crowd. They weren't cheering what he was saying, but they weren't booing either. So on he plunged. He was strangely comforted by the presence of players from the first championship team.

"So what do we do?" He paused for effect. "First, as

of this moment, I am rescinding the state of emergency order and am instructing Colonel Glanton and his Instant Reaction Force to abandon their checkpoints and to end their patrolling of the streets. The DPS and local police and sheriff's office will resume their duties, according to law." B.A. stopped talking and gazed at the audience, giving them a look that demanded they respond. And, slowly at first, then growing rapidly, the crowd was soon on its feet cheering the coach-cum-governor, showering him with approval.

B.A. was speaking louder and his face was red. "I have instructed the attorney general and the Federal Bureau of Investigation to begin a wide investigation into D-L Financial Group. There is a serious question about the fiscal behavior of this company, including the manner in which they obtained this football franchise from Conrad Hunter and his brother Emmett. Also, today I informed the State Department in D.C. that D-L Financial had been passing information to the Japanese, in return for access to their markets and a deal memo agreeing to sell *this football team* to the Japanese. They are drug smugglers, gun runners *and* just about anything else you can name. Also, I believe we have enough proof in our possession to link the heads of D-L Financial with the assassination attempt on my life."

The crowd fell into a shocked silence.

"D-L Financial is run by greedy men who have no respect for the rules of the game. Our *country* seems to be run these days by the same kind of men. But, as I've often told my friend, Phil Elliott, here from the championship team, the game is stronger than all of us."

Governor B. A. Quinlan grinned at the crowd and waved.

"You all *enjoy* the game now."

He turned in a full circle, waving to the whole stadium, then he stepped off the podium and signaled for Phil and Jo Bob to walk on either side.

They drove back out of the stadium.

Another Day,
Another Dead Body

Phil and Jo Bob were with the governor in his limo. No one said anything for quite a while. No one had to.

"What's going to happen to Delma?" Phil broke the silence.

"The grand jury will be dismissed," B.A. said. "And Wade Hampton will be given the option of resigning his office or be charged and tried publicly on several counts of conspiracy to extort. Delma will be pardoned as soon as the paperwork is done and I sign the pardon."

"I don't think I could survive another week like this, Coach," Phil sighed.

"Why haven't we stayed in touch?" B.A. was suddenly sentimental as the limo pulled to a stop in front of the hospital where Bob Tracy was recuperating.

"What do people like us have in common, except that we played football a long time ago, when we were very young," Phil said. "And, as I recall, you and the Hunters ran me out of Texas and warned me never to return."

"It's strange how time changes one's perspective." B.A. stared at his shoes. His eyes were sad. "Those were the greatest days of all."

"We were young, Coach," Jo Bob said. "If life isn't wonderful when you're young and healthy, it cuts down the chances that life will be more fun when you grow old."

"I'll settle for being allowed to grow old," Phil decided.

"Me too, Phillip." Governor B. A. Quinlan's face

broke into a broad smile, as he shook hands with his former players. "When you come to Austin, visit me. Phil, by the way, you shouldn't be having any more trouble from that judge in Purgatory. He is going to be called up to Austin to appear before the Judicial Review Board."

The governor stepped out and the FBI man closed the door.

"Where should I drop you boys?" the driver asked.

Jo Bob gave him the directions to Wilson's Ranch. They had left one car there for Elliott and Jo Bob to use.

"I hope the next twenty years are quieter than the last twenty have been," Phil said. "I was damn proud of myself just for surviving my twenties and thirties. Now I am halfway through my forties and everything is getting tougher to endure."

They sat in the back of the limo. It was raining hard. The leading edge of Ida was affecting the weather clear to Dallas in the north and to El Paso in the west. Ida was going to come ashore at Brownsville and travel right up the Rio Grande Valley, raising hell all the way.

Jo Bob and Phil got out of the limo at Wilson's house. It was strangely quiet without the constant chatter, yelling and screaming, crying and laughing of all the children.

Suddenly, Jo Bob snatched his revolver from his shoulder holster. Phil stopped and waited to learn what was bothering Jo Bob to the point he had drawn his gun.

"The front door is open and the glass is broken near the lock," Jo Bob pointed out. "The question is why are they here?"

"No, Jo Bob, the important question is, are they *still* here?" Phil said. "And, if so, what the hell do we do about it?"

"We kill them first," Jo Bob said. "Then, if time permits, we ask them what they are doing and who sent them."

The sheriff eased the door open, his pistol cocked and held in the shooting position. Williams went through the door and Phil followed, doing his best to hide behind his large friend.

They were both in the living room, back to back, checking out hallways and entrances to rooms off the living room.

Phil was looking down the long hallway with the bedrooms on both sides. Suddenly, a man appeared at the end of the hall. He was coming out of John and Susan's bedroom and didn't see Phil in the living room until he had taken several steps down the hallway. He was trapped.

The man drew his pistol, aimed at the ex-football player and Phil Elliott prepared to die. The man's gun was almost up to shooting position when Jo Bob fired off a string of six rounds and hit the intruder in the chest with every shot. The man collapsed like a sack of ashes. Jo Bob walked over to the body. "He's one of Glanton's mercs," he announced.

The man was wearing the tailored camouflage with the peculiar insignia of PMI. Fortunately, there were no more of them around.

Phil and Jo Bob searched the dead man, finding a thick roll of fifty-dollar bills, a five-gram vial of cocaine, his wallet with his driver's license, probably phony, and a folded sheet of paper with a list of names photocopied on it.

Phil found the list and looked it over first, then handed it to Jo Bob.

"Tell me that don't set your teeth on edge," Phil said. "And I'll bet that's the short list."

"Whatever list it is, *we're* on it," Jo Bob replied and read the instructions on the top of the page. *"Shoot on sight."*

"You can't say he didn't try," Williams said. "What do we do with the body?"

"What do we do about the *carpet*?" Phil asked. "Jane's going to kick your ass for blowing this guy's blood and guts all over the wall and carpeting."

"Let's just decide about the body now, Elliott." Jo Bob said. "Please?"

They wrapped the dead man in a large sheet of plastic and stuck him in the trunk. Then they both looked through the house again, making certain the guy had come alone. All that was left behind was the blood and guts on the wall and floor.

Then they headed for Kerrville, dumping the body about fifty miles away from Wilson's off on a one-lane road that ran several miles back into the woods. The coyotes and wild dogs would make short work of the body.

Sitting in the front seat, they both knew they would follow this road until the end. They had to.

It had been a long, long road and both Phil and Jo Bob wondered if they would live to see the end. Or *know* the end when they saw it.

But neither one of them had ever walked away from a game before it was over.

The End—*Then*

Phil Elliott woke in severe pain to the ringing of his phone. It was a struggle to crawl across the bed to reach the phone.

Head Coach B. A. Quinlan's secretary was on the phone. The coach wanted to see Phil at 11:00 A.M. in his office. Normally, a call from B.A. would be cause for concern, but yesterday in New York Phil had played a splendid game, making key catches that set up touchdowns and had scored a touchdown himself that should have won the game had not Delma fumbled the ball deep in Dallas territory.

It took Elliott fifteen minutes just to get out of bed, swallow a couple of pain pills and limp into the bathroom. He ran hot water in the tub and climbed in, letting the moist heat do what it could with the damaged muscles, joints, and ligaments.

Phil had difficulty dressing, once he got out of the tub. His back and legs were so crippled he had to lay on his back to pull on his pants, shoes, and socks.

The codeine number four compound was kicking in and the minor aches and pains were soothed, but nothing short of morphine would stop the agony of his smashed, broken, chipped, fractured, and generally mutilated spine, ribs, and back muscles.

When he reached the North Dallas Towers and the offices of the football team, Elliott was slowly beginning to loosen up, which always improved his state of mind. He still limped noticeably, his knee sore and swollen.

The team doctor had drained the fluid off that knee and then gave him a shot of Xylocaine and cortisone. Now those drugs were wearing off and Elliott was beginning to feel the additional damage he had done to himself by playing and using the needle to keep him out on the field. Elliott *was* tough and he got the ball without a thought of the consequences, which were almost always injurious to his body and mind. Lately, Elliott had been wondering what this kind of abuse was doing to his spirit and his soul. There was just too much violence and he was a part of it. But he would worry about that another time—today he had to meet with B. A. Quinlan, the head coach.

He waited out in the lobby for a few minutes, then a phone call to the receptionist summoned Elliott to the head coach's presence. Phil had played so well in New York that he was certain B.A. was going to discuss his character, since his play had been flawless. Then, after a full discussion about the problems of Phil's attitude, B.A. would tell him that "attitude" was that immeasurable something that makes a great professional football player. In short, B. A. Quinlan was going to tell Phil that he would remain on the bench until his attitude improved.

If they would tell him what "the right attitude" was, Elliott would certainly try and have one. But B.A. never did. Nobody did.

B.A.'s secretary, Ruth, opened the door to the coach's office and stood aside to let Elliott pass.

Nothing had prepared him for what was waiting inside.

"Phil," B.A. said, after a long moment of shuffling papers and avoiding eye contact, "where were you last Tuesday, until approximately eight A.M. Wednesday morning?" He never looked up.

Phil Elliott tried to assess the situation. By all standards he could contrive, it didn't look good.

Conrad Hunter sat at B.A.'s right hand, Clinton Foote at his left. To the left of Clinton Foote sat Ray March, who was in charge of the league's internal security. March was ex-FBI, as were the others on his staff. Their primary job was surveillance of players and investigations of misconduct. They had connections with the local law in all of the league cities.

Emmett Hunter wasn't present, but a ruddy-faced, alcoholic attorney named O'Malley was there, glaring out from the heavy shrubbery that made up his eyebrows. The only man Elliott didn't recognize was a stocky man in his mid-forties, wearing a poorly styled brown-and-yellow checked wool sport coat.

His name was George Rindquist and he was the snitch. He had been following Elliott all week, taking notes and photographs, once breaking into Phil's house to obtain a small amount of marijuana, and, another time, breaking into Elliott's car to photograph the few joints Phil had lying loose in the glovebox.

Officially, this was an investigation of a player for using illegal drugs, but Phil Elliott had also been seeing and sleeping with Emmett Hunter's fiancée, Joanne Remington.

It was not a pretty scene. The commissioner had already suspended Elliott before he was even advised he was being investigated. Rindquist was a Dallas vice cop who moonlighted for the team by spying on players and collecting all sorts of information for possible use against any player who gave the team trouble.

Elliott had gone too far and he was out. The meeting was a mere formality and Phil left before it was concluded. He was suspended indefinitely from professional football for violating the morals clause.

Clinton Foote advised Phil that Rindquist had an extensive police file on Elliott and the best thing he could do would be to make himself scarce around Dallas.

Phil Elliott left with just that thought in mind. He was going to Lacota and Charlotte Caulder.

As he walked across the lot toward his car, Phil was stopped by Seth Maxwell who pulled up in his blue Cadillac convertible.

All Maxwell wanted to know was if Phil had mentioned his name as a person who often smoked marijuana with Elliott.

Phil told him no and asked Maxwell how he knew that Elliott would be at B.A.'s office that morning and how Seth knew what the meeting was about.

Seth Maxwell never replied. He just rolled up the electric window, drove out of the parking lot and headed north on the expressway.

Phil Elliott stopped by his house just long enough to

pack a bag and pick up his color TV. He left everything
else behind. It was all part and parcel of the life he had
just left and he wanted to take very little of that violence
and madness with him to Charlotte Caulder's ranch.

Phil had met Charlotte just a week earlier, when she
had attended a team party with Bob Beaudreau. He had
escaped with her from a bar brawl that Alan Claridge
had started at Tony Perelli's Rock City nightclub. She
had come with Beaudreau but Elliott had spirited her
away in the violence and confusion of the fight that
started after Claridge got up on stage, took off his clothes
and waved his dick at the crowd.

It should have been obvious from that scene that Alan
Claridge's future was in politics.

The gate to Charlotte's ranch was open and Phil drove
through.

He wasn't surprised to see Beaudreau's Lincoln parked
near Charlotte's house. Beaudreau had not taken kindly
to Charlotte preferring Phil over him. Earlier in the
week, Phil had driven up to the gate to find Beaudreau
screaming every racial epithet in his limited vocabulary at
David Clarke, the black man who lived in the bunkhouse
and helped run the ranch, because Clarke wouldn't let
Beaudreau onto the property. Clarke was only doing
what Charlotte had requested, but Beaudreau was raging. Phil intervened and finally bounced Beaudreau off
his burnt orange Lincoln. Beaudreau swore that Elliott
and Clarke would be sorry.

Phil walked up to the house, expecting again to have to
intervene in an argument between Beaudreau and Clarke.
But inside the house was quiet. Deadly quiet.

Elliott found Beaudreau in the den, his .357 magnum
lying on a magazine on the coffee table, his boots and
pant cuffs soaked with blood.

He had killed them both: Charlotte Caulder and David
Clarke. He had emptied his .357 magnum, blowing them
to doll rags and exploding Phil Elliott's known universe.

It was so long ago and so frightfully near.

It had been the end of everything . . . then.

The End—Now

They had been driving in rain since they left Wilson's. Hurricane Ida hit Brownsville and was moving up the Rio Grande. The sky was black; the winds and rain increased hourly.

Gates Ford's helicopter was sitting in the Purgatory Square in front of the sanctuary church when Jo Bob and Phil drove in from Dallas.

There was the usual polyglot of people crowded around the building, but something was amiss. There was an undertone of anguish and frenetic activity that neither Jo Bob nor Phil could quite comprehend.

"Everybody's probably at Doc's drinking coffee and making plans," Jo Bob said. "Nobody's gonna be outside in this weather." The rain pounded on the car roof.

"There's Doc at the church," Phil said. "And Gates Ford and Satler Lomax. Swing over there and let's find out what's going on."

Jo Bob Williams, High Sheriff of Purgatory County, was back on his own turf and not a moment too soon. The two men jumped from the car out into the driving rain.

Elliott followed Jo Bob into the sanctuary church as the crowd parted like the Red Sea. They caught up with Ford, Lomax, and Doc at the altar. Gates was kneeling over the priest who was flat on his back, spread-eagled on the floor.

The aliens were yelling and crying and chattering in unintelligible Spanish and mongrel Tex-Mex borderese.

Doc had his back to Elliott and Jo Bob as they approached, talking to L. Ray Prescott, who was grimacing at the scene on the floor. L. Ray had his badge pinned on the vest pocket of his western-cut coat and his Colt .45 automatic shoved into his wide leather belt with the Texas Bullriding Champion's buckle. Jo Bob had deputized L. Ray to keep things under control until Jo Bob returned from the reunion.

L. Ray Prescott had a relatively quiet tour of duty since returning from his disastrous trip to Bahia. The Abbott brothers hadn't come into town since the day Jo Bob made Matthew Abbott let his wife out of the car trunk and ride in the front seat. There had been no action at all—until today.

"What the hell is going on here, L. Ray?" Jo Bob asked, as he reached the steps to the altar.

"All hell broke loose here before sunup, Jo Bob." L. Ray spoke without looking up.

Elliott followed Prescott's gaze to the prostrate priest.

The priest had been held down, spread-eagled; his hands and feet were nailed to the floor.

Doc was working on him, trying to remove the nails without further damaging the priest.

"It was them boys from the military institute," L. Ray said.

Phil Elliott looked around. The church windows were all broken out, the altar had been smashed, as had the few small icons this poor parish could afford. The pews had been riddled with automatic weapons fire.

"They just seemed to go berserk. They been ridin' along the border, shootin' every Meskin they can find, killin' most of 'em, too. It's been hell, Jo Bob. Happened before we knew it. They was like crazy people."

"What happened here?" Jo Bob asked, wincing at the sight of the priest.

"Just what you see. They shot some more poor damn Meskins, then rode and . . . and . . ." L. Ray turned away from the priest. ". . . and nailed him, just the way you see. Goddamn, Jo Bob!"

"How many they got left at PMI?" Jo Bob wanted to know.

Gates Ford spoke up. "Not that many, we think. Glanton's had to disband his troops after the governor's speech. But I'm sure there's enough to still do some serious damage."

"We're going to call for support," Satler Lomax said.

"The hell you are," Jo Bob thundered. "You're in *my* territory now."

Ford and Lomax exchanged glances. Elliott waited for the rest of the news.

"They've got two women hostages," Satler said. "One of 'em's ours."

"Who's the other?" Phil wanted to know.

Doc now had the priest's hands free. The priest had a thick cloth clamped between his teeth, to bite on against the pain and to muffle his cries.

"Let me put it this way, Phil," Gates Ford said. "You might not have to worry about your ex-wife taking you to court anymore."

Inside the PMI

"Terrorism and drug smuggling is a sanctioned covert strategy for Latin America," Ross Denham explained to the men inside the small building. "The official policy had to be put on hold since the Justice Department went after Noriega in Panama. So, we have just continued the policy on a private basis, until the mess with Noriega is straightened out or forgotten. Fortunately, the public's attention span is about fifteen minutes."

"Well, I don't care about the drug policy," James High, Texas banking commissioner, said. "All I know is that you need a large amount of cash deposited in your D-L Financial Group member banks and savings and loans. The FDIC, FSLIC, and the House Ethics Committee have suddenly become interested in every transaction you guys have made. I am afraid that the late Congressman Claridge left us twisting in the wind when he died."

"Don't worry," Denham said, waving his hand blithely in the direction of the runway outside the building. "There is more money on that plane than you can imagine. I am talking *billions* of dollars. We have the laundry runs set up, as soon as we get paid for the product."

"We'll be bigger than United Fruit," Laughlin said. "We just ain't got no bananas."

Beaudreau broke into a chorus of "Yes, We Have No Bananas."

"Well, I just want to expand a little on what Mr. High said about the S&Ls," Steve Peterson said. "After

Hartman killed himself and you put me in charge of your Dallas branch, I went down there and spent the whole afternoon and night going over the books." Peterson shook his head. "There is absolutely no way to juggle the books and make the institution solvent. Unless we get some clean cash in there soon, there is no way to make the cash-to-loan ratio even close. It won't take a genius to figure it out. The first federal examiner that walks through the front door will nail us to the floor."

"They're unloading the solution to that problem, right now," Denham said. "Beaudreau has already given us the delivery and payment schedules. You will have plenty of cash in three weeks, at the outside. It would be sooner, but we always run the money offshore. It will come to you *clean,* from our shell operations in the Bahamas. We'll also run money through our Nevada casinos that our partners in New Jersey will wash for twenty percent."

"That's right," Beaudreau said. "All my product sales are in bulk, nothing less than two hundred kilos. I don't like to hold on to that shit very long. I'm set to deliver to my buyers as soon as that plane is unloaded."

"Well, we better hurry up and move the stuff out of here," Louis Lafler said. "In case you haven't noticed, it's been raining like hell for almost a day. The water is already over the low water bridge at Frio Creek. This is flash flood country. That river out there could rise thirty feet in an hour and that would cover the River Road, then there would be no way out."

"Get the women out of the closet," Denham ordered.

Bob Beaudreau walked to the closet with a movement similar to an overfed duck crossing a barnyard. He unlocked the door and Courtnay Howard-Elliott and the matron who'd been watching her stepped slowly into the room, squinting their eyes against the light. They had been in the closet five hours.

Denham was about to order the women to sit down when he stopped, cocked his head, and listened intently, trying to hear over the incessant pounding of the rain.

"Did any of you hear a noise?" Denham asked. "It sounded like some sort of bang, a gunshot." He paused, then turned quickly toward the door. "There it is again."

"I can't hear a thing," Bobby Laughlin said. "It's probably one of the trucks acting up."

Suddenly, the door to the building flew open and wind and rain blew into the room, scattering papers and scaring everyone. They had good cause to be scared, because sailing in with the wind and rain were Sheriff Jo Bob Williams, Phil Elliott, and L. Ray Prescott.

All three men were armed. Jo Bob with a revolver. Elliott had a nine-millimeter automatic that Gates Ford gave him. L. Ray was carrying a twelve-gauge three-inch magnum automatic shotgun with an eighteen-inch barrel.

"Against the wall, motherfuckers!" Jo Bob yelled over the sounds of the storm. "Search 'em, L. Ray, and toss any weapons you find over here on the floor."

Now, from outside the sound of gunshots grew nearer, as Gates Ford, Satler Lomax and their men inexorably advanced across the runway toward the plane. Glanton's men were no match for them.

"Goddammit!" Denham said. "Ten more minutes and we'd have been out of here."

Shortly, the firing stopped. Glanton surrendered and ordered his men to do the same.

The door to the outside opened again and Gates Ford walked inside, closing out the raging weather behind him.

"Good work, boys," Ford said. "I'll take over from here." Ford's MAC-10 machine pistol was in his right hand.

"Fuck you, motherfucker," Jo Bob replied. "These people are under arrest here in Purgatory County. You can have them *after* we are done with them.

"Which, for at least one I see here, will likely be never." Elliott was giving Bob Beaudreau a furious look. The intensity of the sad anger caused by this man and Elliott's hatred for him was making Elliott nauseous.

"Sheriff," Gates Ford said. "I don't need to remind you that the drug laws rescinded the Posse Comitatus Act and gave the federal law enforcement agencies, the military, and the intelligence community automatic jurisdiction in *any case involving drugs* and *drug trafficking.*"

Satler Lomax blew into the room, then closed the door.

"The trucks are ready to go and we've set the explosives in the pumping station." Lomax stopped to catch his breath. He had been a busy man. "The pipeline scheme is a master stroke. Once they got that fully operational, they could have sent their product all over the U.S. and Canada, using those hollow cleaning pigs, just by leasing them on various oil pipelines. They have a computer on line that would've been handling all the schedules, leases, payments, and accounts receivable. Two or three men could have run a nationwide drug network. The cost savings alone in man-hours is incredible."

Denham's eyes lit up. His computerized system of drug dealing was ingenious. He was proud, listening to Lomax's enthusiastic respect for Denham's genius mind. "The *real* genius is the whole operation is exactly like an oil company."

They all turned to him. Denham dropped his hands and moved away from the wall, expounding on the foolproof design of his operation.

"My information collection and vetting operation at ICC, which was paid for by tax dollars and enjoyed complete exemption from antitrust, was the whole key," Denham bragged. "I have access to every law enforcement and intelligence agency computer in D.C. and all the major cities. I can tap into NSA at Fort Meade or the Agency at Langley, right from this room." He pointed to the computer terminal on the desk and looked at Gates. "I knew you and Lomax were sent by the Watchers, before you did. I also know that you are *specifically prohibited from arresting Mr. Laughlin or myself.*"

"Hey! Motherfucker!" Jo Bob waved Denham back to the wall. "I'm the one who has your asses in a bag and I've got no plans to do anything but drop them in the Tri-County Jail."

"Wait a minute, Sheriff." Gates Ford spoke carefully. "This is a national security problem. He's right. My orders are to watch and record his behavior, but under no circumstances am I to arrest him without clearance from Langley."

"Too late, motherfucker!" Jo Bob said. "I already put all these guys under arrest."

The muzzle of Gates Ford's MAC-10 swung slowly toward Jo Bob. The movement was almost imperceptible. *Almost.*

Jo Bob pushed the barrel of his revolver into Ford's face.

"You can be certain you will be the first one killed, motherfucker," Jo Bob snarled.

"Sheriff," Satler Lomax said. "Our orders are to make certain Glanton and his men are neutralized and the survivors taken to Southern Command for debriefing. As far as I am concerned, nobody in this room even exists and I didn't see one ounce of cocaine. So, if you'll excuse me, I'll see to my men. We had some casualties." Lomax turned toward the door.

"Wait a minute!" Elliott said to Lomax, then turned to Jo Bob. "There's something wrong here." Phil studied Ford for a long moment. Then Elliott finally spoke. "Jo Bob, this is too neat. Everything fell into place too quickly. Too many things happened to pressure D-L and too much information was passed along too easily. It's *you*," he said to Gates Ford.

"You are a good reporter," Ford said. "Good instincts. But right now, we have you trapped in this building."

"Your people killed David Stein and Tony Perelli," Phil accused Ford.

"The Heavy Squad, Phil." Gates smiled. "We needed to sow a little chaos to get these guys moving too fast and making mistakes, while it provided us with extra cover. It's always easier for us to work when the system is in shambles."

"Pete Ruiz was working for you, *all the time*." Phil turned angry. "You told the guy to kill the governor! What about Claridge and Hartman? You kill them, too?"

"Phil, we had our orders. We did what we were ordered to do," Ford said. His eyes moved around the room, trying to figure the odds of surviving a firefight in a twenty-by-twenty room. They weren't good. Jo Bob still had his cocked pistol in Ford's face. "Denham and Laughlin were out of control, Phil. They were making their own side deals and not reporting to the Agency. We were sent to stop them from making their own foreign policy in Latin America."

Elliott could only whisper. "They work for the Agency? Denham and Laughlin?"

"*Did* work. Now they've been . . . uh . . . fired."

"How do you plan to do it?" Elliott asked.

"We're taking their cocaine," Ford said. "Then, in the

next few weeks, the FDIC, FSLIC, SEC, IRS, and FBI will be all over D-L Financial Group."

"You treasonous, vile, opportunistic communist!" Denham screamed. "You can't run far enough that I won't find you."

"You will be busy doing time on Uncle Sam at a federal prison somewhere," Gates said. "We'll be taking the cocaine out of here, Sheriff."

"Not if I blow your head off." Jo Bob was confused and angry. It was a very dangerous mood for everybody in the room.

"Take it easy, Jo Bob." Elliott soothed. "Let me have your radio." He took Jo Bob's hand radio and stepped into the tiny corner office.

The rest of the people watched Elliott talk into the radio, listen a moment, then talk some more. Nobody could hear what he was saying.

"Should we try and stop him, Ford?" Satler asked.

"Who can he call with *that* radio?" Gates said. "And, even if he did reach somebody, what is he going to tell them?"

Phil Elliott was calling Ruby Prescott at her house upriver. He was asking how fast the river was rising. Finally, Elliott stepped out of the small cubicle and handed Jo Bob his radio back.

"They've got us outgunned and outsmarted, Jo Bob," Phil said. "Let them take the trucks and go."

Jo Bob ground his teeth and frowned, as he thought his way through the situation. Their position was not strong.

"He's right, Jo Bob," Ford said. "Let us win and get the hell out of here. There are worse things."

"We trusted you," Jo Bob said. "Both of you."

"You were my teammate in college," Elliott said to Ford. "And you were with us on the football team," he said to Lomax. There was an air of wonder to his words.

"Maybe this'll teach you something, Phil," Gates Ford said. "All that teammate stuff is a lot of bullshit. At least, in the real world."

"All right, motherfuckers," Jo Bob ordered suddenly. "Get out and don't ever come back to Purgatory."

Lomax opened the door and Denham, Laughlin, Lafler, High, and Steve Peterson followed Bob Beaudreau out into the teeth of the storm. Phil could see several men with their weapons pointed at the door, just a few feet away from the small building.

Soon, over the roar of the wind and the pounding of the rain, they could hear the truck engines, as one by one they passed the small building on the route to the gate that led directly onto River Road.

"What'll you do with the cocaine, Gates?" Elliott asked.

"Use Beaudreau and sell it to his customers," Ford replied. "We can finance a nice little war with that kind of money."

"Where?" Phil asked.

"Wherever they tell us." Ford shrugged. "Well, I guess I'm off, too."

"Wait a second, Ford," Elliott said. "What's to stop you from killing us, too?"

"What's the point?" Ford said. "You gonna write about this? No one'll publish it. And if they do, no one'll believe it. And the ex-Mrs. Elliott? Not a very reliable witness, I'd say. And just in case, I'll just mention a little matter of a first-husband bigamy. With everybody but you, Phil, the threat of a jail sentence will usually buy a reasonable period of silence."

"What about me and L. Ray?" Jo Bob wanted to know.

"Hell, Jo Bob," Gates Ford said, grinning. "I don't even know L. Ray. And you're just too damn *big* to kill."

And with that, he opened the door and disappeared into the pouring rain.

"Well, they're getting away," Courtnay said. "All the dirty bastards."

"Not for long," Phil replied.

"Did you call my wife, when you took Jo Bob's radio?" L. Ray asked.

Phil nodded. "The river is rising a foot every ten minutes, clear up by your place. All the low-water bridges are covered with six to ten feet of water. Once they get on River Road, they're trapped."

"Well, what about us?" Courtnay demanded.

Jo Bob smiled. "I used to play around here when I was a little boy. I know a nice little cave on a nice high hill. We'll be okay there."

As Jo Bob was speaking, Ruby called on the radio.

"You boys better be on some high ground," Ruby said. "A rise just flashed through here that had to be ten foot high."

"Okay, Ruby," Jo Bob said, and led them out the hangar and down into a ravine that cut back under the cyclone fence that surrounded the airstrip. Within minutes they were safely in the cave.

Jo Bob turned to the others. "That rise will be a thirty-foot wall of water by the time it gets this far downriver. It'll knock those trucks off River Road like they were toys."

They all sat quiet for a moment, Phil, Jo Bob, L. Ray, Courtnay, and the matron, trying to imagine the horror that was facing the convoy.

In fact, it was almost impossible to imagine. The convoy was heading downriver when the thirty-foot wall of water overtook them, tossing the big deuce-and-a-half trucks around like they were matchsticks. The cascade of water thundered down the canyon drowning out the voices of the men swearing, screaming, praying, and calling for help. Some got free of their trucks and hung on to trees. But eventually, another rise roared down the canyon and swept the last of them away.

The dying Hurricane Ida had dropped sixty inches of rain on the Purgatory watershed in twenty-four hours.

In the last three hours, the Purgatory River had risen sixty-two feet, wiping away everything in its path: the truck convoy and every single building in the River Ranch Estates development.

Dreams—*An Epilogue*

The school bus wound through the hills. The road ran high above the fast-moving blue-white water of Indigo Creek, Michigan.

Phil Elliott heard the bus engine through the open window of the extra room he used as his office. He had plenty of time to walk down the hillside to the road before the bus arrived.

Pulling on his tan goose-down vest, Elliott started down the narrow driveway to the county road, a mile away.

There was a letter from John Wilson, commenting on the events in Texas. Things were not yet calm, maybe never would be. Courtnay was working for Felice McShane at the Railroad Commission. Dickie Blades, Dallas's great hope for the future, had died of acute cocaine poisoning. Clinton Foote used the tragedy to his advantage, announcing that "cocaine abuse was God's way of telling football teams they overpaid their players." There was another letter from Grant Grinnell. He had enjoyed Phil's piece on the reunion—even if no one would publish it—and wondered if Phil couldn't expand it to a book.

The school bus pulled alongside Phil and stopped. The door opened and a tall, lean, good-looking sixteen-year-old with dark eyes and hair jumped down next to his father. Scott grabbed his father around the neck, laughing while he did it. The boy had grown to the size of the man.

"How was school?" Phil asked, as he threw his arm over the boy's shoulder.

"Same ol', same ol', Dad," Scott said, his eyes laughing. "How did you handle women, Dad?"

"Nervously, at first. Then badly," Phil said. "And finally, not at all."

"Do you think they should be treated equally?" Scott asked.

"Is that what *she* said?"

Scott nodded.

"I'd ask her to define *equal*," Phil advised. "And then I'd ask, equal to *what?*"

"I did that, Dad. She wants 'til tomorrow to decide on her answer."

"That's perfect, son." Phil smiled, as they walked side by side up the mountain. "By tomorrow, you can work up a whole new set of questions on another subject."

That night Phil Elliott dreamt that he was again young and healthy and playing football with all his old teammates. He ran routes with speed and grace, jumping high and catching the ball with an ease that comes only with youth and health, and stays only in dreams and memory.

They were all there: Charlotte, Joanne, and Courtnay were in the stands, while Maxwell, Jo Bob, Claridge and Crawford, Delma, John Wilson and Dave Purdue were on the field.

At some level of his subconscious, Phil was aware that he was dreaming and he was trying not to break that slender thread that held him just outside the conscious world. He wanted to linger in that dreamworld, as long as he possibly could.

After all, *dreams* were the stuff of a good life.

About the Author

PETER GENT attended Michigan State University on a basketball scholarship. He was awarded the Big Ten Medal for academic and athletic achievement and graduated in 1964 with honors in communication arts. He signed with the Dallas Cowboys in 1964 and played flanker and tight end for five years.

Since 1972, he has authored four novels, cowrote the screenplay to his first novel *North Dallas 40,* and has written numerous newspaper and magazine articles.

Mr. Gent lives in Michigan with his son, Carter Davis Gent.

Revised and updated with over 75 all
new sports records and photographs!

THE ILLUSTRATED
SPORTS RECORD BOOK
Zander Hollander and David Schulz

Here, in a single book, are more than 350
all-time sports records with stories and
photos so vivid it's like "being there." All the
sports classics are here: Babe Ruth, Wilt
Chamberlain, Muhammad Ali ... plus the
stories of such active stars as Dwight Gooden
and Wayne Gretzky. This is the authoritative
book on what the great records are, and
who set them—an engrossing, fun-filled
reference guide filled with anecdotes of
hundreds of renowned athletes whose
remarkable records remain as fresh as when
they were set.

There's an epidemic with 27 million victims. And no visible symptoms.

It's an epidemic of people who can't read.

Believe it or not, 27 million Americans are functionally illiterate, about one adult in five.

The solution to this problem is you... when you join the fight against illiteracy. So call the Coalition for Literacy at toll-free **1-800-228-8813** and volunteer.

Volunteer Against Illiteracy. The only degree you need is a degree of caring.